Praise for

ASHES TO ASHES

"Leaves competition in the dust. Hoag capably demonstrates just why she has become one of the hottest names in the suspense genre."
—*People* (Page-turner of the Week)

"A compelling, ultimately startling story."
—*Chicago Sun-Times*

"*ASHES TO ASHES* is the kind of attention-grabber that will make first-time Hoag readers scramble to read all her other books." —*Fort Worth Star-Telegram*

"Without a doubt, Tami Hoag is one of the most intense suspense writers around. Her stories . . . have a way of burrowing into the dark parts of the unconscious and planting seeds of terror."
—*Chicago Tribune*

"If page-turner is a term too easily used, Ms. Hoag has restored its legitimacy." —*Cincinnati Enquirer*

"Patricia Cornwell wrote thrillers that had readers turning the pages until 3 A.M. Now Hoag is keeping readers up all hours." —*Sun-Sentinel*, Fort Lauderdale

"A winning psychological thriller that will attract fans of Thomas Harris." —*Booklist*

"Hoag has a way of sneaking up on the reader in superior thriller tradition." —*Publishers Weekly*

A THIN DARK LINE

"A THIN DARK LINE is chilling, it's atmospheric, it's even romantic; but the novel's best achievement is its making readers constantly interrogate their ideas about justice and revenge, their own presumptions of guilt and innocence." —*Us* magazine

"This mystery defies you to put it down, and when you're done you're damned glad you didn't."
—*The Detroit News/Free Press*

"Hoag deftly demonstrates that the search for the truth is rarely straightforward. Important clues are cunningly buried, and the book's tension is as sustained as it is palpable." —*Chicago Tribune*

"Hoag's tale, with plenty of twists and turns, is a great way to spend a quiet weekend."
—*The Orlando Sentinel*

"Hoag writes big, full stories with complex characters and situations. She doesn't shrink from the raw side of crime and the dark side of human nature."
—*The Cincinnati Post*

"Hoag tells her story masterfully." —*Mostly Murder*

"With a flair for dialect and regional atmosphere, Hoag captures the essence of the Cajun family and working relationships while injecting suspense and heart-pounding terror into a violent tangle of justice, innocence, treachery, and public opinion. A thoroughly engrossing read." —*Booklist*

"Killer suspense."
—*Booknews* from The Poisoned Pen

BANTAM BOOKS BY TAMI HOAG

ASHES TO ASHES

A THIN DARK LINE

GUILTY AS SIN

NIGHT SINS

DARK PARADISE

CRY WOLF

STILL WATERS

LUCKY'S LADY

SARAH'S SIN

TAMI
HOAG

STILL
WATERS

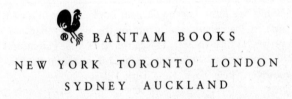

BANTAM BOOKS

NEW YORK TORONTO LONDON
SYDNEY AUCKLAND

ISBN 0-7394-0382-6

Bantam Books are published by Bantam Books, a division of Random
House, Inc. Its trademark, consisting of the words "Bantam Books"
and the portrayal of a rooster, is Registered in U.S. Patent and Trademark Office and in other countries. Marca Registrada. Bantam Books,
1540 Broadway, New York, New York 10036.

PRINTED IN THE UNITED STATES OF AMERICA

To Nita and Andrea
for believing, pushing, prodding . . .
For all you do, this one's for you.

ACKNOWLEDGMENTS

My sincere thanks go to Mower County Sheriff Wayne Goodnature and to Deputy Sheriff and brother-in-law extraordinaire Barry Reburn for their time, enthusiasm, and expertise. Also to my in-laws, who tolerate talk of police procedure, murder, and mayhem at family functions as if it were a normal kind of thing. Thanks, too, to Sandy Forstner of the *Stewartville Star* for taking time out of his schedule to give me his insights into the life of a small town newspaper. And lastly, to Boozer, my canine pal for the past fourteen years, for graciously lending his own unique presence to the book.

Altissima quaeque flumina minimo sono labi.
The deepest rivers flow with the least sound.

Still waters run deep.

—LATIN PROVERB

STILL WATERS

O N E

L IFE'S A BITCH AND THEN YOU DIE."

The words had no sooner slipped from Elizabeth Stuart's lips than the slim stiletto heel of her Italian sandal glanced off an especially large chunk of rock. She stumbled, swore with the fluency of one raised on a cattle ranch in West Texas, and gamely pressed on, limping. She had endured too much in her life to let a little thing like this break her, bodily or otherwise—two broken marriages, countless broken hearts, broken dreams that lay scattered in her wake like the wreckage of a plane crash. This was nothing by comparison.

Still, she couldn't seem to keep a sheen of tears from glossing over her eyes. It was life's little insults heaped one on top of another that tended to get to her. The odd major catastrophe—like getting dumped and dragged through the mud by the man she had pledged to love until death? Shoot, she could buck up and take that. She was a trooper. She was a fighter. Get her sixteen-year-old gas-guzzling boat of a car hung up on the side of a country road on the way to the tumbledown hovel she was currently calling home? That was just plain too much.

She sniffed and swiped a hand beneath her nose, gritting her teeth against the urge to cry. Lord have mercy, if she started crying over this, if she let the dam crack and the tears start to flow, she'd likely drown. And she would ruin her Elizabeth Arden mascara, which she was nearly out of and couldn't afford to replace. Life would go on, she told herself grimly, beating back the tears with her lashes. Life would go on, for better or worse, whether Brock Stuart divorced her or her Eldorado was stuck or whatever other shit was flung merrily into her path by that bastard Fate. All she had to do was keep putting one foot in front of the other. What she stepped in along the way couldn't matter. She either had to keep moving on or curl up in a big ball of misery and die.

The Eldorado was a good half mile behind her, hanging off the edge of the road like a drunken cowboy sliding off his horse. Elizabeth glanced back at it, scowling, then set her sights forward again. If she could get past the fact that she was madder than a wet cat, she'd note that the view was lovely. The rolling countryside of south-eastern Minnesota was beautiful. Not in a spectacular, breathtaking way. Not in the wild, desolate way of West Texas, but in a gentle way, a peaceful way. Like Vermont without the mountains. The rippling hills were bathed in a palette of springtime greens—young corn and oats, alfalfa and wild grass, all swaying in the early evening breeze. Occasional islands of trees broke the monotony of farm fields. Maples, cottonwoods, oaks. Their leaves turned inward, undersides flashing silver as the wind shook them.

To the south, the pastureland sloped down to Still Creek, the meandering puddle of water the nearest town had been named for. The banks were steep, the creek itself shallow and muddy, probably twenty feet across. Dragonflies skimmed above the surface and weeping willows bowed across it, their slender, pendulous branches fluttering like ribbons. In the part of Texas Elizabeth was from, Still Creek would have been called a river and it would have been coveted by all who lived near it and guarded jealously by the ranchers who owned land along its banks. Here, where water was plentiful, Still Creek was insignificant, just another facet of the pretty landscape.

Above the pastoral beauty of Still Creek and its environs, the sky hung like a curtain of lead, threatening an evening shower. Elizabeth muttered a curse under her breath and tried to limp a little faster. She was at least a mile from home. The nearest farm belonged to one of the Amish families the area was famous for. She doubted she would get much in the way of help there. They would have no phone to call a tow truck, no tractor to pull her car out of the ditch. They wouldn't even have a cold beer to console her with. In short, they would be about as much good to her as a bunch of eunuchs at an orgy.

"Look on the bright side, sugar," she said, hiking the strap of her Gucci handbag up on her shoulder. "If this was West Texas and you were stranded in the middle of nowhere, it'd take you the better part of a week to walk home."

God, Brock would have loved seeing her reduced to this, she thought, casting another dubious look at the swelling clouds. Limping down the road from a little jerkwater town toward a house he wouldn't deem fit for dogs, rain pouring down over her, ruining her favorite Armani silk blouse. She could picture him, perfect and gorgeous, handsome enough to make Mel Gibson look homely, snickering at her in that mean, superior way of his, like a spoiled little rich kid who'd taken up all his toys and kicked the poor neighbor girl out in the street.

For a man so filthy rich, he could be a petty bastard. But there was no point in reviewing that fact now. She snagged back a handful of wind-tossed black hair with her free hand and tucked it behind her ear as she hefted her Kmart vinyl briefcase, and kept on walking, gravel biting into the bottoms of her feet through the thin soles of her sandals.

There was a message in that, she reckoned. People who had to walk through life wore sensible shoes with thick rubber soles, and fat white cotton socks. Rich people wore red kid Ferragamo sandals with pencil-slim heels and had chauffeurs take them where they needed to go. Rich people had no need for sensible shoes or rain-coats. She was no longer a rich person.

That in itself wasn't as devastating as it might have been had she been rich all her life. She had been rich for only a few short years, the five years she'd been married to Brock, who had taken a modest family fortune and parlayed it into a disgusting amount of money in the media business. His knack for turning failing newspapers, television, and radio stations into blue-chip businesses had put him on a financial par with the likes of Ted Turner. Brock Stuart had more money than most third world countries.

It had been easy enough to get used to that life-style, Elizabeth reflected, brushing a speck of lint off the lapel of her red silk blouse. She had a taste for champagne and a natural love of French lingerie. She'd been a whiz at picking out trinkets from Tiffany's and designer gowns. But she still knew how to wear faded jeans. She could still dance the two-step and belt down Lone Star beer. She still knew how to wear boots. Unfortunately, hers were a mile down the road lying on the back porch with a heap of battered sneakers.

Just ahead, on the north side of the road, stood the tidy Amish farm she had already disregarded as a source of help. The yard was empty. The house was dark, its curtainless multipaned windows giving it an air of abandonment. Long, plain wooden benches were stacked like cordwood on the front porch. The only sign of life was a fat ginger cat sitting on the top bench, licking its paw.

On the south side of the road a freshly laid gravel drive led across the field to the construction site of what was being touted as the finest resort south of the Twin Cities. The paradox was not lost on Elizabeth. The tourists who came to see the Amish and their simple, rustic way of life would be staying just across the road in twentieth-century splendor. In addition to the hotel itself, there would be tennis courts, a golf course. There was even a rumor going around that Still Creek would be dammed and swollen into a small man-made lake that would be stocked with fish and lined up with paddleboats.

The resort was in a stage of construction that made it look like nothing more than a big, ugly skeleton, but Elizabeth had seen the sketches of the finished product in a back issue of the *Clarion*. She could say with certainty that the Still Waters resort was going to be big and vulgar, not unlike the man who was building it—Jarrold Jarvis. She labeled the style Early French Brothel, an incongruous blend of French Provincial, English Tudor, and Moorish monstrosity. It would look as out of place here as a Las Vegas casino.

She groaned as she caught sight of Jarvis's powder-yellow Lincoln Town Car parked near the rusting white trailer that served as office for the construction site. When it came to overbearing swine, Jarrold Jarvis was king pig around Still Creek. He'd made his money in highway construction, scratching his way up from the bottom rung of the ladder to a position where he could afford to dabble in the tourist trade with a little venture like Still Waters. His journey from poverty to prosperity had left him with a survival-of-the-fittest mentality that, in his opinion, allowed him to lord it over anyone he thought inferior to him, genetically or financially—which meant most everyone in Still Creek.

Elizabeth knew a lot of men around town had come to the erroneous conclusion that because she had suffered the great misfortune of having been married twice, she was an easy lay. Jarrold Jarvis was the only one who'd actually had the gall to come right out and say so to her face. He had insulted her in one rancid breath and propositioned her in the next. He was the last man she could think of—except Brock—whom she would want to be rescued by. But as thunder began to rumble in the distance and the belly of the slate-colored clouds sagged a little lower, she turned in at the driveway and limped determinedly down it. There was no telling how long it might be before she would be able to afford another Armani silk blouse.

The building site had an eerie kind of quiet about it. The work crews had long since called it a day. The hammers and saws were silent. Nature itself seemed to be holding its breath in the face of the modern wound that was being inflicted on it. A large chunk of the perfect meadow had been sliced away, bulldozed to make room for rooms with a view. The soft green grass had been peeled back to reveal rich black dirt that was now rutted with tire tracks and littered with the evidence of man's intrusion—discarded food wrappers, crumpled soda cans, trampled yellow invoices, an abandoned leather glove.

No one answered Elizabeth's knock on the office door. "Mr. Jarvis?" she called, carefully descending the beat-up metal steps. She wasn't sure what she dreaded more—silence or having him answer.

"Mr. Jarvis?" Her voice carried across the meadow and faded away unanswered.

Heaving a sigh, she wandered up along the driver's side of the Lincoln, the heels of her sandals sinking down into the thick, coarse gravel of the drive. Her gaze scanned the building site once again in the waning light. Jarvis might have caught a ride with his contractor or foreman. Or he might have just walked into the surrounding woods to take a leak or something.

Now, there was an unpleasant prospect—catching Jarrold Jarvis with his knickers down. Elizabeth hung back beside the car, grimacing at the idea. Jarvis was a big man with a build that spoke of a sedentary life and a fondness for fat and cholesterol. He might have looked like some hot stud once upon a time, but years and calories had stretched him into a waddling tub of lard, sort of like Orson Welles after he let himself go. If there was anything even remotely interesting inside his shorts, it was completely overshadowed by his belly.

Just about convinced that she'd rather be drenched with rain and struck dead by lightning than ask him for a ride home, she started to turn away from the car. Her heart leapt into her throat as her gaze caught on the figure of a man sitting in the front seat.

"Jesus H. Christ!" she gasped, clutching at her heart

as she stumbled back a step, then lurched forward. "You obnoxious son of a—"

She grabbed the handle of the door and fumbled with it, adrenaline pumping through her, fear and anger making her fingers clumsy. "Of all the rotten things to do! I'm standing here, yelling my fool head off, and you sit there like a big old jackass looking at my butt! By God, Jarrold Jarvis, if these weren't my favorite Ferragamo sandals—"

The rest of her tirade was lost, jammed somewhere in her throat with the bitter taste of terror as the Lincoln's door swung open and Jarrold Jarvis spilled out onto the fresh white gravel at her feet, his fat throat slit from ear to ear.

TWO

Mmm . . . yes . . . you know how good that feels right there . . . mmm . . . Dane . . .

Dane Jantzen slid his open mouth across his partner's belly upward to the underside of her right breast. His tongue flicked out to tease her nipple, leaving a wet trail on her skin. The dampness glistened in the soft light from the chrome torchiere lamp that stood in the corner of the bedroom. He blew softly across the moistened spot, then slowly drew her distended nipple into his mouth and sucked.

He enjoyed the taste of Ann Markham. He didn't agree with her politics, and her openly avaricious ambition left a bitter taste in his mouth. Professionally, they didn't really like each other. But then, those were the very reasons they were ideal partners in bed. Neither was angling for commitment. Neither wanted anything from the other but a good lay and complete discretion.

They'd been honest about that from the first. Ann had her sights set on the state attorney general's office in St. Paul. Dane had his set on eternal bachelorhood. They were both involved in careers where their private lives had to withstand public scrutiny. They couldn't afford gossip and they couldn't abide ties. What they had found was, to Dane's way of thinking, the perfect arrangement.

He had shackled himself once to a woman who valued status above all. Once had been plenty. While he had liked domestic life well enough, he hadn't liked it well enough to risk again experiencing the kind of pain Tricia had dealt him when she'd decided to trade him in for a more ambitious man. The pain of betrayal and rejection that, after all these years, still cut at him in unguarded moments.

He had given her his heart when he'd been too young to know better, too young to think that she wouldn't love him forever. Too young to believe that he wouldn't play football for the rest of his life, basking in the glory of public adoration and the undying devotion of his beautiful wife. Then his knee had gone and his career with it, and Tricia had given his heart back to him without apology or any sign of regret. And he had gone home to Still Creek with a bitter lesson learned: The path of true love was a treacherous one, littered with the carcasses of those who had been cast aside along the way. He had no intention of traveling that road again.

He told himself it was simply because he hated to lose. Whether the game was football or work or women, he couldn't hack losing. It stuck in his throat like a chicken bone. Besides, it was easier being single. He had no expectations to live up to but his own, no definition of success or failure or wealth or worthiness but his own. He was content with his position as sheriff of Tyler County, where nothing much ever happened and he was free to take a day off now and again to go fishing. He was content with his quiet, well-ordered life and his small farm outside of Still Creek. He was content with his affair with Ann.

They'd met at a seminar for the Southeastern Minnesota Drug Task Force two years before, when she had been new to the Olmsted County attorney's office in Rochester and he had been fresh from his victory over Boyd Ellstrom in the race for Tyler County sheriff. The physical attraction had been immediate, strong, and mutual. Over dinner that evening they had each made their desires clear and they had set the ground rules for their relationship—no strings, no demands, no threat of marriage. They had then driven out to Ann's secluded house in Rochester's Weatherhill area and spent the night engaged in blistering hot sex.

The arrangement had worked well for both of them. Ann's home was half a county away from the watchful eyes of Dane's conservative constituents. They never ran afoul of each other in the court system. They never bored each other with small talk or phony sentiment. They gave each other good, honest, mutually satisfying sex with none of the usual cumbersome emotional baggage attached.

"Oh, Dane, please," she whispered in the breathless voice she used when she wanted something *really* badly.

"In a hurry tonight?" he murmured dryly.

"Just hungry," she said, licking her lips. "The Baylor case starts tomorrow."

A slow smile spread across Dane's mouth. Ann was never better in bed than the night before the start of a big case. The adrenaline, he knew, was for her job, for the excitement of the battle, not for him. But he benefitted just the same.

"How do you want it?" he whispered against her lips, easing himself just barely inside her.

"Hard and fast," she gasped, her eyes glittering with reckless excitement as she stared up at him. "Really hard."

Dane groaned as he settled his mouth over hers. He was in for one hell of an evening.

Ann was as hot and unrestrained in bed as she was cool and reserved in her professional world. The contrast never failed to give Dane a little extra rush when he was inside her. When he wasn't, it only made him acutely aware that she was a consummate actress and a hypocrite, playing whatever role she needed to play to get what she wanted. Typical woman. But at the moment he didn't give a damn. He heaved against her one final time and came in a hot rush of satisfaction.

The satisfaction would be short-lived. It always was. There was that burst, that instant when his body reached its climax, that was sweet and good, but it always fell short of what some other part of him wanted. He would be physically sated. Ann never failed him that way. His body never failed him that way. And he told himself that was all he wanted—the physical release. But as he eased himself down on top of her, he couldn't quite escape the faint hollow feeling in his gut. In that single unguarded moment when a man was at his weakest, he couldn't quite deny the need. He wouldn't name it, wouldn't make a move to do anything about it, wouldn't see it as anything other than a weakness, but he couldn't deny it was there.

"You screw good for a country boy." Ann's voice, still breathless in the afterglow, cut through Dane's moment of introspection like a razor.

He flashed her a grin that was just short of being cold. "Aw, shucks, ma'am, it's all that practice we get on sheep at an early age," he drawled with biting sarcasm.

Ann gave a throaty chuckle. She enjoyed prodding him about being a hick from the sticks. She knew it hit a nerve. He'd caught the feral gleam of satisfaction in her eyes more than once when a barb had stuck and spiked his temper. He suspected it was a calculated defense, a way of keeping an emotional buffer between them. The buffer he appreciated, the method pissed him off.

"You baaad boy," she said, snickering.

"Better sheep than city bitches."

She reached a hand up and stroked his head the way she might pet a favorite dog. "Now, don't get nasty, darling."

"I thought that was what we came here for."

She laughed again. Her perfectly manicured fingers skated down Dane's back to his buttocks. She squeezed his ass and arched up beneath him, her body tightening around his cock, enticing him to hardness again.

"That's right, Sheriff Jantzen," Ann murmured, her eyelids drooping to half-mast as she savored the sensation of him swelling inside her. "So let's get down to business."

Dane moved against her, his eyes narrowed, mouth set in a grim line. No, he didn't like Ann Markham much, but he liked what she did for him. She kept him sexually appeased and emotionally on guard, and that, he insisted, was all he really wanted from any woman.

On the chrome-and-glass stand beside the bed a pager went off.

"Dammit!"

"Shit!"

"Yours or mine?" Ann asked, all business in the blink of an eye. Dane disengaged, and she scrambled out from under him and rose up on her knees, scraping her tumbled bangs out of her eyes as she reached toward the stand.

"Mine," Dane barked. He swung his long legs over the side of the bed and reached for the phone. "This had better be nothing short of murder."

Ann chuckled. "Murder in Tyler County. That'll be the day. People down there die of boredom, not mayhem."

Dane growled in reply, a sound that might have been either agreement or rebuttal, but was in any event unpleasant.

"Lorraine, this is my night off." He snarled into the mouthpiece through gritted teeth, annoyance ringing in his every word.

The woman on the other end of the line completely disregarded his tone of voice and the threat implicit in it and rushed eagerly into her news, as breathless as if she'd just run a mile to get to the phone. "Dane, you're not going to believe this. Someone's gone and killed Jarrold Jarvis. They found him out at Still Waters."

"Killed?" Dane murmured, his annoyance jelling into a cold lump in his stomach. He straightened his spine and squared his broad shoulders, coming unconsciously to attention. He drove a hand into his hair, slicking it back from his forehead. "You mean he died. He had a heart attack or something."

"Oh, no. I wish that was what I meant, but Mark was very clear. He said killed."

Killed. Murdered. Christ. There hadn't been a murder in Tyler County in decades. The idea stunned him, numbed him like a blow between the eyes. With an effort he cut a narrow line through the haze in his brain and forced his mind to function in its official capacity.

"How?"

The dispatcher hummed a note of anxiety. Dane could picture Lorraine Worth's penciled-in eyebrows drawing together above the rims of her rhinestone-studded glasses. When she finally spit it out, her voice had dropped to the near whisper people of her generation reserved for tragedy and scandal. "His throat was cut. Mark said his throat had been cut . . . from ear to ear."

THREE

DANE TURNED HIS BLACK-AND-WHITE BRONCO IN at the drive to the Still Waters resort and gunned the engine. A crowd had already gathered, and he had to swerve off onto the rutted, hard-packed dirt to find a place to park among the cars and TV station news vans. He swore as he climbed down out of the truck and strode across the uneven ground of the construction site, pain biting into his bum left knee with every step, telling him better than any meteorologist that there was a storm brewing. He ignored the pain and glared at the people who had come to catch a glimpse of death.

Someone had killed Jarrold Jarvis. No matter how many times he replayed the message in his head, it still didn't seem real to him. He hadn't particularly liked the man—no one had—but he wouldn't have wished him dead, and he couldn't think of anyone who would have—not sincerely enough to carry it through. Jarvis was—had been—a blowhard and a bully, a man who liked to throw his considerable weight around and bask in the limelight like a beached walrus in the sun, but those weren't reasons enough to kill him.

The fact remained, someone had not only wished him dead, but had taken the necessary steps to make that wish become a reality.

Already the scene of the crime had taken on a ghoulish, circus atmosphere. Every rube in the county with a police scanner had come to gawk. Three black-and-white Tyler County cruisers were parked at haphazard angles around Jarvis's Lincoln, like covered wagons circled around the pioneers to protect them from Indian attacks, only the worst attack had already taken place. Death had been dealt. Their job now was to protect the body from the vultures. The deputies stood guard around the fringes of the scene, nervously discouraging onlookers from getting too close. Floodlights on the cars combined with utility lights strung up on the naked skeleton of the resort building to illuminate the tableau with a constant harsh white light that was punctuated by the flashing blue and red of the cruiser beacons. Above it all, Mother Nature added to the display with strobes of lightning.

At a glance, Dane estimated nearly fifty people in attendance and about half of them were headed his way with bright eyes, raised voices, and cameras. Reporters. Christ. As a life form, he ranked them slightly above child molesters. They would ask stupid, obvious questions and expect answers he couldn't possibly give. They would dog his heels like a pack of rabid mongrels, slavering shamelessly over every scrap he tossed them. One of the reasons he had left L.A. after his retirement from football had been to shake the damn press that had crowded in on his personal life and the three-ring circus of his divorce. Now they were here too, invading his county, sniffing around for blood and dirt. He looked down at the ground as hand-held lights threatened to blind him.

"Sheriff Jantzen, does this come as a shock?"

"Sheriff, did he have any enemies?"

"Do you have any suspects?"

"Were there any witnesses?"

Dane ignored the questions being hurled at him from all sides, knowing that if he paused, if he offered one sentence in answer and gave them an opening, they would pounce. Chief Deputy Mark Kaufman shouldered aside two of the reporters and reached him first. Kaufman was a short, stocky man of thirty-five with a receding line of coffee-brown hair and perpetually worried eyes. His khaki uniform shirt was sweat-stained, and dust streaked his black trousers. He cracked his knuckles one at a time as he fell into step with Dane. "Jeez, we thought you'd never get here."

"Who found him?" Dane demanded in a low voice.

"Elizabeth Stuart. She's that gal that bought the *Clarion*. Moved into the old Drewes place." He shook his head like a man who'd been dazed. "Brother, she's a looker, let me tell you."

Dane's steps faltered at the sound of helicopter blades beating the air. As he glanced up, a spotlight poured down on them. Squinting, he managed to catch a glimpse of the call letters of a Twin Cities television station emblazoned across the side of the chopper. The machine hovered above them, another vulture looking for its share of the victim.

"Judas Priest," he snapped. "Don't they have enough crime of their own to report on?"

He didn't wait for an answer from his deputy, but pushed his way past another half-dozen people, all barking for his attention. Kenny Spencer, the young deputy trying to hold his section of the throng at bay, was clearly relieved to see him and eagerly stepped back to let him into the circle of calm that had been established around the crime scene. The eye of the storm.

"Evening, Sheriff," he said, nodding and swallowing nervously, his Adam's apple bobbing in his throat as his gaze darted from Dane to the reporters. His long, thin face was chalky-white and gleaming with sweat.

"Hell of a way to spend the evening, huh, Kenny?"

Kenny couldn't quite muster a smile. At twenty-three, death was something he had seen rarely. The car accident that had claimed Milo Thornson last winter. Edith Baines after her heart attack at the Sons of Norway dance. But this was an entirely different kind of thing. This death had been deliberate and vicious. Someone had literally ripped the life from Jarrold Jarvis, had cut his throat and drained it out of him in a torrent of blood.

Kenny shuddered at the thought as his supper threatened a return trip from his stomach. He swallowed hard and turned a grayer shade of pale.

Dane gave his deputy a pat on the shoulder and forced himself to take another step toward the Lincoln. He didn't blame the kid for being rattled. He wasn't exactly looking forward to this himself. Death was never pretty and it was never pleasant. He'd been a deputy for seven years and a sheriff for two, but somehow he had never really believed he would have to face death in its most brutal form. Not here.

Murder had no business in Still Creek. It had been a fact of life he had grown almost blasé about during his years in Oakland and L.A. The headlines had been so commonplace in the newspaper, he hadn't bothered to do much more than scan the stories on his way to the comics. But murder didn't belong here. People in Still Creek didn't lock their doors. They left their keys in their cars. They never hesitated to stop to help a stranger. Murder wasn't something that happened in Tyler County. It was something to read about in the city papers. It was something that occasionally shocked everyone in Rochester, the nearest "big" town of sixty thousand people. It was a fact on the nightly news that everyone frowned about and worried over in the most abstract of ways, something that happened out in the big world, where everything was going to hell in a hand basket. But it didn't directly touch the lives of the residents of Tyler County. Until now.

Dane's broad shoulders rose and fell as he planted his hands at his waist and heaved a sigh. He tried to take in the scene with the eyes of a police officer—objective, observant. But he couldn't fend off the initial shock of seeing a man lying dead and knowing another human being had caused that death. The tremors reached the very bedrock of his life. His face, however, remained impassive as he squatted down beside the body.

Jarvis lay bellydown on the gravel like a fat dead seal, his arms at his sides. His feet were still inside the car.

With one hand he gingerly lifted the man's right shoulder and took a look. The wound was obvious and ugly, a deep slash across the throat that revealed more of the inner workings of the human body than Dane cared to see. The fine layers of skin at the edges of the gash had curled back slightly, giving the impression of a macabre smile on hideously distorted lips, lips painted with dark maroon congealed blood.

He had died quickly, too quickly to have reconciled himself to his fate, Dane thought, tearing his gaze away from the wound and taking in the dazed expression in the dark eyes, the mouth open in shock, as if he had started to cry out, only to find it too late.

Jarvis hadn't been a handsome man alive. Somewhere around fifty, he had a jowly, mushed-in face, thick lips that were perpetually curved into a horseshoe-shaped frown. He had worn his carrot-red hair slicked back with Vitalis in a modified pompadour that looked as incongruous on his big head as a beanie would have. Death had not improved him any. His skin had begun to lose the chalky-white cast of recent death, taking on a faint pink tint instead, a shade that clashed ghoulishly with his blood, the blood that had begun to harden on the front of his yellow dress shirt, stiffening the sodden fabric like an overdose of starch.

For just a second Dane could see in his mind's eye what must have happened the instant the blade had sliced across the man's throat. His stomach tightened at the sea of blood flowing in his imagination.

"Jesus," he murmured, letting go of Jarvis's shoulder. Rigor mortis had yet to set in, and the body slumped back into place limply, two hundred sixty pounds of lifeless flesh and fat. Dane sat back on his heels and raked his hands back through his hair.

"I guess Jarrold won't be cheating at poker anymore."

Boyd Ellstrom leaned against the back door of the Lincoln, his arms folded across his chest. The beginnings of a paunch strained the buttons of his uniform shirt and spilled over the waistband of his black trousers. At forty-two he had finally outgrown the baby face that had plagued him most of his life. Now he simply looked petulant, his full lips perpetually turned down in a pout that suddenly made Dane think of Jarvis.

"Good job, Ellstrom," he drawled sardonically as he rose. "Dust the car for prints with your butt. The BCA boys will love you."

The deputy made a sour face as he pushed himself away from the Lincoln. "You called the BCA? This is our case, Dane. We don't need them."

"Yeah, I can see how professionally you're handling it," Dane said dryly.

"Well, I sure as hell wouldn't have called in outsiders."

"It wasn't your choice, was it?"

"Not this time."

Dane ground his teeth, biting back a retort. He didn't need to get into a fight with one of his own deputies in front of the press. He merely stared at Ellstrom. A flicker of uneasiness crossed Ellstrom's fleshy face, then he turned and swaggered away with his thumbs hooked into his belt.

Tamping down his temper, Dane moved away from the car; ostensibly looking for clues, all the while wondering why Boyd Ellstrom had remained on the Tyler County force after he'd lost the race for the sheriff's office. The man had fifteen years experience; he could have gone anywhere in the state and gotten a better job than the one he had here.

"Boyd says you called in the BCA."

"They're the experts," Dane said, his voice soft and deadly. He turned his scowl on his chief deputy and ticked his reasons off on his fingers one by one. "We've got no lab, we've got no forensics team, we've got no one who has seen a murder anywhere but on television. I don't think anyone here has picked up enough from watching *Columbo* to do this right."

The state Bureau of Criminal Apprehension had been designed for just such circumstances as these. Comprised of specialists who had at their central lab all the latest technology for analyzing evidence, the bureau was at the disposal of every law enforcement center in the state. It was a sheriff's decision whether to call them in or not. As far as Dane could see, a country cop would have to have shit for brains to leave the BCA out of a murder investigation.

"We've never handled a murder. I don't want this fucked up."

Kaufman shrugged and strived to look innocent, raising his hands in surrender. "Hey, me neither. I'll be glad to have them."

Dane's jaw hardened and his eyes narrowed as he stared over at Ellstrom, who was barking at the reporters like an ineffectual guard dog. "We don't all seem to be in agreement on that point."

"Yeah . . . well . . ." Kaufman cracked his knuckles and shuffled his feet. "You know Boyd."

"Yeah, I know Boyd. He couldn't find shit in a cow barn but he thinks he can solve a murder on his own."

Kaufman cleared his throat nervously and stepped a little to one side, diplomatically drawing Dane's eyes away from Boyd Ellstrom. "What do we do until the BCA boys get here?"

"Pray it doesn't rain," Dane said as thunder rumbled overhead and pain bit into his knee. "Don't touch anything. Don't let anybody else touch anything. They'll take care of all the photography, the fingerprinting, physical evidence. We just have to stay out of their way and do whatever they ask. Yeager will be here within the hour. So will the lab."

"Right."

"Where's the Stuart woman?"

Kaufman motioned toward the mob of reporters and gawkers that were pressing in on the scene. "Tough lady. She made me take her back to her car so she could get her camera."

Dane snorted. "Compassionate, huh? Bring her over here."

As the deputy went off toward the crowd, Dane called to mind what facts he knew about Elizabeth Stuart, the new publisher of the Still Creek *Clarion*. Like most everyone in the country, he had heard about her divorce from Atlanta media mogul Brock Stuart. It had been impossible to escape the story. The headlines had been plastered across every sleazy tabloid, told and retold by the radio and television newspeople, detailed in every major paper.

What a world. Every day people died horrible deaths, society was coming apart at the seams because of drugs and AIDS and the pollution of the planet. Wars were being fought with thousands of lives in the balance. And Elizabeth Stuart's divorce had made headlines. For a few short weeks her life as a gold digger had taken precedence over world events.

Dane had absorbed the information with the morbid fascination of a man who had gone through his own version of the battle of the exes. The woman had already been married at least once when she'd managed to snare Stuart. He had tolerated her lavish spending habits the way a billionaire might, but he had eventually objected to her infidelities and had finally called her on them. Naturally, she had tried to lay the blame at his feet. She had hurled all manner of accusations about him, the predominant one being that he nailed anything in skirts. But she hadn't been able to substantiate her case. Naturally, she had portrayed herself as an innocent while she had tried to cut herself a big chunk of his financial pie, but, for once, justice had prevailed. Dane thought Stuart had to be some kind of a saint for giving the woman a nickel after the way she'd treated him. From what he'd seen, she was nothing but trouble with a capital T.

And now she was here, in Still Creek, Minnesota, tangled up in the first murder they'd had in thirty-three years. Christ.

"Sheriff"—Kaufman cleared his throat nervously as he led her up by the elbow—"this is Miss—er, Mrs.—um—"

Elizabeth took pity on the deputy. When he'd shown up at her house to pick her up, he'd been tongue-tied the instant he'd set eyes on her. He looked at her now with a shy, lovesick kind of smile, his eyes shining like a spaniel's. Men, she thought, resisting the urge to roll her eyes. She offered her hand to the sheriff. "Elizabeth Stuart, Sheriff Jantzen. I'd say it's a pleasure to meet you, but the circumstances aren't exactly ideal, now, are they?"

Her voice was dark and sultry, Dane thought, warm, a little rough. Smoke and heat. Satin and sex.

She stared up at him with gray eyes fringed by thick black lashes. The spotlight behind her backlit her wild black mane like a holy aura and made her skin look so pale that her mouth stood out like a cherry in the snow. A tiny scar hooked downward from the left corner, tempting a man to trace it with the tip of his finger or the tip of his tongue.

Damn, he thought, no wonder Brock Stuart had fallen for her. He let his gaze wash down over the rest of Elizabeth Stuart with insulting insolence.

A Nikon camera hung on a thick leather strap around her neck, the weight of it pressing her oversize turquoise T-shirt to her full breasts. The jeans she wore were tight and faded. A small waist was accented by a tooled leather belt and a big silver buckle depicting a barrel racer. Gently flared hips met long, long legs. The jeans were tucked into a pair of slightly battered, obviously expensive black cowboy boots that rose nearly to her knees.

"Have you about looked your fill, Sheriff?" Elizabeth drawled sarcastically.

She'd been ogled plenty in her thirty-four years, but it had never unnerved her quite as much as it was doing now. She put it down to the circumstances and stubbornly dismissed the fact that Sheriff Jantzen was a prime example of the male of the species. He had what she called the "lean and hungry look"—a tough athleticism, a certain predatory animal magnetism that radiated from the hard planes of his face and the angular lines of his body, and charged the air around him. He didn't much look the part of a sheriff in his pleated tan Dockers and lavender polo shirt, but there was no mistaking the air of authority. Uniform or no, he was the man in charge, the dominant male.

He lifted his gaze to hers and gave her a long, level stare that told her nothing she could say would embarrass him into behaving if he didn't want to. He had eyes like those of an Arctic wolf—cool blue and keenly watchful. They were set deep beneath a straight brow line that only enhanced his predatory expression. She had the disconcerting feeling that he could see right past her shield of bravado, that he could see clear into her soul if he wanted to. That made him one dangerous man.

"What time did you find the body?" he asked, his voice at once loud enough for her to hear clearly but quiet enough so his words wouldn't reach beyond the deputies.

"I—I don't know," she stammered. "I wasn't wearing a watch."

She could have added that her Rolex was reposing in a pawnshop in Atlanta, but she doubted the man in front of her would have cared. He didn't strike her as the sympathetic sort. His face could have been carved from stone for all the emotion it showed.

"We figure it must have been about eight-thirty," Deputy Kaufman said, recovering from the speechlessness Elizabeth had inspired in him.

"That was more than two hours ago," Dane said sharply.

Kaufman rushed to the lady's defense. "She had to get a buggy ride from the Hauers' to her place to use the phone. You know how Aaron Hauer is about getting involved with outsiders. I don't imagine he hurried any. And then we had to wait for you. . . ." The deputy's explanation trailed off pathetically as his boss fixed him with a steely glare.

Dane turned that same look on Elizabeth. "Did you see who killed him?"

"No. I didn't see anybody, except . . ." Her voice faded away as her gaze flicked toward Jarvis. She rubbed a hand across her mouth.

"He was like that when you found him?"

"No. He was inside the car. I opened the door to talk to him and he—"

She pressed her lips together and gagged down the lump of fear and revulsion that clogged her throat. She couldn't stop the tremor that rattled through her body or the image that flashed through her head—Jarvis falling dead at her feet. *On* her feet, to be precise. His head had landed smack on her toes. The blood from his wound had colored her feet so that she hadn't been able to distinguish her skin from the straps of her red sandals. Bile rose in her throat, and she shivered again.

"So he looked just like this when you left here?" Jantzen asked, all business, no compassion.

She forced herself to glance again at the dead man, expecting to see his glassy eyes staring at her in surprised disbelief, but all that met her gaze was a helmet of oily red hair. "No. That's not how he looked."

Dane turned to his chief deputy. "Who moved the body?" he demanded in a tone that did not invite confession.

Kaufman shuffled his feet on the gravel and cracked his knuckles. "Jeez, Dane, you didn't see him," he mumbled. "We couldn't leave him that way; it wasn't decent."

"Decent?" Dane questioned, his voice deadly calm.

The deputy swallowed hard. "We just turned him over, is all. Hell, it wasn't as if the killer had left him right there."

Dane arched a brow, his temper in grave danger of boiling over. His voice grew even softer. "No? How do we know that, Mark?"

Kaufman closed his eyes, wincing. All his explanations stuck in his throat.

Dane turned on his heel and started to walk back toward the Lincoln.

Elizabeth's mouth dropped open as Jantzen's words sank in. Furious, she bolted forward.

"Just what do you mean by that crack?" she said, impulsively grabbing hold of his arm as she caught up with him.

He looked down at her with disdain, his gaze lingering on her hand, pale and perfectly manicured against his tan skin. Elizabeth felt a shudder of awareness shake her. As casually as she could manage, she removed her hand from his arm and took a half-step away from him. The word "dangerous" drifted through her mind again. She lifted her chin and matched him regal look for regal look.

"Are you implying I had something to do with Jarvis's death?"

"I'm inferring that you may not be telling us the truth," he said. "We won't know for certain until we question you."

Anger flashed in her eyes like quicksilver, and she took a deep breath, obviously intending to tell him just what she thought of him and his theory. Dane casually turned away and motioned for Kenny Spencer to join them. He smiled a nasty smile as he heard the woman behind him choke on her rebuttal. He doubted she had much experience with men turning their backs on her. It gave him tremendous satisfaction to think he might have been the first.

"Kenny, take Ms. Stuart back to the station and wait for me there in my office."

"Yes, sir." The young deputy turned toward Elizabeth expectantly. "Ma'am?"

Elizabeth ignored him. She wheeled on Dane, grabbing his arm again as he started to walk away from her. "Are you arresting me, Sheriff?"

"Not at the moment."

"Then I should be able to come in on my own, later," she argued. "I heard you called in the boys from the state crime lab. I'd like to stay and see them in action. I do have a job to do here, you know."

"I don't give a rat's ass about your job."

"You have no right—"

"I have every right, Mrs. Stuart." He leaned over her, trying to intimidate her with his height and his scowl. "You're a witness in a murder investigation."

"I'm also a member of the press."

"I'll try not to hold that against you."

Thinking of her struggling new business, Elizabeth swung an arm in the direction of the small crowd waiting at the perimeter of the area that had been cordoned off by the deputies. "I have as much right to stay here as the rest of them."

She didn't like the idea of making money off a man's death, but then, that was the news. Nothing on God's green earth was going to bring Jarrold Jarvis back to life, but Jarrold could still help her pay her bills and put food on the table for herself and her son. She wasn't going to let Dane Jantzen take that chance away from her without a fight.

Dane flicked a glance at the reporters and photographers who were waiting like hyenas at the site of a lion's kill. They watched for the opportunity to break past the deputies and snatch a juicy tidbit for their papers or news programs. They listened for every scrap of information they could catch. He could single out the ones who had come down from Minneapolis and St. Paul. They had a certain look—hungry, aggressive, clever. Their eyes gleamed with the same kind of excitement Ann Markham's had at the prospect of fast, hard sex. The others, from the smaller stations and papers in Rochester, Austin, and Winona, would be less assertive but no less persistent in their quest for dirt. That was the pecking order of the press. As far as Dane was concerned, none of them had any right to be here. A man had been killed. It was a tragedy, not a photo opportunity.

Without looking at Elizabeth he gave a curt nod toward the nearest cruiser. "Take her, Kenny."

"No!" Elizabeth whispered furiously, no more eager to be overheard by her colleagues than Dane was. She leaned up toward him until they were nearly nose to nose. *"I found him—"*

"Finders keepers?" Dane snorted, his eyes narrowing in derision. God, she was a cold-blooded bitch, eager to make a nickel off a man any way she could. It didn't even seem to matter to her whether the poor bastard was alive or dead.

He thought of the men she had loved and left, of the way she had tried to milk gold from Brock Stuart. He thought of Tricia trading him in for a younger, more ambitious man and the L.A. press lapping up the story like greedy cats at spilled cream. The reins on his temper slipped a little farther through his hands.

"You think you deserve an exclusive, Mrs. Stuart?" His mouth twisted into a grim smile. "Fine."

Elizabeth gasped as his hand closed around her upper arm. He set off once again toward the body, this time towing her in his wake as though she were a child's pull toy. He stopped, kneeling beside Jarvis and jerking her down with him so violently that she had to let go of her camera and grab the open car door with her free hand to keep from falling on Jarvis. The camera bounced hard off her sternum and the gravel of the drive dug into her knees as she settled with a grunt beside the body.

"You want an exclusive, Mrs. Stuart?" He reached down and rolled the body over without looking at it, his gaze riveted to Elizabeth's face. "Here's a Kodak moment for you, Liz. Snap a few shots for the old scrapbook while you're at it. Be sure to get that charming smile— the one below his second chin."

Tears welled in Elizabeth's eyes as she relived the horror of what she had discovered two long hours before. She choked them back with an effort and glared at Dane Jantzen, in that moment hating him about as much as she hated anything. "Jesus Christ, you're a bastard," she spat out.

"Don't you forget it, honey." He rose, pulling her up with him, and turned to hand her over to Spencer, but Kenny had inadvertently gotten an eyeful of Jarvis and was leaning on the trunk of the Lincoln throwing up on his boots.

"Ellstrom!" Dane barked at the deputy, who stood staring blankly down at the body. "Take Mrs. Stuart to the station and make her comfortable. She'll be giving us a statement later on."

Ellstrom pulled his gaze away from Jarvis. A worry line creased up between his brows. "But the lab guys—"

"Will muddle through without your expert supervision," Dane said dryly, handling Elizabeth over by the elbow.

"I'll give you a statement all right, Sheriff." She jerked her arm free of Ellstrom's clammy grasp and took an aggressive step toward Jantzen. A particularly insulting and vulgar suggestion sprang to mind, but she couldn't get the words past her tongue as she stared up at him. The expression in his eyes was too mocking, too amused. He would undoubtedly laugh at her if she lost control and smirk at her if she backed down. It was a no-win situation. The thing she longed to do most was kick him, but she didn't need to add assaulting an officer to everything else that had gone wrong today.

"At a loss for words, Mrs. Stuart?" he asked, arching a brow.

"No," she snarled through clenched teeth. "I just can't seem to find one bad enough to call you."

"There's a thesaurus on my desk. Feel free to use it."

"Don't tempt me, sugar," she said as she took a step back toward the waiting deputy. "What I'd like to do with it wouldn't exactly be good for the binding."

Dane chuckled in spite of the fact that he disliked her. She had a lot of sass . . . and a backside that could make a man's palms sweat, he observed as she sauntered away with Ellstrom. She moved like sin. And the way she filled out a pair of jeans was enough to make Levi Strauss rise from the dead.

It was too damn bad she was nothing but trouble.

FOUR

BOYD ELLSTROM PILOTED THE CRUISER DOWN THE
drive, away from the resort and the swarm of reporters
that had attempted to descend on the car. That son of a
bitch Jantzen would grab what glory he could with the
press, but Boyd was the one escorting the star witness
away from the crime scene. More than one camera had
captured that on film and videotape. He made a mental
note to get as many copies of the photos as he could.
They would come in handy when the next election rolled
around.

Yessirree, the way he saw it, nothing but good could
come from old Jarrold biting the big one. Dying was
probably the only thing the old fart had ever done that
would benefit others more than it did himself. Jarrold
wasn't going to get anything out of it but a chance to rot
in the ground. Boyd, on the other hand, was looking at a
much rosier future—provided he found a certain IOU
before anyone else stumbled onto it.

The idea of that damned note floating around had
his bowels twisting like a snake in its death throes. He
wished for a Tums.

Jarvis had always kept to himself the names of the
people who owed him money and favors. As much as he
had enjoyed publicly lording it over other people, he had
gotten off just as much on the feeling of playing God,
manipulating with unseen hands, giving and taking at

will. He had kept all the damning evidence hidden away somewhere, producing it like an evil magician when he wanted to apply a little pressure—as he had with Boyd earlier that day.

The fat toad had been walking around town all day with that damned note in his pants pocket. *Boyd Ellstrom: $18,700.* He'd slipped it out and set it on the table at the Coffee Cup just that morning while pretending to hunt for change for a tip. Boyd had just about died at the sight. For the minute and a half that slip of paper had lain on the table, in plan sight of half the town, he had seen his whole cursed life pass before his eyes and swirl right down the toilet. If anyone in Still Creek got wind of him owing Jarvis—or, more important, *why* he owed Jarvis—he could just bend over and kiss his political ass good-bye. Jarvis had merely smiled at him over the rim of his coffee cup, the pig.

Well, he'd died like a pig too, hadn't he? Boyd thought. Like a pig at the slaughterhouse. Poetic justice, that's what that was.

Elizabeth studied the deputy from the corner of her eye, not liking what she could see of his face in the light from the dashboard instruments. He kind of favored Fred Flintstone with his big square head and droopy shoulders. He had the look of a bully about him, the kind of man who sought out positions of authority to give him a sense of power over other people.

She had learned early on in her life to be a quick and shrewd judge of character. It had been essential to her survival as she'd come of age around Bardette, a dusty, hopeless place where the honky-tonk and whorehouse were the only thriving businesses and most of the men were meaner than the rattlesnakes that coiled behind every rock. She had learned to size up a man at glance. Deputy Ellstrom fit into the same category as Jarrold Jarvis had.

The image of Dane Jantzen filled her head in Technicolor memory—handsome, predatory, churlish. What category did he fit into? One all his own, she thought, doing her best to ignore the disturbing shift of feelings inside her—heat and uneasiness, wariness and anger. The last thing she needed right now was to run afoul of a man like Dane Jantzen.

She had come to Still Creek to start her life over, to build up a business and her self-respect and her relationship with her son. They hadn't been here three weeks and she was embroiled in a murder investigation and on the bad side of the sheriff. Pure damn wonderful.

"Did you know him?" she said abruptly, needing to break the silence and her train of thought.

Ellstrom jerked his head in her direction as if he'd forgotten she was sitting there. "Jarrold? Sure I knew him. Everybody did." He said it almost defiantly, daring her to dispute the fact that the dead man had been well known if not well loved.

"This is quite a shock, I guess," she said, intrigued.

He shifted on the seat and mumbled something under his breath as he adjusted the volume control on the police radio. The crackle of static rose like the noise from one of those mechanical ocean wave sound devices guaranteed in the backs of cheap magazines to put people to sleep. It put Elizabeth's teeth on edge. She flinched at the discordant screeching but tuned in automatically when word of the BCA mobile lab's imminent arrival came across the airwaves.

Ellstrom chewed on a swear word, clenching his jaw, his hands on the steering wheel.

"I take it you don't approve," Elizabeth commented, turning sideways on the seat so she could better gauge his responses.

"We could handle this ourselves," he said, still defensive. "Jantzen brings in those city boys and we'll be nothing but gofers. We don't need a bunch of college dickheads poking around."

A sly smile tugged at one corner of Elizabeth's mouth. Dissension among the ranks. She knew without having to ask, Jantzen would hate it. He had the air of the absolute ruler about him.

"Can I quote you on that, Deputy?" she asked, her tone curling automatically into honey and smoke. She wasn't above the prudent use of feminine wiles, as long as she didn't compromise herself. A girl had to use what tools she had at her disposal. If batting a lash or two would loosen a man's tongue, she figured that was his problem, not hers.

An even nastier smile turned the corners of Ellstrom's lips as he considered the ramifications of having Elizabeth Stuart quote him in the *Clarion*. Jantzen would shit a brick. That alone made it worth his while.

He shot her a sideways glance, taking in the big silver eyes and ripe mouth. He'd seen her around town. She had a body that could give a man a fever. He couldn't make up his mind which he would grab first if he got the chance, tits or ass. Either way, a man was guaranteed a good time. It wouldn't hurt him a bit to do her a favor or two, he thought, shifting a little in his seat as the crotch of his pants tightened up, making him forget about his intestinal distress for a moment. Rumor had it she'd be willing to return a man's favor—on her back. His dick twitched at the thought.

"Yeah, sure. Why not." He straightened up behind the wheel, puffing his chest out with self-importance. "Like I said, Jantzen's blowing this investigation calling in outsiders. We can take care of our own in Tyler County."

"My, you certainly do sound like the voice of authority, Deputy," Elizabeth murmured, glad for the poor light so he couldn't see her roll her eyes.

Ellstrom sniffed and nodded. "Yeah, well, I should have beat Jantzen in the last election, you know."

"Is that a fact?"

"He only won because he used to play pro football. Big fucking deal."

Elizabeth's imagination instantly conjured up a picture of Jantzen in full football regalia—pads accenting his shoulders, tight little spandex britches hugging his behind. She cursed herself for having a natural weakness for big, strapping athletic men. Her life would have been a whole hell of a lot tamer if she had been attracted to the anemic, balding, bookish type.

The headlights of the cruiser spotlighted her Eldorado hanging off the south side of the road, abandoned like a beached whale, and she heaved a sigh. Damn car. If it hadn't been for the fact that the Caddy had an undercarriage lower than a sow's belly, she would have driven right on past Still Waters and been home now, blissfully ignorant of Jarrold Jarvis's murder and blissfully ignorant of Dane Jantzen.

Ellstrom slowed the cruiser and gave the car a suspicious glance, showing off his miraculous cop instincts. "That yours?"

"Yep." Elizabeth's heart sank a little as they rolled past the car. She couldn't bring herself to be mad at it. It was the '76 model, a sleek cherry-red boat designed before the days of fuel economy and aerodynamics. The last of the GM ragtops of its day, the Eldorado had held the dubious distinction of being the world's biggest automobile that model year. It sucked gas by the gallon and used oil with the abandon of a Saudi sheikh, but Elizabeth loved every gaudy inch of it. It reminded her of Texas and money, things she had left behind.

"What happened?" Ellstrom asked, an extra touch of male arrogance sneaking into his voice. "Run out of gas?"

"No. It just sort of . . . acts up every once in a while," Elizabeth hedged. Bone-headed male smugness was something she could do without tonight. Tomorrow would be soon enough when she went in search of someone to tow the car back up onto the road. It would be a man, and he would pat her on the head and snicker to himself. In her opinion, the Lord had not seen fit to create nearly enough female tow-truck drivers. But then, he was a man.

"Have any ideas on who might have killed him?" she asked, steering the conversation back on track.

"Do you?" Ellstrom's eyes darted her way. "You're the witness."

"Me? Sugar, I didn't witness much more than my own regurgitated Snickers bar. The place could have been crawling with killers. I sure as hell didn't stick around to see. And I'm not long on theories either, Don't know anyone round here well enough to say whether or not they might kill someone. How about you? You being the man who should have won the election and all, you must know somebody who'd want old Jarrold dead and gone."

Ellstrom's face set into a scowl. Ignoring her, he reached for the microphone of the radio and called in to tell someone named Lorraine that he was bringing in an important witness and she had better have everything ready. Elizabeth settled back in her seat. Deputy Ellstrom's loquaciousness was apparently not going to extend beyond bad-mouthing his boss. Figured. If he spouted theories on suspects, he might actually have to back them up with something other than hot air.

Still Creek had closed up for the night. The imitation gaslights that lined Main Street cast a hazy pinkish glow on the shop fronts that shouldered up against one another on either side of the wide main street. The ornate facades of the buildings that had been constructed in the early 1880s stood like silent sentinels, dark windows staring blankly as the police car cruised past.

A tidy little town, Still Creek was kept spit-and-polish clean out of midwestern habit and for the benefit of the tourists being lured to take in the bucolic scenery and the sights of the many Amish farms in the area. There was no trash in the gutters, no shop fronts in need of paint. Wooden tubs of geraniums sat curbside at regular intervals. The occasional spiffy red park bench tucked up against a building offered respite for those weary of walking from gift shop to gift shop. Windows were decorated either with austere Amish artifacts and quilts that were like works of graphic art or with gaudy Scandinavian rosemaling painted on the window glass in colorful curlicues like frosting on a bakery cake. A banner had been strung up above Main Street advertising the annual

Horse and Buggy Days festival that would begin in one week.

The cruiser rolled slowly past the old building that housed the Still Creek *Clarion*. Like its neighbors to the north and south, it was built of dark brick two stories high with fancy dentils and cornices along the front belying the fact that it was really just a plain old square commercial building with a wet basement and dry rot in the floors. The gold letters arching across the wide first-floor window had been there for ninety-two years, proclaiming to one and all that the *Clarion* printed the truth.

Elizabeth thought of the hours she would put in the next day working on the story of what had happened to her that night. The truth. Looking around her at the sleeping town, she knew instinctively that the truth was going to go far beyond the death of Jarrold Jarvis, and Still Creek would never be the same. But the truth was what she had come here to print. The truth, unadorned and unadulterated.

The courthouse squatted like an enormous toadstool smack in the center of town, surrounded on three sides by Keillor Park. Built in 1882, the year the railroad had come through and Still Creek had won the title of Tyler County seat, it was constructed of native limestone, big square blocks of it stacked stone upon stone by Norwegian and German immigrants whose descendants still lived here. The old-time town square had forced Main Street to skirt around it and, while it was a picturesque arrangement, it wasn't conducive to traffic flow, explaining why the state highway had swung off to the west, missing the heart of Still Creek altogether.

Ellstrom pulled the cruiser into the parking lot and nosed it into a slot up against the side of the building that was marked SHERIFF JANTZEN. Elizabeth felt a smile threaten, but she ironed it out. Whatever this antagonism was between the sheriff and his deputy, it wasn't cute. The gleam in Ellstrom's eye was too malicious to be mistaken for cute.

He led the way into the building through a side door

marked TYLER COUNTY LAW ENFORCEMENT CENTER and down a set of marble stairs and a cool white hall glaring with bare fluorescent overhead lighting. Elizabeth followed him along the corridor and to the right, the heels of her cowboy boots thumping dully against the smooth, hard floor. She wondered what would come next and how long it would take. Trace was supposed to be home by eleven. The large round clock mounted above the dispatcher's station already showed eleven-ten.

"Lorraine," Ellstrom said in a tone of voice that rang with phony authority, "this is Miss Stuart. She's the one found Jarrold. Dane wants her to wait in his office. I have to get back out there and help secure the crime scene." He hitched up his pants and puffed out his chest. Macho and tough, the man in command.

Behind her big U-shaped fake birch desk, Lorraine Worth gave him the cold, hard look of a woman who wasn't fooled by much and certainly wasn't fooled by him. The dispatcher-cum-secretary sat at her post with schoolmarm posture and pinched lips, dressed in something June Cleaver would have worn around the house with a string of pearls at her throat. Her hair rose up an impressive height in a cast-iron bouffant the color of gunmetal. Her eyebrows were penciled on, thick, dark lines drawn in a style intended to make her look stern and to minimize the motherly quality of her eyes. She stated at Ellstrom from behind rhinestone-studded glasses that pinched up on the outside corners like cat's eyes, and somehow managed to look down her straight, long nose at him, even though he towered over her desk.

"The crime lab is about to arrive," she announced imperiously. "You'd better get out there, or there won't be anything left for you to do except sweep up the coffee cups."

Ellstrom narrowed his eyes to slits and scowled at her without noticeable effect, then turned on his heel and stalked away as Lorraine snatched up the receiver of the ringing telephone to her right.

"Tyler County sheriff's office . . . No, the sheriff has

no statement at this time . . . No arrests have been made that I'm aware of," she said, turning an eagle eye on Elizabeth, taking in her appearance in one scathing glance, disapproval tightening her mouth into nothingness. "I wouldn't know anything about the woman and I don't spread gossip, at any rate. Now, I must ask you to hang up. This line has to be left open for emergencies."

She ended the call herself, cradling the receiver with a resounding thump.

"I don't mind telling you, I dislike this business intensely," she said sternly, her gaze still boring through Elizabeth as if she was more than ready to lay the blame at her feet. "There hasn't been a murder in Tyler County in thirty-three years. Not since Olie Grimsrud did in Wendel Svenson, the milk hauler, for having hanky-panky with Leda Grimsrud behind the bulk tank in their milk house. I don't like it a bit."

"I'm not so crazy about it myself," Elizabeth said as the phone at Lorraine's elbow rang again. She didn't like the woman's implication that it was somehow her fault the amazing streak of law and order had ended, but she had caught the glimmer of fear beneath the anger in Lorraine Worth's eyes, and she sighed. Still Creek had been a safe haven for its residents for a long time. Now the ugly reality of a brutal world had intruded. The woman had a right to her anger.

Elizabeth's own nerves were frazzled right down to the nub. She wasn't in the habit of finding dead bodies practically within sight of her own house. The reminder of just how near home she had been made her shiver. She thought of Trace wandering along the road, maybe trying to hitch a ride from wherever he'd gone for the evening, and the nerves in her stomach congealed into a gelid lump.

"Listen, is there a pay phone around here I could use? I need to call my son."

The dispatcher gave her a long look that Elizabeth guessed was intended to communicate the woman's feelings about divorced mothers or women who stumbled across dead bodies, or both, then tilted her bouffant sharply to the left. Murmuring a thank-you, Elizabeth headed in the direction of the pay phone that hung on the far wall while Lorraine snatched up her receiver and singed some other poor curious fool's ear.

The phone at the other end of Elizabeth's call went unanswered for five rings before the answering machine switched on. She swore under her breath. It wasn't unusual for Trace to be late. In fact, it was the rule rather than the exception, one of his little ways of telling her he didn't like their new home, their new life-style, their new codes of conduct. The counselor in Atlanta had told her to give the boy structure; he had failed to mention how to get Trace to accept it.

Elizabeth left her message and hung up with a sigh. Her sweet little boy had been swallowed up by a sullen youth with troubled eyes and broad, tense shoulders; a defiant, belligerent teenager. But speaking with a defiant, belligerent teenager would have been much preferable to wondering where he was on the night of the first murder in Tyler County in thirty-three years.

She dug another quarter out of her purse, dropped it in the phone, and dialed again, then leaned a shoulder against the wall and stared across the room at Lorraine Worth. Frighteningly efficient, she sat at her station as alert as a Doberman on guard duty. On the sixth ring a muffled voice answered.

"Yeah, what? Who? Hmm?"

"Jolynn, it's me," Elizabeth said, lowering her voice to the pitch of conspiracy. "Did I wake you?"

"Stupid question. What are you, a reporter?"

"Wake up and listen. There's been a murder."

"A what?"

"Murder. Somebody killed somebody. I reckon you've seen it happen on television once or twice." She caught Lorraine Worth glaring over at her, her head tilting like a satellite dish tuning in for maximum reception. Elizabeth scowled and turned her back to the woman so she could speak with her editor privately.

It was Jolynn who had talked her into coming to Still Creek after the divorce, Jolynn who had talked her into buying the *Clarion,* Jolynn who was her one and only employee and nearly her only friend. Their friendship went back to El Paso and the University of Texas, a time that seemed a century in the past for all that had happened in between. Elizabeth thanked God it had endured the years of separation. After the divorce she had felt like one of those space-walking astronauts whose cord had been cut loose, just like in *2001: A Space Odyssey.* She had been adrift, in need of a place and something to anchor her to it. There had been Jolynn, telling her to come to Minnesota, where life was quiet and the people were friendly.

A considerable amount of creaking and shuffling in the background sounded from the other end of the line, and Elizabeth easily pictured Jolynn struggling to sit up in her secondhand bed, the old springs groaning and complaining as she heaved herself up against the headboard. Jo was no more than five foot four, but she was "generously proportioned," as she put it, and her old mattress had long since given up any pretense of providing support.

"Oh my God," she whispered. "Are you kidding?"

Elizabeth blew a sigh up into her bangs. "I wish I were, sugar, but I'm not. The man is dead as Kelsey's nuts, and I ought to know, 'cause I found him."

"Jeez Louise," Jo murmured reverently. "I had a migraine. I turned the scanner off and went to bed at nine o'clock. What happened?"

"Somebody killed Jarrold Jarvis out at Still Waters. Can you get out there right away?"

"Yeah, sure. Where are you?"

"At the courthouse. I'm liable to be tied up here awhile. It's a long story."

"I'll bet. God, Jarrold Jarvis. Somebody finally got up the balls to do it."

"The big question is who," Elizabeth said, twisting the telephone cord around her finger. "Can you get out there pronto? The BCA just made the scene. Them and about nine thousand reporters."

"Make it nine thousand and one, boss."

JOLYNN DROPPED THE RECEIVER BACK ON THE TELE-phone and dragged a hand through the mop of chin-length brown curls falling in her eyes, trying to digest the information Elizabeth had given her, trying to make it seem real. Murder. She tugged the sheet up to base of her throat, wadding the fabric in her fist, as if it could somehow protect her from the ugliness of the word.

Dim amber light glowed through the shade of the lamp that squatted on the nightstand. The pale pool of illumination suddenly seemed less than adequate. Dark corners of the shabby, messy room loomed menacingly and she felt transported back to her childhood, when every night shadow had held some evil menace.

"You're not leaving, are you, sweetheart?"

She flinched as if she'd forgotten the man lying beside her. He rolled toward her lazily, caught the edge of the sheet in one hand, and tugged the fabric aside to reveal a plump breast.

Jolynn twisted away from her ex-husband, swinging her legs over the edge of the bed. She let go of the sheet and reached down for the pile of clothes that lay in rumpled drifts across the worn beige carpet.

"Yes, I'm leaving. Sorry, Richard. Duty calls."

Behind her, Rich Cannon pushed himself up onto his knees on the sagging mattress. As Jo stepped into her panties he caught her around the waist from behind and pulled her back against him. "Come on, Jolynn. Dick's ready to play again." His erection poked at her, punctuating his statement like a physical exclamation mark.

"Richard." She groaned his name, disgusted with him and with herself.

She never failed to feel dirty and cheap after one of their little assignations. And she never failed to succumb to his charm the next time he came around. It was one of life's little cycles she couldn't seem to get out of. Like her period, she hated it but was always relieved when it arrived. That was about how she felt regarding Richard.

He had shown up on her back doorstep at eight-thirty, unannounced, unexpected, urgent. And she had taken him to her bed without so much as saying hello.

She grabbed his wrists now as his fingers slid into the tangle of dark curls at the apex of her thighs. He had broad hands with short, thick fingers and uncommonly well-kept fingernails. He hadn't bothered to remove either the wedding ring Susie Jarvis had put on his finger or the watch Jolynn had given him on their own fifth wedding anniversary.

"Now is not the time," she said, trying to pry his hands off her body.

"Don't say that," he grumbled, pouting. "Never say that to me when Susie's out of town."

"I'm afraid your wife chose the wrong day to go on a shopping spree," she said with venom. She couldn't help but resent Susie Jarvis Cannon. Susie had money. She had a nice house, a new car that more than likely ran on all cylinders. She had Jolynn's husband. Not that he was worth much out of bed. It was the principle of the thing that galled Jolynn. Susie had it all.

God, she really would have it all now that her father was dead. That Jarrold Jarvis was Susie's father hit Jolynn like an unpleasant surprise. She supposed she should have felt an ounce of sympathy toward the girl, but she didn't. She doubted Susie would grieve much on her way to the bank to pick up her inheritance.

Pushing herself away from the bed, out of Rich's reach, she grabbed up a wrinkled blue shirt from the Cedar Lanes bowling alley and thrust her arms into the sleeves. Giving up, Rich settled back against the metal headboard that was made to look like genuine walnut. It gave a hollow thump as his weight dented a curve into it. He lit a cigarette as he watched her dress, his eyes lingering on every curve she covered, his gaze disturbingly detached.

Jolynn told herself she imagined the coldness. Then she told herself she was used to it, that she expected it, that it didn't affect her. She had sex with him only because it was easy and habitual; it wasn't as though she were still in love with him or anything.

She pulled her jeans on and sucked in a breath so she could close the button and zipper. She had the kind of figure that had regrettably gone out of fashion with poodle skirts—full breasts, well-rounded hips that had rounded a little more in the five years since her divorce. She was thirty-three and her metabolism was slowing down in direct proportion to the increase in her appetite for junk food. The extra weight added a fullness to her rectangular face that had the benefit of making her look younger than she was. A person had to peer closely to see the tiny lines of stress that had begun to fan out beside her eyes and around her kewpie-doll mouth.

"So what's going on?" Rich asked, finally resigning himself to being something other than the center of attention for the moment.

Dragging a brush through her hair, Jolynn glanced at his reflection in the mirror above her dresser. Thirty-nine, a native son of Still Creek, he was handsome and he still radiated the arrogance he had cultivated as a high school jock—the high point of his life to date. He sat back in her bed as if he owned it, his straw-colored hair tousled, cigarette dangling beneath his mustache, one hand scratching absently through the thicket of rusty-gold curls on his chest. Elizabeth said he looked a little like Robert Redford as the Sundance Kid, only older and debauched. It was an apt description. There was a trace of meanness about his eyes and weakness in the line of his mouth that a person didn't see until the initial dazzle of golden good looks had worn off. He had told her he was going to run for the state representative's seat this fall. Jolynn wondered how many people would catch on to him before they cast their ballots.

Hate surged through her, as it always did when she looked at Rich and saw him for what he really was—the bastard who'd dumped her for a more advantageous marriage, then had the gall to come around expecting her to fall at his feet . . . which she did, again and again.

"Someone killed your dear old daddy-in-law tonight," she said bluntly, reaching for a spray bottle of Charlie on the cluttered dresser top. She spritzed herself generously, hoping to camouflage the scent of sex that lingered on her. Her eyes never left the mirror.

"No," Rich murmured, his face registering shock, but not much in the way of remorse. He set his cigarette aside in the overflowing ashtray on the nightstand, but didn't move from the bed. "Killed him? Huh. I'll be a son of a bitch."

"Yeah, you are. I'd stay to console you," Jo said dryly, grabbing her purse off the dresser, "but I've got a job to do."

"I'd think your new boss would want to take this one," he said. "She's the hotshot headliner from Atlanta, right? I'd think she'd be right out there to grab all the glory herself."

Jo gave him the same look she gave meat that had overstayed its welcome in her refrigerator. "All that thinking could tax your brain, Rich. I don't want you to hurt yourself, but if you'd think again, you might figure out that nobody working on the *Clarion* is going to get any glory unless we're hit and killed by a news van from Minneapolis."

"Then why go?" he said, holding his cigarette between his thumb and forefinger and taking a deep drag off it. The smoke he exhaled briefly wreathed his head in gray, then drifted up to add another layer of grime to the ceiling.

Jolynn looked at him with utter disgust, shaking her head in disbelief at her own stupidity for staying tangled up with him. "You just don't get it, do you, Richard? Some of us don't have wealthy wives to mooch off. Some of us take pride in doing a job. I happen to be good at what I do."

"Yeah," he sneered. "Too bad nobody gives a damn."

She flinched as if he'd struck her. He had always known just where to stick the barb to make it hurt the most; it was one of the few things he really excelled at. Pain bled through her. Her hazel eyes narrowed to slits. "You jerk."

She grabbed the first thing her hand fell on and flung it at him as hard as she could. He fended off the plastic container of Cover Girl face powder with his hands, knocking it aside and sending a mushroom cloud of fine dust into the air.

"Jesus, Jolynn!"

He hauled himself naked from the bed, choking on the combination of smoke and powder, half tripping as the sheet tangled around his knees. Jo turned and made a dash for the bedroom door, but was caught just shy of getting her hand on the doorknob. A strong arm banded across her midsection, and she was pulled back into the curve of Rich's body as he bent over her. She struggled to get away—from Richard, from herself, from her dumpy little bedroom in her dumpy little house.

"Come on, Jolynn," he cajoled, his mustache brushing the shell of her ear, scratchy and soft like the edge of an old shaving brush. He spewed out platitudes with the ease of long practice and little sincerity. "I'm sorry. I didn't mean it. I just don't want you to leave, baby."

"Tough shit. I'm going," she snapped, sniffing back tears. She may have had no pride when it came to sleeping with him, but she damn well wouldn't cry in front of him. She shrugged him off and took another step toward the door.

"I'll be here when you get back," he murmured.

She hesitated with her hand on the tarnished brass knob, dredging up the nerve she never seemed to find when he showed up on her doorstep. "Don't bother."

FIVE

"Y OU'D BETTER WAIT IN THE SHERIFF'S OFFICE."
Lorraine Worth grasped Elizabeth firmly by the elbow
and propelled her through the maze of gray metal desks
toward the door of Dane Jantzen's private lair. Behind
them and beyond the incessant ringing of the phone, Elizabeth could hear a commotion in the outer hall and
guessed that some of the press had decided to stake out
the courthouse, to lay in wait for the sheriff. Lorraine
looked extremely peeved at the prospect of having to
deal with them, her thin lips pressing into a grim white
line, penciled brows slashing down above her cat-eye
glasses like dark bolts of lightning. Without another
word the dispatcher hustled Elizabeth into the office,
thrust a cup of black coffee into her hand, and bolted
back for her station, swinging the door shut behind her.

Elizabeth set the coffee aside and dug a cigarette out
of her purse. A brass plaque on the desk shone up at her
under the glare of the fluorescent light, the words THANK
YOU FOR NOT SMOKING etched in bold black. She flipped it
facedown and lit up. Jantzen could thank someone else
for not smoking. After what she'd been through, she
damn well deserved a cigarette at the very least.

The lighter she used was wafer-thin, twenty-four-carat
gold, engraved on the flat side with the words "To B
from E with Love"—one of the small prizes she had
managed to get away with when Brock had told her to

move out of their penthouse apartment in Stuart Tower. The Nikon now reposing in the visitor's chair with its hideously expensive Hasselblad lens pointing at the ceiling was another. Small victories.

It wasn't that she approved of stealing. She didn't. Beneath her veneer of practical cynicism she was basically a morally upstanding sort of person. What she believed in was justice. But sometimes a person had to make her own. Brock had screwed her eight ways to Sunday in the divorce. She'd come away from the marriage battered and bloodied emotionally. A lighter and a camera didn't seem like much in the way of compensation, but they helped a little.

Trying not to think about it, she prowled around Dane Jantzen's office, the Virginia Slim smoldering in her right hand. She paused in her pacing long enough to bring it to her lips and take a deep, calming drag. She would have sold her soul for a tumbler of the forty-two-year-old malt whiskey Brock had specially flown in from Scotland—of which she had a case in her kitchen cupboard—but the best the dispatcher had been able to manage was coffee. Lorraine Worth probably didn't approve of strong drink; she had that kind of tight-ass Baptist look about her.

Elizabeth eyed the coffee cup perched on the corner of the sturdy oak desk and frowned. Caffeine was the last thing she needed. She wanted nothing more than a long, hot bath, the comfort of her bed, and a few hours of blessed oblivion. But her desires lingered out on the far horizon, shimmering like a mirage. What had already been an endless night was only going to get longer. And when the end of it finally came, and she was allowed to go home, there would be little comfort to be had. She didn't have a bathtub; she had a tin shower stall that was as narrow as a coffin and just about as pleasant to be in. She might have hot water, but it would be tinted orange from rusty old pipes. She had her bed, her big brass whorehouse bed, as Brock had called it, but she wasn't counting on getting much in the way of sleep. She doubted she would be able to close her eyes without see-ing Jarrold Jarvis spring out of his car like a broken jack-in-the-box.

To distract herself from the disturbing images, she continued her tour of Jantzen's office, studying, looking for clues about the man. Not that she cared on a personal level. From what she'd seen, Dane Jantzen was a grade A bastard. It was just good sense to know your adversary, that was all. She'd learned that lesson the hard way. Be-sides, she was going to want every detail she could get for her story. She was a journalist now, albeit at a two-bit weekly newspaper in middle-of-nowhere Minnesota, but a journalist nevertheless, and she was determined to do the job right.

The office was unremarkable. Flat white paint on the walls. One large window that would have given a pan-oramic view of the outer office had the blinds been raised. Industrial-grade gray carpet. A row of black file cabinets. The usual office paraphernalia, including a per-sonal computer. Diplomas and citations hung in simple black frames on one wall. There was nothing here of Dane Jantzen the man, no mounted deer heads or bowl-ing trophies or souvenirs from his football days.

He was neat. Not a good sign. Men who were neat liked to be in control of everything and everyone around them. Brock was fanatically fastidious and he wanted to control the whole blessed world. Dane Jantzen's desk shouted control. Files were labeled, stacked and lined up just so. His blotter was spotless. His pens were all in their little ceramic holder, tips down, arranged left to right by ink color, no doubt.

Beside the telephone was the one personal item in the room—a small wooden picture frame. Dangling her ciga-rette from her lip, Elizabeth lifted the frame and turned it for a look. The photograph was of a young girl, perhaps ten or eleven, just showing signs of growing into a gangly youth. Brown hair sprouted out the sides of her head in pigtails that hung past her shoulders. She was smiling shyly, crinkling her nose, emphasizing the freckles on her cheeks. Dressed in baggy shorts and a blazing orange T-shirt, she stood on a lawn somewhere holding up a sign done in multicolored Magic Markers that read I LOVE YOU, DADDY.

Elizabeth felt a jolt of surprise and something else. *Daddy.* "Holy Mike," she muttered. "Somebody actually married the son of a bitch."

"She has since seen the error of her ways, I assure you."

Elizabeth whirled toward the sound of that sardonic voice, managing to look guilty and knock her coffee to the floor all at once.

"Shit! I'm sorry."

Dane stuck his head out into the hall and calmly called to Lorraine for a towel.

"I was looking for an ashtray," Elizabeth lied, not quite able to meet his steady gaze as he turned back toward her. She stooped down and grabbed the cup, dabbing ineffectually at the stain on the rug with a wadded-up tissue she'd fished out of the pocket of her jeans.

"I don't smoke." He hitched at his slacks and hunkered down in front of her, his mouth twitching at one corner with cynical amusement. "It's not good for you."

She forced a wry laugh, dousing the stub of her cigarette in what coffee was left in the cup. "What is these days besides oat bran and abstinence?"

"Telling the truth, for starters," he said placidly.

She raised her head and sucked in a breath of air, startled by his nearness. He made no move to touch her, but she could feel him just the same, as if he'd reached out and caressed her.

Instinctively she leaned back, but her fanny hit the front of his desk and she realized he had her trapped. It wasn't a pleasant sensation.

"Telling the truth is my business, Sheriff," she said, struggling to sound prim instead of breathless.

"Really? I thought you were a reporter."

"Your towel, Sheriff."

At Lorraine's stern, disapproving voice, Dane pushed

himself to his feet and took the towel the dispatcher thrust at him.

"Thank you, Lorraine."

"I've told those people out there you have nothing further to say, but they aren't leaving. Apparently they're waiting for *her*," she said, stabbing Elizabeth with pointed look.

She rose on shaky legs, setting aside the coffee cup. She opened her mouth to speak, but Dane answered for her.

"She won't have anything to say to them."

Eyes narrowed in annoyance, Elizabeth propped a hand on her hip. "I can speak for myself, thank you very much."

"Not to the press you can't."

"You're not a judge, you can't impose a gag order."

He smiled slightly, wolfishly. "No, but if you push me far enough, I might be tempted to use one of these towels to accomplish the same job." He turned to Lorraine, all the blatant sexuality tamed into a look of authority no sane person would have questioned. "Have Ellstrom roust them out of here. I'll be holding a press conference in the morning."

The secretary nodded smartly and went to do his bidding. Dane dropped the towel to the wet spot on the floor and stepped on it with the toe of his shoe.

"For your information," Elizabeth said defensively, "I had no intention of talking to them tonight."

She wrapped her left arm across her stomach and rubbed at her bottom lip with her right thumb—nervously. No question about that. He wondered what she had to be so skittish about. What she had seen? What she had done? The electricity that sizzled in the air between them every time he got a little too close? No, he doubted that last one. She was far too experienced at wrapping men around her pinky to be shy of him. Unless it was his title that frightened her off.

"Is your refusal to talk to them just professional discourtesy, or are you more concerned about incriminating yourself?"

"Why should I be worried about that?" she challenged him. "You haven't charged me with anything. Or is that your cute little way of telling me you've decided I killed Jarvis, then obligingly called 911?" She crossed both arms in front of her. "Please, Sheriff, I hope I don't look that stupid."

"Naw . . . stupid isn't how you look at all, Mrs. Stuart," he drawled, sliding into the upholstered chair behind his desk.

Because he knew it would rattle her, he let his gaze glide down her from the top of her head to the wet spot on the knee of her tight jeans where the coffee had gotten her on its way to the floor. He was being an asshole and he knew it, but he couldn't seem to help himself. Elizabeth Stuart was just the kind of woman who brought out the bastard in him—beautiful, ambitious, greedy, willing to use herself to get what she wanted, willing to use anyone she knew. His gaze drifted back up and lingered on the swells of her breasts.

"You ought to about have it all memorized by now, hadn't you?" Elizabeth snapped, dropping her hands to her hips.

He didn't apologize for his rudeness. Elizabeth doubted he ever apologized for anything. He nodded toward the visitor's chair in a silent order for her to sit. He sat behind his desk with a kind of negligent grace, elbows braced on the arms of his chair, fingers steepled, brooding eyes staring at her.

"Have a seat, Mrs. Stuart."

"Miss," she corrected him, moving her camera from the chair to the top of a stack of files on the desk. She settled herself and pulled her purse into her lap to hunt for another cigarette.

"You dropped the Mrs. but kept the last name. Is that proper?"

"I don't really care."

"I suppose by that point in time you'd probably lost track of what name to go back to anyway."

That wasn't true, but Elizabeth didn't tell Dane Jantzen. Her roots went back to a cowboy named J. C. Sheldon and a mother who had died before Elizabeth could store up any memories of her. Victoria Collins Sheldon, a beautiful face on a photograph, one framed sepia-toned photograph J.C. had kept with him as they had moved from ranch to ranch. A photograph he had kept beside his bed, wherever his bed happened to be, and gazed at with heart-wrenching longing as Elizabeth stood out in the hall and peeked in at him, wondering why he didn't love her the way he loved that picture. A photograph J.C. had cried over when he'd had too much to drink. A photograph Elizabeth had studied for hours as a skinny, lonely little girl, wondering if she would ever be as pretty, wondering if her mama was an angel, wondering why she'd had to go and die.

But that was all too personal to reveal to this man. Under the cynical hide she had grown over the years lay a wellspring of vulnerability. She seldom acknowledged it, but she knew it was there. She would have had to be a fool to reveal it to Jantzen, and she had ceased being a fool some time ago. So she let Dane Jantzen think what he wanted, and told herself his sarcasm couldn't hurt her.

"I can see how you might have felt you didn't get anything out of him in the divorce so you might as well try to wring a few bucks out of his name," he said bluntly. "That's just business as usual for you, right?"

"I kept the name because my son didn't need another change in his life," she snapped, her cool cracking like a dry twig beneath the weight of his taunt, making a mockery of the platitudes she had calmed herself with just seconds before. She lunged forward on her chair, poised for battle, cigarette clutched in her hand like a stick to hit him with. "He didn't need another reminder that Brock Stuart didn't want him."

And neither did I.

The words hung between them, unspoken but adding

to the emotional tension that thickened the air like humidity. Dane sat back, a little ashamed of himself, not at all pleased that his poking had stripped away a layer of armor and given him a glimpse of the woman behind it. Not at all pleased that that kind of rejection gave them a common bond. He didn't want bonds. The truth was he didn't want Elizabeth Stuart to be anything other than what he had imagined her to be—a cold, calculating, manipulative gold digger, his ex-wife in spades. He didn't want to know that she had a son she cared about, didn't want to know she could be hurt.

Elizabeth forced her stiff shoulders back against the chair, a little shaken, a lot afraid that she had just revealed a weakness. What had happened to her restraint? The stress of the evening was wearing on her, wearing through that hard-earned thick skin in big raw patches. To cover her blunder she turned the cigarette in her hand, planted it between her lips, and lit it as quickly as she could so as not to let Jantzen see her hands shake.

"I'd rather you didn't smoke," he said.

"And I'd rather you weren't a jerk." She took a deliberately deep pull on the cigarette, presented him with her profile, and fired a stream of exhaust into the air, flashing a razor-sharp glance askance at him. "Looks like neither one of us is going to get our wish."

He yanked open a drawer, pulled out a plastic souvenir ashtray from Mount Rushmore, and tossed it across the desk in her general direction.

Elizabeth eyed the ashtray. "What a gentleman."

His mouth curved ever so slightly. "You ought to see what they taught me in charm school."

"Charm?" she scoffed, tapping her ash off on Teddy Roosevelt's head. "I'll bet a dollar you can't even spell it."

Point to Stuart, Dane conceded, grinding his teeth.

"Tell me what happened out there tonight," he said softly, welcoming the stirring of anger. Anger was an emotion he could grasp and wield like a sword. It was safe as long as he could control it.

He pulled a pocket cassette recorder out of his top right desk drawer and clicked it on. "For the record," he explained with a cool smile, tilting his head in mock deference. "This is the statement of Elizabeth Stuart regarding the Jarvis murder."

He plunked the recorder between them on the desk. Elizabeth regarded it with a suspicious look. She abandoned her cigarette to smolder in the ashtray, curling ribbons of smoke fluttering up from it. "I worked late on the ledgers at the paper office," she began without prompting or preamble. "They're a mess. I don't reckon old Larrson had balanced those books since Jesus Christ was in knickers. Took off about quarter to eight. That I know 'cause there's a clock in the office. I live out past Still Waters, about a mile or so east."

"The Drewes place."

She lifted an angular shoulder in an offhand shrug. "So I'm told." She hadn't bought it from a Drewes. No Drewes had lived in it for fifty years or more, but their name had stuck, making everyone who had lived there after them a trespasser of sorts.

She gave the sheriff an assessing look, deciding she'd better tell the tale exactly as it had happened. It was one thing to fib a little to Ellstrom; this man was a whole different breed. "I saw some deer standing in the trees along the north side of the road and I stopped to take a couple of pictures. I got too far off the shoulder and my car got hung up."

She paused, waiting for a sarcastic comment, but none was forthcoming so she pressed on, thankful for small favors.

"I didn't have much choice but to start walking." In Italian sandals with pencil-slim heels. She was going to have blisters for a week.

"Why did you turn in at Still Waters? The Hauer place is closer to the road."

"It didn't look like there was anyone home. Besides, if I have my choice between begging a ride in a Lincoln and begging a ride in an Amish buggy, call me strange, but I'm liable to pick the car every time."

"Had you met Jarvis before?"

She took up her cigarette and pulled at it, sighing out a plume of smoke. "Yeah, I'd met him," she said with a note of resignation that indicated it hadn't been the most pleasurable experience.

"Did he hit on you?"

Her eyes flashed. "That's none of your business," she snapped, tapping the ash off her cigarette with a sharp flick of her forefinger.

He smiled unpleasantly, leaning his forearms on the desk. "I beg to differ, Liz. Did he hit on you?"

"Yes," she said, exasperated. "He did a couple of times. Not that it matters."

"Maybe it matters a lot."

"Only if I killed him, which I didn't."

He gave a shrug. Elizabeth narrowed her eyes at him and stubbed out her cigarette.

"What did you do when he hit on you?"

"I told him to go eat dirt and howl at the moon."

"In so many words?"

"No, not in so many words," she spat out. "I've got more class than that."

"Class?" Dane sat back and lifted one straight brow. "I'll bet a dollar you can't find it in the dictionary."

Elizabeth scowled at him. "You've got a real way about you, Sheriff. How'd you get elected anyway? By threatening the voters with thumbscrews and rubber hoses?"

He bared his teeth in a parody of a smile. "On my looks and my sterling character."

"Sterling?" She gave an unladylike snort and shifted in her chair. "Looks like brass to me."

"And you with such a discerning eye for men. What did Jarvis look like to you—gold?"

"He looked like the butt end of an ugly dog," she said bluntly. "I don't care if he had money coming out his ears. I wasn't interested and I made that clear to him."

"So you walked up to the construction site to ask for a ride home. Jarrold suggested a ride of another sort—"

"The only ride Jarrold might have suggested was a ride to the mortuary. He was dead when I got there," she insisted, intent on steering the sheriff's line of questioning away from his overblown impression of her sex life, a sex life that was nonexistent in reality and notorious in the press. "I looked around for him, yelled my stupid head off, then saw he was sitting in the Lincoln. I was mad 'cause I figured the jerk had been sitting there looking at my backside the whole time, so I yanked the door open to give him a piece of my mind."

She stopped then and shuddered as the memory descended on her like an anvil. The image flashed before her eyes—Jarvis falling out of the car, his head hitting her feet with a sickening soft thud, his black eyes staring up at her with stark surprise, his blood splashing across her bare skin in macabre polka dots. She flinched and tried to swallow the revulsion crowding her throat as waves of heat and cold flushed through her, leaving her feeling dizzy and weak.

With one shaking hand she combed back her hair, anchoring the thick mass at the base of her neck as she rocked forward on the chair, head down. "Oh, God," she murmured, the beginning of a prayer for deliverance.

Dane watched her struggle with the emotions suddenly threatening to overwhelm her. All her sass had deserted her, leaving them both in a dangerous position. He wasn't in the habit of harassing distraught women. He wasn't in the habit of harassing women, period. Leaning back in his chair, he steeled himself against the sight of this tough lady falling apart. She was a witch who'd left a trail of devastated males in her wake, he reminded himself. She could very well have had something to do with Jarvis's death. He told himself so, but he didn't really believe it. The shaking was too natural, the combination of terror, denial, and revulsion in her expression was too spontaneous to be a put-on. He doubted even the infamous Elizabeth Stuart was that good an actress.

"I'm sorry," she whispered, her breath hitching in her throat. She let go of her hair to press her hands together before her like a penitent sinner. "I'm sorry."

Dane watched the rise of tears in her eyes. He felt something like sympathy shift through him and he lashed out at it, telling himself he was doing them both a favor. "That's all right," he said. "But you might as well save the waterworks. I don't go for the damsel-in-distress routine."

Elizabeth snapped her head up and gaped at him, stunned that he could be so cold, so uncaring. She pushed herself out of her chair and leaned across the desk, wincing as her skinned knuckles kissed the smooth wood surface. "It's not a routine, Sheriff Jantzen. I'm sorry, but I don't have a severed head fall on my feet every day of the week. I don't have a repertoire of witty things to say when I find murdered bodies."

"And the press said you had an answer for everything," he said with mock surprise.

She knew he was referring to the smear campaign instigated against her by Brock during the divorce. The power her ex-husband wielded over the press was awesome and terrible. The stain of his influence had spread all over the country—even to Still Creek, Minnesota, apparently—and had left her with a reputation blacker than Texas tea. Brock and his wizard lawyers had taken the truth and twisted it like a Gumby doll. But she wasn't going to fight Brock Stuart's lies tonight. She was too damned tired to care what Dane Jantzen thought of her.

"Don't believe everything you read, sugar," she said softly, straightening away from him.

That one mocking brow sketched upward again, and Elizabeth had to clamp down on the urge to fling herself across the desk and rip it off his face.

"That's an interesting piece of advice coming from a reporter," he said, the calm words belying the fact that she'd struck a bull's-eye.

Don't believe everything you read. Didn't he know that better than most people? Christ, the press had had a field day with his divorce—the divorce from his profession and his wife. And as a professional athlete, he had learned long ago that the differences between reality and journalism laid end to end could reach Mars. He knew better than to believe everything he read at face value, but another part of him knew better than to believe an ambitious woman. His sense of fair play pulled him in one direction, his sense of self-preservation pulled him another.

He watched her move to the end of his desk, her attention on the framed documents on the wall. She had fought back her tears, pushed herself past the panic that had had her shaking in the chair. He had to admire her guts, if nothing else.

His gaze drifted down to the faded denim cupping her ass, and he decided there was definitely more to admire than inner strength. She shifted her weight restlessly from one booted foot to the other and raised both hands to comb her hair back. Her T-shirt tightened across her breasts.

"If I believed only half of what I read about you, I still wouldn't like you," he growled, pushing himself up out of his chair.

"Like I give a rat's ass."

Dane stepped closer, so close that her shoulder brushed his breastbone and the high curve of her cheek was only a breath away from his mouth. "You'd better care, honey, because if I find out you're even remotely mixed up in this murder, I'll nail your pretty ass."

"That's harassment, Sheriff Jantzen," Elizabeth murmured. She wanted to move away from him, but she wouldn't give him the satisfaction.

"It's the truth," he said softly with a chilling smile. "Nobody's going to commit murder in my county and get away with it."

"Are you charging me with something? If you are, do I get to call a lawyer, or don't you have them up here in the Great White North?"

"Oh, we have them. Can't get rid of them any more than we can get rid of welfare cheats and outsiders."

Ruthlessly checking the fine tremors shuddering through her, she turned very slowly, very deliberately, and sauntered away from him. "Oh, for the days when the sheriff could ride undesirables out of town on a rail!"

"Here, here," Dane grumbled, though he had a hell of a time thinking of her as undesirable.

He retreated to his chair again. He picked a red pencil out of the ceramic holder and drummed the eraser end absently against the blotter. "What happened after you found the body?"

"I threw up," Elizabeth admitted candidly. "I imagine one of your lab boys is out there right now scraping up the remains of my Snickers bar, putting it in a Ziploc bag to be microanalyzed or carbon-dated or whatever it is they do with stuff like that."

She dropped back down into her chair, exhausted and tense from trying to act as tough as she talked. The truth was, she could have used a shoulder to cry on, but it had been so long since anyone had offered one, she wasn't sure she would even remember what to do with it. Probably shove it away out of habit and old suspicion, she decided sadly.

She leaned forward and grasped the edge of the seat with both hands, rocking slowly from side to side to relieve a little of her nervous energy as the rest of the memory played through her mind.

She had stood staring at Jarvis, and it had suddenly occurred to her that whoever had killed him might still be there, hiding in the cover of the woods that surrounded the construction site, watching her. And as the tall cottonwoods and oaks seemed to press in on her and the air grew heavy with the scent of blood and evil, she gave in to the panic and ran, tripping and falling because of her heels. She sprawled headlong, the gravel shearing the skin off her knuckles and tearing out the knees of the capri pants she'd bought in Cannes. Hysteria rose up inside her, freezing her lungs and coating her mouth with the taste of copper. Tears streaming down her cheeks, she pushed herself back up and ran on, her breath sawing in and out of lungs that had inhaled too many Virginia Slims in the last few years.

"I ran to the Hauer place," she said flatly, condensing the experience into brief, emotionless sentences. "Aaron Hauer was out in the barn. He gave me a ride home."

"Did he say if he'd seen anything?" Dane asked, the edge gone from his voice. He could see her strength flagging. He probably should have gone in for the kill, but he couldn't bring himself to do it. Some little shred of chivalry made him back off.

"He didn't say much at all. I got the impression he wasn't too pleased to get involved. He started lecturing me on being separate from the world. I told him it was kind of tough to be separate when a dead guy fell on your feet."

Dane tried to picture Aaron Hauer dealing with Elizabeth Stuart and almost chuckled. Two people couldn't have been more different. Aaron, so staunch in the old faith, so reserved, being confronted by Elizabeth, the model of the decadent "English" woman, flamboyant and outspoken, blatantly sexual.

"He took me home, I called 911, changed my clothes, and here we are at the end of a wonderful evening," she said, mustering a big false smile.

The red pencil stilled against the blotter. Dane's eyes narrowed. "Changed clothes? Why?"

"Why?" she repeated, incredulous. "Because I smelled like a horse and there was blood on my feet! Because a dead guy touched me. Because I found a murdered corpse in that outfit and I couldn't stand the idea of wearing those clothes another minute. I took off every stitch I was wearing and threw it in the trash. And let me tell you, that just plain broke my heart 'cause that was my favorite Armani silk blouse."

"It was evidence," Dane growled. "You tampered with evidence."

"I washed my feet too," she sassed. "Is that some kind

of capital offense? For crying out loud, if you want blood to look at, it seems to me there was plenty on Jarrold."

His voice dropped to that silky-soft pitch that raised the hair on the back of her neck. "There might have been plenty on your clothes too."

Elizabeth bit back a half-dozen words ladies weren't supposed to know, tamping down her frustration and capping it with a paper-thin layer of composure. "So we're back to that. I swear, you're worse than a terrier with a rat in its mouth. For the last time, I did not kill him. I'm sorry if that makes your life harder because you can't just pin this rap on the notorious stranger in town, but that's just too damn bad."

"I want those clothes," he said stubbornly. "All of them."

She waved her hands in surrender, slumping back in her chair. "Well, fine, but let me tell you, sugar, you don't look like a 36C, and if the rest of the deputies catch you in French-cut red lace panties, you're liable to have a hard time living it down."

Dane clenched his teeth against a surge of pure unbridled lust. She had just painted one very erotic picture of herself for him.

Elizabeth glanced away the carnal heat in his gaze. "What happens now?" she asked softly.

A loaded question. His libido had a few suggestions that tried to crowd ahead of good sense. He cursed himself for letting sex drag his thoughts away from his job, but he realized that it was in part a defense mechanism. He didn't want to have to deal with what was to come next. He had grown up in Still Creek, knew most of its three thousand residents by sight if not by name. He didn't want murder to have any part in life here.

"Now, you go home, Miss Lizzie," he said, rising.

Elizabeth gave him a skeptical look. "Just like that?"

"Don't take any long vacations."

She rolled her eyes at the cliché as she rose and gathered her belongings.

There was a sharp rap on the door and Lorraine

poked her head into the office. "Dane, Amy just called from the Rochester airport."

His face dropped. "Amy. Shit. I forgot all about her." He sucked in a deep breath and blew it out as he tunneled his fingers back through his hair. Guilt gave him a swift kick, but there wasn't anything to be done about it. "I can't leave here now. Send Kenny to get her."

Lorraine pinched her colorless lips together in silent disapproval and retreated.

"Flying in paramours, Sheriff?" Elizabeth asked, shrugging the straps of her camera and purse over her shoulder. "My, my. What will the taxpayers think?"

He gave her a look. "Amy is my daughter."

The girl with the pigtails. For some reason Elizabeth didn't want to think of him as a father. It made him seem too . . . human. She didn't want to think of him as a single parent because then they would have something in common, and that seemed more dangerous than good.

"See you around, cowboy." She paused with her hand on the doorknob and gave him a mocking smile. "Before I go, do you have a statement for the local press?"

"Not one you could print in the paper."

"Any idea who killed him?"

"Oh, I have my ideas, Miss Stuart." He tapped two fingers to his temple. "I think I'll just keep them up here for now."

"Careful they don't get lost, sugar."

Dane watched her saunter out of his office, not caring that she'd gotten the last word for the moment. He had a feeling he wasn't finished with Miss Elizabeth Stuart. Not by a long shot.

SIX

ELIZABETH FLIPPED ON EVERY LIGHT SWITCH SHE passed, needing to flood the house with brightness and chase away all the sinister shadows that lurked in the corners. The back porch light revealed an ancient chest-type freezer with boxes stacked haphazardly on it and on the warped wooden floor around it, most of them loaded with useless things she had yet to unpack since the move. The kitchen light—two rings of fluorescent glare installed during some tasteless era twenty or thirty years previous—illuminated a good-size room that was hung with peeling orange and yellow wallpaper in a fruit motif. The kitchen cupboards had been painted diarrhea brown. Half of them had doors either missing or hanging drunkenly by one hinge.

The room was a disaster area. A half-dozen cereal boxes stood open on the chipped-Formica-topped table. Trace had forgotten to put the milk away. After a good twelve hours sitting open in a warm room, the carton gave off an aroma, sticky-sweet and sour. Dirty dishes were piled in the stainless steel sink some brainless wonder had installed smack in a corner with no adjacent countertop. The old black-and-orange linoleum had big ragged chunks missing. The floor around the table was littered with a mismatched family of rather large athletic shoes.

"By golly, I'm just gonna have to up and fire that maid."

Elizabeth cast a wry look in the direction of Deputy Kaufman, who had driven her home, catching him checking his receding hairline in the side of the old chrome toaster. He straightened quickly, his apple-round cheeks flushing pink. A nervous laugh rattled out of him, as if she'd just told a joke in a language he didn't quite comprehend. He was about as transparent as a teenager with his first big crush. Elizabeth sighed inwardly.

"Thanks for seeing me home, Deputy. I imagine you'll be wanting to get on home yourself, as late as it is. Your wife will be worried."

"Oh, I'm not married," he rushed to assure her, hope leaping bright in his eyes.

She picked an oven mitt off the table and tapped it thoughtfully against her cheek. "You're not?" She thought the surprise in her voice probably rang true enough for a man. "Well, I can't believe some sweet young thing hasn't scooped you up by now."

The compliment had Kaufman glowing.

"If I hadn't just plain sworn off men . . ." She let the sentence trail off, shaking her head in regret. The deputy's optimism leaked out of him on a sigh. He seemed to shrink a little before her eyes, like a slowly deflating balloon.

Resigned once again to his protect-and-serve role, he glanced around the room, eyes widening as if he had suddenly come out of a trance and was seeing the mess for the first time. He recovered admirably. "Um . . . would you like for me to look through the house? I couldn't help but notice you didn't have the door locked."

"Honey, in this dump, I'm lucky I have doors, period."

What little money she'd had left after the lawyers had finished picking through her divorce settlement had gone to buy the *Clarion,* with a little left over to put away for Trace's college fund. The Drewes place had been the best she could afford, and what a sad statement that was, she thought, looking up at a ceiling that was cracked into a giant spiderweb of lines. It was a far cry from the penthouse in Stuart Tower, where every detail right down to the toilet paper had been picked out by a covey of decorators. It had taken her weeks to get over the feeling that she shouldn't sit down on any of the chairs or sofas. No, the Drewes place was more like the little cockroach haven she had shared with Trace's daddy back in Bardette half a lifetime ago, where the plaster peeled off the walls like giant scabs and someone had stolen every single doorknob in the place and sold it for scrap. At least she hadn't found any rattlesnakes in this house—yet.

"Oh, it just needs a little fixing up," the deputy said charitably.

"That's what the real estate agent told me." Elizabeth's mouth twisted into a grimace as she led the way into a dining room that smelled of *eau de* dead mouse. "I'm starting to see y'all have a true bent for understatement up here."

She followed him through the two main floors of the house, declining the trip to the basement. Any fiend willing to hide out down there could have the place all to himself as far as she was concerned. The search turned up nothing but proof that she was a dismal failure as a housekeeper. No one was hiding in her closet or anywhere else. The house was empty. No sign of a murderer. No sign of Trace.

Kaufman blushed clear to the bald spot on the crown of his head as he collected the clothes Jantzen wanted as evidence, digging the provocative red underwear out of the wastebasket with kitchen tongs. He put the ensemble in a brown paper bag and toted it to the back door.

"Are you sure you'll be all right here alone?" he asked, his brows making a little tent above his puppy eyes. "I'm sure I could get my sister-in-law to come out and stay with you. She used to be in the army."

Elizabeth mustered a smile for him. "No, thanks any-way. My son should be home soon. I'll be fine."

He hummed a little note of worry and shuffled his heavy shoes. "We'll be driving by now and again, so when you hear a car, don't worry. I'd like to set someone to keep watch all night, but we don't have a very big staff—"

"I understand. Really, I'll be fine."

He looked a little depressed at the fact that she wasn't begging him to stay and protect her. Men. She resisted the urge to roll her eyes. Kaufman tipped his head po-litely, his shy blush returning under the dim porch light. "It was nice meeting you."

Elizabeth bit the inside of her cheek. Lord have mercy, she'd just fallen smack into the twilight zone, hadn't she? Exchanging pleasantries with a law officer after a night of murder and mayhem. It couldn't get much weirder than that. She hoped.

She went and stood at the kitchen window, watching as he drove away. Cute guy. And as sweet as he could be—unlike a certain boss of his, she reflected sourly as his taillights glowed off into the distance. She hadn't heard Dane Jantzen express any concern over her well-being. He hadn't made any effort to come out here and see to her safety or peace of mind. Arrogant jerk.

The silence of the house closed in on her abruptly, like a door slamming. She was alone in a house that gave no pretense of being a home.

Alone. The word gnawed at her stomach. She'd never cared much for being alone, but it seemed that was the way she'd lived most of her life. Alone, if not physically, emotionally. Testimony to the fact that everything she wanted most always seemed furthest out of reach. All she had ever really wanted from as far back as she could remember was to be important to somebody, to be loved, to be needed, but that didn't seem to be in the cards for her.

Her daddy had been lost in his need for her dead mother, ignoring Elizabeth and taking what solace he could find in a whiskey bottle. She'd been nothing more to J.C. than an extra piece of baggage to drag along as he'd drifted from ranch to ranch, looking for a job he could stick with until his next big bender. At seventeen she'd been dazzled by Bobby Lee Breland, third best calf roper on the West Texas rodeo circuit. A green-eyed rascal with the devil's grin and more charm than any man had a right to. And she'd been the light of his life . . . for about six months. Their marriage had lasted through his affairs with Miss Texas Barrel Racing and the Panhandle Stampede Queen only because of Elizabeth's determination that Trace have a father. But she'd drawn the line at second runner-up for the Rattlesnake Roundup Days pageant and moved on with her life—alone, nineteen, with a baby, no friends, and no prospects.

It seemed history was repeating itself, she thought as she pulled herself back to the present and looked around the depressing mess that was her kitchen. Brock had cheated on her, she'd been forced to move on, and here she was, in a place where she knew one person, on her own with a son who had become a stranger to her and a future that looked shaky at best.

Tears threatened as Elizabeth looked around the room, her eyes settling on the wall clock. One A.M. Trace should have been home two hours ago. Dammit, tonight of all nights he could have made it home on time. A man had had his throat slit not much more than a mile from here. Her motherly instincts rushed up to clog her throat with fear for her only child.

The killer had to have been nearby still when she'd found the body. She was sure she'd felt someone watching her, felt the evil in the air. He could be there, in the woods, waiting for another victim. And Trace was out on the road on his bike, alone in the dark.

She turned and stared out the kitchen window, straining her eyes against the blackness, seeing nothing but her own reflection in the glass. And she felt it again—that sense of being watched, that feeling of something malicious and malevolent hanging thick in the air, reaching through the window to run bony fingers down her neck and send shivers skittering over her skin. To the west, lightning spread across the sky like cracks in a windshield. Thunder rumbled like distant cannon fire.

Something in the air. Something heavy and violent.

The hair rose up on the back of her neck and she hugged herself against a chill of sudden vulnerability.

The sound of the screen door slapping against the frame went through her like a gunshot. She wheeled and bolted back against the counter, belatedly wishing she'd gotten out the pistol she'd stolen from Brock's collection. Instinctively she reached for something to protect herself with. Her trembling fingers closed on the handle of a steak knife that had been left on the counter to harden with a crust of A-1 Sauce. She pulled the knife up in front of her as the kitchen door swung open and Trace ambled in.

"Shit," he drawled, eye's lighting on the knife. "I figured you might ground me, but stabbing seems a little extreme. I'm only a couple hours late."

Elizabeth's breath left her in a gust that took most of her strength with it. The adrenaline that had had her poised to defend herself rushed out of her, leaving her so weak she thought her knees might buckle. Her heart pounded with a mix of relief and leftover terror.

"You scared the life out of me!" she accused Trace. "A man was killed just down the road from here tonight."

Trace blinked at her. He had never been one to betray his feelings with his expression. From boyhood he had worn one face—serious, brooding. He had inherited her looks more than his father's—the dark hair, which he wore cropped short and parted on the right, the rectangular face with its strong, stubborn chin and short, straight nose. He even had her mouth. His lips were clear-cut and sensuous, more so the older he got. The contrast between that lush mouth and the lean planes of cheeks that were now seeing a razor several times a week was too sexy for a mother to contemplate. Elizabeth regularly thanked God Trace hadn't inherited his daddy's undying hunger for things high-breasted and nubile, because she couldn't see why any female would want to resist him.

He looked at her now, gray-green eyes steady behind the lenses of his Buddy Holly–style glasses. "Well, I didn't kill him," he said blandly. His gaze slid pointedly to her hand. "Did you?"

Elizabeth set the knife down on the counter and tried to rub some of the white out of her knuckles. The fear she'd known the instant before her son had opened the door had diluted to embarrassment, as fear often does. She warded the feeling off, turning her mind away from thoughts of murder, switching it to mother mode.

"You were supposed to be home at eleven. What have you been doing?"

"Nothing," he mumbled, dodging her eyes. His broadening shoulders gave a defensive shrug and he jammed his fists into the pockets of his faded jeans. He was already a couple of inches past Elizabeth's five eight, and was in a transition period between lanky and something sturdier. She doubted any of his shirts would fit him by fall; the white cotton T-shirt he wore now looked so small on him. He shifted from one sneakered foot to the other as she waited for a better answer. "I just been hanging out, that's all," he said at last.

"Where?"

"In town."

"With who?"

"No one!" he barked. He shot her a glare, eyes narrowing in resentment, mouth tightening. "What is this—the goddamn third degree? Want to set me under a spotlight and whip me with a truncheon? I wasn't doing anything!"

Elizabeth bit her tongue and crossed her arms over her chest to keep from walking up to him and shaking him. He was lying. Unlike his father, Trace had never been good at it. Not as a little boy who had had a habit of sneaking into the cookie jar before supper or as a teenager who had gotten himself into far worse trouble than spoiling his appetite. Whether he was a poor liar naturally or by design, Elizabeth had never been able to decide, but whatever the case, lies hung on Trace like a cheap suit. He rolled his shoulders now, uncomfortable with the fit.

She wasn't supposed to call him on it. That's what the counselor in Atlanta had said. They would never build a relationship if they couldn't lay a foundation of trust. Elizabeth had wondered more than once if the man had ever had a son who'd dabbled with drugs and been arrested for joy riding. She doubted it. Malcolm Browne, with his anemic looks and candy-striped bow ties, had always struck her as being strange as a three-dollar bill. But for what he'd soaked Brock for the sessions, she had figured he must be good, smart at least. Half of Atlanta's bluebloods had sent their kids to him to get straightened out. Too bad Brock had kicked them out before the counselor had managed to get the kinks out of Trace. Too bad she had been so damn busy trying to fit in with Atlanta society she couldn't keep him from turning into this surly, angry youth in the first place, she thought as guilt reached in and grabbed her by the heart.

"You can do nothing with no one right here," she said quietly.

"Oh, yeah, these are such luxurious accommodations." Trace sneered. "I just love lying around here. Watch the plaster peel. Smell the dead mice rot under the floor. It's a regular laugh a minute."

Elizabeth sighed and took a step toward him, reaching out with one hand. "I know you're bored, honey—"

"You don't know anything!" He suddenly exploded with all the fury of a bomb, anger rolling out of him in waves. He seemed suddenly bigger, more male, looming over her, his shoulders taut, the muscles in his bare arms standing out in sharp definition as he held his clenched fists waist-high. Behind his glasses his eyes were stormy and burning with frustration.

Elizabeth thought for a millisecond that he might actually strike out at her physically, and the thought sent a tide of nausea surging through her. He had never raised a hand to her. As a little boy he had seldom raised his voice. But his temper had grown unpredictable with the flux of his hormones. And with the use of cocaine. She didn't think he could be using again. He hadn't shown any other signs and didn't have any money. That was probably the best part of being broke; Trace couldn't afford to get into the kind of trouble he'd gravitated toward in Atlanta.

He reined in his burst of emotion and abruptly turned away from her, slamming a cupboard door that bounced back open mockingly. He slammed it twice more, harder and harder, with the same result. Finally he swore and kicked the door below it. "I hate this place!"

He braced his hands against the counter and stood with his back to her, his head down, shoulders heaving as he gulped air. Inadequacy and despair swamped Elizabeth like a tidal wave. This wasn't what she had wanted for them. Even when it had become clear that Brock was going to give her little more than the shit end of the stick in the divorce, she had pictured a better fresh start than this.

It had sounded so good in her head. A small town in Minnesota, a business of her own, working with her old college pal Jolynn. A farmhouse for herself and Trace, a place where they could spend quiet evenings and get to know each other again. Sit on the porch and watch the sun set. Reality was proving to be just one boot in the teeth after another.

What little strength she had left drained out of her and she gave in to the need to touch her child. He was nearly a man now, but she could still see him when he was five with his big sad eyes looking up at her from behind spectacles that seemed too grown-up for his little face. Lord, when did he get to be sixteen? she wondered desperately as she settled a hand at the small of his back. She felt no baby fat left beneath the thin fabric of his T-shirt, only muscle, and it stiffened at her touch.

"Honey, I know things don't look good right now,"

she said softly, rubbing her hand in slow circles designed
to soothe. He gave a harsh, humorless laugh and shook
his head. "They'll come around," Elizabeth promised,
not quite sure whether she was trying to convince her son
or herself. "You'll see. We just have to give it a little time,
that's all."

"Yeah, right." He twisted away from her touch, that
action cutting her more deeply than anything he could
have said. His mouth bent into a parody of a smile and
he blinked furiously at the tears in his eyes. "Like till hell
freezes over. I'm going to bed."

He was through the swinging door before Elizabeth
could draw breath to say good night. The door swung
back into the kitchen, bringing with it the faint perfume
of dead mouse from the dining room, and she stood
there, alone again, thinking back on the night she'd told
Bobby Lee she was leaving him.

She had stood in the kitchen under the glare of the
fluorescent light, the smell of bacon grease and Aqua
Velva settling in a lump at the back of her throat as her
nerves churned in her stomach. Trace was on her hip,
chewing the head off an animal cracker, his big eyes all
watery and scared—a reflection of her own expression,
she was sure. She had dressed to kill in her best cowgirl
outfit, thinking it might make an impression on Bobby
Lee, seeing what all he was going to have to do without—jeans that clung tighter than skin on a sausage and
a fitted western blouse that was exactly the color of a
dandelion and had black piping and a fancy yoke and
French cuffs on the sleeves, her Miss Bardette Barrel Racing buckle on a belt three sizes too big (to emphasize her
tiny waist), her Tony Lama boots, freshly polished and
sprayed with Amway boot shine. She knew she looked
good enough to make a man howl, but that didn't
change the fact that she was just nineteen and scared as
hell.

She stood there in the middle of that kitchen and told
Bobby Lee Breland she'd had it with his messing around,
that she was going to take their son and leave him for

good right that next minute if he didn't do something drastic.

The refrigerator hummed as Bobby Lee remained in the doorway, a bottle of Lone Star dangling from his fingertips, his red shirt hanging open, the tails trailing down over muscular things encased in new blue Wranglers. She would never forget how he looked—like an ad for the bad boys of the pro rodeo circuit, sandy hair falling across his forehead, green eyes hard as emeralds and boring into her, his bare chest and belly tan as leather, shiny with sweat and lined with muscle. She would never forget what he said as he pushed himself away from the door frame and walked past her, grabbing his dusty black Stetson from the table as he headed out.

"Can you be gone by nine? I got me a date with Cee Cee Beaudine."

And he walked out the back door and left her standing there feeling like the only person left on earth.

Just exactly the way she felt now.

HIS ROOM WAS NO BETTER THAN THE REST OF THE house. On the second floor, it overlooked a boggy pasture full of cows. The window had to be propped open with a sawed-off length of broomstick because the old rope on the pulley system was broken, and then the mosquitoes and gnats swarmed in through a rip in the screen to congregate at the light bulb sticking out of the ceiling. The walls were cracked plaster painted the color of cantaloupe. Some other poor slob sentenced to live in this pit of a house had spent hours scratching obscenities and other vital messages into the wood floor with a piece of wire. COUGARS RULE. A.J. + G.L. JOE EATS PUSSY. FUCK TINA ODEGARD. LIFE SUCKS.

Trace flicked on his stereo, then flopped bellydown across his unmade bed, his gaze riveted to one particular piece of wisdom as Axl Rose screeched through the speakers about love and pain. LIFE SUCKS. There was the truth.

He hated Still Creek. Hated the way it looked. Hated the way it smelled. Hated everything about it. He hated the Amish in their stupid hats and stupid clothes, driving their stupid horses all around. He hated the businesses and he hated the people who ran them. Stupid bunch of dickhead Norwegians, that's all they were. They looked at him as though he were from the fucking moon, laughed behind his back at the way he talked.

He knew what they thought. White trash, redneck southerners, that's what they thought. Crackers with a capital C. He'd heard the whispers of gossip about his mother. They all thought she was a tramp. Just because she was pretty. Just because that son of a bitch Brock Buttwipe Stuart had divorced her.

Back in Atlanta nobody had laughed at them. They'd lived in the penthouse of Stuart Tower. Trace had had a closet bigger than this bedroom. He'd had a wall of bookshelves and a big desk with his own computer. The Stuart name meant money and influence in Atlanta. It didn't mean anything in Still Creek but that they were strangers.

Anger burned and roiled in his gut and he tossed over on his back, not sure how to escape it. He felt it more and more lately, eating away at him, churning his insides. Sometimes he just wanted to explode with it, screaming and fighting. But he reined it in and stamped it down, as he'd always done with his feelings. It didn't pay to let people see what you felt. They turned it against you more often than not. Better to show nothing.

Like when that fat jerk Jarvis had turned him down for a job at Still Waters, Trace thought as he stretched over to the nightstand and pulled a stolen pack of Marlboros out of the drawer. He shook one out, leaning on his side as he lit it, then falling on his back again to stare at the geyser of smoke he blew up toward the ceiling. Jarvis had laughed at him, as if he thought he were a baby, and told him to go get a paper route. The anger had boiled inside him then, like scalding steam. All he'd wanted to do was punch in that ugly bulldog face until there wasn't anything left of it but bloody mush. But he hadn't shown it. He'd kept his chin up. He'd stared down the laughing work crew that had been leaning against the side of a rusted Chevy pickup with coffee cups in their hands. He'd walked away like a man.

Don't get mad, get even. That was what Carney said. Carney Fox was about the only person who hadn't given him a hard time since he'd come to this shithole town. Don't get mad, get even. That was his new motto. He said it aloud, testing the sound of it on his ears, then drew another deep drag on the cigarette and shot another cloud of smoke toward the fly-specked ceiling.

He couldn't seem to keep himself from getting mad, but he was working on it. Sometimes it scared him, the way he felt, so full of fury and rage at the injustices that had all but ruined his life. But most of the time he controlled it, the way a man should. He didn't let it show, and that was the important thing. He sometimes wished with all his heart for a nice white line of coke to make it go away, but he was through with that stuff. It made a man weak, and if there was one thing he was never going to be again, it was weak.

HALF A MILE TO THE NORTH, DANE STOOD ON HIS front porch, nursing a beer and staring off toward the old Drewes place. Weariness ached through him and pain pinched his bum knee like a C clamp. Another storm was brewing off to the west, grumbling threats but not making good on them, just like the earlier one that had promised to wash away all the physical evidence at the murder scene, then rolled on toward Wisconsin without so much as dampening the dust.

He tipped his bottle of Miller back and let the cold liquid slide down a throat that was raw from barking orders at his deputies and the press, and thought that thunder was appropriate tonight. It set the mood for evil.

They had worked at Still Waters until after one. The regional BCA agent, Yeager, had still been there sniffing around like a lazy old bird dog, bemoaning the fact that the Still Waters resort was going to be the ruination of a prime turkey hunting spot, when Dane had left to check on Amy and Mrs. Regina Cranston, the woman who was going to cook and clean and maintain a grandmotherly presence in the house for the three weeks his daughter was visiting. Jarvis had been carted off to Davidson's Funeral Home for the night. His Lincoln had been towed to Bill Waterman's junk yard, which served as Tyler county's impound lot. The mobile lab had packed up and taken what evidence they'd found back to the central lab in St. Paul.

Work at the scene had ended, but the real work was just beginning. Dane figured he'd grab an hour's sleep, then return to his office and start trying to find a killer with what information they had. He almost managed to laugh at the lunacy of that. Christ, what did he know about finding killers? Nothing more than what he'd read in textbooks. The worst thing that had ever happened in his tenure as sheriff had been Tillman Amstutz knocking his wife around after imbibing too much peppermint schnapps at the VFW. And Vera had managed to knock Till a good one back, smacking him upside the head with a frozen ring bologna and giving him a concussion.

They had the odd burglary in Tyler County, the occasional drunken fistfight at the Red Rooster bar. There was a class of social lowlifes who dealt pot and pills to one another. But for the most part, law and orderliness was bred into the folks of the Upper Midwest. Now this bastion of upstanding respectability had been breached, and he was the man who had to account for it.

Dane Jantzen, local hero. Captain of the Cougar football team. Star forward of the Cougar basketball team. Only native of Still Creek ever to be seen on national television. Tricia had accused him of wanting to come back here because he would always be a hero in Still Creek; he didn't need ambition or talent here. He could get by the rest of his life on stories of his glory days, when he had been sure-handed and fleet of foot.

Not true. He had come back because this was home, because he needed a place that was comforting and familiar after his career, his identity, had been ripped from him. In L.A. he had been Dane Jantzen, star receiver for the Raiders. Then his knee had gone and in the blink of an eye he was a nobody. The spotlight had gone out fast enough to blind him and he had been left groping around in the dark for something, someone, some clue to who he would be now that the Number 88 jersey had been handed over to another man with great hands and delusions of immortality.

Tricia had been more disappointed over her loss of status as a player's wife than in Dane's loss of mobility due to his blown knee. She had taken solace in the idea that he would go into broadcasting and eventually be a bigger star in the television booth than he had ever been on the field. When he told her he intended to move back to Minnesota, she literally laughed in his face. He'd been her ticket out of Still Creek; she had no intention of going back. She made it very clear she had married the football jersey, not the man inside it.

So he had come home alone, a beaten hero, and slowly built a new career, built a new life, carefully keeping each component separate so that if he lost one, he wouldn't lose them all, carefully keeping himself separate from the process so as not to lose himself in it. He was satisfied with the result.

He was a good sheriff. Whatever people's reasons for voting for him, they had been getting their money's worth to this point. He ran a tight county, kept crime to a minimum. Until tonight. Now he would be put to the test. Now he would have to prove that he hadn't gotten this job on the strength of his ability to run a good crossing pattern and keep his eyes on the ball.

He would do it, he vowed, pushing the doubts aside. He would catch this killer. He would win because winning was the one thing he had always done best. He wouldn't tolerate a loss. Neither would the good folk of Still Creek.

He'd done the right thing calling in the BCA. The lab boys had swarmed over the scene like ants at a picnic, dusting everything in sight for fingerprints, taking video and still pictures, making plaster casts of tire tracks, measuring blood spatters and scraping samples into plastic bags. They had vacuumed Jarvis's Lincoln and would sift through the debris for trace evidence that might make or break the case. Their efficiency was an awesome thing to behold, Dane reflected, taking another long pull on his beer. He only wished he hadn't beheld it in his county.

Tomorrow they would ship the body off to the Hennepin County medical examiner in Minneapolis, where a team of pathologists would determine the cause of death. Not that there was much question about it. Tyler County's coroner, Doc Truman, was a general practitioner who still made house calls in his '57 Buick Roadmaster. He had neither the equipment nor the inclination to handle a detailed autopsy for a murder investigation. He would, as a matter of courtesy, duty, and principle, ride along in the hearse from Davidson's Funeral Home, and stand in on the procedure, but he had told Dane he was more than happy to be relegated to the role of witness this time around.

Witness. The word brought to mind a clear image of Elizabeth Stuart sitting in his office, pale, shaking, gray eyes glazed with tears as she relived the horror of finding the body. Dane swore under his breath. He had wanted to put his arms around her, to offer comfort. He tossed back the last of his beer and set the empty on the porch rail as he looked across the pasture and woods that lay between his house and the old Drewes place. No question about it, she was more dangerous to him vulnerable than sexy. Sex he could handle. Sex he could keep in perspective. Vulnerability was another thing. And need. Need was something he didn't like to think about. He much preferred his other impression of Elizabeth Stuart—the opportunistic alley cat. Comfort was the last thing he wanted to offer her.

"Daddy?"

Dane turned automatically, as if he were used to the title, when the truth was he heard it only over the phone except for the few precious times a year when Amy came to stay with him. His daughter stood at the front door, her long brown hair in disarray around her shoulders, an L.A. Raiders jersey hanging to her knees. She blinked at him sleepily and wandered onto the porch to snuggle against him as naturally as if it were something she did every night of her life. Dane slid an arm around her and leaned his cheek against the top of her head, breathing deep the scents of Love's Baby Soft cologne and strawberry shampoo.

"What are you doing up?" he said softly. "It's way past your bedtime, peanut."

She smiled at him as if she thought he was dear but bordering on senility. "Daddy, I *am* fifteen, you know."

"No way," he scoffed. "You're not more than ten. It wasn't a week ago you were throwing up baby formula on me."

"Gross!" She pretended offense, but ruined it with a pixie giggle. "I'm still on California time, too, you know," she reminded him.

"Hmm . . ." He didn't like to think about that either—that his daughter lived half a continent away with her mother and the man who had taken his place.

Six months after the divorce Tricia had signed a prenuptial agreement with a running back who had two good knees and a yearning to become the next John Madden. Dane told himself he didn't regret losing Tricia, he just regretted losing, period. He told himself he didn't even care that she'd taken him to the cleaners in the divorce. But he would never forgive her for taking his daughter away from him.

He looked down at Amy now, panic seizing his gut as the realization hit him again. She wasn't such a little girl anymore. It seemed she'd grown half a foot since he'd seen her last. The softness of childhood was beginning to melt away from her, revealing the angular bone structure of a fashion model. She wasn't a woman yet either, but somewhere in between, the transition obvious in her face, where her cheeks were beginning to hollow but little-girl freckles still dotted the bridge of her tip-tilted nose.

He'd lost so much time with her. The years had stampeded over him, leaving him with only a handful of memories of pigtails and gap-toothed smiles, of a little sprite who trailed a stuffed rabbit with her everywhere she went. He'd spent so little time being a father to a little girl that he had no idea what to do with a teenager.

A mock frown curled down the corners of his mouth, and he lifted a brow imperiously. "Your mother lets you stay up past midnight?"

"And I shave my legs too," she said with a saucy, teasing look that reminded him too much of Tricia. "*And* I go on dates with boys."

Dane shuddered with true horror and shook his head. "That does it. I'm shipping you off to a convent."

"We're not Catholic."

"Doesn't matter. They're big on taking converts."

Dating. God help him, he wasn't ready for that. His daughter wasn't old enough to date, was she? He wasn't old enough to have a daughter dating, was he? He hadn't really felt that old—until now. In that moment, standing there in the dark in the middle of the night, he felt suddenly very old and very mortal.

"Did someone really get murdered tonight?" Amy's voice cut through the silence, soft with a touch of fear.

"Yeah," Dane murmured. "Someone did."

She shivered delicately against him and tightened her arms around his waist, pressing her cheek against his chest. "I didn't think anything like that would ever happen here."

Dane stared over her head, across the dark expanse of countryside to the south, toward the old Drewes place and Still Waters, and felt the heaviness of evil in the air. The thunder rumbled a little closer than before. Lightning sketched long, bony fingers across the sky.

"Neither did I, sweetheart," he whispered.

"Do you know who did it?"

"No, but I'll find out." He tipped her chin up with his forefinger. "It's on my list of things to do, right after tucking you in."

Amy rolled her eyes. "Daddy, I'm too old to be tucked in."

"Oh, yeah?" He propped his hands on his hips and gave her a look of challenge as she stepped back from him. "Does that mean you think I'm too old to carry you upstairs?"

"Oh, no," she said, giggling, holding her hands up to fend him off as she backed across the porch toward the door. "No, no, you don't."

It was a ritual they had gone through since she turned ten, when she had first decided she had outgrown the piggyback ride. Tradition. The kind of ritual most fathers went through with their daughters on a nightly basis, Dane imagined. One day Amy would be genuinely too old for it, but it damn well wasn't going to be tonight. Too many other aspects of his life seemed suddenly threatened by change; his daughter wasn't going to grow up on him tonight too.

He cut off her route to the door, keeping his eyes on hers, bending down, hands up, ready to catch her or block her. Old instincts from his former life came back to him and for an instant he felt just as quick, just as strong as he had when Kenny Stabler had been throwing him bombs.

"Daddy, I mean it," Amy said, trying to look stern. "I've grown. You'll hurt yourself."

"That does it," Dane growled.

He feinted left, then bolted right, catching her as she tried to slip past him. She squealed a protest as he swung her up in his arms, her long hair and long legs flying as he held her against his chest. They were both laughing when Mrs. Cranston came rushing to the door, armed with a baseball bat, her head crowned by spiny pink curlers, her face shining with a liberal application of Oil of Olay. She was a short woman in her sixties, built like a small tank, with fire in her small dark eyes.

"Sheriff, for heaven's sake!" She clutched her blue chenille robe to her throat with her free hand as she pushed open the screen door with the Louisville Slugger.

"It's okay, Mrs. Cranston," Dane said while Amy buried her face against his shoulder in humiliation. "This is a family tradition. Sorry we woke you."

He stepped sideways through the door and strode across the living room with its soft beige carpet and sturdy masculine furnishings. Mrs. Cranston, shuffling along behind him in a pair of fuzzy slippers, said, "I thought you might be the killer."

"He is," Amy muttered through her teeth. "I'm going to die of embarrassment."

Dane ignored the comment and shot a look at his housekeeper's weapon. "Well, it's nice to know you're ready to protect us, Mrs. Cranston."

She pulled up at the door to the guest bedroom and rested the bat across her massive bosom. "I was a switch hitter on the all-ladies team back during WW II."

"Armed and dangerous." He shifted his daughter in his arms and started up the stairs, calling back over his shoulder, "Remember to have me deputize you."

The housekeeper giggled before she caught herself and sniffed. "Oh, pshaw."

Dane turned his concentration to making it to the second floor of the house. Halfway up the stairs he was reminded of the cruel reality that Kenny Stabler hadn't thrown him a bomb in over a decade. Pain clutched at what cartilage remained in his left knee and he tried to bite back a grimace without much success.

Amy caught the look and frowned at him as she threaded her fingers together at the back of his neck. "I told you so."

"You can't tell me anything," he grumbled. "I'm your old man." He groaned as they gained the landing and an old back injury made its presence known. "Emphasis on the *old*."

"See?" she said as he set her on her feet on the smooth oak floor. She tugged down the bottom of her jersey and tucked a strand of hair behind her ear. "We're both too old for this."

Dane sighed and scratched at a mosquito bite on his neck. "Humor me, will you? I don't get to play Daddy very often."

Amy bit her lip and looked entirely too perceptive and too sympathetic, too wise to be a child. "I wish you weren't so alone, Daddy," she said softly.

The sentiment hit Dane like a linebacker out of nowhere, knocking him mentally off balance. Automatically, his hand reached down for the polished stair railing, as if to steady himself. Christ, the whole damn world was shifting beneath his feet tonight. That aspect of his personal life was a totally separate issue from his relationship with his daughter. He had honestly never thought of the two coming together in any context.

He shook it off and forced a grin. "Who could put up with me?"

She shrugged and stepped closer to slide her arms around his waist, her face earnest and somber as she rested her chin against his chest and stared up at him. "I could, and if I could, then—"

"You don't count. You're related, you have to put up with me." Dane dropped a kiss on her forehead and gently pushed her and her subject of discussion away. "Go to bed. It's late."

Amy backed toward the door to her room, looking frustrated, looking as if she had a lot more to say but knew this wasn't the time to say it. "Good night, Daddy," she said with a sigh of resignation.

" 'Night, peanut."

He stood in the hall until the beam of light shining out from under her door went out. Then he turned slowly and made his way back down the stairs, his eyes scanning the photographs of Amy that marched down the stairwell in chronological order, from when she was a bright-eyed baby, to a toddler with a scrape on her chin—the result of her determination to run down the sidewalk when her legs hadn't yet quite gotten the hang of walking—then a grade-school student. He stopped before he came to the junior high photos and went back to the last picture taken before Tricia had ripped their family apart.

Amy at six. A smile that showed an incongruous mix of baby teeth and permanent teeth. Crooked pigtails and bangs in her eyes. Not long after that picture had been taken, Tricia had severed their relationship as brutally as if she'd taken a knife to him.

Knife. His mind seized on the word greedily, eager to turn his thoughts away from his personal life. He had a murder to solve, and now seemed as good a time as any to get started. He padded down the stairs and slipped out of the house soundlessly, locking the door behind him.

SEVEN

MORNING BROKE SO FRESH AND PRETTY IT WAS almost impossible for Elizabeth to believe the events of the previous night had happened. Almost. Bird song drifted through the open window on a rain-washed breeze and pink-tinted beams of sunlight. The heavy malevolence that had hung in the air as she'd stood over the body of Jarrold Jarvis had passed with the storm during the night.

Perhaps, if she had slept at all, she might have been able to convince herself that finding the victim of a brutal murder had been nothing more than a nightmare. But she hadn't slept. She'd gone upstairs after using up every last drop of hot water in the tank trying to scour the taint of Jarvis's death off her, turned Trace's stereo off and covered him with a blanket as he lay sleeping in his clothes. She had considered emptying the ashtray he had stashed under his bed, but she left it. Compared to some forms of rebellion he'd already tried, this one was minor.

For a time she just stood in his doorway and watched him sleep, needing to be near him even if he wouldn't have wanted her there. Aching to be closer to him as the chasm of the generation gap yawned between them. He was all she had, her only family—not counting J.C., who was living out the last of his days in a V.A. home in Amarillo, his mind so pickled by years of drinking that he didn't even remember he had a daughter.

Trace was hers, the baby she had given birth to when she'd been little more than a child herself, the little boy whose scrapes she had tended, whose tears she had dried. They had drifted apart over the last few years, the whirl-wind of life in Atlanta's social stratosphere pulling them away from each other. But they had come back down to earth with a crash, and now it was just the two of them again, and Elizabeth wanted to cling to him, to hold him to her for comfort. Only she hadn't figured out how to get him to let her that close.

She stood in his doorway and looked across the room at him, fear knotting in her stomach at the thought that emotionally he might always be half a room away with a barren no-man's-land between them. Then she went off to her own room with her memories of murder and a bottle of Brock's imported forty-two-year-old scotch. Now she felt as if someone had filled her head with sand. It lolled on her shoulders as she dropped her legs over the edge of the bed and struggled into a sitting position.

"Oh, Lord," she groaned as the room swirled once around her. She squeezed her eyes shut and ran her tongue over her teeth, grimacing at the taste of old sweat socks in her mouth. "I'd beg for mercy and promise to never do it again, but we both know I'd be breaking a commandment."

A pounding was going on somewhere behind her ears that had her contemplating the possibility of crawling back into bed and staying there for the next five years or so. But there was a day to face, and it was liable to be a doozy. Today the shit would hit the fan. News of Jarvis's untimely demise would spread through Still Creek over doughnuts at the Coffee Cup. The phone lines would be humming with it. People would want details and an-swers. And since it was her job to ferret out those details and print those answers, she would have to haul her fanny out of bed and go scrub the fur off her teeth.

Gingerly she put her fingers to her temples, holding her head in place as she rose unsteadily to her feet. The pounding grew louder, more real, more like the sound of knuckles on wood. She grimaced as her foot hit a puddle of water and she remembered too late that she had left the window open during the storm, craving for the cleansing feeling of windblown rain to wash away the cloying scent of death that seemed burned in her nostrils.

Squinting against the bright, pretty morning, she leaned heavily on the windowsill and peered down at the yard. A bony sorrel horse was tied to the light post, harness hanging on its gaunt frame, one hind leg cocked as it dozed. A boxy black Amish buggy stood behind it, looking too much like an old-fashioned hearse to suit Elizabeth. The pounding came again, this time drawing her gaze to the door that was directly below her.

An Amishman stood on her back porch stoop. He must have sensed her presence, because he took a step back and looked up at her, drawing his wide-brimmed straw hat off to reveal a head of silky blond hair. Aaron Hauer. The man who had been her reluctant taxi driver the night before, taking her home in his buggy so she could call the sheriff's department to report the murder.

He looked nearer to forty than thirty, a tall, rawboned man with a face from "American Gothic," austere and joyless. His jaw was trimmed with a thin stubble of pale whiskers. He stared up at her, regarding her with a kind of subtle disdain through the lenses of a pair of old-fashioned rimless spectacles.

"Mr. Hauer," she called, wincing a little at the rusty sound of her voice and the ringing it set off in her head. She offered what would have to pass for a smile as she clutched the neck of her nightgown together in a fist, hoping he couldn't see enough through the fine white silk that would offend his Christian sensibilities. "What are you doing out at this hour?"

"The sun is up," he declared, as if that were an excuse for getting people out of bed.

Elizabeth glanced to the east, sucking a breath in through her teeth as the rays stabbed into her eyeballs like needles. "Dawn. By golly, it is. Funny, I didn't hear it crack."

Her sarcasm was lost on Hauer. He looked up at her expectantly. "I come to look at your kitchen, Elizabeth Stuart."

"My—?" The mere effort of trying to make sense of this episode was giving her a case of vertigo. She tipped her head back against the window frame and let out a slow, deliberate breath in an attempt to calm the squall churning through her stomach. She had no memory of asking him to come back, but she had no intention of arguing about it from this position either. "Just give me a second here, sugar," she called, not risking another look. "I'll be down in two shakes." Down on the floor, puking up whatever dregs remained in her stomach, she thought bleakly as she moved away from the window.

She made her way across the room, sloshing through the puddle again, gritting her teeth against the urge to moan. Moaning was a luxury she didn't have time for. She would have to deal with Aaron Hauer, then call Jolynn to come and get her. She intended to camp out on Sheriff Jantzen's doorstep until he gave her something she could print in the *Clarion*.

Holding her breath to ward off the dizziness, she bent over and dug through her closet, pulling out a pair of jeans and a gray UTEP T-shirt that was so old and faded the insignia across the front was little more than a shadow—a bleak reminder of how long it had been since she'd walked the hallowed halls of the University of Texas at El Paso. The outfit was hardly high fashion, but it would do for the moment. After she sent Mr. Hauer on his way, she would come back and rummage through for something with a Fortune 500 look about it. Something appropriately businesslike. Something that would make Dane Jantzen sit up and wipe the smirk off his face.

Aaron Hauer was still standing patiently at the back door when Elizabeth arrived some ten minutes later. She figured anyone who came calling before the coffeepot kicked in could damn well cool his heels until she'd had a chance to pee and run a brush through her hair.

She leaned a shoulder against the door frame, needing to prop herself up. "What can I do for you, Mr. Hauer?"

"Aaron Hauer," he corrected her, his voice rising and falling with the heavy accent of the German dialect his people spoke among themselves. His gaze was somber and steady behind the lenses of his spectacles. "My people, we don't believe in titles. Titles are *Hochmut,* proud. Pride is a sin."

"Really? My, well, I guess I'll have to add that one to my list."

He sighed briefly, no doubt already appalled by the list of her sins, Elizabeth thought. She was a far cry from the Amish women she'd seen around town in their long dresses and concealing bonnets, their eyes downcast demurely, voices hushed.

"I come to look at your kitchen, Elizabeth Stuart."

"So you said." She scratched a hand back through her hair, rubbing at her scalp as if she might jar loose some memory of inviting him back to her house. None came.

Aaron held up the doorknob that had fallen off as he'd knocked. One corner of his mouth quirked upward in a wry smile that transformed his face and complemented the tiny spark of humor hiding in his eyes. "I'm thinking you're needing a carpenter."

The laugh that rolled out of Elizabeth was spontaneous. She didn't even try to hold it back, though it made her head pound like a bass drum. So the Amish could be opportunistic just like everyone else. At her insistence, Aaron Hauer had come into her house last night to stay with her while she called the sheriff's office. Obviously, he'd taken one look at the way the place was falling down around her ears and started adding up the dollar signs.

"Sugar," she drawled, "what I need here is a stick of dynamite and a big fat insurance policy, but I'll be damned If I can afford either one." She sobered and sent him a look of genuine apology. "I'm afraid I can't afford a carpenter either, for that matter."

He frowned a little, tilting his head to the side, his

gaze narrowing. "You can't know that. I have yet to tell you my price."

"If it's more than a cup of coffee, I can't afford you."

"We'll see." He picked up his carpenter's box and pulled the screen door open, inviting himself in. "My consultation fee is a cup of coffee. You can manage that, I guess."

He moved past her and into the kitchen as if he had every right to be there. Elizabeth followed, mouth hanging open, caught between amusement and irritation. "You've got a golden future as a Fuller Brush man just waiting for you, honey."

Aaron ignored her. He set his toolbox on the table between cereal boxes and surveyed the room with a critical eye. The place was a shambles. It looked even worse in the light of day than it had the night before under the glare of artificial light. The only thing saving it from total disgrace was the scent of fresh coffee wafting from the electric pot on the counter. He didn't approve of electricity, but coffee was something else again.

"You can't cook in this kitchen," he declared.

Elizabeth went to a cupboard with a door that hung by one hinge and pulled out a pair of mismatched coffee mugs. "I've got news for you, Aaron. I couldn't cook in Wolfgang Puck's kitchen."

He glanced at her, straight brows pulling together in suspicion. "Who is this Wolfgang?"

"Nobody you'd know. Only a world-renowned chef and restaurateur."

He shrugged, largely unconcerned with anyone who lived outside a ten-mile radius of his community. Oh, he read in *The Budget* news of Amishmen who lived in other parts of the country, but the English didn't concern him. They could keep their fashions and their wars and such to themselves. He wasn't one for restaurants either. His nieces and nephews liked to go to the Dairy Queen in Still Creek for French fries and ice-cream cones once or twice a summer, but he never enjoyed taking them. Too many tourists staring, pointing, shooting their pictures as if they thought Amish were little more than animals in a zoo.

He accepted the mug of coffee Elizabeth offered him with a softly murmured *"Danki,"* and lifted the cup to his lips with no small amount of trepidation. If her housekeeping skills were anything to go by, he was in for an unpleasant shock. But the coffee was smooth and rich, and he sipped it, his brows lifted in surprise.

Elizabeth gave an offended sniff. "You don't have to look so shocked. I can measure out Folger's Crystals with the best of them."

"You make a good cup of coffee too," he said with a decisive nod.

She shook her head and chuckled to herself. "Thanks. Maybe I should have made Brock's coffee for him," she murmured reflectively as she dug through the rubble on the counter for a cigarette and a book of matches. "He might have decided I was good for something."

"Brock?"

"My husband—formerly."

"You are a widow?"

Her gray eyes narrowed with malicious glee as she stared up through a cloud of smoke. "I wish," she said with relish.

Aaron watched her with a kind of stern bewilderment, tucking his chin back, instinctively knowing he should take a dim view of her attitude even though he didn't understand what she was talking about.

"I'm divorced," Elizabeth explained, tapping ash into a microwave tray that still bore traces of the overcooked lasagna that had been packaged in it.

Aaron grunted his disapproval as he set his cup aside and muttered "English" half under his breath. Marriage was meant by God for life. A man and woman joined in partnership to work and to bring forth children, to remain as companions until death. He had no sympathy for people who took the Lord's word so lightly and disposed of marriage partners as easily and as often as they traded in their automobiles.

"How about you?" Elizabeth asked, naturally curious about this odd man who had invaded her kitchen. She hadn't lived in Still Creek long enough to encounter any of its Amish residents up close and personal—until last night, and then small talk had seemed inappropriate to say the very least.

He stood across from her, his hands tucked into the deep pockets of his homemade black trousers. Like every Amishman she'd seen, he wore a cotton shirt that was a warm shade of blue, buttoned to the throat and trimmed with a set of black suspenders. For the first time she realized he was attractive in an unkempt sort of way. He kind of favored Nick Nolte in *Cape Fear*—taut, unsmiling, but not without appeal. His face was long with prominent cheekbones, a straight blade of a nose, a tightly compressed mouth. The expression he wore had the same kind of brooding quality that was all the rage in *GQ* these days. With a shave and a haircut he would have looked like any respectable yuppie male. He could have even kept his retro-look glasses as trappings of the upwardly mobile. Elizabeth almost laughed at the irony, but she doubted Aaron would find it amusing. A sense of humor probably wasn't high on his list of attributes.

He made her think of an English professor she'd had at UTEP. Philip Barton. Indomitable, uncompromising, with straw-colored hair and eyes that burned with the intensity of lasers. She'd had a huge crush on him. The allure of the aloof. He'd taken her to bed and given her a C minus on her D. H. Lawrence paper. A man of high principles.

"My wife is dead," Aaron Hauer said succinctly, and turned away from her.

The words hit Elizabeth with the force of a lead pipe, knocking the breath from her. "I'm sorry," she mumbled.

If he heard her, he ignored her automatic statement of sympathy. He went to work inspecting the cupboards, his shoulders rigid, jaw set, gaze so intent on the cabinetry, Elizabeth wondered if he saw it at all or if he was looking right through it to some distant memory. She thought she could feel his pain radiating from him like an aura, and she envied him a little. He must have loved the woman he'd lost. That was more than she could say about her ex-husband. Brock had never loved her. He had loved possessing her, but he hadn't loved *her,* and she knew for a fact he didn't mourn her passing from his life.

"*Ya,* I can fix these for you," Aaron said absently. His long-fingered hands stroked the frame of an open cupboard as a man might stroke a woman's hair, gently, fondly. "Better to build new. There is no craftsmanship here."

"I can't even afford to have them fixed, let alone replace them," Elizabeth said. She sank down on a chrome-legged chair that was undoubtedly as old as she was. The red vinyl seat was cracked and torn, and mice had long ago made off with the stuffing, but it took the weight off her blistered, aching feet and stopped the room from tilting like the deck of a listing ship. "I'm not just trying to horse-trade with you here, Aaron. The fact of the matter is, I'm pretty much broke."

"So are your cupboards,"

"The place was vandalized a couple of times before I bought it," she said, not wanting him to think all this wreckage was due to her lack of domestic skills.

"The young people from town used it as a place to have their drinking parties," Aaron said, looking over his meticulously arranged toolbox for the proper size screwdriver. "A good spot for that." His mouth tightened against the bitterness. "Hidden. Out of town. No one to bother them but Amish."

It angered him beyond words, though he spoke of it as if he thought teenagers should be expected to ruin property as a part of their coming of age. The way the English raised their children was nothing short of barbaric in his mind. They had no principles, no scruples, no respect for anyone or anything, no fear of God or of punishment. They disrupted other people's lives and paid no consequences. But as he took his screwdriver to the hinge of one cupboard door, he calmed his temper and tried to see the good. If no one had ruined Elizabeth Stuart's cupboards, then he wouldn't have the job of fixing them.

"There are other ways of paying besides money, Elizabeth Stuart," he said, turning his thoughts back to the matter at hand.

A jolt of shock went through Elizabeth and she sat up ramrod-straight on her chair. Christ in a miniskirt! Not only could Amishmen be opportunistic, they could be lewd and lascivious too. Trading work for sexual favors. This certainly brought new meaning to the idea of having a handyman.

She stared at him, agog, wondering just what it was about her that brought out this side of a man. It wasn't as if she had set out to entice him—unless Amishmen simply went on the assumption that all "English" women were easy. In fact, all she'd tried to do since he had arrived was send him home. But here he was, calm as you please, suggesting—

"You have a windmill you are not making use of," he said, putting his weight into the task of wrenching a screw free from the wood and half a dozen coats of paint.

Elizabeth blinked. "I do?"

"*Ya.*" He pulled the screw free, examined it briefly, tucked it into the deep pocket of his trousers, and went to work on another. "Silas Hostetler is by way of needing a new windmill. And Silas has a young black gelding I might could use to replace my old sorrel."

"Ah . . ." So it wasn't her body he was after. She wasn't sure if she should be offended or relieved.

"We have a deal, then?" Aaron pulled another screw free and pocketed it before casting her a look over his shoulder.

She sat with one leg tucked up on her chair, hands around her ankle, arms framing her breasts, plumping them up beneath the man's thin undershirt she wore. She looked wild and wicked to him with her black hair tumbling around her shoulders, unbound and uncovered. Sinful, he told himself. A woman's hair was her glory and only for her husband to see.

But Elizabeth Stuart had no husband.

And he had no wife. As much as he still thought of himself as married, his Siri was with God and he was alone on this earth.

He tore his gaze away from her, turning back to the cupboard. He had no intention of involving himself with an English woman. No matter that she obviously needed a man to look after her, or that her eyes were the color of the sky just before dawn. He had come here for other reasons, practical reasons.

"I guess we do have us a deal." Elizabeth pushed herself up out of the chair, a little bewildered that something good could happen this easily. Her life was Murphy's Law in practice. That she could get her kitchen fixed up for the price of a worthless old windmill seemed too good to be true. But then, the windmill wasn't worthless to an Amishman.

Don't look a gift horse in the mouth, sugar, even if he's hitched to an Amish buggy.

"Where I come from we shake on deals, Aaron Hauer," she said, offering her hand.

He looked at it as if he suspected her of having a joy buzzer tucked into her palm. Reluctantly he set his screwdriver down and accepted her offer, sighing as if it pained him to touch her. Elizabeth's mouth twitched into a wry smile. She didn't doubt that he'd never shaken hands with a woman before, certainly not an "English" woman. It gave her a little feeling of triumph to be the first.

His hand was warm and dry, callused, tough. Tremendous strength was there, but the potential for gentleness too, and artistry. She thought of the way he'd rubbed his fingers over the cabinet and figured some lucky Amish maid was going to get herself a good husband one of these days, when he was finished mourning the wife who had died.

"Thank you, Aaron Hauer," she said softly. His gaze caught on hers for an instant and something subtle charged the air between them. It wasn't attraction, precisely, or need, or even understanding. Elizabeth couldn't give it a name other than awareness, and even that seemed too strong. *Odd* was what it was. Then he pulled his hand back and glanced away from her, and whatever it had been was gone.

"I've got to go change for work," she said, backing toward the dining room door. "Town's liable to be damn near on fire with news of the murder." He frowned at her language and turned back to his work without comment. Elizabeth watched him, bewildered. "You don't seem overly concerned that a man was killed within shouting distance of your house."

He grimaced as he twisted at another stubborn screw. "What goes on in the world of the English is of no concern to me." He muttered something in German as he fought to loosen the screw. The wood gave up its stubborn hold and he had the hardware free with a few expert flicks of the wrist.

Elizabeth went on watching him, amazed at his calm. He spoke as if their two worlds existed on parallel planes that couldn't touch, couldn't become entwined with each other even as they themselves were disproving that theory. That a killer might not discriminate between Amish and English the way he did apparently hadn't occurred to Aaron Hauer. Elizabeth doubted Amish throats would be any more resistant to a blade than Jarrold Jarvis's had been, but she envied Aaron his insulation of faith. It would have been nice to cite a Bible verse and absolve herself of any involvement in what had happened. But she couldn't do that. Even if she hadn't found the body, she was still a reporter.

"You'll have to introduce yourself to Trace," she said, mentally shifting gears as she moved sideways toward the phone that hung on the kitchen wall. She would call Jo for a ride, then call the guy Deputy Kaufman had said would pull her car out of the ditch—what was his name?

Jurgen something. "Trace is my son," she clarified. "It's against his religion to get up before noon.

"Help yourself to any food you find that doesn't look like a science experiment. Chee-tos is probably the best you're gonna do. I hope you don't have anything against artificial colors and preservatives, 'cause that's about all we live on. I'd burn you some toast, but I've got to make a couple of calls, then I'm off to look for truth and justice."

"And what will you do with it when you find it?" a low, soft male voice said in a tone laced with sardonic amusement.

Elizabeth swung around toward the back door, her heart jamming up in her throat. Dane Jantzen stood leaning against her refrigerator, as if he had much more important things to save his energy for besides good posture. He was in uniform—or as near to it as he probably ever came—pleated black trousers and a tailored khaki shirt and tie, badge and name tag pinned to his wide chest.

"I'll tell the world," she said, annoyed with herself for taking the time to stare at him.

"And make a buck off it," he commented mildly.

Elizabeth reined in her temper as she lifted her chin and crossed her arms defensively. "That's right, Sheriff. It's called free enterprise."

He gave a little snort and straightened away from the refrigerator to wander the kitchen, his narrow gaze scanning the cluttered countertop. "That's what you call it."

She sucked in a breath to tell him off, but bit her tongue before the words could come spewing out. She wouldn't give him the satisfaction of rising to the bait. He enjoyed it too much, the arrogant jerk. She watched him for a minute as he browsed the contents of a doorless cupboard as if the brand of canned vegetables she bought might give him a vital clue.

"Alphabet soup," he said, flashing a nasty smile as he fingered the Campbell's can. "Boning up on your spelling skills?"

"Do you have a warrant?" she snapped, leaning toward him.

"Do I have reason to need one?" he asked quietly.

Elizabeth ground her teeth. "What you need is a personality transplant."

Dane chuckled. "Have a donor in mind?"

"Attila the Hun would be an improvement, but I'm not fussy."

"So I've been told."

The words cut. Dane cursed himself for caring, but he couldn't help it. He enjoyed sparring with Elizabeth Stuart. She had a sassy tongue and a sharp wit. But he didn't enjoy seeing the sudden flash of hurt in her eyes, and he wasn't proud of himself for being the cause. Dammit, he had expected her to sling another barb back at him; he hadn't expected her to retreat. He would have thought her skin was thicker than that for all the papers had said about her during the divorce.

Don't believe everything you read, sugar. Her words echoed back to him, though he didn't care to hear them, didn't care to hear the truth in them. She backed away from him, her expression carefully closed, precisely arranged to reveal none of the emotions that had flashed automatically across her face seconds before. The need to apologize rose up inside him, but the words all jammed at the back of his throat and he couldn't seem to force them past his tongue. Apologizing wasn't something he did well or often.

"*Wie gehts*, Dane Jantzen."

Dane's attention went for the first time to Aaron Hauer. He had been aware of the Amishman's presence, had seen the horse and buggy in the yard, had seen Aaron himself working on a cupboard door, but his focus had homed in on Elizabeth, his senses tuned into her, intensely aware and wary.

"Good morning, Aaron." He nodded at the cupboards, sliding his hands into his pockets and leaning a hip against the counter. "I'd say you've got your work cut out for you here."

Aaron lifted a door down, carefully scrutinizing the edge. It was too warped to plane. He would have to replace it. *"Ya,"* he said after a few moments. "Plenty of good needs doing here."

The censure in his voice was so subtle, Dane almost dismissed it as a figment of his guilty conscience. Aaron watched him a second longer, his gaze somber and steady, before turning back to his work. Dane rolled his shoulders, shrugging off the feeling of being accused, and stepped back into the role he was comfortable with, the one that went along with the badge he was wearing.

"Plenty of bad going on around here last night," he said. "You didn't happen to see anything, did you?"

The Amishman selected a pair of pliers from his carpenter's box as carefully as a dentist selecting the proper tool for extracting a tooth. He turned back to the cupboard and set to work removing the broken latch. "No."

Dane drew in a long, slow breath, willing patience. The Amish adhered to a strict hear-no-evil see-no-evil speak-no-evil policy that could be infuriating to an officer of the law. They bore no witness to anyone but God Himself. Even when violence was directed at them they simply turned the other cheek and went on with their lives as if nothing had happened. Aaron was a perfect example.

"A man was killed. Murdered," Dane said, trying to impart the gravity of the situation and knowing it probably wouldn't make any difference. Aaron went on working as if he hadn't understood a word. "This is serious stuff, Aaron. Jarrold Jarvis got his throat cut last night. If you saw anything—a man, a car, anything—I need to know."

Aaron winced a little, though whether it was the image of a man being murdered that pained him or the fact that the cupboard latch had cracked between the teeth of the pliers, Dane couldn't tell.

"I cannot help you, Dane Jantzen," he said, frowning at the broken latch before he tossed it away into the plastic dish Elizabeth had been using for an ashtray.

"Can't or won't?"

He heaved a weary sigh and pushed his glasses up on his nose. "There was no car," he said, looking down at the cupboard door. "There was no man."

Dane's gaze sharpened. "How about a woman?"

Elizabeth's patience snapped. "Oh, for pity's sake, all right, I confess," she said. "I snuck up on a two-hundred-sixty-pound man, got him in a choke hold, and, for no earthly reason, did him in with my fingernail file. You see," she went on, digging out a second cigarette and tossing the pack back onto the table, "what y'all don't know is that I've been trying to treat my PMS with steroids and it's just made me plumb crazy. I'm fixing to plead insanity due to hormones as my defense."

"Careful, Miss Stuart," Dane warned with a smile. "Anything you say can and will be used against you."

She tipped her head back and fired a stream of smoke into his face. "Tell me something I don't already know."

"All right." He nodded. "You're coming with me."

Elizabeth took a step back, her bravado vaporizing as her imagination ran rampant. She was a stranger here, a woman with a reputation, a woman without an alibi. She had been at the scene of the crime, had the victim's blood on her shoes, and Dane Jantzen was a county sheriff in a county where two bums pissing in the street was a crime wave. Visions of women-in-prison movies flashed through her head. Mother Mary on a motorcycle, talk about life going from bad to worse.

Dane wagged his head in disgust. Every time he thought he had this woman pegged as tough, her armor cracked. She was looking up at him as if he'd just told her he sacrificed children on a daily basis. He plucked the microwave tray off the counter and stuck it under her smoldering cigarette before the inch of ash dropped off.

"You need a ride to town," he reminded her with no small amount of exasperation. "As I recall, you managed to drive that battleship you call a car off a perfectly straight road and, unless those steroids you're taking have given you Herculean strength and you've pulled it out of the ditch with your lovely bare hands, it's still sitting there."

"Here I thought you stopped by just to satisfy your daily requirement for harassing people. I wouldn't have suspected you had a big capacity for common courtesy."

"It's damage control," Dane corrected her. "The press conference starts at nine. I want to know where your mouth is."

Elizabeth narrowed her eyes. "Well, it won't be kissing your ass. I can get my own ride, thank you very much."

She turned with a toss of her aching head, bent on making a grand exit if it killed her, but a hand closed on her elbow and swung her back around. She was a hairbreadth from his chest, her gaze almost level with the polished brass name plate that read SHERIFF JANTZEN in bold black letters. Slowly, defiantly, she raised her head and stared up at him, and the world tilted a little on its axis.

She told herself it was a combination of her hangover and his height in cowboy boots, but the little voice of truth inside her clucked its tongue. The fact of the matter was he was too damn close and too damn male. The effect was unsetting in the extreme. She wished with all her heart to be anywhere else with anyone else.

"It wasn't an offer," he said, his voice silky soft. "It was an order. You're coming with me. Now."

EIGHT

God Almighty, you have just cornered the market on charm, haven't you?" Elizabeth shot her most scathing glare across the cab of the Bronco as it rumbled down the gravel road. She suspected it had no effect at all, it being hidden behind the lenses of her Ray-Bans, but the intent was there, burning in the air between them.

Dane bared his teeth. "Charm is my middle name."

"Really? I would have thought it was something that started with an A."

"Admirable?"

"Arrogant. Annoying. Ass—"

"Tut-tut, Ms. Stuart," he clucked in mock affront. "Such language is unbecoming to a lady of your quality."

Elizabeth snarled at him. "You wouldn't know quality if it spit in your face."

She dug through her purse—the one item she had managed to grab as Dane had all but dragged her out of the house—and pulled out her compact and a tube of Passion Poppy lipstick. Snapping open the mirror, she watched her reflection bob up and down as she tried to put some color on her lips. "You could have given me ten minutes to change and put on a little makeup—"

"I've never known a woman who could make up her mind in ten minutes, let alone her face—"

"—but no, you've got to play Mr. Macho and drag me

off at the crack of dawn for a press conference that doesn't start for hours. You know, you'd'a been a real hit in Nazi Germany. You could have been the poster boy for the SS."

"Jesus Christ," he grumbled. "I don't think denying you the time to put on mascara constitutes cruel and unusual punishment."

"No, that part comes now," Elizabeth said dryly. "Having to suffer your delightful company all the way to town, riding in this lumber wagon while I shove my best tube of Estee Lauder lipstick up my nose."

Dane hit the brakes and sent the Bronco skidding to a halt. A little yelp of surprise escaped from Elizabeth as her purse went flying and her body hurtled toward the dash. She stuck out a hand to save herself, broke a nail, and thumped her head on the windshield just the same.

"Dammit to Hades, I spent ten dollars on these nails!" She shoved her sunglasses up on top of her head and examined the broken fingernail, running her thumb over its jagged edge.

Her nails were the one indulgence she allowed herself these days. She had always seen a good manicure as the mark of a true lady, and she clung to that symbol now that she couldn't afford any of the other trappings of sophistication. She had skipped lunch three times in the last week so she could have Ingrid Syverson at the Fashion-Aire Beauty Salon put on a triple coat of Vivacious Red. Now the whole effect was ruined.

"I told you to wear a seat belt," Dane growled.

And she had refused just to irk him.

"You're a maniac, that's what you are," she grumbled, picking up her slim gold compact and checking her reflection before stuffing it back into her purse along with a handful of junk that had flown out onto the floor. Lighter, tampons, coupons for frozen pizza at the Piggly Wiggly, five loose Junior Mints, and eighty-three cents.

"No," Dane corrected her, the muscles in his jaw working as tension clenched his teeth together. "What I am is dead tired. I got an hour's sleep last night. I got to go home long enough to make sure some lunatic with a knife hadn't added my daughter to his list of things to do, then I spent the rest of the night at the station being hounded by reporters and racking my brain over who would have wanted to make Jarrold Jarvis shorter by a head." He turned toward Elizabeth with a look that had her unconsciously bracing herself against the door. "I'm a man whose patience is running seriously in the red, and the last thing I need is some southern belle whining to me about her goddamn fingernails."

Elizabeth straightened her sunglasses and primly resettled herself on the seat, smoothing her old UTEP T-shirt as if it were her finest designer blouse. She tucked a strand of hair behind her ear, collecting her poise as silence settled like dust in the cab of the truck.

"I do not whine," she said stiffly, presenting him with her profile. "I pout."

"Pouting is generally a silent endeavor," Dane remarked. He slid the stick back into gear and the Bronco began to roll forward once more. "Maybe you're out of practice."

Damn but if she didn't have to give him the last word. Why couldn't he have sent Deputy Kaufman to pick her up? That sweet little puppy-eyed man would have let her change clothes. Shoot, she probably could have shampooed her hair and shaved her legs too, for that matter. He would have inquired after her feelings instead of laying into her with fangs bared, like a bad-tempered wolf.

She snuck a glance at Dane out of the corner of her eye. He *did* look tired. His face was drawn, the skin stretched taut over the bones. He had shaved, but there wasn't much to be done about the lines of tension digging in around his mouth and eyes. A little trickle of sympathy leaked through Elizabeth. She supposed he had reason to be churlish. The weight of what had happened rested squarely on his shoulders, and, while they certainly looked strong enough to carry a load, that didn't make it fun.

"Did your daughter make it in all right?" She kicked

herself for asking, but the words had snuck out of her mouth without permission. She had told herself she didn't want to know anything about his personal life, didn't want to draw any parallels between her life and his, but the horse was out of the barn now.

He shot her a suspicious look, like a wild dog wary of a handout from a stranger. "Yeah, fine."

"She lives out of state, I guess."

"Los Angeles."

"That's a long way. Must be hard," she murmured. Distance had never been a problem for Bobby Lee, she mused bitterly. He had never made any attempt to see Trace after she had moved out. But then, she doubted Bobby Lee kept a picture of their son in a frame on his desk either. Just that one little sign of fatherly caring put Dane Jantzen in a whole different league for her. She might have thought he was a jerk deluxe in every other way, but she couldn't help admiring a man who cared about his daughter.

"Yeah," Dane admitted reluctantly. "It's tough. I don't get to spend much time with her as it is. Now I've got this murder—"

He checked himself abruptly. The last thing he needed to do was confide in this woman. Christ, what was he thinking? That she might sympathize because she was a single parent too? Fat chance that she would side with him. She was a mother, not a father. She had custody, not visitation. If there were comparisons to be drawn between his situation and hers, then surely she had more in common with Tricia than she did with him.

"Any leads on a suspect yet?" she asked.

He was glad for the change in subject. "Trying to get a scoop for the *Clarion*?"

"I'm trying to make conversation."

"I thought you were going to pout. I'd really prefer if you pouted, actually."

Elizabeth tilted her head to one side. "Well, we're not big on courting to each other's preferences, you and I, now, are we?"

Dane gave a snort. "Not so far."

She studied him quietly for a moment, reflecting with some wonder on the antagonism that had instantly sprung up between them. She generally got on famously with men—as long as she wasn't married to them. A smile, a batted lash, a flirtatious word and she had the garden-variety man eating out of her hand. This one was more liable to bite her hand off. Her fingers curled protectively into fists against the soft leather of her Gucci bag.

"I'm not asking anything you won't tell at the press conference," she said. "And I sure as hell can't run off and print it anywhere right now, can I?" She glanced around the Bronco, which was outfitted with all the paraphernalia of a standard police cruiser, including the wire-mesh barrier between the front- and backseats. "I'm what you might call a captive audience."

Dane rubbed a hand over his jaw, fighting off a yawn. What would it hurt to give her the same official statement he intended to give the rest of the press? He could consider it a practice run. Eyes on the road, he hit the blinker and turned onto the highway.

"We think it was a transient," he said flatly. "Murderrobbery. He caught Jarvis alone after hours. Killed him. You came along before he had a chance to steal the car."

The idea sent a shudder through Elizabeth. If she'd gotten there a little sooner, she would indeed have been a witness—or another victim. She remembered again the feeling of being watched as she'd stood there staring down at the body, and her skin crawled beneath a cold wave of pinpricks. Fear gripped her throat, and she had to nearly spit the words out of her mouth.

"His wallet was gone?"

"Empty. And the glove compartment had been rifled."

"Maybe Jarrold was just out of cash."

Dane shook his head. "Jarrold was never out of cash. Some men measure masculinity by the length of their cock; Jarrold Jarvis measured it by how big a wad a man carried in his hip pocket. I saw him at the Coffee Cup yesterday. Phyllis would have liked to have taken a frying pan after him. He paid for a dollar-ninety-eight check with a hundred and cleaned out her till. She had to send Renita to the bank and wait tables herself while *All My Children* was on. That's just about motive enough for Phyllis to have killed him herself. She gets cranky when she misses her soaps."

Elizabeth nibbled at her ragged fingernail as she turned the possibilities over in her mind. "So what was this transient doing out to Still Waters? It's hardly on the way to anyplace. He'd have to be some piss-poor retarded kind of mugger to be looking for a victim out in the country like that."

"He's not a mugger by trade. He's a man who saw an opportunity and acted on it. We get our share of drifters through here in the summer. Looking for farm work and odd jobs. There's been a guy hanging around town since April or so. Came down from the Iron Range. Said he was looking for work, but more like he was looking for trouble. He's been skirting the edges of having his butt thrown in jail since the day he got here."

"This drifter have a name?"

"Yep."

"You gonna share it with me?"

"Nope."

"Is he in custody?" she asked, professional interest taking a backseat to her personal fears. She couldn't shake the feeling that the killer had seen her, had stood there and watched her, had been out there in the night as she'd waited for Trace to come home. She had sensed him, had felt the heaviness in the air, the electric tension of something dark and menacing.

"Not at the moment," Dane said. "I've got every deputy in the county beating the bushes for him. If he's gone to ground around here, we'll find him." And the case would be closed and everyone in Still Creek could go back to business as usual. He could take a few days off to get his first crop of hay in and to just be with his daughter. "We'll get him."

"How'd he know Jarvis?"

"He tried to hire on at Still Waters and got turned down."

"You think that's a motive to kill?"

"Depends on the man. In New York, Chicago, there are kids—sixteen, seventeen years old—willing to cut your throat if they happen to like the jacket you're wearing. This guy had the opportunity to see Jarrold flashing his cash around. Money will motivate people to do a lot of things."

"Ain't that a fact," Elizabeth murmured. A picture of Brock flashed through her mind. The man had more money than God and he'd still gone rabid at the idea of more. She doubted he would have let anything stand in his way of marrying that brainless twit of a European princess, Marissa Mount-Zaverzee. Marry-and-Mount-Me. Bags of money there. Rumor had it her daddy had bought their titles, that their blood was no more blue than a dirt farmer's, but that didn't make their money any less green.

"Know a little something about that, do you?" Dane eased off on the gas as they reached the edge of town, and shot her a hard glance.

Elizabeth was ready to snap back, but she caught something in his look, a cynicism that was old and ingrained, a bitterness that had to have predated her arrival in his life. She narrowed her eyes in speculation.

"Put the screws to you in the divorce, didn't she?"

He flinched as if she'd reached across the cab and pinched him hard. A ghost of a smile curled the corner of her mouth. It held no joy or humor, only weariness and the kind of knowledge she would gladly have done without.

"My luck," she said on a long sigh, wishing for a cigarette. She had enough to deal with just scraping by through life right now. She surely didn't need a man with an ax to grind climbing on top of everything. She already felt as though she were in the middle of a stampede, fighting to keep her feet under her. Then along came

Dane Jantzen, weighed down by a load of old emotional baggage, kicking at her for spite's sake.

She rolled her window down and let the cool morning air wash over her for a minute while she stewed. This would have been a good time to let things slide, she reflected, but she was sick of taking the blame for other people's sins. Besides, she'd never been much good at keeping her mouth shut when she had the need to say something.

"I'm not your ex-wife, Sheriff—"

"Thank God."

She scowled at him as her temper simmered a little hotter, the flames of righteous indignation leaping up inside her. "I'll second that," she said, " 'cause dollars to doughnuts, you've got to be pure D hell to live with. But I don't need to be taking all kinds of shit from you because Mrs. Dane Jantzen got herself some shark lawyer and cleaned your pockets for you. That's your fault, sugar, not mine."

"Yeah," Dane drawled. "I guess you've got enough faults without me adding to them."

Elizabeth gave a sniff and shook her head as they turned off Main Street and headed west on Itasca, skirting around an Amish buggy that was plodding toward the Piggly Wiggly. A round-faced boy no more than five peered out at them from the dark interior, eyes eager and owlish. He raised a chubby hand to wave, and his mother frowned at him and rattled off something in German.

"While wallowing in your sad and bitter past, you seem to have taken a wrong turn," Elizabeth said sarcastically. "We're nowhere near the courthouse."

"We're not going to the courthouse. I have to stop at the Jarvis place first. Helen Jarvis called in to say someone trashed their mailbox last night."

"No fooling?" She sobered and shifted sideways on the seat. "The killer adding insult to injury?"

"Seems pretty juvenile."

"I don't think our prison system is overflowing with psychologically mature men."

He hit the blinker again and turned left, easing the Bronco to a stop in front of a glorified split-foyer house that had been overdressed with a row of fake Doric columns along the front. It had the look of a low-rent Tara, complete with a little grinning black-jockey hitching post standing beside the front step, as if Ashley Wilkes might actually ride up, tie his horse to it, and stay to chat about The War. Pink plastic flamingos lurked in the juniper bushes, their long necks bent at unnatural angles. Smack in the middle of the front yard, amid a riotous patch of pink petunias, stood an enormous carved stone fountain that would have looked more at home in Versailles.

At the end of the curving drive, the mailbox—encased in white imitation wrought-iron filigree—was in a sad state. It stood crumpled over sideways, like a skinny kid who'd had the wind knocked out of him by the class bully. The frame was twisted and scabs of paint were missing in a manner that suggested someone had tried to beat it to death with a tire iron.

The complete picture of Jarrold Jarvis's home had a weird, incongruous, surreal quality about it that made Elizabeth shiver in distaste. If the king and queen of tacky had needed a palace, she thought, this would have been it.

"Christ in a miniskirt," she muttered, leaning ahead. "I'll bet you a nickel they've got a black velvet painting of Elvis hanging over the imitation Louis XIV settee."

"You lose." Dane pulled the keys from the ignition and palmed them, flashing her a wry grin. "It's a bullfighter. Wait here."

"Wait here!" Elizabeth wailed.

He slammed his door on the rest of her indignant protest and started for the house. Elizabeth scrambled down out of the truck, pushing her sunglasses up on her nose and hitching her purse strap over her shoulder. If he thought she was going to stay in the car like some recalcitrant child and miss out on meeting the bereaved Mrs.

Jarvis, he had another think coming. In the first place, that she offer her condolences was only decent. In the second place, she wanted to see what kind of woman had married a pig like Jarrold. Then there was the matter of her job.

She took one step toward the house, and Dane wheeled on her with a look that could have frozen molten lava. It stopped her in her tracks, discretion, for once, winning out over impulse. She shrugged and showed him a big, phony smile.

"Just stretching my legs," she said meekly.

Dane snarled a little under his breath, backing toward the house until he was certain she wasn't going to follow him. He couldn't think of many more distasteful things than facing a new widow with a reporter in tow. God only knew what the amazing Miss Stuart might come up with—*I'm sorry for your loss, Mrs. Jarvis. By the way, did your husband sleep around or anything? Just for the record. The public has a right to know.*

Helen Toller Jarvis met him at the front door with a cherry Jell-O mold in hand. Short and moon-faced, she looked to be near fifty and was hardened rather than well preserved, as if the layer of plumpness under her skin had solidified into something more dense than fat. Her face was stretched unnaturally taut, the result of being the only recipient of a face-lift in all of Still Creek.

She was dry-eyed and pale, her skin looking waxy beneath a layer of makeup that had been applied with a lavish hand. Two shades of blue shadow arched over her eyes in a monochromatic rainbow that went to her brow line. Rouge dotted her cheeks in spots of hectic red. Her hair, dyed a shade of peach that brought to mind fiberglass insulation, rose up in a teased and sprayed cone, looking impervious to any disaster—natural or manmade. Tragedy might drive Helen to her knees, but her beehive would survive.

A low buzz of activity sounded in the house behind her. News of Jarrold's death had hit the grapevine, and the women of Still Creek had begun to arrive with food in hand to offer comfort and shore up the grieving with tuna casserole and applesauce cake.

"Dane," she said, the corners of her lips flicking up in an automatic smile. "I thought you might be another woman from the church. We have enough Jell-O to last the year already. Mavis Grimsrud brought this one."

She lifted the jiggling red mass to give him a better look. It was molded in the shape of a fish with bulging maraschino cherry eyes and fruit cocktail innards showing through the transparent sides. Dane tucked his chin and clenched his teeth against a grimace.

"I don't know why people think we need Jell-O when someone dies," Helen said, her piping voice hovering somewhere between chipper and shrill. She looked up at him, her eyes a little glazed from shock or tranquilizers, over-plucked brows tugging together like a pair of thin question marks. "Why do you think that is, Dane?"

"I—a—" He shrugged, at a loss. He had expected her to have questions about Jarrold, the case, the senselessness of murder. Jell-O was out of his realm.

"I suppose everyone has a box in their cupboard," she mused absently. She balanced the plate on one forearm and picked at a cherry eye with a long coral fingernail. "If you know that trick with ice cubes, you can have it ready in a flash. Now, a hot dish, that's something else. Arnetta McBaine brought one by made with Tater Tots. She told me once she keeps a casserole in her freezer for emergencies."

Dane drew in a long, patient breath. "Helen, how are you doing? Do you need anything?"

She snapped out of her fog with a half-laugh of embarrassment. "I'm fine," she said, her voice fluttering like Glinda the Good Witch from the *Wizard of Oz*. Her lips tightened against her teeth and her eyes squinted into nothingness. "Jarrold is the one not doing too well. And my mailbox. My poor mailbox isn't well at all."

"I know. Lorraine told me you'd called. I thought I'd drop by myself—"

"Excuse me, Mrs. Jarvis. I just wanted to offer my condolences."

Dane jerked around, eyes blazing. Elizabeth stepped past him on the stoop and offered her hand to the Widow Jarvis.

Helen's wispy brows scaled her forehead again. "I'm sorry," she chirped. "Do I know you?"

"No, and I'm terribly sorry we have to meet under these circumstances. I'm Elizabeth Stuart."

"Elizabeth—?"

For an instant Helen Jarvis went still while the cogs of her brain slipped into gear. The lull before the storm. Elizabeth saw the sudden flash of recognition, then fury in the woman's tiny eyes, the rise of natural color beneath the clown dots of rouge on her cheeks. She pulled her hand back and braced herself for she knew not what.

"You're that woman," Helen said, her voice suddenly so low and rough, she sounded like the devil talking through Linda Blair in *The Exorcist*. Elizabeth took a cautious step back, the short hairs rising on the back of her neck. "You're that *southern* woman." She hissed the word as if it were one of the foulest in her vocabulary.

"I'm from Texas, actually," Elizabeth said weakly.

Helen edged out onto the step, a wild sound rumbling in her throat like a poodle growling. Her body was rigid and trembling visibly, her face flushing red as rage bubbled up inside her. If a human could have imitated a volcano about to blow, Elizabeth figured this was about what it would look like, right down to the fiery cone of hair thrusting up from the top of her head. It was a frightening thing to behold, and she could only stand and watch, like a deer caught in headlights, too flabbergasted to think of anything else.

"You bitch!" Helen exploded, fury blasting out of her in waves. "How dare you come to this house! How dare you!"

Before Elizabeth could draw breath to answer, the Jell-O mold came flying at her. The plate dropped away en route, like a booster off a rocket, and shattered on the concrete of the terrace. The gelatin bass kept coming. It hit her square in the chest and burst like an overripe melon, spewing fruit cocktail and shards of Jell-O in all directions. Elizabeth fell back with a gasp of astonishment, arms spread wide as if she'd been shot.

Dane snarled a curse under his breath as globs of red goo pelted his clean shirt. He grabbed Helen by her rigid shoulders and turned her back toward the house.

The doorway was suddenly overflowing, ladies from Our Savior's Lutheran Church spilling out onto the terrace, their faces frozen in various expressions of horror and excitement according to their personal bent. Mavis Grimsrud, who bore a notable resemblance to Ma Kettle, let out a shriek at the sight of Elizabeth, though whether it was concern for Elizabeth or for her own dismembered Jell-O masterpiece was difficult to tell.

"Grandma Schummacher's plate!" she wailed as her gaze fell to the terrace. She hitched up her cotton housedress to her knees in one meaty fist and squatted down to pick up the slivers of china.

Dane herded Helen around her, singling out Kathleen Gunderson with his gaze. "Kathleen, take Helen inside and see that she lays down."

"Lie down," Helen growled, digging her heels in every step of the way into the foyer. "Talk to that slut about lying down."

Kathleen, a dainty woman Helen's own age, took a firm hold of her friend's arm and dragged her another step into the house, her mouth tightening with disapproval. "Helen, for heaven's sake, there's no need to air that dirty laundry now."

"Dirty laundry! I gave her some dirty laundry!" Helen's shrill little-girl voice ended in a squeak and giggling uncontrollably she went off into the nether reaches of the house with Kathleen.

"Judas H.," Dane muttered. He turned and pinned Edith Truman with a look.

She raised a hand, needing no order. "I'll go call Doc."

The rest of the women lingered around the doorway, eyes on Elizabeth. No one rushed out to console her or to help her brush the mess off her clothes. Not one voice was raised in inquiry or sympathy or explanation. They stood up against the side of the Jarvis home as if they were guarding the portal against a foreign invasion, their gazes ranging from carefully blank to wary to accusatory.

Elizabeth stood just off the terrace, staring back at them, reading their expressions. The faces were new, but the sentiment etched there was no different from what she'd seen on the faces of the Atlanta Junior League ladies the day news of her impending divorce had hit the grapevine. She was an outsider. She was unwelcome here. Separation stretched like an invisible gulf between them, yawning wide, with no one willing to reach across to her. She was alone.

The feeling was nothing new, but somehow it managed to hit her with an unexpected amount of hurt. Being snubbed by Atlanta's upper crust when Brock's propaganda campaign against her had been at its peak hadn't broken her. But standing here next to Jarrold Jarvis's lawn jockey with cherry Jell-O dripping down her and the venerable matrons of Our Savior's Lutheran Church looking down their noses at her had tears crowding her throat.

"Why don't you ladies go in and make some coffee," Dane suggested.

He held Mavis's elbow as she hefted herself up, the final remains of Grandma Schummacher's plate crunching under her orthopedic shoes. Great, he thought, as if the town wasn't already buzzing with news of the murder; now there would be this tale to tell and retell. How "that southern woman" made poor Helen Jarvis lose her mind.

As the last of the church ladies went into the house and the door swung shut behind them, Dane wheeled around. "Dammit, I told you to wait—"

The rest of his diatribe jammed in his throat. Elizabeth

was standing there in her faded jeans and college T-shirt, scraping red Jell-O off herself, blinking back tears. Tears. Shit. He could take her tantrums and tirades. Her tart tongue kept her just where he wanted her—at arm's length. But tears. He hadn't expected tears, had never been sure what to do about them. Something suspiciously like tenderness sprang unexpectedly to life inside him, and he winced as if it were a thorn.

"Well," she said on a shaky breath, trying to force one of her cocky grins. "So much for paying my respects."

One fat crystalline drop rolled over her lashes onto her cheek. She swiped at it angrily, leaving a globby smear of gelatin. Dane swore under his breath. He stepped off the terrace, pulling an immaculate white handkerchief from his hip pocket.

"You really bring out the best in people," he grumbled, rubbing at the mess on her cheek, focusing on the task instead of on the almost overwhelming desire to take her in his arms and hold her. Soft. He was going soft in his old age.

Elizabeth almost managed to chuckle. He had meant it facetiously, of course. Hadn't given a thought to the fact that he was actually being nice to her for once in his accursed life, she was sure. But he was. There was sympathy in his eyes behind the annoyance, and he had positioned himself between her and the house, shielding her from view of anyone peering out between the Levolors.

"Could you rub a little harder?" she asked as he mushed her cheek up against the side of her nose. "I've never been partial to having skin there, and I think you've about got it scraped right off."

Dane scowled at her but gentled his touch.

"Thank you," she murmured, reaching up to take the handkerchief from him. "I'll get the rest, if you don't mind."

The rest was on her chest. The idea of letting his hand drift down to touch her breasts wafted through her mind as she looked up at him, as her fingertips bumped against his on her cheek. Just a quick vignette of involuntary fantasy, a fleeting image of those long, elegant fingers brushing against her.

Dane glanced down at the globules of Jell-O clinging to the upper slopes of her breasts. His mind raced ahead to imagine what it might be like if she were naked and he were to gently rub those cool, glittering bits of sweetness over her skin, then lean down and let his mouth follow the trail. . . . Heat drifted through him, the core of it curling like a fist in the pit of his belly.

His gaze drifted back up and caught on hers. She blinked, like someone trying to come out of a trance, and the tip of her tongue skimmed across her bottom lip.

He wanted to kiss her. For an instant he couldn't see any reason not to lean down and taste that mouth. It was a matter of simple, unbridled lust, he told himself. A male wanting a female. Nothing complicated, nothing emotional. She made him hot, and his body wanted a chance to do something about it.

He cupped her cheek, catching his thumb beneath her chin and tilting her face to a better angle.

"Dane!"

Edith Truman's voice cut through the sensual haze. Dane shook off the spell and turned around. Edith stood at the door with a dishtowel knotted in her hands, looking like his grandmother come out to call him in for pie. Having been married to Doc Truman for nearly sixty years, she had seen more than her share of human trauma and was luckily a woman who thrived during times of crisis. Her eyes were bright as she leaned out the door.

"Mark just called to see if you were still here. They're getting things set up for the press conference, and apparently there's some disagreement over who gets to sit at the head table."

Dane raised a hand in a gesture that managed to combine acknowledgment and resignation. "I'm on my way." He glanced over his shoulder at Elizabeth.

"Come on, trouble," he said, starting for the truck. "It's showtime."

"Would you mind dropping me off at Jolynn's?" Elizabeth asked, falling in step beside him. "I might attract undue attention if I show up at your little soiree looking like this."

Dane imagined she would attract attention if she showed up in a nun's habit, but he kept that comment to himself and muttered a grudging yes.

"You're a prince," Elizabeth said, climbing into the cab of the Bronco. She bit back a chuckle at the look he shot her. He wanted her to think he wasn't anything but a tough, ornery son of a gun with a badge. He didn't much like the idea that she had caught a glimpse of something nicer in him.

"Don't spread it around," he grumbled, sliding behind the wheel. "I'm not running a taxi service either, so don't expect me to hang around and wait for you while you try to decide what the latest fashion for a press conference is."

"No, sir." She saluted him smartly, winning another disgruntled snarl for her efforts, then she relaxed against the seat and studied him for a minute as he started the truck and headed south again. "Much as it pains me to be civil to you," she said soberly, "I do thank you."

"For what?"

She toyed with the strap of the seat belt, uncomfortable, uncertain of her footing on this ground. She could stand toe-to-toe and fight with him. This was much trickier. It skirted the edges of liking him, and that seemed unwise. "For being decent," she said at last.

"I'm midwestern, it's ingrained."

"It wasn't ingrained in any of those women standing on that veranda."

"You're new here," Dane said, feeling a little embarrassed that he had to make excuses for his townspeople. "They don't know anything about you except—"

"Except that I'm a notorious, man-hopping divorcee from the South," Elizabeth finished, her mouth twisting at the injustice. "They know what they've read and they know I'm not one of them. I'm familiar with the routine,

Sheriff. I've been through other versions of it before. Let me tell you, sugar, these old gals have got nothing on the ladies of Atlanta. I'm just not holding up as well these days, that's all."

Dane looked at her, his curiosity stirring at the remembered pain in her eyes. For a minute he forgot that he didn't want to get to know the woman behind the infamous legend. "I can't imagine that you didn't fit in in Atlanta."

She arched a brow. "Why? Because I have a drawl? Well, it's the wrong drawl, and I've got the wrong bloodlines, and I was born in the wrong town. The only thing I did right was marry money and enough of it so that all those little blueblooded belles had to put up with me and smile while they were at it. But then, that's one of the traits of a true southern belle—she can cut you right down to the bone all the while looking like butter wouldn't melt in her mouth. I am here to say it, darlin', God didn't make a more vicious creature than an Atlanta Junior Leaguer with a mood on. Every minute I lived there I had the feeling they didn't figure I knew enough not to wear white shoes after Labor Day."

Dane steered the Bronco over to the curb across the street from Jolynn Nielsen's house and let the engine idle. "Why can't you wear white shoes after Labor Day?"

Elizabeth laughed, the tension dissipating. "Honey, you will never make it into the Junior League."

It sounded to him like nobody should want to. The picture Elizabeth painted was of an enclave of bitches waiting with claws extended to pounce on the first person to pick up the wrong fork at dinner. He rolled his eyes. "I'm crushed."

"And I'm grateful." She smiled at him softly and held his handkerchief out to him. "Thanks. See you at the press conference, cowboy."

He dropped the handkerchief in the litter basket that hung from a knob on his door, then shot her a parting look. "*Please* don't get into any more trouble," he said tightly.

She batted her lashes in innocence as she settled her purse strap on her shoulder and slid down out of the truck. "Trouble? Who? Me?"

NINE

"CHRIST ALMIGHTY, SHE CAME RIGHT AT ME," Elizabeth said, dragging her T-shirt off over her head. "Came right at me looking like Tammy Faye Baker in a frenzy—all crazed and bug-eyed, with this big cone of hair and makeup done like she got caught in an explosion at the cosmetics counter in Woolworth's. I never had anything like that happen in all my born days."

With a grimace of distaste Jolynn lifted the discarded shirt off her bed, gingerly pinching the neck band between thumb and forefinger, and dropped it to the floor.

"I guess now I know how the Panhandle Rodeo Queen must have felt that time I caught her in bed with Bobby Lee and I took after him with the pellet gun we used to shoot rats with." Elizabeth shivered, recalling again the wild look on Helen Jarvis's face as she'd launched that plate. "Shook me something terrible."

She went to her friend's closet and stood there in her jeans and bra, eyes scanning the array of blouses for something suitable for a news conference. The closet wasn't offering much. That Jolynn's wardrobe had suffered in the years since her divorce was readily apparent. There wasn't a suit or linen blouse to be had. Jo was partial to men's flannel shirts for winter and men's work shirts for summer. Uncomplicated, unflattering, the costumes seemed to suit Jolynn's general air of being downtrodden. Elizabeth made a mental note to drag her off on a shopping trip as soon things settled down and they were making a little money. She dug to the back of the closet and plucked out an oversize imitation gold lamé blouse. It was a bit much for day wear, but it was better than a castoff from the friendly staff at Harley's Texaco.

"This'll do."

Jolynn frowned. "Hey, that's my good Christmas blouse!"

"I'll be careful."

"Burn a hole in it and we won't have to wait for lung cancer to do you in—I'll kill you myself."

"If we can sell enough newspapers between now and Christmas, I'll buy you two of the real thing as a bonus," Elizabeth said, slipping the blouse on and starting on the fake rhinestone buttons. "Provided some crazed woman doesn't do me in first," she added, shuddering again. Her fingers stilled on the third button, and she looked up at Jolynn, eyes full of confusion and traces of hurt. "I can't figure it, Jo. I only found the body, I didn't kill him. What'd I ever do to Helen Jarvis to make her throw a Jell-O fish at me?"

Jolynn sat down on the bed and busied herself tracing a pattern in the dust on the nightstand. She'd known Elizabeth since their college days in El Paso when she had been an army brat off her father's short leash for the first time in her life and Elizabeth had been a struggling young single mother taking classes and working two jobs. They had forged a bond then that had lasted through good times and bad, through changes in fortune and changes in marital status. She figured she knew Elizabeth better than anyone, and she knew how what she had to say was going to sting. For all her don't-give-a-damn attitude, Elizabeth had a heart more tender than most and an ego that had been sorely abused of late.

"It's not what you did to Helen," she said hesitantly. "It's what Helen thinks you did with Jarrold." Elizabeth blinked at her in confusion and Jo pressed on, her mouth twisting a little on the taste of the words. "The rumor going around this morning is that you and Jarrold had been meeting out at Still Waters to do the horizontal hokey-pokey."

Elizabeth's jaw dropped. "I hardly knew the man!" she protested, jerking back a step as if Jolynn had lashed out at her physically. "And what I did know I loathed and despised!"

Jolynn drew a sad face in the table dust. "Yeah, well . . . so the story goes. I don't doubt but that Helen is more upset about the rumors than she is about Jarrold lying cold on a slab down at Davidson's. You're up-staging her grieving-widow act."

"Eeewwl" Elizabeth shook herself, the very thought of having sex with Jarrold Jarvis making her skin crawl. "Where'd you hear all this?"

"At the Coffee Cup. I stopped in, hoping to catch that BCA guy having breakfast."

"And did you?"

"No, but Phyllis filled me in on this latest tidbit. Everybody knows you found the body."

"And everybody knows I'll just drop my panties for anything with testosterone," Elizabeth said bitterly. She shook her head and blew out a breath. "Doesn't matter what he looks like, acts like, smells like. If he's got a third leg and walks upright, I'll be there with bells on."

A storm cloud and jagged line of lightning joined the sad face on the nightstand. Jo's heart squeezed a little. "Phyllis set a few people straight." Not that they had listened or cared. In Jolynn's experience, people were much more eager to believe the worst than the truth. In a town the size of Still Creek, gossip was served up and devoured as an essential part of the daily diet.

"Well, God bless Phyllis anyway." Elizabeth slumped down on the bed beside her friend and stared across the room at her reflection in the dresser mirror. Her eyes were bloodshot, and she could have benefited greatly from a generous application of her Elizabeth Arden concealer. With the gold blouse and twinkling buttons, she looked like a pathetic refugee from a bad New Year's party. A sense of despair ballooned inside her, hollow and aching. She raked a hand back through her hair and heaved another sigh.

"I really wanted things to be different here," she said quietly, letting a little of that despair trickle out in hope of relieving the pressure. "I wanted this place to be like some kind of magic kingdom where nobody ever heard of Brock Stuart and people didn't snap up ugly likes dogs after meat scraps." She managed a little laugh. "Instead of Oz, I feel down the rabbit hole. Dead bodies, women throwing food at me, the lord high sheriff dragging me around like a captured fugitive. Lord love a duck, I should have moved to Outer goddamn Mongolia."

Jolynn gave her an affectionate bump with her shoulder. "You wouldn't like it. You can't get good candy bars there. They make everything out of rancid yak milk."

A weak smile tugged at Elizabeth's lips and she chuckled. She had one friend. That counted for something. "Is that a fact?"

"You bet." Jo pulled open the drawer on the nightstand and rummaged through her stash. "Snickers or Baby Ruth?"

"Snickers."

She pulled out a candy bar for Elizabeth and one for herself. They sat in companionable silence for a moment, consoling themselves with chocolate.

"How'd it go at the scene?" Elizabeth asked.

Jo peeled back a little more of the candy wrapper and cleared her throat. "It was kind of like being at a party, only more macabre. There was this weird sort of festival atmosphere, reporters swarming all around, chatting, drinking coffee. The crime lab guys were a hoot."

"Did you learn anything?"

"Aside from a couple of truly tasteless jokes about severed heads? Not much." She took another bite of Baby Ruth and talked around it. "I thought this was interesting—he wasn't killed in the car. All the blood was spilled on a spot to the south and west of the building site."

Elizabeth worked a peanut between her molars as her

brain chewed on the information. "So why put him back in the car? Jantzen says they think some drifter killed him for his pocket money. Why would the guy take the time to put the body back in the car—especially if was going to steal the Lincoln too?"

"Maybe he wanted company on the trip to Des Moines."

"Jolynn!"

"No, really," she insisted, shifting on the bed like a kid settling in for a good ghost story. Her small hazel eyes were bright as glass marbles with enthusiasm for the topic. "Why not take the body? Take old Jarrold and the car and boot it into another jurisdiction. Ditch the corpse in one spot, the car in another, the murder weapon some-place else. That kind of stuff screws the cops up royally. It's what all the great serial killers do."

Elizabeth gave her a look. "You been reading up on it, have you?"

Jolynn shrugged without remorse and took another bite of her candy bar. "It's a fascinating subject, if you've got the stomach for it."

"Which I don't. Any whispers of who did it?"

She shook her head, sending a mass of overpermed curls tumbling into her eyes. She raked them back with her free hand. "Not a word. I managed to get a second with Yeager after the hoopla had died down. He's the regional BCA man. Cute guy." The corners of her kewpie-doll mouth curled upward, and she dropped her gaze to her lap, concentrating much too hard on picking up a crumb of chocolate and popping it in her mouth. Yeager probably hadn't even noticed she was female. There was really no point in acting like a teenager with a crush. "All he could talk about was what a shame it was they cut down that woods to build Still Waters. He says it was a prime turkey-hunting spot."

"That's not what was getting hunted there last night."

Sobering, Jo toyed with the ragged ends of her candy wrapper. "No."

Silence descended between them again. A moment of

quiet in memory of the dead. Most everyone would have respect for Jarrold Jarvis in death, Elizabeth reflected, even if they hadn't in life. That's the way people were—perverse, hypocritical. It was almost enough to make her join a convent. Almost. If it weren't for the fact that nuns didn't drink or smoke or get their nails done in Vivacious Red . . . And then there was that celibacy thing. Even though she'd sworn off men for the time being, that didn't mean she would want to sleep alone forever.

"So what's the story on Jantzen anyway?" she asked, wishing instantly she would just bite her stupid tongue off and be done with it. She wasn't supposed to want to know more about him.

Jolynn arched a brow. "Great Dane?"

Elizabeth scowled and picked at a long-dried fleck of white paint on the leg of her jeans. "I haven't seen anything about him that's all that great," she grumbled, feigning disinterest.

Her friend howled, laughing, rocking back on the bed and slapping her thigh. "Oh, come on! The man could cut a swath through Hollywood, and you know it."

"If he's so fabulous, how come you're not after him?" she asked peevishly.

Jolynn didn't bat an eye at the remark. "It doesn't matter who's after him," she said. "He's not playing."

"Get out," Elizabeth scoffed, giving her a shove. "Do not try to tell me he's gay. If he's gay, I'm the queen of England."

"He's not gay. He just doesn't go for local girls," Jolynn explained, shredding the loose pieces of her candy bar wrapper methodically as she spoke. "He married his hometown sweetheart way back when. Played pro football for the Raiders for a few years. Then he blew his knee, blew his career, and the wife blew him off. Rumor has it, he's seeing someone from out of town, but he manages to keep his private life very separate from his public one—which is no mean feat in a town this size. Why?" she asked, casting Elizabeth a sly look as she nibbled at a peanut. "You interested?"

"Hardly," Elizabeth sniffed. "I've done sworn off men. He's been hounding me, that's all. About the murder and everything."

She scanned the room in order to avoid the mental image of Dane Jantzen bending over her with his handkerchief, shielding her from the scathing gazes of the ladies of Lutheran guild, wiping the Jell-O off her with a look of disgruntled sympathy in his eyes.

Jolynn wasn't any more talented domestically than Elizabeth herself. The bed wasn't made. The hamper beside the dresser was overflowing, the clothes looking as though they were trying to escape before they could be subjected to the tortures of the washing machine. A mountain of notes, books, and junk-food wrappers rose up on the back of the nightstand behind the telephone, the alarm clock, and a dirty ashtray.

The nightstand jerked her gaze back when she would have looked on.

"How's your headache?" she asked innocently.

"My what?" Jo bit off a chunk of nougat, but froze in mid-chew as she followed Elizabeth's meaningful gaze to the ashtray. She squeezed her eyes shut for moment as she mentally called Rich Cannon a dozen of her favorite names. He couldn't even go to the effort of cleaning up after himself, the lazy bum. He came in, took what he wanted and left, leaving half a dozen cigarette butts and the toilet seat up.

"Don't say it," she muttered through her teeth, her self-esteem sliding down somewhere around her feet.

Elizabeth ignored the request. That Rich Cannon thought he could just swagger in and have Jo service him galled her no end. And that Jolynn let him get away with it galled her even worse. "You deserve better, Jolynn."

Appetite gone, Jo set her candy bar aside and pushed herself to her feet, wiping her hands on her jeans. "Yeah," she said, looking down at her battered Reeboks. "Don't we all."

"He was here when I called you last night, wasn't he?" Elizabeth had been too distracted to notice anything odd in Jolynn's voice during the call. She'd been too caught up in her own nightmare to think her best, and nearly her only friend had been lying to her.

Jolynn didn't answer, which was answer enough.

"How did he take the news of his father-in-law's demise?"

She gave a shrug of affected indifference. "With a grunt and a snort. His usual show of sensitivity."

The image wasn't difficult to conjure up. From what Elizabeth had seen, Rich Cannon had no concern for anyone or anything that didn't directly affect Rich Cannon. He certainly didn't show any sign of caring for Jolynn. She was a convenience to him, one he took advantage of without compunction or remorse.

"He's using you, Jolynn."

"There's a news flash." She plucked up the damning evidence and dumped it in the wastebasket, ashtray and all, sending up a fine plume of tobacco ash. "Well, I'm using him too, you know," she pointed out as she straightened. "Did you ever think of that? The man is hung like Secretariat. Sometimes it's worth a bit of personal degradation to go for a little pony ride."

Elizabeth refrained from comment. Jolynn had a look of desperate revelation in her eyes, as if this particular defense had only just occurred to her. Elizabeth didn't have it in her to call her on it. At any rate, there wasn't time.

"Come on, sugar," she said wearily, abandoning half her Snickers bar on the night table. "We've got us a circus to go to."

THE COURTROOM WAS STANDING ROOM ONLY. LORraine Worth stood guard at the door beside Kenny Spencer, checking press credentials with an eagle eye and turning away curious civilians, of which there were many. The hallway was lined with Still Creek residents eager for news or perhaps a glimpse of a suspect. They stood in knots of three and four, casting eager, expectant looks at every stranger who walked by.

Elizabeth imagined the room had changed little since the 1800s. Soft blue plaster rose up from a skirt of rich walnut wainscoting, fine lines and cracks in the walls denoting age like a matron's wrinkles. Stern men from other eras stared down at the crowd from heavy, ornate gilt frames. Old globe lights hung from a ceiling where ancient fans made a feeble attempt to stir the stuffy air. The Tyler County courtroom didn't look any more ready for the intrusion of the modern world than did the town of Still Creek itself with its quaint Victorian architecture and Amish buggies trudging the streets.

At the front of the room a podium bristling with microphones had been set up directly in front of the judge's bench. The prosecutor's table had been pulled forward to flank it and provided room for three people, their places marked with hand-lettered placards made from folded pieces of poster board—Sheriff Jantzen, Agent Yeager, Deputy Kaufman. Only the end chair was taken. Mark Kaufman sat behind the table, cracking his knuckles and looking like a man with a fear of public speaking waiting to address the U.N. He caught Elizabeth's eye and flashed her a wave and a nervous smile.

Lights and cameras crowded around the front of the room in a veritable forest of high technology. There was a general din of excitement as reporters, eager for something to do, grilled one another while they waited for the festivities to begin. Elizabeth and Jolynn slipped into seats at the back of the room just as Dane walked in at the front.

The noise level rose like a wave rolling into shore as the reporters caught sight of him coming out of judge's chambers. Questions were tossed out in the hope of getting something out of him other than the official statement. He ignored them.

The town VIPs had been given seats in the jury box and Charlie Wilder, the mayor, and Bidy Masters, head of the town council, popped up out of their chairs as

Dane walked by them. He checked his stride and turned reluctantly to face the pair.

Charlie was plump and jovial, the kind of man people enjoyed voting for. He owned Hardware Hank's and ran sales continuously, which helped endear him to people as well as keeping him from going under. The sales were often on items people had little use for, like Veg-O-Matics and Epilady hair removal devices, but as long as there was a sale on something, folks were more inclined to shop in town than drive to Rochester for cheaper prices at the big discount stores.

Nobody enjoyed voting for Bidy, a thin, sour-faced man with stooping, hollow shoulders that, coupled with his long, somber face, gave him the appearance of a vulture. But hardly anyone wanted to run for the town council, let alone be the head of it, and Bidy was conscientious and business-minded if not pleasant. Horse and Buggy Days had been his idea—not as a festival that would give locals an opportunity to have fun and relax, but as a tourist attraction that would draw in money from outside the community. He had a shrewd head for the tourist industry, and it was a sure bet he wasn't going to see murder as a long-term boost to the economy.

"Dane, can we have a word?" Charlie asked, leaning his belly against the rail of the jury box.

Bidy leaned in close too, beady eyes fastened hard on Dane's face. "We're wondering how soon you might have this wrapped up."

"The press conference? Shouldn't take more than half an hour."

"No, no," Charlie said. "This murder business. We heard there was a suspect at large. Have you got him yet?"

"No."

"Well, can you give us a time frame here, Dane?" The mayor gave one of his belly-jiggling chuckles that were calculated to soften edges regardless of the topic. He probably could have announced to the whole town he was a devoted neo-Nazi and everyone would think it was just fine as long as Charlie was laughing and smiling. "Are we looking at a day? Two?"

Dane tried to stretch his threadbare patience a little further, but couldn't quite manage to cover his sarcasm. "If you mean, will we have him before the Miss Horse and Buggy Days pageant begins, the answer is—we'll do our level best."

Charlie had the grace to blush. Bidy narrowed his eyes and worked his thin mouth like a toothless hag sucking on her gums.

"A shame about Jarrold," Charlie said, tossing in the sentiment in an attempt to look less mercenary.

Dane tipped his head and moved away from the pair, stepping around a light stand and through the gate that led to the spectator seating, where the esteemed members of the press were shouting at him, hands raised like frenzied bidders at the stock exchange. Christ, he hated reporters.

Elizabeth watched him bear down on her. Whatever had transpired since he had dropped her off at Jolynn's had not improved his humor. His mouth was set in a grim line, his eyes fierce beneath ominously lowered brows. He cut in at her row, stepping around people. Bending down, he closed a hand around her upper arm, his face no more than inches from hers.

"I want you closer to me," he said in a low voice.

An instinctive thrill rushed through her. Elizabeth steeled herself against it and forced a cocky smile. "Really, darlin'," she whispered, "don't you think you ought to see to this press conference first? What will people say?"

Nothing they're not saying already, Dane thought, his jaw tightening as he bit back the words. He had overheard the secretarial scuttlebutt at the water cooler on his way in and had nearly taken Tina Odegard's head off for gossiping on taxpayers' time. He told himself he didn't need his staff spreading rumors, but there had been something more to his anger that he didn't care to examine too closely, something vaguely proprietary that had risen up at the snide suggestion that Elizabeth had been sexually involved with Jarrold Jarvis.

"I'm sure you'll manage to incite a riot," he said sardonically. "I want you where I can have you yanked out of here if things get out of hand."

Any retort she might have made was lost as he hauled her up out of her chair and ushered her toward the front of the room. Heat rose in her cheeks as she heard her name ripple through the crowd. They stopped at the front row and Dane fixed a reporter from the Rochester *Post-Bulletin* with a steely glare.

"This seat is reserved," he growled.

The man started to protest as he shuffled through his notes, but then he looked up and swallowed his words in one gulp. Murmuring apologetically, he slid from the seat and motioned Elizabeth into it. She gave him a wan smile, then shot a glare at Dane.

"Thank you *so* much for making a spectacle of me," she hissed under her breath.

Dane flashed his teeth. "Oh, I can't take any credit for that," he whispered. "Thank whoever dressed you."

She plucked at a rhinestone button. "The way I see it, my being in Jolynn's best Christmas blouse is your fault."

"Yeah, well, I'll be glad to help you out of it later if you ask me real nice."

Elizabeth narrowed her eyes, not liking the warmth spreading through her any more than she liked the man who was causing it. "I'll ask you to go take a flying leap."

"Sorry, no time." He scanned the crowd, squinting as camera flashes went off around them, finally locking on Bret Yeager as the BCA agent trundled in a side door wearing his usual air of distraction and juggling an armload of papers. "Enjoy the show, Miss Stuart." He flashed her one last mocking smile. "I'd say you've got the best seat in the house, but I wouldn't want you to get a big head."

"Jerk," Elizabeth grumbled as he walked away. She

plunked down on the commandeered spot and dug her reporter's notebook out of her purse as Dane stepped up to the podium and addressed the crowd.

He read his statement with eloquence and authority, and Elizabeth caught herself thinking about the comment Jolynn had made earlier. There were plenty of professional athletes who made a beeline from the field of play to the silver screen—or at least the TV screen. She wondered why he hadn't. Lord knew he had the looks and the voice.

"Probably won't take direction," she muttered to herself, doodling little footballs on her notepad.

Yeager moved to the mike as Dane finished. The agent carried a messy sheaf of papers, which he plunked down on the stand, then promptly ignored. He was six feet tall and stocky, and most resembled an unmade bed. His tie was crooked and a little spike of sandy hair stuck straight up from the crown of his head. He expanded on procedure for a few minutes, talked about lab techniques, then opened the floor for questions, but Elizabeth wasn't listening. She was too busy wondering about the wife who had dumped Dane after his career had ended. Had he left L.A. because of her or in spite of her?

". . . Mrs. Stuart?"

The mention of her name snapped her back to the matter at hand. She looked around sharply, like a student in class who had been called on while daydreaming. It seemed as if every eye in the place were trained on her, waiting, watching, homing in with sharp scrutiny. She shifted in her chair, turning to the man next to her.

"I'm sorry," she murmured. "Did someone say my name?"

The silence broke abruptly as another voice shouted out a question. "Is it true, Mrs. Stuart, that you not only found the body, but were personally involved with the deceased?"

Elizabeth swung around in confusion, looking to confront the face behind the voice. A burly, bearded man rose from his chair down the row and thrust a tape recorder at her, repeating the question, his voice booming to be heard above the sudden rise of sound. Then another man rose and a flash went off in her face. She shrank back from it, reaching back with a hand to find some support, only to have fingers close on her elbow. She swung around again and more faces loomed in on her, all of them looking wild, mouths moving, voices pouring out in a stream of babble.

Instantly she was back in Atlanta, in the Fulton County courthouse, reporters pressing in on her, shouting at her.

"*Is it true you were sleeping with your son's best friend?*"

"*Is it true you seduced Mr. Stuart's business associates?*"

"*Can you produce any evidence to substantiate your claims of conspiracy?*"

"*What about the photographs?*"

"*What about the videotapes?*"

"*Mrs. Stuart—!*"

"*Mrs. Stuart—!*"

The sound pounded on her ears as the crowd began to close around her. Elizabeth felt panic rise in her throat, and she jumped to her feet. She desperately needed to escape—anywhere, any way. She dropped her notebook and dove ahead, trying to cut a path between two photographers, shoving them in opposite directions, slapping at their cameras with her hands.

Then her eyes focused on one face in the blur—Dane's. His expression was furious as he shouted at the people around her. Elizabeth didn't hear a word he said. She grabbed the hand he held out to her and let him pull her away from the melee. She stumbled up the steps past the witness stand and into the judge's chambers. The door slammed behind her and she wheeled around, eyes wide, mouth tearing open as she tried to suck in a startled breath.

"Stay here," he commanded. "I'll be right back."

He went out into the courtroom before the look of

terror on her face could persuade him otherwise. Anger burned through him as he scanned the crowd. The deputies had restored a certain amount of order, herding people back to their seats, but excitement still charged the air. The scent of the kill, he thought bitterly. Fucking reporters. Goddamn fucking reporters.

The noise level died abruptly as he grabbed the podium with both hands and roared a command for quiet into the microphones, his volume setting off a series of feedback shrieks in the amplifiers. One intrepid fool raised a hand to ask a question, but the arm fell like a wilting weed as Dane turned his full attention on the man.

"Miss Stuart has no statement for the media," he said softly, his voice barely a whisper rasping out of the speakers. Still, it reached every corner of the room, fell on every ear, lifted every neck hair. "Is that understood, ladies and gentlemen of the *esteemed* press?"

Several seconds of silence passed before a reporter from the *Tribune* spoke up. "What about freedom of the press, Sheriff?"

Dane met the man's gaze evenly. "The first amendment doesn't give you the right to harass or coerce statements out of witnesses. If Miss Stuart has anything to say, she'll say it to me and no one else. She is a part of an ongoing murder investigation. Anyone bothering her will have to answer to me. Have I made myself perfectly clear?"

He glanced around the room to find most eyes on their steno pads or electronic equipment. At the table beside him, Kaufman was cracking his knuckles and sweating like a horse. Yeager slumped back in his chair, dark eyes glowing, rubbing a hand across his mouth to hide a grin of unabashed delight.

"This press conference is over," Dane murmured.

Silence followed him into the judge's chambers. Elizabeth had retreated to a corner near a floor-to-ceiling bookcase that was crammed with dusty leather-bound tomes on jurisprudence. She stood with her back to the wall, one arm banded across her middle, the other fist pressed to her lips.

Dane crossed the shadowed room, head down, eyes on the woman before him. She was nothing but a bundle of trouble, but at the moment he couldn't direct any of his anger at her.

"I—I know you don't like me," she stammered. "But I'll give you a dollar to forget about that for a minute and put your arms around me."

He bit back a groan as compassion eclipsed his need to keep his distance from her. No matter what she'd done or who she'd done it with, he couldn't take the thought of her being emotionally hacked to pieces by media mongrels. He put his arms around her gingerly and patted her back, and blatantly ignored the warmth rising in him. Proximity, that's all it was. Proximity and basic human kindness.

"It's nothing personal," Elizabeth assured him as his clean male scent filled her head. He was so strong and solid. She thought about doubling her offer, to buy a little more time, but squashed the idea. She couldn't let herself weaken, couldn't rely on anyone to hold her up, especially Dane Jantzen, lone-wolf misogynist Jantzen with his ornery moods and his grudge against divorcees.

"I'm sorry I caused such a commotion," she said, her voice hoarse with suppressed emotion as she pushed herself away from him.

Dane sat down on the corner of Judge Clauson's massive walnut desk and gave her a wry smile, shaking his head in wonder. "Lady, I sincerely doubt you could walk into a roomful of blind monks without causing a commotion."

A chuckle managed to find its way past the knot in Elizabeth's chest. She sniffed hard and wiped the tears from her cheeks with the back of her hand, glad she hadn't gotten time to put that mascara on after all. She would have looked like Rocky Raccoon by now.

"I'm gonna take that as a compliment," she said. "Whether you meant for it or not." He didn't say, but he didn't take it back either, which was better than nothing, she supposed. Feeling calmer now, she sniffed again and offered an apologetic little smile. "I'm sorry I overreacted out there. It's just that all those voices and cameras and . . . It brought back . . ."

She pulled in a deep breath and shook off the rest of what she had been about to say. She didn't have the energy for it, and she doubted Dane wanted to hear it anyway. "I just can't get attacked but once a day or I get skittish. Thanks for saving me—again."

Dane shrugged lazily. "We protect and serve. Are you okay now?"

"Oh, sure." She grinned, tossing her hair back over her shoulder. "I'm right as rain. I should be more used to that kind of thing by now, I suppose."

"No one should have to get used to it. I never got used to it," he admitted candidly, a wry smile flipping up one corner of his mouth as he recalled his own brushes with the press.

"I saw that look once," Elizabeth said, sliding into the high-back leather swivel chair behind the desk. She crossed her legs and moved the chair side to side, pushing off with the toe of her sneaker. "It was on the face of a cat sitting next to an empty goldfish bowl. What'd you do? Cut up some poor shrimp from the *L.A. Times* and feed him to your pet tiger?"

"Not quite. I cultivated a reputation for having a short and violent temper. Not many people were willing to call me on it at the time."

Or now, Elizabeth was willing to bet. He was a man who seemed to keep his control on a tight leash, yet an undercurrent of something wild and dangerous ran just beneath the surface. Something dangerous and exciting.

Dangerous thinking, Elizabeth.

"Well," she said, springing up out of the chair to pace along the bookshelves. "I don't think anyone is liable to buy that routine from me unless I start waving a gun around or something. I think I'll just rely on the kindness of my local sheriff's department."

"It's what you pay your taxes for." He went to a door opposite the one they had come in through and held it open. "Come along, Miss Stuart. Agent Yeager has a few more questions for you."

Elizabeth nibbled her bottom lip as she hitched her purse strap up on her shoulder. For a second there she had almost thought they were going to be friends. A dozen questions had sprung to mind. She had wanted to ask him about being an athlete in the spotlight and about his own divorce, wondering if a football star splitting with his wife engendered the kind of hoopla a media mogul did. But in the blink of an eye he was back to business and she was back to being a witness. As she passed him in the doorway and headed down a flight of service stairs, she couldn't quite decide if that made her happy or sad.

"THAT WENT WELL ENOUGH—EXCEPT FOR THAT LIT-tle rhubarb at the end." Bret Yeager sprawled in the visitor's chair with his Top-Siders propped on Dane's desk. "You just jumped right in there with both feet, didn't you?"

Amusement was in his voice, and Dane shot him a look intended to back him off. It had no effect. Yeager just grinned at him. He was the picture of rumpled relaxation, his tan chinos creased from too many wearings without washings in between, his plaid sport shirt looking as though it had been snatched out of the laundry basket without benefit of seeing an iron. His sun-streaked brown hair hadn't known a comb anytime recently.

"I told you, son," he drawled with no thought to the fact that Dane was three years past his own thirty-six. "Throw 'em a bone. Give 'em a suspect. They'll gnaw on that for all it's worth and leave you alone for a while."

Oklahoma twanged in his speech, though he hadn't lived there in years. Bret considered himself a vagabond of sorts, drifting across America in pursuit of justice. Sort of like Paladin or that Kung Fu character. Taking into account his penchant for philosophizing and his general dislike of violence, he thought the latter might be a more accurate comparison.

His career had taken him from Oklahoma City to St. Louis and up the Mississippi to Minneapolis, with a blessedly brief stopover in the hell that was the south side of Chicago. He had lost his taste for violent crime around the time he'd lost count of the bodies he'd seen and the bereaved he'd had to speak those awful words to—*We regret to inform you* . . . The position of BCA agent to this pretty little corner of the world had seemed just the thing to him. Tyler County was a sportsman's paradise with trout streams crisscrossing acres of woods and farmland that abounded with deer and game birds. The people were honest and hardworking. The pace was slow. There hadn't been a murder in Tyler County in thirty-three years. Until now.

On that grim reminder, he dragged his feet off the desk. He sat up and rubbed a hand back through his hair, watching as Dane paced the room like a caged tiger. "Relax a little, will you? I'm getting worn out watching you."

The big yellow dog sprawled in a boneless heap beneath his chair lifted its head and whined in agreement.

"Hear that? You're wearing out my dog too."

Dane glanced at the dog as the big Labrador groaned and dropped his head to his paws, falling into an instant sleep. "That wouldn't take much from what I've seen. Is he good for anything besides peeing on tires?"

"Ol' Boozer?" Yeager straightened in his chair, ready to defend his longtime companion. "Why, he's just a dynamo when duck season rolls around. You ought to see him. He'll swim a mile and he's got a mouth soft as butter. He's just saving his energy now, is all."

Dane arched a brow as the dog rolled onto his side and belched.

"I don't think anybody is going to be satisfied for long with a suspect at large," he said, turning his attention back to the matter at hand. "I know I'll be a lot happier once we've brought Carney Fox in and closed the case."

"Yeah, you and the press too. You just wait. They'll be there shooting rolls of film like a pack of tourists at Disneyland when we haul Carney's sorry butt in, then they'll trot on home and we'll never see them again."

"Fine by me," Dane said. "The less I see of reporters, the better."

He ignored the image of Elizabeth that quickly flashed through his mind and planted himself in front of the time line taped to his wall. He had made LeRoy Johnson open up the Piggly Wiggly at two in the morning so he could commandeer a roll of butcher paper for the purpose. A strip of the waxy white paper now stretched the length of the wall, notes made in his own neat hand chronicling everything that had happened the night before, as well as statements that had been made about the time leading up to Jarrold Jarvis's death. He homed in on his favorite tidbit, given by Eugene Harrison, who had been sitting in the Red Rooster spending his unemployment check on Old Milwaukee. *4:20—Carney Fox pays for a pack of cigarettes. Talks about going to Still Waters "on business."*

That all but put Fox at the scene of the crime. All they needed was a fingerprint, a strand of hair, a knife with his name on it, and they would have a closed case. Fox was a troublemaker. Had been since the day he'd rolled into town in his '81 Chevy with his hair greased back and a cocky sneer curling the corners of his lips. Dane couldn't say he'd be sad to put Fox behind bars for good. Then Still Creek could get back to business as usual and the Miss Horse and Buggy Days pageant could go on without fear of being disrupted by something as unpleasant as a capital crime.

A sharp rap sounded on the door, then Lorraine poked her head into the office. She gave Yeager a scathing once-over, ironing his clothes with her gaze. He smiled lazily, rubbed a hand over his rumpled shirt, and scratched his belly.

"That Stuart woman is wondering if you're ready for her."

Dane let out a long, controlled breath. He had needed a moment's respite after their little heart-to-heart in chambers and had left Elizabeth cooling her heels at Lorraine's desk. It seemed his moment was over.

"Send her in, Lorraine."

Lorraine hesitated, pressing her thin lips into a line as she contemplated speaking her mind. Her eyes narrowed behind the lenses of her cat-eye glasses.

"Yes, Lorraine?" Dane prodded.

"It's not my place to criticize, but that woman is as brazen as they come," she said, her cheeks coloring. "Calling the deputies 'honey' and 'sugar.' It's disgraceful."

Yeager grinned up at her. "She's from down south. It's just her way, darlin'," he said in an exaggerated drawl. He winked at Dane as Lorraine lifted her bouffant to its full impressive height and gave an imperious sniff.

"I think she's sweet on me," he said with a chuckle as the door thumped shut.

Dane laughed. "Not."

"It's nice to see you boys are having such a good time while some of us are wasting the day away waiting on you." Elizabeth slipped into the office and stood with her arms crossed and her back up against the wall.

Yeager straightened up out of his chair, the grin dropping off his face as he cleared his throat. "Agent Bret Yeager, ma'am," he said politely, offering his hand. "I'm awful sorry we kept you waiting. Hope it didn't trouble you none."

Elizabeth shook his hand, responding automatically to Yeager's down-home charm. She shot Dane a sideways look. "Well, it's nice to see *some* people have more manners than God gave a goat. It's a pleasure to meet you, Agent Yeager."

"Pleasure's all mine, ma'am."

Dane rolled his eyes. "Before you start telling her

she's pretty as a bald-faced heifer, can we get down to business?"

Yeager grinned. "Would you care to sit, Ms. Stuart?"

Elizabeth glanced at the chair the agent motioned to and the huge yellow dog that lay beneath it, and shook her head. "No, thanks. I just want to get going. We're putting together a special edition of the paper."

"I'll be brief, then." Yeager leaned over the desk, frowning as his eyes scanned a freshly typed document. "You state here that it was approximately seven-thirty when you left your office and headed out of town. You're sure you didn't see anyone around? Not necessarily at Still Waters, but maybe going by on the road or maybe a cloud of dust in the distance—a car going the other way?"

Elizabeth tipped her head. "Sorry. Whoever did it either left before I got there or after I'd gone for help. The only car I saw was the Lincoln."

"In the past—before the murder—did you ever happen to hear Mr. Jarvis say anything about being on the outs with someone? Someone who worked for him, someone he might have fired or turned down for a job?"

"I didn't know Mr. Jarvis," Elizabeth said coolly, her back straightening against the wall. "He grabbed my ass once in the paper office and I belted him for it. I don't know how y'all get on in Minnesota, but where I come from, that kind of thing doesn't exactly constitute friendship."

"I didn't mean anything by it, ma'am," Yeager assured her, lifting a hand to stem the defensive stream. "I didn't mean a thing. It's just that this is a small town. People overhear conversations, pick up a little gossip here and there. I thought maybe with you being a reporter and all . . ."

"No," she whispered, her gaze falling once again on the sleeping dog. Had to be Yeager's, she thought absently. Jantzen wouldn't have a dog like that, a fat old friendly sleepy dog. He'd have something big and mean—a German shepherd, a wolf. A wolf with blue eyes, and they'd communicate telepathically.

"No, I didn't overhear anything," she said softly. She lifted her head and met Yeager's curious gaze, not even trying to hide the weariness she was sure was showing through. "And I wish to God I hadn't seen anything. Now, if you don't have any more questions, I've got a job to do."

He scribbled something on her statement with a ballpoint pen and nodded. "You're free to go, ma'am."

"Am I free to ask some questions of my own?"

"Sure."

She turned toward Dane. She didn't know cop protocol. The BCA man might have seniority on the case, but it was Jantzen she wanted the answers from. This was his town, his county. He was the man in charge, protocol or no. "You're sold on this transient theory. Is this drifter your only suspect?"

One corner of his mouth tugged upward sardonically, "Aside from you? Yes."

"Why is that?" she asked, ignoring the jibe. "From all I've been told, Jarvis wasn't a popular man. There must be someone else who might have wanted him dead."

"You're not too popular yourself," Dane countered. "But Helen Jarvis and her Jell-O fish notwithstanding, I don't think anybody in Still Creek is going to kill you."

The wild look in the Widow Jarvis's eyes flashed in Elizabeth's mind, and she shuddered inwardly. That platter might have been a knife. She had no doubt Helen Jarvis would have hurled it with just as much zeal.

"You think you know them all that well?" she asked.

"I've lived here almost all my life," Dane said. "The only people in Still Creek I can't vouch for are strangers."

Elizabeth met the challenge in his gaze evenly. "Sometimes the people we think we know best are strangers inside."

"A dramatic line," he commented mildly. "Maybe you should be writing fiction."

He straightened away from the desk and stretched, dismissing her, dismissing her line of questioning. He stepped past her without a word of apology and pulled the door open.

"Now, if you'll excuse us, Miss Stuart, we've got a suspect to catch."

TEN

THEY WERE DOING A BOOMING BUSINESS AT
Elaine's Coffee Cup. Though she hated to think of someone getting murdered—even Jarrold Jarvis—Phyllis Jaffrey had to admit it was good for business. The place had
been full all day. Reporters running in and out, drinking
coffee by the gallon and eating everything in sight.
Townsfolk congregating for support and speculation
over strawberry pie. She'd had to ask two tables of regu-
lars to get up and leave so she could seat the tour group
of elderly matrons from Edina for lunch. Between tourism and murder she was making enough money to contemplate a winter vacation to Phoenix to visit her
predecessor, Elaine.

Elaine had taken her lumbago and her brace of poo-
dles and flown south the day after her retirement party
back in '72. She had left the restaurant business behind,
but the restaurant itself still bore her name and probably
always would. People in small towns didn't like
change—Phyllis included. She had kept the same old
booths, reupholstering them in the same serviceable
brown vinyl when the need arose. The counter was the
same one that had been installed in the late 1800s when
the Coffee Cup had been the first ice cream parlor south
of Rochester.

When the linoleum had finally given out in '83 Phyllis
had intended to replace it with something as close to the

same as possible, but, having a shrewd head for business and seeing that tourism was going to be the next big thing in these parts, she had told Bob Griege to tear up the old stuff and restore the original narrow-board oak floor beneath. No one had objected. If things had to change in Still Creek, folks generally preferred to go backward instead of forward.

She listened to the music of the cash register ringing up another few dollars and sighed a sigh of supreme contentment. There was turmoil in the air along with the scent of French fries and coffee. Invigorating stuff. She didn't even mind that her feet felt like two big throbbing snowshoes or that she'd missed her soaps. There was enough going on around her to make *All My Children* seem dull by comparison.

The reporters had run off after the press conference to write up their articles, but the booths and tables were still mostly filled. The clatter of silverware and china accented the steady undercurrent of murmured gossip. Then the front door swung open and for one long, taut second all sound ceased, as if the whole place had taken in a big gulp of air and held it.

Elizabeth Stuart stepped inside, and the tension level rose like the mercury in a thermometer plunged into boiling water. Every eye in the place swung her way. The men would have looked anyway, Phyllis thought. Men *always* turned to look at Elizabeth, no matter how old or how married they were. It was some kind of primal instinct. But the women looked too. The lead player of their conversations had just had the gall to show her face in the most public place in town.

Resentment had run hard against Elizabeth from her first day in Still Creek. News that a divorced woman had bought the *Clarion* had swept through the town like fire. That she was beautiful, wore tight jeans, and drove a cherry-red drop-top Cadillac added fuel to that fire. That she had a notorious past *and* an accent sent the fire raging out of control.

Being contrary, Phyllis had been determined to like

Elizabeth. To her relief, she had discovered there was a lot to like. She watched now as her young friend stood in the doorway, absorbing the waves of hostility, and Phyllis's heart went out to her. She bustled out from her post at the kitchen door and wound her way through the maze of tables with the grace of a lifetime waitress, crepe-soled shoes swooshing silently across the polished floor, the ties of her ruffled muslin apron fluttering behind her.

Elizabeth caught sight of Phyllis bearing down on her, her mouth puckered into a plum-colored knot, determination blazing in her eyes, hair standing out like an abused Brillo pad around her head. Phyllis wasn't more than five feet, even in her thick-soled waitress shoes, but she projected the aura of a much larger person. She had to be sixty if she was a day, but age, while it had boiled her body down to sinew and gristle, had done nothing to diminish the power of her personality. She was ornery and outspoken and had a face like a Pekingese—round and flat with a tiny nose and big watery brown eyes. Elizabeth had never been so glad to see anyone in her life.

"Jolynn has a booth at the back," Phyllis said in a voice as rough as gravel. Grabbing Elizabeth's arm, she propelled her toward the rear of the restaurant.

Chin up, Elizabeth walked past the tables of townsfolk, pretending to ignore their hostile stares. Regardless of what they thought, she hadn't done anything wrong. She wouldn't pretend she had. Conversations resumed in her wake like the Red Sea closing up behind Moses and the Israelites.

"Guess I'm the talk of the town," she said through her teeth.

Phyllis gave a growl. "Idiots. I told I don't know how many people—'If she was going to have an affair with a rich married man, don't you think she'd have picked someone better-looking than Jarrold?' "

"I don't guess they think I'm that discriminating."

"Oh, for crying in the beer," Phyllis grumbled. "They think just because Rosemary Toller Shafer had a fling with him way back before she let herself go, some other beautiful woman might too, but it's hardly the same thing, if you ask me. Rosemary did it only to spite Helen and Garth."

Elizabeth turned and stared down at her, mouth dropping open.

Phyllis pinched Renita Henning's arm as they passed the mayor's table. The plump blond waitress nearly doused Charlie Wilder's lap with decaf as she yelped and jumped. "I'm taking a break," Phyllis barked. "Go get Christine out of the storeroom and tell her to stop whining about her corns. *I've* got corns so big you could feed a dairy herd with them. I don't want to hear any more about her puny corns."

"You pinched me!" the girl whined, rubbing her arm.

Phyllis gave her the evil eye. "Oh, for the love of Mike, I was just getting your attention. When I pinch you, you'll know it. Now, bring us three diet Cokes and don't be dawdling at the counter, talking to Alice Wilson about getting a home perm. Your hair is just fine the way it is." Phyllis sniffed and swung around, bumping Elizabeth back into step like a goat herding a sheep through a pen. "I don't know what's the matter with kids these days," she grumbled. "All they do is complain. Soft, that's what they are. Watch too much TV."

They slid into the back booth—Jolynn and Elizabeth on one side, Phyllis across the table from them. The booths were old-fashioned with high backs that blocked much of the view, effectively swallowing up the occupants and keeping them from sight of most everyone else in the room. A blessing, Elizabeth thought, sinking down into the squishy-soft upholstery. She'd been as much of a celebrity as she cared to be for one day.

Renita brought their Cokes in tall glasses with ice and set them on the Formica-topped table, careful not to spill a drop, then pulled a damp cloth from the pocket of her ruffled apron and wiped the table anyway, earning herself a look of approval from her boss. After she had deposited three paper-wrapped straws in a neat row, she turned and marched away down the back hall, presumably to go in search of the corn-inflicted Christine. Elizabeth watched the girl disappear, then jerked around toward Phyllis.

"Are you telling me Jarrold Jarvis *did* have an affair with someone?" she whispered, leaning across the table.

Phyllis ripped one end off her straw wrapper and blew the paper tube across the table. "*An* affair?" She gave a little snort.

"With this Rosemary person."

"Oh, that." She waved a hand as she dunked her straw into her glass and took a long pull on her Coke. "That was nearly twenty years ago. Everybody in town knows that story."

"Except me," Elizabeth said as she watched Jolynn nod sagely.

"It was back when Jarrold was still in partnership with Garth Shafer in the road-construction business," Phyllis explained. "Jarrold's wife and Garth's wife are sisters. The Toller girls. Like day and night, they always were. Helen was little miss everything in high school, but a tramp the likes of which you've never seen. She'd do anything on a dare." She waved again and sucked on her drink. "Anyway, that was a coon's age ago. Helen married Jarrold and Rosemary married Garth, and they were all just famous friends. Then Helen started flashing diamond rings around like they were hen's eggs and getting pretty high on herself because Jarrold had taken her on one of them cruises to Aruba and bought them all new living room furniture and I don't know what all. They just seemed to be rolling in dough, while Garth wouldn't let Rosemary buy so much as a decent hat for Easter. Next thing you know, it's all around that Rosemary and Jarrold are going at it in his office after hours. And it was true too. That youngest Shafer boy is the spitting image of Jarrold, poor kid."

Phyllis sat back, toeing her shoes off under the table and stretching her arches, her lined face relaxing into an expression of uncomplicated pleasure.

Elizabeth stared at her, amazed. "But that gives all kinds of people reason to kill Jarvis. Helen, Rosemary, the old business partner—"

Phyllis rolled her eyes. "It was twenty years ago. People might move that slow down south, but up here we take care of things a little quicker."

"What happened?"

"Nothing much. Jarrold bought out Garth's half of the business and got to be rich as Roosevelt. Garth started the Ford dealership. Helen and Rosemary haven't spoken to each other since."

"That's it?" Elizabeth asked in disbelief. "There wasn't a fight or threats or a divorce or anything?"

"This is Minnesota," Phyllis said. "We don't go in for big dramatic scenes. Too embarrassing. We keep our feelings to ourselves. And divorce . . ." She frowned. "Well, it's still more than a little bit of a scandal to get divorced around here. Back then it was practically unheard of."

Elizabeth sat back and took a sip of her soda. Where she came from there would have been a fistfight at the very least and gunplay wouldn't have been a big surprise. Around Bardette people said what they thought and let their tempers run close to the surface. Steam was blown off and forgotten on a regular basis. She tried to imagine what it might be like for all those people to bottle up those kinds of feelings—hate, humiliation, resentment. What might happen after twenty years of bitterness fermenting inside a person?

"Phyllis is right," Jolynn said. "That's all old news. Jarrold's done it with a zillion other women since then. Everyone knows he cheated on Helen—Helen included."

"Maybe Helen got fed up with it," Elizabeth suggested.

"And killed the fat goose that laid the golden eggs?" Jo shook her head.

"Fat geese have fat insurance policies."

"True," Jolynn conceded. "But I can't see Helen doing the deed."

"I can," Elizabeth grumbled, shivering.

Jo shook her head again. "She's too short."

"You don't have to be tall to hire yourself a killer."

"Like Carney Fox?" She sat back into the corner of the booth, crossed her arms over the front of her bowling shirt, and hummed a note of consideration as the wheels of her mind started turning. Fox's name hadn't been mentioned by anyone connected with the sheriff's department, but it hadn't taken anyone long to figure out who the "unnamed transient" being sought for questioning was. Carney Fox was the obvious choice. He had drifted into town in April and hovered on the edge of trouble ever since. His reputation, coupled with the fact that no one had seen him since Wednesday afternoon, made him the prime suspect.

"I don't see it, myself," Phyllis muttered. She sucked her Coke dry and rubbed the wet ring the glass had left on the table. "Helen got too much mileage out of being Jarrold's wife. She's always had to be the center of attention, no matter if what's going on around her is good or bad. If you ask me, Carney Fox did it on his own just out of meanness." She leaned across the table, her head tilted to an angle of conspiracy. "He's from the Iron Range, you know. They're peculiar up there."

Elizabeth lifted a brow. "What's the Iron Range?"

"Up north," Jolynn explained. "Northern Minnesota, where they used to do big business mining taconite— low-grade iron ore."

"Hardly anything up there but wolves and Indians," Phyllis said. "And people living on the dole."

"Major unemployment problems," Jo interjected. "Taconite isn't worth much anymore with the U.S. steel business being what it is."

"Jantzen told me this guy came down here looking for work." Elizabeth took another absent sip of her drink, tracing a fingertip up and down the side of the sweating glass.

"I guess he found it," Jolynn said. "If you call slitting

people's throats and stealing their pocket money a profession."

"I just think it's awful easy to blame the stranger in town," Elizabeth said. "There had to be other people who hated Jarvis."

"Oh, you bet." Phyllis chuckled. "Everyone with their name in that little black book of his. But I can't see anyone going to the trouble of killing him. Not anyone from Still Creek. That's just not our way. Get mad and don't say anything. That's how—"

Jo and Elizabeth leaned forward simultaneously, like a pair of bird dogs spotting a quail, eyes bright. "Black book?"

Phyllis smiled a cat-in-the-cream smile, the fine lines of her face creasing deeper. People didn't always realize it, but she was in a position to know most everything about most everybody in town, since the Coffee Cup was the place to talk things over and Phyllis had no moral compunction about eavesdropping.

"Jarrold loaned people money—people the bank wouldn't trust or people who didn't trust the bank, people needing money for things they didn't want anyone to know about. And he kept their names in a little black book." She nodded toward the booth across the way, the only booth in the place that was empty now. "Jarrold did most of his business right there," she said proudly.

Elizabeth turned toward Jolynn. "Jantzen said the glove compartment of Jarvis's Lincoln had been gone through. They figured the killer was looking for cash."

"What if he wasn't?" Jo murmured.

For a long moment they sat looking at each other, excitement crackling in the air between them as possibilities and motives tumbled through their heads.

Jolynn glanced at her watch. "Shit, we don't have time to work on this. If we're going to get the mockup of the special edition done and over to Grafton, we've got to haul ass, boss."

The days of local newspapers printing their own editions off a Linotype machine had come and gone. It was the age of the personal computer—even in remote burgs like Still Creek. Part of Elizabeth's initial investment in the *Clarion* had been two new IBM personal systems for herself and Jolynn. They did their own typesetting, but the actual printing of the paper was done at a large central press in Grafton. The foreman had promised to squeeze their special edition in between the regular appointments of a half-dozen other local newspapers. Time on the presses was carefully doled out. Elizabeth had had to beg and cajole to get them worked in.

Jolynn was right, they would have to put the juicy information Phyllis had given them on the shelf for later consideration, but consider it she would. Maybe Dane Jantzen was going to be happy pinning this murder on a drifter and closing the case, but she wanted the truth. The *Clarion* might not reach millions or pack the political wallop Brock Stuart's newspapers did, but, by God, it would print the truth—not what was easiest or least offensive or most sensational or the word according to Brock. The truth. And if she had to stir the mud beneath the surface of Still Creek to get at it, then that was what she would do.

Dog-tired and bone-weary, dane slumped down into his chair. He couldn't remember feeling this exhausted since his last training camp with the Raiders, when age and injury had made death seem preferable. His eyelids fell like blackout curtains and he dropped his head back and groaned. He'd spent the worst part of the afternoon tramping up and down the steep hills of Hudson Woods, literally beating the bushes for any sign of Carney Fox. It was now 6:45 and he had nothing to show for his efforts but a tear in the leg of his jeans, a piercing pain in his knee, and a mood that was blacker than pitch.

They'd been over nearly every square inch of Tyler County since the murder and found not hide nor hair of their quarry. Weasly little shit. He was probably halfway to Canada by now, crawling his way along through drainpipes like a sewer rat. If there had been any doubt in Dane's mind that Carney had done the killing, this would have sealed the issue. A man didn't go to ground unless he had some reason to hide.

Dane was willing to bet when the fingerprint information came back from the lab in St. Paul, there would be a nice fat Carney print among the dozens of incidentals left in and on Jarvis's Lincoln. Then he'd nail Carney's bony little butt to the wall. Provided they could find him.

He rubbed his hands over his face and slicked his hair back, peeling his gritty eyes open to take in the carnage of his once-immaculate office. Foam cups were on every available surface. One had tipped over on a mountain of paperwork, dotting the top report with rippling brown coffee stains. Half-eaten sandwiches had been abandoned here and there, candy wrappers strewn through dozens of statements, cake crumbs scattered like dust over the black-and-white blow-ups of the crime scene. The scent of male sweat hung in the air, and just beneath it lay the insidious aroma of dog.

Yeager and his damn bird dog. The agent had taken the dog with them to Hudson Woods. It had gotten hair all over the backseat of the Bronco, and the only thing the worthless mutt had done was wear himself out marking trees.

"Christ, I'll be glad when this is over," Dane whispered, lifting his gaze to the ceiling.

He wanted his life back, his nice, orderly, peaceful life. But he wouldn't get it back tonight. He still had every available man out hunting for his suspect. Yeager had taken over the operation in the field for the evening. Dane was grabbing five minutes to choke down a sandwich and call Amy. Then he would be on his way to Minneapolis to witness the autopsy. The call had come down from the Hennepin County M.E.'s office midafternoon that they would be squeezing Jarvis in as after-dinner entertainment.

The only other man Dane could spare for the job was

Ellstrom, and even though the cause of death seemed more than obvious, he didn't trust Ellstrom not to screw up on some essential detail. Besides, he felt a certain obligation. This was his county. A man under his protection had been murdered. It seemed only right that he witness the proceedings in person.

He looked down at his blotter and the neatly wrapped ham salad sandwich Lorraine had left for him and grimaced.

The door swung open as he reached for the phone, and Elizabeth Stuart ambled in. She had traded Jo Neilsen's gold lamé Christmas blouse for a plain white cotton T-shirt, which she wore tucked into her jeans.

He could just make out the scalloped outline of her bra. He had been present when Kaufman had been cataloging the items of clothing she had discarded after finding the body. The lady had some kind of taste in underwear. Sensuous, sexy, expensive.

Expensive. The word cooled his ardor with a chill reminder of who Elizabeth Stuart was and what kind of woman she was—expensive, ambitious, the kind who attached herself to men who could afford to buy her imported lace panties.

"Don't they knock on doors where you come from?" he asked irritably.

Elizabeth slowly paced the length of the time line that was taped to the wall, mentally photographing details from the corner of her eye. "I didn't want to risk the return of the formidable Miz Worth to her desk. I got the feeling she doesn't much care for me."

"She's gone for the day. You're safe."

He pushed himself out of his chair and moved to block her path along the time line. Elizabeth pulled herself up just short of running into him. Foolish, she told herself. He wasn't about to give an inch. All she'd done by challenging him was put herself too blasted close.

"I thought you had a hot date with a deadline."

"We finished."

She stepped back and dropped into the visitor's chair,

frowning as he chose to sit on the edge of the desk directly in front of her rather than behind the expanse of oak. He had changed out of the dress clothes he'd worn for the press conference, trading them for a chambray work shirt, faded jeans, and battered leather work boots.

"I came by some information that might be of use to you," she said.

"What kind of information?"

"The kind that gives a whole lot of other people motive to kill Jarrold Jarvis. It seems he did a little loan-sharking on the side," she said. "Loaned people money, kept their names in a little black book."

The tension fell out of Dane's shoulders. "Oh, that." He got up and wandered away from the desk, trying to work a kink out of the shoulder he had separated twice during the '79 season.

Elizabeth stared up at him in disbelief. "What do you mean— 'Oh, that'? You knew?"

"Of course I knew, this is a small town. Jarrold was a source of money if you needed it bad enough. It's nothing."

"Nothing!" She catapulted herself up out of the chair and took a step toward him. "How can you say it's nothing? What if one of those upstanding citizens got tired of paying him back? What if old Jarrold was putting the screws to somebody who couldn't cough up the cash so they offed him?"

"*Offed him?*" Dane gave her a look. "Where do you get this stuff—television?"

"The point is, any one of those people might have killed him," she insisted.

"We *know* who killed him."

"You know who you *want* to have killed him."

Irritation pulled Dane's brows together. "What's that supposed to mean?"

"It means you'd rather pin the rap on some poor fool wandered down from the steel belt than look in your own backyard—"

"It's the *Iron Range*," he corrected her impatiently. "And I don't have to look in my own backyard."

"Afraid of what you might find?"

"No," he said, moving half a step closer to her, his hands jammed at the waist of his jeans. "I know exactly what I'll find. That's why I don't have to look there. I have a suspect who had motive and opportunity and I have no doubt he had the means too. Why should I go looking for something more? You think I don't have better things to do than sit around here dreaming up murder mysteries?"

"Even if Fox did kill him, that doesn't mean he wasn't just the hitter—"

"Fox?" Dane snapped. "Who the fuck gave you that name?"

Elizabeth rolled her eyes. "Everybody in town figured it out in about two seconds."

He rubbed a hand over his face and slicked his hair back, squeezing his eyes shut like a man in the grip of a muscle spasm. "Shit."

Elizabeth pressed on with her theory. "Someone could have paid him—"

Dane gave a bark of laughter. "Jesus, what are you—some kind of conspiracy nut? You think Lee Harvey Oswald was a fall guy? You think man walking on the moon was a hoax? You think Reagan knew about Iran-Contra?"

"Yes," Elizabeth said with a decisive nod. "I never did like that man—not even on *Death Valley Days*."

Dane rolled his eyes heavenward and ground his teeth. Lord, why did he have to be saddled with a murder and Elizabeth Stuart all at the same time? He wasn't in the mood for this, didn't have the patience for it. Reining in his temper, he drew a long, slow breath. She was only trying to help, he realized that. It wasn't entirely her fault his blood pressure was moving into the red zone.

"Most crime is simple," he said in the same tone of false equanimity he might use with an annoying two-year-old. "Most criminals are stupid. Carney Fox killed

Jarrold Jarvis for his money and for the sheer fun of it and vamoosed. End of story."

Elizabeth stared up at him, incredulous, barely controlling the urge to grab him and shake him. She felt full of the truth, brimming with motives and secrets, enthusiastic to do her part for justice, but the man in charge of justice didn't want to hear what she had to say. "You're not going to do anything with my information? You're not going to look for this book or question anybody or—"

"No."

"Unbelievable," she muttered, shaking her head as if dazed. "You don't care that one of your most prominent citizens was a loan shark—"

"He was not a loan shark—"

"You don't care that a dozen different people had reason to want him dead." He drew breath for another protest, but Elizabeth didn't wait to hear it. "You don't care about finding the truth," she said, caught between cynicism and disbelief. "All you care about is closing this up in minimum time with minimum fuss."

"I don't care about running my ass ragged over some half-baked theory."

"You want to blame some outsider and close the case. Keep your little tourist town looking squeaky-clean no matter what kind of dirt there is under the rug." She narrowed her eyes and looked at him with disgust. "You're lazy, that's what you are."

"Oh, yeah?" Dane snarled, his temper spiking upward as her accusation hit a nerve that had been rubbed raw long ago. "Well, you talk too damn much."

And they had gotten too damn close. They realized it at exactly the same second, Dane thought. She was standing no more than a hairbreadth away, her breasts rising and falling as she gulped air. A flush of color stained her cheeks and her eyes widened, the pupils dilating as she stared up at him.

He tried to tell himself to back off, but he couldn't. Wouldn't. Something more powerful than common sense pulled him toward her, heated his blood, drew his eyes to her mouth. That lush, lush mouth. That tantalizing little scar crooked at the corner of her lips. He had wanted a taste of her from the moment he'd first laid eyes on her, and now, he couldn't think of a single reason he shouldn't take that taste.

Her lips parted slightly and Dane took the action as a silent invitation, dropping his mouth to hers before she could tell him different.

Soft, sweet. All he had imagined. More than he had bargained for. A warning bell sounded somewhere in the back of his mind, but desire swept through like a flood and drowned the alarm, leaving nothing but that incredible heat in its wake. He tangled a fist in her hair and tilted her head back, giving him better access, a better angle.

Elizabeth gasped slightly at the shock of their bodies coming together, at the surprise of his lips touching hers, and he took advantage, sliding his tongue slowly into the warm, wet cavern of her mouth. He kissed her slowly, deeply, taking her, possessing her, staking a claim. He swept a hand down her back and over her buttocks, cupping her, lifting her into him.

Elizabeth trembled and groaned, barely aware that she had made the sound. She couldn't remember the last time a man had touched her like this, made her want like this. It thrilled her and frightened her and made her burn with shame.

She'd sworn off men, sworn off *this* man in particular. He was dangerous in a way that had nothing to do with the laws of man and everything to do with the laws of nature. He thought she was what Brock and the press had painted her to be—an easy lay, an expensive whore.

She uncurled the fists she had wound into his shirt and pressed her hands flat against his chest as she wrenched her mouth away from his.

"And here I thought we didn't agree on anything," Dane murmured.

A tremor of hurt shuddered through Elizabeth. At that

moment she hated him just about as much as she hated anything. Hated him for thinking what everyone thought. Hated him for making her want. Hated him for making her hate herself.

"We don't," she whispered bitterly.

He lifted a hand and gently brushed a strand of hair from the curve of her cheek. "Liar."

Slowly, seductively, he traced the tip of his thumb along her cheek to touch the corner of her mouth and the scar that hooked down from it. Desire jumped along her nerve endings. Anger flared right behind it. Gaze locked on his, she tilted her chin down and bit him.

Dane hissed a breath in through his teeth and jerked his hand back. Elizabeth started to back away from him, but his left hand still rested on the curve of her hip. His fingers tightened, holding her in place.

"Doc Truman called."

The announcement boomed loud as thunder across the office. Elizabeth bolted, swinging toward the door and the oversize figure of Deputy Ellstrom that blocked it.

Ellstrom looked from Elizabeth's guilty face to his boss. Jantzen sat back against the edge of his desk, anger and arrogance radiating from him like steam. He had his fists jammed into the pockets of his jeans, but the pose didn't do much to hide the fact that the man was hard as a pike.

That bastard gets everything, Boyd thought bitterly, his stomach churning. Power, position, women. People around town still bowed down to him because he used to be able to catch a football. Well, that wouldn't last. Boyd was a man with a plan. He'd come out on top . . . if he could just find that damned note. Nerves twisted his intestines like bony hands wringing out a dishrag.

"Deputy." Dane's gaze locked on Ellstrom. "Do you possess the motor skills and base intelligence required to raise your fist and knock on a door before you open it?"

Ellstrom chewed back a retort. It wouldn't do him any good to mouth off now. He had thought he could get some use out of the Stuart woman, having her quote him in the paper and whatnot, but it was plain what side of the bed she was playing on. Jantzen was primed and ready. In another minute he would have been getting his wick dipped, the lucky son of a bitch. "Doc Truman called," he said again.

Elizabeth strained against the urge to run away in humiliation. Ellstrom took half a step back from the doorway, making an opening that wasn't quite wide enough for her to walk through without turning sideways. She could feel his eyes on her and knew if she cared to look she would see that damned smug disdain, that knowing male contemptuousness that made her mad enough to choke. He and Jantzen would probably have a good snicker about this after she left. It wouldn't matter that they hated each other. Men unfailingly banded together when it came to sports and women.

"Excuse me, Deputy," she snarled. "Your belly's in the way."

Ellstrom grunted in affront and took another step back, his frown cutting deeper lines into his fleshy face. Elizabeth brushed past him, taking her first step through the doorway, when Jantzen's voice stopped her.

"This discussion isn't over, Miss Stuart." He spoke casually, but a thread of steel lay under the deceptive laziness of his tone. A promise. A threat.

Elizabeth shot him a malevolent look over her shoulder. "It is as far as I'm concerned. You can do something with the information I gave you or you can sit around with your thumb up your ass. I'm going looking for the truth, whether you want me to find it or not."

AARON WAS STILL AT THE HOUSE WHEN ELIZABETH FInally made it home. He looked up as she walked into the kitchen, glancing at her over the tops of his spectacles as he carefully cleaned his tools and put them away in his toolbox.

"It's past seven," she said, slinging her purse over the

back of a chair. Too tired to give a rip about decorum, she straddled the chair and sank down onto the cracked seat, dropping her chin on her hands on the chair's back. "I thought you'd be long gone by now."

Aaron picked a fleck of brown paint off the end of a screwdriver, then wiped the tool with a flannel rag he carried for the purpose, his mouth turned down in concentration. A man kept his tools as he kept his life—neat and orderly. He slid the screwdriver into its proper place in the box. "A good day's work for a day's wage," he said.

Elizabeth gave a weary hoot of laughter. "You don't belong to a union, do you?"

He didn't get the joke, but he smiled a little just the same. It seemed the thing to do. "I belong to the church, to the *Gemei*," he said, taking up a pair of pliers and beginning the process of inspecting and cleaning once more. He glanced at Elizabeth out of the corner of his eye. She looked ready to fall asleep where she sat, straddling the kitchen chair like a man, her wild black hair falling around her in decadent disarray. "You are yourself late, Elizabeth Stuart. You don't belong to no union neither, I'm guessing."

She tipped her head back and beamed a smile at him. "You know what they say, sugar. No rest for the wicked. Nobody punches a time clock on a murder investigation."

She stretched her back and sighed, slowly pushing herself up from the chair. *Wicked.* The word played through Aaron's head as his gaze caught on the sinuous movements of her body. He should have thought of her as wicked, an English *Windfliegel,* a hussy, but he didn't, not really. She seemed unconscious of the way she moved, the way her breasts shifted beneath the white undershirt, the way her hair swung around her. She wasn't trying to tempt him. The temptation was within himself.

He had been too long without a wife.

" 'Course," Elizabeth went on as she pulled a bottle of

the stolen scotch from the cupboard, "if Jantzen has his way, this'll all be wrapped up faster than you can spit and whistle."

She peered into an array of tumblers that had been left out on the counter, selected one that looked mostly clean, and poured herself a hefty dollop of the Highland's finest. The first sip went down as smooth as the liquid gold it resembled, spreading a welcome warmth through her belly and soothing the ragged edges of her nerves.

"He wants it all wrapped up with a neat little bow," she murmured, turning around to face the table once again. She leaned back against the counter and crossed her arms in front of her, cradling the whiskey glass against her chest so that the malty aroma teased her nostrils like expensive perfume. "Never mind if justice is done."

" 'Justice is mine, sayeth the Lord,' " Aaron quoted, arranging his pliers to his satisfaction.

"Is that what your people would do? Leave it up to God to punish the killer?"

" 'Stand not in judgment of your fellow man.' " He folded his flannel rag neatly and slipped it into its own compartment in the carryall, then turned to face her, sliding his long hands into the deep pockets of his trousers. He regarded her somberly, a certain sad weariness darkening his eyes. "We can't bring back the dead, no matter what. Gone to God, they are. It don't make no difference what we do."

He was thinking about his dead wife, Elizabeth supposed. The idea tugged at her heart. But this was hardly the same thing. "It makes a difference if an innocent man goes to jail," she said.

He nodded. "And so we let God decide what happens. *Es waar Gotters Wille.* God's will. God's plan," he murmured almost to himself, his vision seeming to turn inward. "God's plan."

He wrapped one hand around the smooth wooden handle of his tool carrier and turned toward the door.

"Tomorrow I will be back, Elizabeth Stuart. Plenty of work needs doing here."

"You've done a lot already," Elizabeth said. The cupboard doors had all disappeared. The faucet had stopped dripping. Someone had cleared the rubble from the table and done the dishes. She had no illusions that someone was Trace. "I feel like I should at least offer you dinner. Would you care to stay?"

Aaron cast a dubious glance at Elizabeth standing beside the stove. The two didn't look compatible to him. "*Danki,* no."

"You're a smart man, Aaron," she said with a rueful look. "I never did get the hang of cooking. I was just gonna have me some Chee-tos and a tuna sandwich. If the tuna hasn't gone bad."

"It has," he muttered, turning once again for the door.

Elizabeth followed him out, carrying her scotch against her like a toddler with a bottle of milk. "Thanks again for the work, Aaron. It's nice to have one person seem neighborly around here."

Aaron paused at the bottom of the steps and glanced up at her. One corner of his mouth twitched up as if he somehow found her words ironically humorous, but he said nothing. She watched as he walked to his buggy and stowed his box away under the seat. Within a minute the bony sorrel horse was trotting west down the road, the black buggy rattling along behind it. The sun was sliding down in the sky, bathing the rolling countryside in amber. A red-winged blackbird sitting on the telephone pole sang his song, then quiet settled in. The evening breeze brought the scent of new-mown hay from somewhere. The world seemed as still as if nothing at all had happened during the course of the day.

Aaron Hauer would go home and sleep peacefully, separate from the turmoil that had swallowed up Elizabeth's life. It was the way of the Amish—to let the world go on, to be oblivious to it. But it seemed to Elizabeth that the people of Still Creek weren't so very different. They were separatists, too, in their own way. They wanted to pin the blame on outsiders and get on with their lives as if nothing had happened.

Sinking down on the top step, she took a sip of her drink and leaned her head against the peeling green frame of the screen door. Maybe Dane was right. Maybe Carney Fox was guilty as sin. Maybe it was a stranger who had brought trouble here. But it seemed to her just as likely that someone else was behind the crime.

Preconceived ideas. That was what it all boiled down to. Dane had decided Fox was a troublemaker, that no one he knew could be a killer. He had lived here almost all his life, had developed his impressions of the towns-people from childhood on. They were friends, acquain-tances, relatives. He wouldn't be able to look at them without having his perception colored by the past.

Just the way he couldn't look at her without her al-leged past rising up to cloud the view, she thought.

Her whole body trembled at the memory of the way he'd kissed her. Her hand was shaking as she raised the glass to her lips and took another sip of scotch to wash away the flavor of him.

The truth. She had come to this town wanting nothing more than to print the truth, like the slogan of the *Clarion* said. To live without the shadow of lies shrouding her. But as she sat on her back stoop watching the day slip into night, it wasn't the truth of the crime she con-fronted. It was the truth inside herself. The truth that had blared in her ears as Dane Jantzen had held her against him, as he had wiped the Jell-O off her face that morn-ing, as he had looked into her eyes after the fiasco at the press conference and asked her if she was all right.

She wanted him.

Somehow that scared her more than the idea of look-ing for a killer.

ELEVEN

D ANE WOKE WITH A JOLT AS THE ALARM ON THE
stand beside his bed went off. He slammed his fist down
on the button, silencing the thing, then lifted his head
from his pillow and peered through the slit of one eye.
Five A.M. The red zeros glowed at him like a pair of de-
monic eyes. Three hours of sleep. Three hours of restless
sleep, haunted by erotic dreams of Elizabeth. He groaned
and slapped the clock away.

He slowly eased himself up into a sitting position. All
the old war wounds roused from slumber and grabbed
hold of him. Dane grimaced and groaned as his shoulder
throbbed and his lower back seized up where bone spurs
were digging in their rowels. The name of every defensive
back he had ever encountered scrolled across his memory
to be cursed and condemned to eternal hell.

Slowly he swung his legs over the side of the bed,
stripping away the tangled sheet, and rose, straightening
a little more with each step across the hunter-green carpet. He imagined he looked like time-lapse photographs
of the progression of man from his apelike ancestors as
he made his way toward the oak dresser across the room.
By the time he arrived he was upright, but a glance in the
mirror told him he looked less than civilized. He slicked
his hair back out of his eyes and took in the dark streaks
beneath them and the shadow of beard on his cheeks. He

looked more like a killer than the sheriff who was out to catch one.

After a quick shower and shave he pulled on a pair of jeans and a shirt and padded down the hall in his stocking feet to Amy's room. He cracked open the door and looked in, his heart jamming up against the base of his throat as he watched her sleep. In the dim light leaking through the shade her face looked soft, angelic, young. A mix of guilt and panic stirred through him. He had hardly spent an hour with her since she had arrived, and every hour that passed took them nearer to the day she would fly back to Los Angeles.

Silently, he slipped into the room he had let her decorate herself the first time she had come to stay with him. The walls were covered with violet-sprigged paper. The carpet was purple. The furnishings, curtains, bedclothes, were white and frilly, symbols of pint-sized femininity. Dane felt like a giant sliding between a curvy little white iron chair and the foot of the canopied bed.

He eased himself down on the edge of the mattress and reached out to brush a strand of long chestnut hair from his daughter's cheek. She mumbled a protest in her sleep, rubbed at her nose, and turned onto her side. The next minute, as if she sensed his presence, she opened her eyes, fluttering lashes that were long and delicately curled.

"Hey, peanut," Dane whispered, smiling softly. "I didn't mean to wake you."

Amy looked up at him, reading the lines of strain in his face even through the sleep in her eyes. "What time is it?" she asked, sitting up and slipping directly into his embrace, too sleepy to deny the childish urge.

"Early," Dane murmured, rubbing a hand over her hair just as he had done when she had been five. "I have to get to work. I just wanted to stop in and kiss you good-bye."

She made a pained face and propped herself back against a mountain of lace-trimmed pillows. "You're working too hard."

Guilt nipped him a little harder. "I'm sorry, honey. I don't have a choice."

"I know," she said, looking down as she straightened the number on her Raiders jersey. "I just wish you didn't have to."

"Me too. I wish I could just take the next three weeks off and spend the whole time with you, but I have to see to this case first."

"Is it almost over? Mrs. Cranston says you know who did it, you just haven't caught him yet."

"We'll get him. Maybe today. Then I'll come home early and we'll toss the old football around. How's that sound?" he asked, grinning at the prospect.

It was another of their traditions, one Amy had started at the tender age of six, during her tomboy phase, when she had gotten into the trophy case and snuck out his game ball from the 1980 win over the Giants that had sealed the Raiders' playoff berth. She'd taken it out in the yard to impress the neighborhood boys. A window on the garage had gotten broken and a furious Tricia sent the kids home, leaving Amy on the back step to repent the error of her ways.

Dane could still remember the look of abject misery on Amy's little face when he had come home. The football sat at her feet, scuffed and dirty. She looked up at him, her chin propped on her hands, her eyes swimming with tears. Her hair was in pigtails, crooked, with one of the ribbons missing. There was a smudge of dirt on her button nose.

She looked up at him, bottom lip quivering and said, "Daddy, I wish I was a boy so you would play with me."

They played that night until the sun went down, and Amy went to bed with that dirty old football instead of her favorite stuffed rabbit. So had begun the tradition.

Amy saw the anticipation in his face and felt terrible. Then she watched the joy wash out of his expression and felt even worse. "I'm sorry, Daddy. I can't," she said, holding up her hands, fingers spread wide to display her perfectly manicured nails. "I can't wreck my fingernails—I've got cheerleading camp as soon as I get back home. If I had to go with broken nails, I'd just die, I'd be so embarrassed. And I have a shot at being head cheerleader for the junior varsity this year. But if I don't look just right . . ."

She trailed off and dropped her hands to her lap, her heart sinking deeper and deeper as she watched her father's face. He didn't understand. She had hurt his feelings and that was the last thing she ever wanted to do. He was so sweet, but she despaired of his ever figuring out that she wouldn't be ten years old forever.

"I'm sorry, Daddy," she murmured, nipping at her lower lip.

"No, it's okay." Dane jolted out of his state of shock, embarrassed by the look of sympathy on his daughter's face. He made a face and mussed her hair to cover the awkwardness. Inside, he was reeling, stunned by how much it hurt to have that one stupid ritual taken away from him.

"Fingernails," he scoffed. He got her in a headlock with his left arm and tickled her ribs with his free hand, sending her into a fit of shrieks and giggles, while he tried to gloss over the raw feeling inside with indifference. It didn't matter. It was just a game. Hadn't he had enough football to last him?

"I knew we should have traded you in for a boy at the hospital," he said.

"Oh, yeah?" Amy bounced away from him on the bed. She got up on her knees and held a pillow in front of her like a shield. "Well, I'm a million times better than any dumb boy."

"Oh, yeah?" Dane answered, taking a little comfort. This, too, was ritual. "Says who?"

"Says my old man."

She tossed the pillow at him. Dane caught it and dropped it on the bed as he stood, sobering. He sighed and combed his hair back with his fingers. "I have to go."

Amy stood up on the bed and walked across the mattress to kiss her father's cheek. "Catch him today, Daddy. Tomorrow we can go riding."

Dane kissed her back and left the room, wondering what his constituents would think if he told them that was as strong an incentive for him as seeing justice done.

"GOOD MORNING."

Elizabeth looked up from the mountain of paperwork on her desk, surprised that anyone would be walking in at seven-thirty in the morning. She had come into the office at seven to take advantage of the quiet and work on the books while she waited for Jo to return from Grafton. Problems with the press had backed up the schedule and the special edition hadn't been run until after midnight. Jo had called to say she would be spending the night in Grafton and driving back early in the morning.

Rich Cannon stood on the other side of the wooden counter, trying to look like an aspiring politician as he waited for her. Crisp white shirt. Tie, neatly knotted— bloodred. An interesting color choice, Elizabeth thought, arching a brow. He waited expectantly, freshly groomed and clipped, mustache trimmed, phony smile firmly in place. Despite the spit and polish, Elizabeth doubted he would go very far in politics. He looked too much like what he was—an aging former high school jock trying to skate through life on laurels that had long ago dried up and blown away.

She sat still for a long moment, just looking at him across the dim, dusky expanse of the high-ceilinged old room, her expression stony, waiting for his facade to slip.

His mouth tightened a little, twitching his mustache at the corners. "Is Jolynn here?"

"No."

Slowly she rose from the ancient creaking desk chair and closed the distance between them with an insultingly laconic stride, the heels of her Italian pumps beating a slow tattoo across the battered wooden floor as her olive calf-length pleated skirt swished gracefully from side to side. Rich wasn't long on patience. She could see the muscles of his jaw clench as he waited for her, and she smiled inwardly, a nasty sort of smile.

"She's on her way back from Grafton with the special edition of the paper," she said, resting her arms on the countertop beside the flowering fuchsia plant she'd bought to brighten up the place. "In case you've been too busy looking in the mirror, trimming that crumb duster under your nose, your wife's daddy met a most abrupt end the other night."

"I'm aware of that, yes," he said sardonically.

Elizabeth batted her lashes in mock surprise. "Oh, my, I suppose that leaves you in charge of Big Daddy's affairs, doesn't it?"

"I'll be managing the construction business until we can find someone to take over," Rich said. He had practiced and polished that line for the press, wanting to sound properly grave, yet official and in control. Jarrold's death was providing him with a good opportunity to establish his public image. "It's more work than I care to take on, what with my campaign just beginning."

"Even without it, from what I hear." Elizabeth flashed him a smile that held not one ounce of amity. Rich's smile vanished altogether. She chuckled. "Aw, that's all right, sugar. The capacity to deftly avoid real work is one of the first requirements for politics. You ought to just shine like a new penny."

He drew a quick breath in a manner that suggested his shirt was a little too tight in the chest. "Will Jo be back soon?"

"Why? You fixin' to have a little morning quickie?"

His patience cracked like thin ice. Color rose into his face as he automatically glanced around to see if anyone might have stepped into the room in time to catch her words. His eyes narrowed, showing a hardness he wouldn't have wanted the general public to see. He leaned across the counter, lifting a short, thick finger in warning. "Now, look here," he growled, the practiced tone of control gone, "maybe that's the kind of thing people just blurt out in Georgia, or wherever the hell you come from—"

"No," Elizabeth snapped, batting his hand away from under her nose. Her temper rushed to the fore, ever ready to do battle for a just cause and damn the consequences. Jolynn wouldn't appreciate her interference, but then, Jolynn wasn't here to stop her.

"You look here, Richie." She leaned toward him, eyes flashing silver. "Why Jolynn hasn't clipped your wings for you, I don't know. But so help me, I'll do it for her if you come sniffing around here expecting—"

"I just wanted to talk to her," he said in exasperation, lifting both big square hands in surrender. "I don't know what she's told you about me, but—"

Elizabeth sniffed. "She didn't have to tell me nothing, hotshot. I can spot your kind a mile off."

Rich took a step back, reeling in his temper yet again, fighting to maintain a semblance of cool. He didn't like Elizabeth Stuart. She was a bitch and she had a tongue like a tungsten steel razor blade. He would have told her to fuck off if it hadn't been for the fact that she owned the only newspaper in town.

"Look," he said, congratulating himself on his grasp of diplomacy. "Jolynn and I have a little arrangement."

"I know what you and Jolynn *have.*"

"Yeah, well, it's none of your business."

Elizabeth arched a brow. "Isn't it? Seems to me that folks in these parts are just a little too tight-assed to vote for a man who's diddling his ex-wife every chance he gets."

His color deepened and his brows pulled a little lower over his eyes. "Don't threaten me," he warned. "Jolynn won't blow the whistle on me. We mean too much to each other."

A whoop of laughter burst out of Elizabeth before she could even think to contain it. Not that she would have tried. If the man thought he could slide past her with a line like that, he was an even bigger jerk than she'd pegged him for from the beginning. She laughed until her eyes teared up while Rich stood glaring at her.

"Oh, that's the worst joke I've heard in a long time, sugar," she said, her voice still hoarse with laughter. "You'd better bone up before you hit the campaign trail."

Rich choked down his temper and retreated a step toward the door. "Have her call me when she gets in."

"Shoring up your alibi for the night ol' Jarrold bought the farm?" She tapped a forefinger to her temple and nodded sagely. "Good thinking."

He went still, eyes narrowing. "Are you saying you think I'm a suspect?"

"No, but now that you mention it, you had a lot to gain. Little Susie gets herself a big chunk of the cheesecake, I imagine."

"We've got enough money."

Elizabeth laughed again, slapping a hand against the counter. "Lord have mercy! Nobody ever has enough money. Then again, maybe you just wanted the business to yourself. Or maybe Jarrold had something on you in that little black book of his."

A muscle twitched in his jaw and his color heightened another notch, making him look as though his necktie was strangling him. He held himself rigid, fists clenching at his sides until he hid them in the pockets of his charcoal slacks. "I'm running for public office, Ms. Stuart," he said tightly. "It wouldn't be very smart of me to kill the man who was backing me."

A wicked smile curled up one corner of Elizabeth's mouth. "Whoever said you were smart?"

He made a sound in his throat as he took an aggressive step forward—the leash of his restraint choking him as he strained against it. "You know, you've got a real attitude problem," he said, pulling his hand out of his pocket to point a thick, blunt-tipped finger at her again. Rage shuddered just beneath the surface of his voice. "People around here don't like strangers bulling their way in, shooting their mouths off. You aren't going to make yourself many friends."

"I wouldn't want you for a friend."

Nothing but meanness and petulance was in his eyes now, and in the set of his mouth. His gaze held hers just long enough to set off a tingle of nerves at the base of her neck. "You wouldn't want me for an enemy either," he said darkly.

The door swung open, a breath of morning air sweeping in and cutting across the hot, stagnant tension that had built up like a wall between them. Dane walked in and Elizabeth caught herself letting out a sigh of relief. Lord, as if she'd ever thought she'd be glad to see him.

"Morning, Sheriff." She flashed him a smile that was entirely too bright.

"Miss Stuart." His gaze slid from her to Cannon. Rich looked mad as a bull. His face was red and his eyes were watery. It was the same way he'd looked back in their high school basketball days when a call had gone against him—whether he'd been guilty of the foul or not. Only the cause this time wasn't a referee, it was Elizabeth. She certainly had a way with people.

"Dane." Rich tipped his chin up to a cocky angle that was more challenge than acknowledgment.

Cannon had seen him as a rival twenty years ago and had never quite been able to let go of that high school mentality. When Dane had returned home at the end of his professional football career, Rich had picked up right where they'd left off—always trying to prove something, to one-up him, to be richer, more important, more popular. Once a jerk, always a jerk.

"Rich. I need to have you stop by today for a little chat about Jarrold."

Cannon gave a snort of disbelief. "Christ, Dane, I'm not a suspect, am I?"

Dane shrugged, "It's just routine. We're charting everything he did on the day of the murder. Where he went, who he talked to. And we need fingerprints from everyone who might have been in the Lincoln recently—so we can eliminate friends and family and zero in on the killer."

"I thought everybody knew the killer was Carney Fox."

"Technicalities," Dane said, baring his teeth. One of the good things about being a cop in a small town was that everybody knew everything that was going on. It was also one of the drawbacks of being a cop in a small town.

"Yeah, sure, I'll stop in," Rich said, working up another of his cocky grins. "Just for the record, I have an alibi. I was with Jolynn." He flashed Elizabeth a hard-eyed look as he turned up the obnoxious factor of his smile a notch. "We were working on publicity ideas for my campaign."

"Right," Dane said flatly, knowing exactly what Rich had been working on. He pinched the bridge of his nose and fought off a yawn. "Catch you later, Rich."

Cannon backed out of the office, looking as smug as a kid who'd gotten out of detention by telling the principal a whopping lie.

Dane shook his head and leaned back against the counter. "I don't know who he thinks he's fooling. Everyone in town knows he's screwing Jolynn on the side."

"I suppose you think that makes him some kind of stud," Elizabeth said defensively, more than ready to go to bat for her friend again. She didn't condone the affair, but she'd be damned if she let anyone else run Jolynn down.

He tossed her a look over his shoulder. "I think it makes him a two-timing son of a bitch."

"Well," she said grudgingly, "it's nice to see you have *some* standards."

Dane ignored the barb. He turned toward her, laying both arms on the counter as his gaze drifted over her figure. She looked almost prim in her long skirt and lace-trimmed blouse, her hair caught back at the sides with a pair of tortoiseshell combs.

"Oh, I have standards, Miss Stuart. And you meet some of the more interesting ones."

She met every requirement regarding sex, and he had decided that was all right as long as he didn't think of her any other way.

"I am *so* flattered," she drawled. "But if you think flattery is going to get you anywhere, you'd better think again, cowboy. I'm not interested."

She started to draw back from the counter. She should have been able to make a clean getaway, but he caught her by the wrist before she could do more than shift her weight backward.

"You were interested last night," he murmured, stroking her where her pulse was jumping in her veins.

"I think you've got me confused with your hormones, sugar," she said, her bravado diluted by breathlessness.

He leaned a little closer, drew her a little closer to him by exerting the slightest pressure on her wrist. "If there's one thing that seldom gets confusing in this life, it's hormones," he said. "Trust me, Liz, ours are speaking the same language."

Damn him for a dog, but he was right. She cursed her body for having no shame, no pride, no intelligence when it came to picking men. But she had no intention of giving in, not with a man who thought so little of her as this one.

"Well, how about the rest of you?" she asked. "Do your ears understand a plain old American no, or do I need to send for an interpreter? I'm not interested."

He released her and gave her an inch of breathing room, straightening his shoulders. "We'll see," he murmured, watching her, the gleam in his eye turning speculative.

"We'll see donkeys fly," Elizabeth snapped, sassier now that he wasn't touching her.

Dane laughed, genuine humor easing the lines of stress from his face. "Christ, you're something else. Do they raise all the women in Texas like you—bodies built for sin and mouths that shoot like six-guns?"

Elizabeth couldn't help but smile. The threat of intimacy was gone, replaced by the threat of liking him. He had a certain charm about him when he wasn't being a jackass.

"Naw," she drawled. " 'Course, all good Texas girls are bred to be beauty queens. My luck, I got my daddy's gift of gab. Made me a washout for pageants."

"I'll bet." He chuckled a little over the idea of Elizabeth smarting off to some old judge who liked her a little too well in her bathing suit. As much as she had irritated him with her brash talk, he had to admit it was refreshing. The lady spoke her mind, which seemed infinitely preferable to coy game-playing as far as Dane was concerned. There was plenty about her he was determined not to like, but her impertinence wasn't on the list.

"Me, now, I was cut out to be a rodeo queen," she said.

"Is that a fact?"

"It is. I was Miss Bardette Barrel Racing two years running, which is tougher than any old beauty pageant because a girl has to look good, ride hard, and dance the Cotton-eyed Joe—all the while fending off cowboys left and right. I'd like to see Miss Prissy America manage that."

"I can't imagine you doing that," Dane said, straight-faced.

"What? Riding barrel horses?"

"Fending off cowboys."

Elizabeth scowled at him, not about to admit that she hadn't fended off Bobby Lee Breland and that she had a son to prove it. "Did you come in here for a reason, Sheriff Jantzen? Other than to insult me and ogle my cleavage?"

He had walked in because he'd glanced in the window and seen fire in her eyes as she snapped at Rich Cannon, but Dane didn't see any reason to tell her that. He had reacted instantly, instinctively, to the idea of Cannon sniffing around her, but he didn't care to examine that motive too closely, and he didn't care to have Elizabeth

examine it at all. He wanted to keep things simple between them—chemistry and sex.

"I was wondering if everything went all right last
night," he said smoothly. He lifted a round glass paperweight from the counter and rolled it idly from hand to
hand, setting off a blizzard of imitation snow inside the
decorative ball.

"Like what?" Elizabeth asked suspiciously.

"No odd phone calls? No late-night visitors?"

Uneasiness rippled down her spine, and she sobered.
"You think the killer might be watching me?"

"It's common knowledge you were the first person on
the scene, and we haven't exactly made it clear whether
you saw anything incriminating or not."

"You're telling me I'm a sitting duck?" she said, anger
creeping up the back of her throat to mingle bitterly with
the taste of fear.

"No. I'm telling you to be careful," Dane said. "I'm
telling you not to go off half cocked, 'investigating' on
your own." He set down the paperweight, letting the
miniature snowstorm subside, and reached across the
counter to flick a forefinger down the slope of her nose.
"Stick that pretty nose of yours in the wrong foxhole and
it could get bitten off. While you're stumbling around
trying to root out conspiracies, the real killer's loose out
there."

"Somebody around here has to investigate," Elizabeth
said irritably. "I don't see you doing it."

"You're not supposed to see me, sweetheart."

"Oh, don't try to make me think you're actually doing
your job," she challenged him, crossing her arms. "We
both know how dedicated you are to digging up dirt in
this town. Loansharking by a prominent businessman.
Half the male population running around with their
pants down around their knees, bopping every female in
sight. You just turn a blind eye and let it slide on past,
Mr. Bigshot Hometown Hero."

"Don't try to tell me I'm *not* doing my job," Dane
said tightly. His temper snapped at its leash, his tolerance

wearing thin on three hours sleep. "I spent half the night watching a pathologist fillet Jarrold Jarvis, got home in time to kiss my daughter good-night, then spent a few hours on horseback *doing my job*."

He didn't give her the satisfaction of telling her *she* was the reason he'd been in the saddle half the night. He had taken it upon himself to keep watch over her, just in case Fox decided to pay a visit. He had saddled up his gelding and ridden across the field that separated his land from hers, parking himself just inside the woods behind her house, hidden, silent, and spent the night chiding himself for caring whether she got her throat cut or not.

"Jarvis wasn't a loan shark," he said. "And adultery isn't against the law. You, of all people, should know that." The shot hit its mark. He actually saw her flinch and told himself he was glad. All things considered, it was probably best if they stayed pissed off at each other. He tipped his head in mock deference as he pushed open the door. "Watch your back, Miss Stuart."

"'CAUSE OF DEATH: MASSIVE BLOOD LOSS. PROBABLE weapon: a thin sharp blade.' There's a surprise," Yeager drawled sarcastically.

He sat with his battered Top-Siders propped on the edge of Dane's desk, reading Dane's notes from the autopsy aloud. He wore a tie because there were interviews to be conducted and ties were de rigueur for agents, but the strip of fabric was too short and he had a feeling part of his collar was caught under it at the back of his neck. He didn't really care. He never had his back to anyone when he was conducting an interview anyway.

"There anything of interest in here, or can I save myself the trouble?" he asked, fanning through the pages on the yellow legal pad.

"Nothing you didn't see for yourself," Dane said, stepping over the prone body of Boozer the Wonder Dog. The Labrador grunted and rolled halfway onto his back, paws curled against himself.

Dane gave a little growl of disgust as he slid into his chair. He rubbed a hand across his eyes and worked his mouth against the taste of stale coffee. He'd been on the phone half the morning and had actually been looking forward to going back out on the search for Carney Fox, just to get some air. But the little scumball had finally been run to ground at a biker bar down in Loring, a trashy little burg stuck down between the hills along the Iowa border. Kaufman and Spencer were on their way in with him.

"I talked to the lab boys though," he said. "Jarvis was on warfarin. According to his doctor in Rochester, he'd been having some problems with phlebitis."

Yeager perked up, pleased to have something to play with. "Ooh, blood thinner. That could solve our problem with time of death."

Dane nodded. "Yeah, it could have been earlier, but it's hard to say. Since we can't place Fox at the scene, it doesn't matter at this point." He frowned as he stared down at Yeager's dog. "It doesn't make sense. If he was out there, say six, six-thirty, and did the deed, why the hasty retreat? Why go to the trouble of putting the body in the car and then leave it like that? I don't get it."

"You don't have to get it, son," Yeager said, grinning as he pulled his feet down and leaned forward on his chair. The end of his tie swung across a danish he'd left on a pile of statements, picking up a glob of lemon filling on the tip. He swiped it off and licked his finger clean, dark eyes dancing. "You just have to prove it beyond a reasonable doubt. Any word on trace evidence?"

"Nothing great. Your basic stuff in the car—dirt, food particles, sawdust. He had blue cotton fibers on the back of his shirt. Probably from a work shirt." Dane arched a brow. "Not too many of those at a construction site, are there? And we've got no shortage of fingerprints, clear or otherwise. Jarvis used that Lincoln as a rolling office. There were people in and out of it all day every day."

"We need to match only one set of prints," Yeager reminded him.

Dane conceded the point with a nod. They needed only Fox's prints, another piece or two of physical evidence, a little bit of luck, and they could close the books on this mess. It would be simple, neat, the way he liked things.

He ignored the accusing image of Elizabeth that came to mind and blamed the twinge of uneasiness in his stomach on too much coffee.

CARNEY FOX WAS THE PICTURE OF INSOLENT DISINTERest, ignoring the deputies that prowled the room awaiting the arrival of their boss. He sat at the long table, idly picking at a scab on his elbow. He slouched in his chair, looking as if he might slide right down out of it and onto the floor beneath the table in a boneless heap of apathy. Small and wiry, he lacked the stature to be physically imposing. Snottiness was his best alternative, and he excelled at it.

"You want to call a lawyer?"

He didn't raise his head, but lifted his gaze from his scab to the fat-ass deputy sitting across the table from him. Ellstrom. They had crossed paths once or twice since he'd hit town. Carney had little respect for lawmen in general and less for Boyd Ellstrom. He twisted his sharp-featured face into a snide look that had come naturally to him since birth and gave a hacking little bark of a laugh. "Why should I?"

Ellstrom glanced up from the yellow pad he was scribbling on and scowled. " 'Cause your dick's in a wringer, shithead."

Carney combed a hand over his greased-back dark red hair, arrogant and unconcerned, gaze still locked on Ellstrom's jowly face, dark eyes twinkling with secret amusement. "I don't think so."

Naw, the way Carney saw it, he was sitting pretty. He cackled to himself as Ellstrom tossed down his pen, heaved his bulk up out of his chair, and walked away.

"Fuck!" Carney choked and waved a hand in front of

his face. "Jesus, Ellstrom! Did something crawl up inside you and die?"

Ellstrom shot him a glare. "Shut up, asshole."

The door to the interrogation room swung open and Carney glanced up as Jantzen walked in, looking ready to kick some butt. He was the one lawman in this hick town Carney made a point to steer clear of. The BCA guy came in behind him, rumpled and bleary-eyed, his hair standing up in a rooster tail at the back of his head. Jantzen gave an order to one of the deputies who had run Carney in—Spencer—and the deputy left the room. Kaufman and Ellstrom stayed, Ellstrom standing back along the wall directly across from him, a frown cutting a deep horseshoe above his double chin, his gaze mean and dark as Carney sneered at him.

"Do you want a lawyer present?" Jantzen asked quietly, sliding into the chair at the head of the table, directly to Carney's right.

Carney shifted a little in his seat. There was something about the way Jantzen stared at a person that gave you the creeps. It wasn't that he had a lot to worry about, Carney assured himself. He figured he was holding all the cards. He sniffed and tipped his head to a cocky angle. "You charging me with something?"

Yeager smiled at him. "Naw, this is what we call a 'non-custodial' interview, Carney. Just want to ask you some questions, is all. See if you can help us out."

Ellstrom gave a derisive snort. Carney shrugged his bony shoulders, grinning back at the BCA agent, showing off an alarming array of crooked teeth. "Ask me anything you want," he said magnanimously.

"Hey, that's the spirit!" Yeager laughed.

Dane sat stone-faced. He'd be damned if he was going to play pals with this little lowlife. At twenty-two Fox had an adult record of petty offenses sprinkled with a serious charge or two that he'd never been nailed for, including assault and possession of a controlled substance with intent to distribute. God only knew what kind of juvenile record he might have amassed. The sheriff's office up in St. Louis County had no doubt been glad to see the last of him.

For a long moment Dane simply stared at him, cataloguing every aspect of him—the furtive dark eyes, the thin, bony face, the grimy brown plaid shirt with the sleeves cut off to reveal arms that were nothing but bone and knots of sinew. Carney Fox was the kind of slimy little rodent that slinked through life, always on the brink of trouble, always slipping out of the noose at the last second. The way Dane saw it, justice would be served all the way around if he was guilty. He stared at the little rat and willed him to be guilty.

"I hear you went out to Still Waters Wednesday," he said at last.

Carney jerked up his pointy chin, a truculent gleam in his eye. "Says who?"

"You left the Red Rooster at four-twenty. Said you were going to Still Waters on business."

"Did anybody see me there?" The question was a challenge. Carney folded his arms over his chest and laughed as he watched Jantzen's face darken. That answered his one big question—whether or not the Stuart woman had seen anything besides Jarvis's big dead carcass.

"Were you there?"

Carney pulled a face and shrugged.

Dane rested his hands, palms down, fingers splayed, on the tabletop. His voice softened to a deadly pitch. "Do you know anything about the Jarvis murder?"

Carney let his gaze wander across the other faces in the room—Yeager, Kaufman, Ellstrom. He let the anticipation build.

"You didn't get along with Jarvis, did you, Carney?" Yeager said.

Yeager was the only one in the room still looking cool and friendly. Kaufman was back in the corner, cracking his knuckles. Ellstrom hulked by the door, scowling, red creeping up the sides of his face as he rubbed a hand against his belly. And Jantzen sat there, still as a statue, staring at him with those spooky blue eyes like some kind of a wolf. A shiver wiggled down Carney's back. He hunched his shoulders defensively.

"He was an asshole."

"Aside from having that in common," Dane said dryly, "you didn't get along with him. He wouldn't hire you on a couple months back. You made a big scene about it." He smiled unpleasantly. "Lots of witnesses there."

"So?" Carney challenged. "So I didn't get the job. Big fuckin' deal. I got other prospects."

"Right. Like spending the rest of your worthless life rotting in prison."

Carney sniffed. "You got nothing on me, Jantzen."

Dane leaned toward his suspect, never blinking, until only a scant six inches of stale air and Carney's rancid breath separated them. "Well, I don't like you, Carney," he said silkily. "So you're off to a bad start right there."

Carney swallowed hard, his bravado a little shaky now. Damn those spooky eyes. He held still as long as he could stand it, then scraped his chair back and stood up. "Go fuck yourself, Jantzen," he sneered, digging a cigarette out of the pack of Marlboros tucked into his shirt pocket.

"Why should I when you're doing such a good job of it for me?" Dane said, rising slowly from his chair.

He took a casual step toward Fox, looking relaxed, lazy. Carney held his ground, eyes wary, like a skittish horse. Faster than the kid could blink, Dane's hand snaked out. He snatched the cigarette from Carney's lip and hurled it aside, then charged, backing Fox up so fast he stumbled and smacked the back of his head against the wall.

"I want a straight answer, you little piece of shit," Dane snarled, towering over him, looking ready to tear out his throat. "Are you listening to me, Carney? It's third down and you're so deep in your own end you're about to get the goal post up your ass. Punt, Carney. Were you out there?"

His back against the cold hard plaster wall, his courage beating a hasty retreat, Carney blurted out the tried and true line that had saved his butt more than once. "I got an alibi! I was with a friend."

Dane's eyes narrowed as anger bubbled in his gut like hot acid. An alibi. Swell. Now he would have to ferret out some other shitheel and go through this all over again. "Not that I believe you have any," he growled, "but does this friend have a name?"

"Stuart. Trace Stuart."

TWELVE

D ANE STEPPED OUT OF THE COURTHOUSE AND
squinted against the late afternoon sun. It was a beautiful
day. All things considered, he would rather have been in
his hayfield mowing alfalfa, or down at the creek dipping
a pole into the water. But neither of those things was in
the cards. As he put on a pair of mirrored sunglasses, a
trio of reporters rushed up to him, pens poised.

"Sheriff, is it true a suspect has been questioned and
released?"

"No arrests have been made," he said flatly, and continued on his way. They started to tag after him, but he
turned slowly and lifted his sunglasses. "I don't have
anything more to say," he murmured.

As Dane saw it, one of the few good things about
reporters was that they were quick studies. In the two
days since the murder they had learned very quickly
when to test him and when to back off. They backed off.

He took the path that cut catercorner across Keillor
Park, trying to work off some of his tension with long,
purposeful strides. Several members of the Lion's Club
were working on the bandshell, draping red-white-and-
blue bunting and fumbling around with sound equipment and power cords, preparing for the Miss Horse and
Buggy Days pageant.

A pair of Amish children watched from a buggy that
had been tied to the hitching post at the end of the Piggly

Wiggly parking lot, towheads poking around the side of the buggy, eyes bright with curiosity, mouths ringed with the telltale red of cherry Popsicles. They looked amazed by the preparations being made for a festival that celebrated their presence in Tyler County. A festival that would bring money to Still Creek and nothing but more hassles for the Amish.

There were members of their sect who benefitted from tourism. Those who sold handcrafted goods through the town's shops, the young carpenters who had been signed on to work on the interior of the Still Waters resort to add a touch of "authenticity," the more liberal of the group who allowed tours of their homes and farms. But for the most part the tourism they had attracted was nothing more than trouble for them.

Dane made it a policy to keep channels open between his office and the Amish community. Despite the fact that they almost never called on him, they were his responsibility as much as anyone else in Tyler County. They were also his neighbors, and several were friends. He was well aware of the problems tourism had brought them. The interruptions of their private lives by outsiders who saw them as curiosities, who photographed them and stared at them and mocked them as if they were devoid of intelligence or human feeling just because they chose a simpler life. Then there were the tensions among their ranks as young people abandoned the *Ordnung,* the old church standards, and defected from the *Unserem Weg,* the Amish way of life; lured by shiny new cars and the promise of money and leisure time.

To the Amish, Horse and Buggy Days was a bad joke, an irony. But Dane supposed it was really just a part of the system of checks and balances that kept the two cultures living in harmony. The Amish had come to Still Creek from Ohio in the mid-seventies when the price of land had been high and the price of crops low. Farmers had been going broke. Cash rich, the Amish had bought up farms left and right, prospering in their isolationism while the rural communities around them slowly died from the economic crunch of the agriculture crisis. Then men like Jarrold Jarvis and Bidy Masters had grabbed on to the idea of tourism, and the scales had balanced.

"Dane! Dane Jantzen!"

Dane turned and winced inwardly as Charlie Wilder and Bidy Masters bore down on him, scowls on their faces and newspapers in hand.

"Have you *seen* this?" Bidy demanded, shaking the paper in front of him like a rattle. "It's a disgrace! It's an outrage!"

Charlie unfolded his issue and held it up for Dane to see. The banner headline read *Local Entrepreneur Murdered: Still Waters Churning*. The news was certainly no surprise. Dane suspected it was the source that had the backs of the town council up. It was the special edition of the *Clarion*.

"It's bad enough having this all over the city papers," Bidy complained, his vulture face pulled into the lines of extreme displeasure usually associated with an acid stomach. "But do we have to put up with it in our own town?"

Dane pulled off his sunglasses and pinched the bridge of his nose. He needed this like he needed a kick in the balls. "Murder is news, Bidy. The *Clarion* is a newspaper."

"*Our* newspaper," Bidy said bitterly. "Now we've got some foreigner coming in, printing stuff like this."

Charlie gave one of his little icebreaker chuckles, but his smile was so forced it looked as if it might crack his round face. "It casts a bad light on Still Creek, Dane. The chamber of commerce mails this paper out as part of the tourism package. Thank God we read the thing before Ida Mae went ahead and sent them. Think of the effect this could have on Horse and Buggy Days! We've already been getting calls—people expressing concerns about coming down from the Cities."

"You'll have to take your complaints to the publisher, boys," Dane said on a sigh. "Freedom of the press is guaranteed by the Constitution. As long as she's printing the truth, it's out of my hands."

It might have been out of his hands, but it was on the tongues of nearly everyone in the Coffee Cup. Dane caught snatches of criticism and complaint as he strode through the diner looking for Amy. A sense of betrayal colored the comments. It was one thing for the bigger papers to report bad news, it was quite something else for their own beloved newsless little *Clarion* to splash murder and mayhem across its front page. The *Clarion* was supposed to talk about all things good and small-town—local 4-H clubs preparing for the county fair, the town council breaking ground for the new library, fire prevention week, Horse and Buggy Days.

Dane dismissed the topic from his mind as he slid into a booth across from his daughter. God knew, he had enough on his mind without worrying about the *Clarion*, and he meant to forget all of it while he snatched a few minutes for himself.

Amy gave him a smile that rivaled the sun's brilliance and a little of the weariness that was dragging him down lifted away. She had selected a booth at the back of the restaurant and sat with her back to the wall and her canvas sneakers on the seat, the latest issue of *Glamour* splayed across her knees. Her long hair was pulled over one shoulder and secured in a fashionably loose ponytail with a scrap of ecru lace that matched her cotton off-the-shoulder summer sweater. The sun had already teased out the freckles on her upturned nose, he thought, then reminded himself that she was seldom without sun, living in California.

"Hi, stranger," she said, wiggling her fingers at him. "How's it going?"

"Hi, peanut." He reached across the table and gave her hand a squeeze, frowning a little as he caught sight of the bright orange polish on her fingernails. "Things are getting pretty bad when you have to make an appointment to see your old man, huh?"

"I know you're busy," she said, sympathy plain on her face and in her voice. "It's okay."

Dane's frown darkened. "It's not okay."

He got precious little time with her as it was. She would be with him for three weeks before heading back to L.A. and Tricia and Stepdaddy. Three crummy weeks. The idea galled him. She was *his* daughter, his baby, as much a part of him as she was of Tricia, yet time for him was doled out in miserly snatches because her mother was ambitious and wanted something "better" than he could provide.

Three weeks. Hell, the way this case was going, he might not get to sleep for three weeks, let alone get to spend time with his daughter. He studied her now, as if he were trying to memorize her features, and his eyes narrowed.

"Is your hair turning red?"

Amy grinned and fluffed at it with orange-tipped fingers. "God, Dad, I thought you'd *never* notice! Mom let me get highlights for my birthday. Don't you love it?"

Dane bit down on the word no, taking a more diplomatic tack. "Aren't you a little young to be coloring your hair?"

"Daddy . . ." She slanted him that look that declared him hopelessly *un*cool. They were going to have it out about this age business before too long, but she couldn't bring herself to start the argument now. He seemed too tired and frustrated—and that stirred not only compassion in her, but caution as well. His fuse would most likely be burning short.

Phyllis Jaffrey swooped in on the booth in her soundless shoes and shoved a plate under Dane's nose.

"What's this?" he asked, eyeing the cheeseburger suspiciously.

Phyllis ignored him while she set a tall glass in front of Amy. "Here's your Coke, sweetheart," she said, a smile in her gravelly voice. She gave Amy's shoulder a squeeze with one bony little hand. "It's the real thing. You're too young and skinny to be drinking that diet stuff." She slid

Dane a wry sideways look. "It's a bacon cheeseburger with the works, Sherlock. You look like you could use a good dose of fat and cholesterol. On the house."

Dane managed a grin for the woman who had been feeding him cheeseburgers since he'd been captain of the junior varsity football team. "Officers accepting favors and gratuities is against the law, Phyllis."

Phyllis sniffed as she hugged her empty tray across her middle. "I don't do gratuities, Sheriff. I do cheeseburgers."

"Amen."

He groaned with heartfelt appreciation as he sank his teeth into the burger. It was no fast-food travesty, but a solid quarter pound of lean, home-grown beef on a bun that had been baked fresh that morning. His stomach growled impatiently for it as he chewed. Breakfast had been five cups of black coffee and half a bottle of Tylenol. He hadn't had any time—or appetite—for lunch. His little chats with Carney Fox and Trace Stuart had occupied most of the afternoon and had left him with a bad taste in his mouth.

The party line was that Carney and Trace had been together all of Wednesday evening. There were other witnesses to corroborate the story concerning the hours from nine o'clock on, but no one had seen them earlier. The Stuart kid was lying. Dane would have bet the farm on it, but he couldn't prove it and he hadn't been able to crack the boy's story.

Trace Stuart. Christ, he was up to his neck in Stuarts. He wondered if Elizabeth knew her son was hanging out with a slimeball like Carney Fox while she was stumbling over dead bodies and digging up dirt on the respectable citizens of Still Creek. The kid was headed for trouble if that was the kind of company he was going to keep. Apparently, trouble ran in the family.

The boy was sixteen. Dane couldn't quite reconcile the image he had of Elizabeth as a sexy, tempting woman with the image of a mother of a sixteen-year-old. She must have been little more than a girl when she'd had him. He started to wonder what that story was, but caught himself and broke off from that train of thought. He was spending time with his daughter now. This was a separate part of his life.

"So how did you get into town?" he asked, glancing up as Amy sneaked a French fry off his plate.

"Mrs. Cranston's guild has to clean the church for the Jarvis funeral. I bummed a ride." She nipped the last of the potato and delicately licked the salt off her fingertips.

"Good," Dane grunted. "I don't want you staying at the farm alone."

Amy rolled her eyes. "Daddy—"

"End of discussion," he declared, both his tone and his expression brooking no disobedience. "I know how grown-up you think you are. Jarrold Jarvis was grown-up too, and he's dead now."

"Do you think you're looking for a serial killer?" she asked, her voice hushed with a combination of horror and excitement. She tossed her magazine aside and swung around to face him, learning forward eagerly, eyes wide, elbows on the table.

"No, but I'm not taking any chances. You're the only daughter I have."

She gave him one of her pixie smiles. "I wouldn't have to be if you got married again."

Dane squeezed his eyes shut and groaned. When he opened them again she was still staring at him, eyes bright with expectation. He pulled a paper napkin from the dispenser and eased back against the cushion of the booth, carefully wiping a thin line of ketchup from his index finger. "That's not likely, sweetheart," he said softly.

"Well," Amy mused, propping her chin on her hand, her expression turning pensive, "it would help if you would get a girlfriend. Mrs. Cranston says you never date anyone from around here. She says rumor has it you're seeing someone in Rochester, but no one seems to think it's serious because you never bring her down here."

"Mrs. Cranston should mind her own business," Dane grumbled.

"I suppose it's just sex," she speculated in the most casual of tones. She sipped on her Coke while Dane turned puce. "That's so passé, Daddy. People need relationships, someone they can care about. I mean, I suppose sex is great, but—"

Dane held up a hand to cut her off. From the corner of his eye he could see his daughter's offhand remarks had snagged the attention of several other restaurant patrons. Ears tipped and lifted like radar dishes to catch whatever other sage wisdom Amy might have brought with her from California.

"I don't want to talk about sex," he said tightly. He didn't even want her to know what sex was.

Amy blinked at him. "Oh. Well, okay." With a shrug she moved back to the heart of the matter. Her big lake-blue eyes darkened and softened with heartfelt emotion. "I don't like to think of you all alone," she said softly. "I want you to be happy."

Dane couldn't say anything for a few moments. Just as it had the first time she had brought it up, the topic had hit him broadside, knocking him off balance. The sincerity in his daughter's statement kicked his feet out from under him altogether. As he looked at her, a knot of emotion tightened in his chest. Panic tightened it another degree. She was growing up too fast, slipping away from him, offering him comfort and concern when he still wanted to be reading her bedtime stories.

She reached across the table and brushed her fingertips over his knuckles, her pretty mouth curving into a tender smile that held too much understanding.

"I am happy," he murmured in a tone so flat he didn't even convince himself. He *was* happy, he insisted, as happy as he could reasonably expect to be. He had his life neatly arranged, just the way he wanted it—his job, the farm, recreational sex with Ann Markham, peace and quiet, no complications. Everything had been in its proper place until the Jarvis murder . . . and Elizabeth.

"You're not so old," Amy said earnestly. "You could get remarried and have a whole second family."

And go through this again? he thought. The pain of having a child taken away from him by circumstance and years? The terrible sensation of sitting across from her and not knowing quite who she was or how she had become that person, knowing the time to find out was running through his hands like sand? *Not on your life.*

Amy sat back and stretched her arms to the sides, dropping the air of gravity like a rock. She could tell by the look on her father's face, she wasn't going to get anywhere. He kept the door closed on his private life. She wanted him to be more open, to treat her more like a friend and less like a child the way her stepfather did, but she said nothing along those lines. Instead, she changed the subject with what seemed to be the capriciousness of youth. "I met someone today while I was waiting outside your office," she said, eyes twinkling. "He was *so* cute."

Dane's brows tugged together in irritation. "One of my deputies?" If he caught one of his deputies flirting with his baby girl, by God, there would be hell to pay.

"I don't think so. I didn't get his name. Anyway, it reminded me that I saw a poster for a dance that's coming up during that Amish days thing, and I thought that if I were to meet this guy again and if we hit it off, maybe I could ask him—"

"No." The word came out automatically, surprising Dane almost as much as it surprised his daughter.

Some of Amy's animation shorted out. She had kind of hoped to slide this past him on lighthearted enthusiasm, but he'd cut her off at the pass. The Argument loomed nearer. She could feel it coming, could feel the dread rise in her chest. She curled her fingers around the edge of the tabletop and braced herself. "But Daddy—"

"I said no." Dane knew he was acting completely on instinct and the fear of having his child grow up. He was probably being unreasonable and undoubtedly being unfashionable, but he didn't give a damn. He couldn't seem to control much of anything else that was going on around him these days, but he could control this. "I don't care what your mother lets you do. I think you're too young to date and you're not dating anyone while you're staying with me. Is that clear?"

She stared at him for a moment, looking crushed and angry. A sheen of tears glazed her eyes.

"Yes, that's clear, *sir,*" Amy said softly, her voice trembling with temper and hurt. From the corner of her eye she could see people staring at them, and she could have died from embarrassment. There would be no argument here, she thought bitterly. God had spoken. And she was just a little girl in pigtails who would be grounded for the rest of her life if she talked back in public.

"You know, Daddy," she said tightly as she slowly gathered her purse and fashion magazine and slid from the booth. "One of these days you're going to have to figure out that I'm not eleven and we don't live in the Stone Age."

Dane sat back, kicking himself mentally. The last thing he wanted was hard feelings between them. "Amy—"

"I have to go meet Mrs. Cranston now," she said, battling the urge to cry. Head down, book and purse clutched against her chest, she hurried out.

"Amy—" Dane twisted around in his seat and watched her walk away, his cheeseburger hardening into a rock in his stomach. All he wanted was to keep her near him, and he had just succeeded brilliantly in driving her away.

He thought of going after her but decided against it. He knew that last look she'd given him—she had inherited it from him. She was angry and she wanted to be left alone to stew and lick her wounds. Wounds he had inflicted. He picked up a limp French fry, dropped it back onto the plate, and shoved the plate away. "Shit."

•   •   •

ELIZABETH SLAMMED THE DOOR OF THE CADILLAC AND stormed out of the shed she was using for a garage. She headed for the house, the wind whirling her skirt around her legs and tossing her hair. Another storm was brewing—in the atmosphere and inside her—and it was very clear which held more fury. She hadn't been this angry since she'd caught Brock in the Jacuzzi with two of his female administrative aides. She hadn't been this scared since she couldn't remember when. Not even finding Jarrold Jarvis had frightened her as badly as this.

Aaron sat on the back steps, a newspaper in his hands, his somber gaze on her as she approached. He rose slowly as she neared and Elizabeth scrambled mentally for something civil to say. She wished he were gone. She didn't want any witness to the battle that was about to take place.

"You're looking like the wet hen that's mad, I'm thinking," he said blandly.

"*Mad* is too small a word, sugar." She pulled up at the bottom of the steps, trying to rein in her emotions to a point where she could hang on and control them and not just fly into screaming hysterics. She was shaking inside and out, and she folded her arms across her middle to try to control that too. "My son has developed a knack for raising my blood pressure that is unsurpassed. I'm afraid we're about to have us a knockdown drag-out hiss-spitting rhubarb here, Aaron. You might want to take your toolbox and skedaddle if you don't care to hear the Lord's name taken in vain."

"He's not here," Aaron said calmly.

"The Lord?"

"Your son."

"Oh, great."

Elizabeth turned around in a circle, flopping her arms at her sides in an attempt to burn off some of the agitation twisting inside her. She'd been primed and ready for a fight, building a head of steam all afternoon, rehearsing her lines on the drive home. But as much as she'd been spoiling for a confrontation, the need to just see Trace, to touch him and look at his face and hear his voice, had been equally strong. But he was gone. She tried not to let herself see the symbolism in his absence. If she got any more distraught or depressed, she was liable to throw up.

After a minute of pacing she found a spot beside the steps and leaned against the side of the house, arms crossed once again. She stared past the farmyard, not seeing the outbuildings, gray and sagging like wet cardboard, or the bright orange basketball hoop Trace had nailed to the end of the shed. She looked past all that to the thick dark woods that marked the northern edge of her property, but she didn't see the jack-in-the-pulpit that grew at the base of the nearest black walnut tree either, or the pair of squirrels that chased each other up the trunk of a silver maple. She saw only darkness, a barrier, a wilderness, and she felt those things inside her as she thought of Trace.

"What am I gonna do with that boy?" she murmured, not even aware she had spoken the words aloud.

"Children need purpose and discipline," Aaron said, thinking Trace Stuart had neither.

Elizabeth gave a harsh laugh and wiped a tear that was clinging to her lashes. "Yeah? Well, you tell me how to discipline someone who's sixteen, full of testosterone, and outweighs me by forty pounds."

He didn't have an answer for that. He couldn't tell her to go back and give birth and start all over with the boy, which was the only answer Aaron could see. The English knew nothing of raising children. Theirs grew up as wild as grass, without purpose or a sense of the order of life. Amish children were taught from the cradle to love God, to obey their parents, to take joy in work, and to guard their way of life.

"You don't get this?" Elizabeth asked, genuinely bewildered as she turned and looked up at him over the rusted stair railing. "Amish teenagers don't rebel?"

He lifted his shoulders a fraction. "*Ya*, they have their time of *rumschpringe*—running around—before they join the church. Some of the boys fancy up their buggies with mirrors and such, stay out late, sneak off to see the moving pictures in town."

Some of the boys. Not him, Elizabeth thought. He could never have been anything but devout with his long martyr's face and somber eyes. "That doesn't seem like much, compared."

Fear sprang up inside her again, spurting through what calm she had managed, like floodwater forcing itself through the weak spots in a sandbag dam. She brought a hand up to her mouth to press back the sound of despair, rubbing off the last of her lipstick. Tears filled her eyes.

"My son is hanging around with the fella they think killed Jarrold Jarvis," she admitted in a strangled voice. "Trace gave him an alibi."

Christ in a miniskirt, her life was turning into one long, living nightmare. Horrible, outrageous things were going on all around her, and she was powerless to stop them. All she seemed able to do was stand by and report it all in the paper. Now she would have to print that her son had sprung the sheriff's only suspect in the only murder in Tyler County in thirty-three years.

"They caught the man what done this terrible sin?" Aaron asked idly, easing himself back down on the top step.

"Jantzen thinks so."

"Good, then. It's all over."

Elizabeth almost laughed as she shook her head. She pulled the combs from her hair and let it tumble free around her shoulders. "Hardly," she said.

Aaron waited, expecting something more, but she let the subject drop. She climbed the stairs, looking weary as a grandmother, and sat down on the step beside him with a long, soul-deep sigh. The hem of her skirt fell to brush the tops of her feet. She looked almost modest for once, certainly more feminine than he had seen her. She sat quietly, staring toward her dilapidated outbuildings, where the wind was playing with a barn door, smacking it against the side of the building—*thwak! thump,*

thump, thump, thwak! thump, thump, thump . . .

"What'cha reading there, Aaron?" she asked at last, a lopsided smile lifting one corner of her mouth. "Not the *Clarion?*"

He flipped up the top end of the paper in his hands. *"The Budget."*

Elizabeth glanced at the first page. The masthead read: *Serving the Sugarcreek Area and Amish-Mennonite Communities Throughout the Americas. Sugarcreek, Tuscarawas County, Ohio.* There were no pictures, only columns of what looked to be newsy letters from around the country. "Got any murders in there?"

He gave her a stern look, brows drawing together above the rims of his spectacles. "No."

"What's it about?"

"The weather, the crops, who visited, who was born, who died."

Not much different from what the *Clarion* had been until she had come along, Elizabeth thought. Exactly what some people thought the *Clarion* should be still. Charlie Wilder came instantly to mind. He had stormed into the office that afternoon, wanting to know why the special edition had held nothing but news of the murder.

"There isn't a word in here about the Lady Cougar drill team preparing for their Horse and Buggy Days performance!" he huffed.

Elizabeth had been in no mood to take his petty complaints. She supposed she should have bitten her tongue for once, but the words were out before she could make any effort to stop them. "Have they killed anybody recently?"

Poor old Charlie turned red as a radish. "Of course not!"

"Well, there you go, sugar. When they kill somebody, they'll get a special edition too."

Of course, Charlie's point had been that the *Clarion* wasn't the place for bad news. Elizabeth narrowed her eyes as she looked at Aaron Hauer's Amish paper. "What's the worst news in there?"

"David Treyer's cousin down in Kalona, Iowa, bought himself a tractor."

She fell into a coughing fit, trying to contain herself. Aaron didn't seem to think the subject was amusing. The utter gravity of his expression told her tractor-buying was a serious offense as far as he was concerned, and she was determined not to offend him by laughing at the ways of his people. She had too good an idea of what it was like to be looked at with derision and ridicule.

"That's bad?" she managed to ask, wiping her eyes with one hand while she dug the other into her purse in search of a cigarette.

"Tractors are not Plain," Aaron said sternly.

She lit up and took a deep drag that should have been calming but burned her throat instead. Her gaze drifted away from the Amishman beside her to the west, where the sun was sliding down in the sky. A buggy rattled past on the road, harness jangling, wheels chattering on the gravel. From her vantage point Elizabeth could look just past it and see the framework of Still Waters in the distance. The construction site was deserted, and would be until after the funeral of its mastermind; then the building would go on, the resort would be completed—much to the benefit of Helen Jarvis and Rich and Susie Cannon.

"How about that?" Elizabeth asked quietly, motioning toward Still Waters with her cigarette as she exhaled a plume of smoke into the early evening air. "That's not liable to be plain by anyone's standards, certainly not by Amish standards. How do y'all feel about that?"

She studied his face as he looked past her. There was tension in the lines beside his eyes and the grooves that were carved into his lean cheeks on either side of his mouth like a pair of parenthesis. But he betrayed nothing with his answer.

"The English do what they will."

"I'm English and I'm not so sure I want it there," Elizabeth said candidly. "It's not like an inn or that big barn they got fixed up over in Fillmore County for a restaurant and all. This'll be bigger, louder. Tennis courts, a golf course. They're even talking about a man-made lake. Something about it doesn't seem right."

"It isn't." Aaron bit off the words. Still Waters was an intrusion, an offense. He had thought so from the first, but he sure had never expected to find an ally in this woman sitting beside him.

He looked down at her, at the honesty in her clear gray eyes, and something hit him in the chest with the same force as the old barn door banging against the side of the barn. Understanding, empathy, friendship. They were alike in some ways, he and this English woman with her accent and her strange ways that didn't fit in here. An odd thought, that one, that he would have any-thing in common with this decadent female. But the con-nection seemed real to him now, and he knew a powerful urge to reach out to her.

That need fought against everything Amish in him. To touch her would be a sin. Wanting her was just as bad. The tug-of-war inside him made him angry. There should have been no question of wanting. He should have been more steadfast to the *Ordnung,* more staunch, unswerv-ing, incorruptible.

He jerked away from her abruptly, breaking the eye contact, breaking the spell. With remarkably steady hands he folded his paper in sharp, even sections and tucked it into the toolbox at his feet.

"I have to go now."

Before Elizabeth could form any kind of comment, he was on his feet and halfway across the yard. She watched him go, a little baffled but not inclined to think on it overmuch. She had enough trouble figuring out the na-tive Minnesotans. What went on in the minds of the Amish could remain beyond her ken.

There was no time to dwell on it anyway, she thought, tamping her cigarette out on the cement step. She pushed herself to her feet and smoothed her hands down the front of her skirt as Dane Jantzen's Bronco wheeled into the yard.

He climbed down out of the truck looking fit to kill somebody, brows ominously low, eyes blazing blue fire, granite jaw set. He stalked across the yard like a gunslinger fixing to draw his Colt and drop her where she stood. Elizabeth leaned a shoulder against the screen door too tired for dramatics, and waited until he was at the bottom of the steps to say a word.

"You got a mood on, sugar?"

Dane's jaw clenched as he looked up at her. She stood there leaning against the door as casual and calm as Scarlett on the steps of Tara, as if she weren't the bane of his existence, as if her son weren't tagging after the worst piece of dirt in six counties, taking lessons in comportment and how to lie to the authorities.

"Yeah, I've got a mood on, *sugar*," he growled, climbing the steps.

She stood her ground and he pressed his luck, recklessness rising to surface above fatigue and frustration and everything else he was feeling. He moved to within an inch of her, trapping her between his body and the door, and heat flared up in the narrow space between them, adding fuel to the fire of his temper. He resented wanting her, resented that desire getting in the way of his job.

"Is your son here?" he asked.

"No," she murmured. "No, he's not."

The sass vanished before his eyes. She looked suddenly smaller, more fragile. *Fragile.* That word took precedence over the others. It reached out and struck a chord somewhere inside him, making him shift his weight back away from her, wary, not quite sure how to proceed. Dammit, he liked it so much better when she spit in his face. He could handle that Elizabeth. He could push her and spar with her and never forget to keep his distance emotionally. He wanted that tonight, wanted a fight to take his mind off Amy and the mess of things he'd made with her. But this Elizabeth was a whole different ball game, and Dane wasn't sure he knew the rules.

"I wish he were here," she said wistfully, her voice

huskier than usual. She tried for a smile, but it trembled on her lips and she turned away from him and went into the house.

Dane followed at a distance. The kitchen had been partially dismantled. Not that it seemed any more a mess than it had been before the upper cupboards had been ripped from the wall. Elizabeth moved around the rubble, oblivious to it. She dropped her purse on a piece of plywood that formed a makeshift table over a pair of sawhorses and went to the counter, where a half-dozen bottles of scotch stood nestled out of harm's way. She selected one that was about half empty and poured two fingers' worth into a glass with a picture of Speedy Gonzales on it. She didn't turn back to face him until she had swallowed half of it.

"Scotland forever," she said, raising the glass in salute. "Best malt whiskey money can buy. Distilled in the Highlands and strained through the Stuart plaid. Costs enough to raise Bonnie Prince Charlie from the dead. 'Course, in the Highland tradition, I stole it," she admitted audaciously. "Want some?"

"No."

"No drinking on duty? Too bad." She drained the glass, then stood for a long moment staring at the smiling Mexican mouse on the side, tracing a forefinger across his sombrero. "I didn't know he was running around with Carney Fox," she said at last.

"Has he been in trouble before?"

Her gaze darted to his. "Is he in trouble now?"

"He's on the ragged edge of it. I think Fox killed Jarvis. Trace says he and Carney were together, here, shooting baskets out back. I think he's lying."

Elizabeth gave a sad little laugh. "He's not very good at it, is he? Not like his daddy was. By golly, Bobby Lee could smear shit on toast, tell you it was honey, and you'd eat it and thank him after. Not Trace. He can't skip brushing his teeth without looking guilty about it." She set her glass aside and rubbed her upper arms as if she were chilled. Her expression turned from reflective to earnest. "He's not a bad kid. Really, he's not. He's just got problems."

"Such as?"

"Such as a daddy he hasn't seen since before he can remember and a stepdaddy who thought adopting him would be politically correct and good publicity, then discovered raising a boy was more trouble and mess than he wanted to bother with."

"You make it sound like you didn't have anything to do with it." The sarcasm was a defense. Dane didn't want to feel sorry for her or empathize with her as a parent. He was too fresh from his encounter with Amy, had spent too much time afterward dwelling on thoughts of Tricia. "Where were you while he was getting screwed up by the men in his life? Out on a date?"

Elizabeth flinched as if he'd reached out and cut her. "You bastard," she whispered, raw fury seeping through her like blood from the wound. It was bad enough to have him strike like that when she was ready for it. This was a sucker punch below the belt, hitting her when her guard was down, when she was letting him see something of herself. Her hands curled into fists at her sides as she moved across the room toward him. "You son of a bitch."

Dane arched a brow. "The truth hurts, Liz?"

"The truth." She sneered the word. "You wouldn't know the truth if it kicked you in the teeth. You don't know anything about me. How dare you judge me? You weren't there."

"No," he said, unmoved. "I was on the sidelines with the rest of America, getting the play-by-play on the news."

Elizabeth glared up at him. They were standing nearly toe to toe. Her body was rigid and trembling with righteous indignation. He stood there, calm as you please, looking down at her with disdain, as if he thought he was so much better than she was, chaste of mind and pure of heart.

"And you swallowed up every word of it, didn't

you?" she said, furious as she thought back on the conversation they'd had in the judge's chambers just the day before. "You went through it too—the hounding, the half truths, the outright lies. But you believed every bit of it about me, didn't you?"

He didn't say a word, but the answer was plain on his face. Elizabeth shook her head in disgust. "Hypocrite.

"Well, I don't care what you heard," she said contemptuously. "I don't care what the press said. You want the truth? Well, here it is: I never, *never* cheated on Brock Stuart. Not once. Not even when he flaunted his little girlfriends in front of me. Not even when he told me to leave. I was stupid enough to think at least one of us should live by the vows we'd taken. Stupid enough to think I'd get justice in the end, if nothing else."

She went on with her testimony even though her voice sounded ready to fail her, reedy and hoarse, catching on the emotion that clogged her throat and hardened in her chest like cement.

"I gave that man everything I had, everything I was. I gave him myself. I gave him my son. And all I ever asked for was that he love me. Do you understand me?" she asked, looking as bewildered and hurt as she had when she had first seen the truth herself. "That's the one big sin I committed. I was naïve enough to think a man like Brock Stuart could love me. But he didn't. Brock Stuart doesn't love anybody but Brock Stuart, and God save the poor fool who thinks otherwise.

"He married me because he thought it would be good for his image—the boss marries his poor but pretty underling. A Cinderella story for the press. He singled me out and swept me off my feet with a determination that seemed ruthless even then, but poor, besotted little me, I was too busy falling in love to think about it. I was too busy thinking that maybe, for once in my whole miserable life, a man might actually love me and be decent to me.

"I'm sure he thought it was pretty hilarious, that he could blind me with a little kindness and dazzle me with diamonds. I bought the whole routine, hook, line, and sinker—flying to Paris for dinner, weekends in Monte Carlo, trinkets from Cartier. Turns a girl's head, you know, especially when the best gift she ever got from a man before that was a divorce.

"Yep," she said with a bitter smile. "He had me believing in fairy tales, then he found himself a real princess and Cinderella went out on her ear. But that *wasn't* good for his image—throwing a woman and child into the streets—so he changed the story to suit him. He gave me a reputation, bought me some lovers I hadn't even had the satisfaction of meeting let alone screwing. And it was a real multimedia slam campaign, let me tell you. Surveillance photos, grainy videotapes of a woman who looked like me doing things Masters and Johnson never even dreamed of."

She paused and tried to steady herself against the onslaught of ugly memories, ugly accusations, but they pounded in on her along with the faces of Atlanta's upper crust, looking at her as if she were something they should have a servant scrape off their shoe, calling her names under their breath. *Slut. Whore. We knew she was nothing but trash. Poor Brock. Poor Brock.*

She pressed her fists against her temples and sucked in a breath around the lump in her throat. "Brock Stuart took the truth and he bent it and twisted it and handed it down to the press like Moses on the goddamn mountain," she said, glaring up at Dane. "And they kissed his ass and told him it smelled like a rose because he *owns* them. *That's* the truth, Sheriff Jantzen," she said bitterly as tears spilled down her cheeks. "Believe it or don't. I don't give a damn."

But she did. She cared what he thought and it made her so damn mad she could hardly see straight. With a tormented cry she struck out at him, her fists drumming against his chest, pounding at him. She shoved him, moving him not one inch—which only made her angrier.

"Get out!" she shouted, her eyes burning and her mouth twisting. "Damn you, just get out!"

Dane stood there open-mouthed as she turned abruptly away from him and went back to the counter, where she stood with her shoulders rigid and her head down, hands braced against the ledge. His chest hurt where she'd hit him. He deserved worse.

Christ, she was telling the truth. He'd seen it in her eyes, heard it in her voice. The sound of it hung in the still air of the shabby little kitchen.

He should have just left. He should have obeyed her order and walked out the door. The cynic in him told him that was what a smart man would do—walk away. Walk away from Elizabeth Stuart and every dangerous thing she awakened inside him. But his conscience wouldn't let him.

He crossed the room slowly, like a man going to his doom, stopping just behind her. She didn't turn to face him, didn't acknowledge his presence in any way. She just stood there, staring out the window as day softened into dusk over the rolling pastureland.

"Elizabeth." He murmured her name, realizing with some surprise that it was the first time he'd said it aloud. He had called her Miss Stuart for the most part, Liz when he was feeling especially sarcastic. Never Elizabeth, never anything so soft and feminine. It suited her. Beneath the tough-cookie act lay a tender heart, feminine hopes, delicate dreams—to be loved, to be cherished instead of used and derided.

She was right. He was a hypocrite, and for the most selfish of reasons—to protect himself. His sense of honor labeled him contemptible. He liked to think he was a better man than that, but the proof of the truth stood before him now, trembling as she tried to shoulder the burden.

"Elizabeth," he murmured again, stepping closer, catching the faintest hint of her perfume—elusive, sweet, sad. "I'm sorry."

"Oh, yeah?" she whispered derisively. "Tell someone who cares."

"I care."

She made a little sound of disbelief and reached for the scotch bottle. Dane caught her hand before she could wrap her fingers around its neck. They curled into a fist, and she tried to pull away from him, but he held fast.

Elizabeth glared at him over her shoulder. She didn't want his sympathy or his contrition. She didn't want him saying he cared. He wasn't the kind of man who gave himself to a woman in anything but the physical sense, and as much as her body might have wanted that, she didn't think her heart could stand it.

"I don't need your pity," she said, lifting her chin. "I don't want anything from you."

Christ, she was beautiful. Dane had never denied that, but it had never taken hold of him in quite the same way either. She looked up at him, defiant and stubborn and proud. Something shifted inside him as he stared down at her, and he suddenly wanted to be the one protecting her from hurt instead of dealing it out.

Dangerous thinking. Guilty or innocent, she still wasn't the woman for him. She would take too much— too much energy, too much effort. She would want things he couldn't give her. Once a woman developed a taste for champagne, she wouldn't go back to a beer budget for long. Guilty or innocent, she was still expensive, still ambitious.

Guilty or innocent, he still wanted her. He couldn't get this close without wanting her. He damn well couldn't touch her without wanting her.

"I don't want you," she whispered. There was no conviction in her voice. Lip service to her pride, nothing more.

"Liar." The word slipped from him on a breath as he leaned closer. "You don't want to want me."

"Same thing."

"The hell it is. Believe me. I know."

For one long moment everything caught and held— words, breaths, gazes were suspended as the truth of the matter hung in the charged air between them. Silence rang in Elizabeth's ears, then the old Frigidaire kicked in with a thump and a hum, and, outside, the wind hurled the door against the barn again—*thwak! thump, thump, thump* . . . The sound did nothing to break the tension in the room.

Slowly, he reached up with his free hand and slid his fingers into her hair, turning her face as he lowered his. She shuddered as his lips claimed hers and all pretense of resistance melted away. She wanted him. She was too tired to deny the need to be held and touched. She'd been alone so very long.

"I'm sorry," he whispered again, each syllable a caress against her lips.

Elizabeth stared up at him. She wasn't sure what he was apologizing for—being a bastard, making her want him, giving in to that need himself. She didn't ask. For someone so keen on knowing the truth, she was inclined toward ignorance now. This truth wasn't liable to be anything she wanted to hear. It wasn't liable to matter. It wouldn't change what was about to pass between them.

She stretched up toward him, and he brought his mouth down on hers. Elizabeth welcomed him, welcomed the sensual fog that was filling her mind.

Her left hand was still entwined with his right, arms were trapped between their bodies. He turned her hand and brought it against him, molding her fingers along his erection. Then he turned her hand and pressed it to her own body, wringing a gasp from her. The sense of doing something forbidden only added fuel to the fire inside her.

"Want me," Dane whispered. "Say you want me."

Elizabeth panted, her lungs grabbing air and puffing it out between swollen, parted lips. "I . . . want . . . you . . . "

Power surged through him. And passion. And something he wouldn't put a name to. Everything else in the world ceased to exist, leaving just the two of them and desire. She was the only woman in the world, and she was going to be his.

He let go of her hand and caught her skirt, crushing

the fabric in his fists as he raised the hem. Elizabeth arched into his touch, helpless to do anything else but gasp for breath. The edge of the counter was biting into her back, but she was only dimly aware of the discomfort. Her focus was on the hunger that was threatening to devour them both.

She gave herself over completely. And when the end came in an explosion of sensation and desperation, she sobbed, frightened by the intensity of it.

The idea terrified her. He couldn't mean that much to her. He couldn't mean anything because she was pretty sure she didn't mean anything to him.

She turned away from his gaze, not wanting him to see the bleakness she was certain he would find in her eyes. Hiding from him. She focused her attention on mundane things—the way the last of the daylight fell in through the window in a dusty gold column, a gold that almost matched the color of the stolen scotch that sat on the counter. God Almighty, they were in the kitchen. She felt stupid as the realization struck her. She hadn't even noticed. She'd been so caught up in need that their surroundings had receded into oblivion. Not once had it entered her mind that they were making love in the kitchen.

No. Not making love, Elizabeth. Having sex. Love wasn't going to enter into this partnership. She wouldn't delude herself into thinking otherwise. Dane Jantzen didn't love her. Why that fact should have made her feel all hollow and achy inside, she couldn't imagine. She should have been used to being used by now.

Dane eased himself away from her, hating leaving the warmth of her body, hating more breaking the deeper connection between them—the one he wouldn't have admitted to feeling even to himself. He arranged himself and zipped his jeans automatically as his mind puzzled over what they had just done. What *he* had just done.

Christ, he'd taken her in the damn kitchen. Standing up. He hadn't even given her the courtesy of comfort. He hadn't even undressed her. What a bastard he was, accusing her of being a whore, then taking her while the truth of her innocence was still hanging in the air around them like the scent of fresh spring rain.

The cynic in him tried to remind him that she had allowed it. But she didn't look happy about it. She looked embarrassed and ashamed.

He lifted a hand to touch her hair and she moved a step away, just out of reach. "Elizabeth—"

"Maybe you should go now," she murmured. "Like I asked you to before."

Dane slicked his hands back over his hair and sighed. He didn't need more complications in his life right now. He didn't need a woman like Elizabeth. But he'd sure as hell had her, and he couldn't just walk away.

"That didn't go quite the way I thought it would," he said softly.

Her eyes widened, and anger flared in them. "Are you saying you came here expecting to—?"

"No. I'm saying I've been thinking about it since the moment I first saw you," Dane admitted candidly. He brushed back her hair, dropped his hand, and carefully touched his thumb to the scar at the corner of her mouth, wondering how long it would be before she told him how she came by it.

"Isn't that just like a man?" she complained.

"I wanted it," he said bluntly. "You wanted it." When she started to protest, he pressed a finger to her lips. "Don't say you didn't, Elizabeth. Your panties will tell a different tale."

She narrowed her eyes and fumed, and Dane thought of how bleak those eyes had looked a minute earlier. "I didn't mean for it to happen this way."

"I don't think it should have happened at all."

"Hush," he whispered, bending his head to kiss her cheek. "Don't say that."

He told himself he didn't want her to regret their intimacy because he didn't want this to be his only taste of her. That was the truth. Part of it.

"There's no reason we shouldn't be lovers," he said.

The words came as a surprise to him, but not the logic behind them. If they set the ground rules now, if they both knew what they were getting, then they could both walk away unscathed in the end. It was simple, neat, the way he liked things.

"Well, for starters, I hate you," Elizabeth said matter-of-factly.

Dane gave her a grin. "You'll get over it."

She shook her head, thinking of the bigger issue. "I don't think so. I don't need the trouble. Besides, I've sworn off men." She backed away a step and lifted her shoulders in an apologetic shrug. "Sorry."

Dane took a step back too, his expression closed. Elizabeth figured he wasn't used to ladies saying no, and he probably didn't like it, but that was tough. He stood there for a moment, a gleam of speculation in his eyes. But he doused it and took another step toward the door, and Elizabeth caught herself wishing he would try a little harder to change her mind.

"You know where to find me," he said as if it didn't matter much to him one way or the other.

She congratulated herself on her resolve as she watched him drive out onto the road and disappear in a cloud of dust and a glow of taillights. But even as she stood there, resolute, there was a hollow pang in her chest.

The telephone interrupted her melancholy, ringing as suddenly and loudly as the starting gate bell at Churchill Downs. Elizabeth jumped to answer it, thinking—hoping—it would be Trace. Her temper had burned off, but not the need to see him and talk to him and try to reach him. She snatched up the receiver on the kitchen wall, smiling with a premature sense of relief. "Hi, honey, I—"

"Bitch."

The word stopped her cold. She just stood there, stunned, her brain scrambling to shift gears. The silence on the line became so absolute, she almost had herself convinced she'd imagined the voice. Then it came again, like a dog growling, low and menacing, eerie and evil.

"Bitch."

Elizabeth opened her mouth and closed it like a fish gasping for air. No sound came out, no air went in. The sense of violation was sudden and sickening. Someone was invading her home. She looked around wildly, as if she expected to see the caller standing in her kitchen doorway. There was no one. The house was dusky and silent. She was alone. The word brought with it an oppressive sense of dread and vulnerability. Alone.

"Whore," the voice growled.

Shaken and shaking, Elizabeth turned and slammed the receiver back in its cradle, then jerked it back up and dropped it to the floor.

"Whore."

She stared in horror at the receiver swinging down along the baseboard, too terrified to rationalize an unbroken connection. Then she jammed both hands down on the cradle and kicked the receiver as if to make sure it was dead this time. A dozen irrational thoughts ran through her head—it was Helen Jarvis doing her exorcist voice, it was Brock tormenting her, someone had seen her with Dane through the kitchen window, the killer was still running loose—

The killer was still running loose. And she was the next worst thing to being a witness.

We haven't exactly made it clear whether you saw anything incriminating or not. . . .

A loud bang sounded beyond the back door, jolting Elizabeth to action. She stumbled away from the phone and ran for the stairs to her room, slamming her shoulder into the doorjamb as she lurched toward the nightstand. She fell to her knees and yanked open the drawer. Her fingers fumbled through a tangle of scarves and scented lace-edged hankies, finally grasping cold hard steel.

The gun was Brock's. One from his collection. A stainless-steel pearl-handled Israeli Desert Eagle .357 Magnum automatic. Elizabeth closed both hands around it and lifted it out of the drawer. The thing was unwieldy and weighed a ton, but she felt safer with it in her hands than she did without it. She sank down onto the rug with her back against the bed, and clutched the gun to her, the flat side against her chest, barrel pointed toward the wall. And she sat there and waited as day faded into night, with nothing but fear and silence for companions.

MIDNIGHT HAD COME AND GONE BEFORE TRACE rolled his sleek racing bike into the old tumbledown shed they were using for a garage. He propped the bike against a stack of bald tires, trudged out of the shed and across the weedy lawn, hands stuffed into the pockets of his jeans.

He didn't like coming home to this house. He especially didn't like coming home when he knew his mom was liable to grill him like a cheese sandwich. *Where you been, Trace? Who with? Doing what?* He would have liked to have harbored some hope that she wouldn't know anything about the sheriff hauling him in and him providing Carney with an alibi, but that was about as likely as a snowstorm in hell. Aside from being a reporter, she was a mom, and moms sniffed out stuff like that quicker than a hound on a trail.

Determined to prolong the inevitable, he sat down on the back step, dug a cigarette out of the pocket on his T-shirt, and fished a book of Red Rooster matches from his jeans. He lit up and took a deep drag, fighting the urge to cough it all out. He didn't really care for smoking, didn't think it was a habit he would keep for long, but he would keep it for a while because it made him feel tougher, more like a man. He knew it wasn't good for him, but since nothing much going on his life at the moment seemed good, he had a hard time caring.

He took another long pull and concentrated on the sound of a door banging against the barn while his lungs burned. There was another storm brewing. Lightning flashed across the night sky like a strobe, and thunder grumbled in the distance, a mirror image of what he was feeling inside—turmoil, anger, uneasiness, as though something were about to happen but he didn't know what, couldn't say how the feelings would escape. Restless, he smashed the cigarette on the cement step and flung the butt out into the yard, pretending it was a basketball and he was the star guard of the Duke Blue Devils shooting a three-pointer to win the NCAA tournament at the final buzzer of triple overtime.

Of course, he wasn't. He was a long, long way from it, and that knowledge weighed on him like a stone. He wouldn't go to Duke to be a Blue Devil or anything else. He was stuck here, in Minnesota, in a dump of a house with no friends but Carney Fox. Christ, did life get any worse than that?

"Well, if it isn't the Lone Stranger."

Trace winced at the edge in his mother's voice. Life did indeed get worse. His stomach churned at the thought of what would come. They would end up fighting, like always. She would try to get him to talk to her, he would push her away. They didn't seem to be able to do anything else. It was as though they were caught up in a continuous loop of time, like on *Star Trek*, where they just kept on reliving the same conversation over and over.

He looked over his shoulder at her and his eyes widened at the sight of the gun she held propped against her left shoulder as she stood in the doorway with her arms crossed over her chest. It flashed silver as a beam of the yard light caught on it, flashed as bright and dangerous as the lightning overhead. Trace bolted to his feet and swung around.

"Jesus, Mom, what are you doing with that thing?"

Elizabeth glanced down at the Desert Eagle as if she had grown so used to its weight in her hand she had forgotten about it. She debated telling Trace about the call, but it seemed less menacing now that he was here with her. It was just a call. A voice on the phone. A shiver ran down her arms at the memory of that voice, raising goose bumps in its wake.

"I was feeling a little jumpy," she said. She nudged the screen door open with her hip and stepped outside, her eyes going automatically to the sky. The wind had picked up and shook the trees like pompons, rattling their leaves together. The barn door banged and thumped.

"They've got a suspect for Jarvis's murder," she said, dropping her gaze to her son. "But then, you've heard all about that, now, haven't you?"

Trace looked away, the muscles in his jaw working. He jammed his hands at the waist of his jeans and sighed the sigh of the oppressed teenager. "Why don't you just go ahead and do it?" he challenged.

"Do what?"

"Bitch me out and get it over with."

Elizabeth pressed her lips together and tamped down the urge to do just that. She didn't want to fight with him, really, she didn't. Beneath the urge to rail at him and shake him and scream out all her frustration, what she really wanted was to hold him to her and take them both back to some point in the past before everything had started to go wrong between them. Back before Atlanta, before Brock and all his money, back to San Antonio, where they had come as close as they ever had to living a normal life. She wanted to go back to a time when he had still been sweet and trusting, and she had felt in control, the all-knowing, all-powerful mama, able to heal hurts and hug away tears. It seemed the years had taken away whatever power she had had or Trace had imagined she had had. He was sixteen now, nearly half her age, and perfectly able to see she wasn't anything but mortal and couldn't fix things with a kiss.

"Trace, I can't hear about you giving out an alibi for Carney Fox and not be upset about it," she said. "He's a suspect in a murder investigation."

"Yeah, well, he didn't do it."

"You know that for a fact?"

He glanced away, dodging her question, dodging her gaze. Lightning flashed as bright as a spotlight on his face, illuminating what he didn't want her to see—the brooding look, the secrets. Elizabeth felt her heart sink, and a mother's panic seized her by the throat and squeezed. She descended the steps and rushed toward him, driven by a need that threatened to overwhelm her. Trace started to turn away, but she caught him by the arm with her left hand and held on, her fingers biting into firm young muscle.

"Answer me, dammit!" she snapped, raising her voice to be heard above the gathering storm. "Do you know he didn't kill Jarrold Jarvis? Were you there?"

Trace jerked away, wrenching his arm free and rubbing at it, scowling. "He didn't do it. We were playing basketball."

It was the same line he had fed Dane, and Elizabeth imagined Dane had heard the same flatness, the same ring of falseness she was hearing now. He was lying. Good God in heaven, he was lying about a possible murderer. Her son, her baby, the child she had held in her arms and dreamed such dreams for. Thunder cracked overhead and another flash of lightning cast everything in sharp, eerie relief, like a scene from an old Hitchcock movie, turning those dreams into a nightmare. The child had grown into someone she didn't know, couldn't reach; the baby was a face in her mind, a small voice calling to her from the end of a long, dark tunnel.

"Dammit, Trace!" she sobbed as the rain began to fall. "Tell me the truth!"

But he just looked at her, silent, drawing into himself, pulling his cloak of adolescent isolationism around himself like a force field. The rain streaked down across the lenses of his glasses and turned his T-shirt transparent in big splotches.

"I'm going to bed," he said, backing away, his voice soft between the rumbles from heaven.

Elizabeth was rooted to the spot, the rain pouring down over her, drenching her, beating against her skin like a thousand fingers. She watched him disappear into the dark house, panic tearing at her inside, clawing to get out. She wanted to run after him, to grab him, to scream, but it wouldn't do any good. She couldn't reach him—not emotionally, not the way she wanted to, needed to—and she couldn't stand the idea of trying, only to fail. Tonight of all nights, she didn't have the strength for it.

So she stood in the rain, crying, the water pelting against her face like rocks, the weight of it dragging at her skirt. She stood until the strength drained out of her legs, then she sank to the ground and sat there, her hair hanging in wet ropes around her face, the Desert Eagle tucked against her as she hugged herself and rocked and wished with all her heart that this was a just a nightmare instead of her life.

THIRTEEN

THE SMELL OF CARAMEL ROLLS TURNED THE WARM air in the kitchen buttery and sweet. Dane shouldered open the door and shuffled in, bleary-eyed, the tails of his black polo shirt hanging outside his jeans. It was after seven. He had overslept and was irritated with himself because of it. It was irrational to think he should be able to function in top form on little or no rest while the burden of a murder investigation weighed down on him, but he caught himself thinking it just the same. Great Dane, the hero, the gridiron god, possessed of superhuman strength and character. He gave a bitter half laugh as he poured himself a cup of Mrs. Cranston's strong black coffee.

Mrs. Cranston straightened away from the oven, red-faced from the heat and the strain of bending her bulk in two. Her small hands were encased in a pair of enormous blue oven mits, and between them stretched a cookie sheet lined with steaming sweet rolls.

"I'll have these iced and ready in no time, Sheriff," she said, bustling to the table in the center of the light, airy room.

He leaned back against the counter and watched her go about her business setting the rolls on wire racks on the table to cool. She looked made for the scene: plump and grandmotherly, a sunny smile in a sunny yellow kitchen while country music played in the background.

The kitchen door swung open and Amy started into the room, hesitating as she caught sight of him.

"Morning, peanut," he said, hoping her temper had cooled off during the night. When she met his greeting with nothing more than a stony look, Dane knew he wasn't going to get his wish.

She greeted Mrs. Cranston with notable enthusiasm, slid onto a chair at the table, and plucked up one of the freshly iced rolls to nibble at it.

"Heather asked me to spend the night," she said without preamble, her gaze locking hard on Dane's. "I told her I'd have to get permission from my father, since I'm just a child."

Dane pinched the bridge of his nose and bit back a reprimand at her tone. He was being punished for the unpardonable sin of wanting his daughter to remain his daughter. His natural inclination was to fight back. He didn't suffer insubordination lightly in his professional life and seldom encountered it elsewhere. But he held himself in check, a part of him feeling he deserved to be punished, if not for the way he had treated Amy, for the way he had treated Elizabeth.

"Fine," he said at last.

Amy took another tiny bite of her roll, barely tasting it as she met her father's steady gaze. "She and Aunt Mary are going to Rochester, shopping. They said they'd pick me up at nine."

"What about our ride?" Dane asked. "I thought I could make some time this afternoon, after the funeral."

Spite outweighed remorse by a narrow margin. Amy lifted one shoulder in a negligent shrug and looked down at her breakfast so she wouldn't have to see the hurt in her father's eyes.

"We'll just have to make it some other time, I guess," she said, trying her hardest to sound as though it didn't matter to her in the least, despite the fact that she'd been looking forward to it. Riding was something they had always shared, just the two of them, because her mother wouldn't come within a mile of a horse. She didn't like the idea of anything intruding on that tradition, but she had a point to make, she reminded herself, steeling her resolve against the urge to go across the room and hug him. She was not a little girl anymore, and she would not be treated like one.

She unfolded herself from the kitchen chair, abandoning the half-eaten roll on the table. "I have to go fix my hair," she said, and made what she thought was a regal exit—head up, shoulders back.

Dane watched her go, feeling his neatly ordered world shifting yet again, and not liking it one bit.

Mrs. Cranston glanced up from icing the last of the caramel rolls, the lines of her face softened by sympathy. "It's not always easy being a grown-up," she said gently.

"You've got that right, Mrs. Cranston," he grumbled, setting his coffee mug aside on the counter. "All in all, I'd rather be playing football."

THE CONSTRUCTION SITE SMELLED OF SAWDUST AND mud. The rain-washed trees along the perimeter shook themselves in the early morning breeze. A meadowlark sang a solo somewhere down along the creek. If you weren't looking at what would become the Still Waters resort, Elizabeth reflected, it was a pretty morning. Cool and blue and breezy. Clouds as puffy and ragged-edged as shredded cotton drifted aimlessly above. The sun had come up above a horizon done in watercolor shades. Now it slanted its beams across the field of young corn to the east, enticing it to grow better than "knee-high by the Fourth of July," as the old farmer's saying went.

Standing there in the beautiful, peaceful quiet, it was hard to believe life could be complicated.

Elizabeth raised her stolen Nikon and took a wide-angle shot of the eastern horizon and the Amishman trudging across a distant field behind a pair of work-horses. It might make a nice picture for the next issue of the *Clarion*. They could do a story about the weather and how it affected both farming and tourism—provided no one was killed in the meantime.

She hiked her purse strap up on her shoulder and cursed the Desert Eagle she had seen fit to tuck into the Gucci bag. The damn thing was as heavy as an anvil, but she wasn't disgusted enough to leave it behind. The phone call had rattled her. It didn't matter how much her brain tried to discount the incident now, in the light of day. It did no good to tell herself she had overreacted. Every time she did, she heard that voice, heard the malevolence in it, felt it touch her like a cold, bony finger. She had crouched by her bed with the pistol until Trace had come home.

She sighed now as the thought of the confrontation they'd had. She hadn't gotten anywhere with him. Not an inch. He had pulled up the drawbridge at the mention of Carney Fox and refused to let her across it. Frustration burned through her. He was hiding something. A half-wit could have seen it. If it had something to do with Carney Fox, and if Carney Fox had something to do with the murder . . .

She jerked around and snapped a series of pictures of the construction site: the office trailer, the rutted parking area, the superstructure. *Still Waters in the Aftermath* she would call this series. She would put it on the front page and give Charlie Wilder a stroke. That would make her popular.

The yellow police tapes had been broken and lay like discarded ribbons in the mud around the spot where Jarvis had met his end. Nothing else marked the place. The blood had washed away the first night during the storm. Still, Elizabeth took a shot of it, then she pointed the camera down toward the creek and snapped off another round of nature photos. She was about to lower the camera when a figure to the west caught her eye. Fiddling with the monstrous lens, she zoomed in.

It looked like Aaron Hauer, though he was too far away for her to make out one Amishman from the next. The set of the shoulders, the tilt of the head, made her think it was him. He was kneeling beneath the shade of a maple tree that stood up the hill from the creek. His head was bowed, his wide-brimmed straw hat in his hands.

The camera clicked and whirred before Elizabeth could catch herself. The man, whoever he was, was praying. She had no business capturing such a private moment on film. Amish people praying wasn't news, and her taking pictures of it made her no better than the tourists who thought they had the right to intrude on the lives of people like Aaron Hauer.

The man stood and settled his hat on his head, then walked away, losing himself in the trees that covered that part of the hillside. Elizabeth lowered her camera and started down the hill toward the creek. Aaron's wife was dead. Maybe she was spending eternity under that maple tree with a view of the creek.

It wasn't morbid fascination that had Elizabeth skidding down the hillside, the legs of her jeans soaking up the moisture that clung to the thick grass, but caring. She liked Aaron. Under the layers of grim, pious duty, there was a man with strengths and vulnerabilities like any man. If she could learn more about him, she could be a better friend to him. To her way of thinking, both of them needed all the friends they could get.

The feet of untold scores of trout fishermen and truants had tramped a path in the tall grass along the bank, but that was the only sign they had left behind. There was no litter. The stream itself ran sluggishly along, bottle-green with dragonflies skimming the surface in search of a waterbug breakfast. In the shallows along the bank, marsh marigolds grew in profusion, bright butter-yellow with velvet-green leaves the size of lily pads. On the opposite bank, a deer stood behind a lacy curtain of weeping willow branches and stared across at Elizabeth with limpid eyes, then turned and glided away, graceful and silent.

What a beautiful place to be laid to rest. So peaceful. So far away from the troubles of the world.

Elizabeth turned from the creek and looked up the hill

to the shady spot where the mourner had knelt to pay his respects and say his prayers. Wild violets grew around the base of the tree. Some had been picked and placed in small bouquets on the ground where three stone markers stood side by side, a large one flanked by two smaller. Siri Hauer, Beloved Wife. Ana Hauer, Gemma Hauer, Beloved Daughter, the smaller ones read.

She kneeled beside one little grave. Two tiny birds carved from wood nestled in the grass at the base of the marker. She traced the tip of a finger across one dainty wing and ached for her strange, quiet Amish friend. She had complained to him about her son. At least she still had Trace with her, no matter how distant he seemed, no matter how difficult to reach. Aaron Hauer could touch his daughters only with prayer . . . and violets.

SOMEONE HAD PITCHED A BRICK THROUGH THE PLATE glass window of the *Clarion* office. Shattered glass was strewn across the floor. What still clung to the frame of the window hung in pointed shards, like crystal stalactites. The gaping hole had let in the rain and wind, which had left the office looking like the dubious survivor of a hurricane. The old wood floor gleamed with puddles. Leftover copies of the special edition had blown all over. But Elizabeth doubted it was the wind that had dumped boxes of old type all over the floor or smashed the monitor of her computer or ripped to shreds the fuchsia plant she had splurged on to congratulate herself for buying the *Clarion.*

Jolynn, who had found the mess, sat on her desktop because her chair was just so much kindling, her eyes bright with interest as she scanned the scene and calculated the possibilities.

"Could be the work of your caller," she said, lifting her morning can of Pepsi to her lips.

"Could be," Elizabeth murmured, peeling a strip of wet paper off the counter and dropping it to the floor. "I hope so. I'd hate to think there's a whole band of crazy people out there waiting to draw a bead on me."

"Yeah, well, the special edition didn't exactly endear you to a lot of people."

"They bought it, though, didn't they?" Elizabeth said with disgust.

Jolynn shrugged and swiped her tangled bangs out of her eyes. "I guess it was like driving by an accident. They didn't want to look, but they couldn't help themselves."

"Hypocrites," she muttered. "That's what they are."

"Someone was mad enough to make a statement about it."

"Yeah, if that was their reason."

"You think maybe someone was trying to scare you?"

"They managed that, sugar. That's for damn sure." She hefted her purse up onto the counter. "Maybe somebody was looking for something."

"Like what?" Jo said on a half laugh. "Our hidden millions? My stash of candy bars?" She reached over the edge of her desk and yanked the top drawer open, breathing an exaggerated sigh of relief as she pulled out a Baby Ruth.

"Like Jarvis's black book," Elizabeth said, leaning against the counter. "Did you mention it to anyone?"

"No. I've been thinking about who might be in it, but I haven't approached anybody yet. Have you?"

"I mentioned it yesterday," she said, watching carefully for Jolynn's reaction. "To Rich."

"Rich? Rich Cannon?" Jolynn gave a hoot of laughter. "You think Rich killed Jarrold? No way!"

"Why not? He stood to gain."

"He stood to gain more kissing Jarrold's ass. Rich is too lazy and too stupid to run Jarrold's business himself," she declared. "They had a symbiotic relationship, you know, like those slimy little remora things that suck all the crud off sharks. Jarrold provided Rich with a fat income for a minimum amount of actual work, Rich was Jarrold's trick pony, his pretty front man for the construction business, handsome husband for Susie the

Shrill." She shook her head again as she stripped back the wrapper on her candy bar like a banana peel. "Rich couldn't have killed Jarrold. He wouldn't have the inclination, the guts, or the stomach for it. Take it from me. I've known him too long."

Elizabeth wasn't convinced. "I don't know, sugar, ass-kissing can get old after a while. Especially if the ass is as fat and ugly as Jarrold's."

Jolynn scrunched her face up and groaned. "God, what an image. You should be a writer."

Bret Yeager stuck his head into the office through what had been the window, a laconic smile stretching across his square, honest face as his gaze landed softly on Jolynn. "Morning, ladies," he drawled. "Can we come in?"

"Lord, honey," Elizabeth clucked, crunching across the broken glass in her cowboy boots to shoo him back. "Don't be sticking your head in through there! Didn't you see *Ghost?* Tony Goldwyn practically got himself decapitated that way."

"There's a lot of that going around," Boyd Ellstrom said flatly as he pulled the door open and swaggered in. Yeager and his dog followed, Yeager whistling softly as he took in the wreckage. The dog sniffed out a dry, clean corner and curled up in a ball to sleep.

Elizabeth darted a look at Ellstrom. He stared back at her, looking just as smug and obnoxious as he had the night he'd walked in on her and Dane. "Yeah, well, I don't want it happening here," she said.

"Why not?" he asked sarcastically. "You could do a special edition."

Yeager played diplomat, stepping in between them with an apologetic smile for Elizabeth. "Don't mind him, Miss Stuart. He's ticked because the sheriff chewed him out yesterday for giving you that quote." Behind him, Ellstrom's Flintstone face turned a dull red. "We're here to take your statements and have a look around."

"Is this BCA business, Agent Yeager?"

"Well, naw, not exactly," he said, rolling his shoulders

a little. He was wearing a tan dress shirt that had come straight from the package. The way he hooked a finger inside the collar and tugged made Elizabeth think he might have forgotten to get all the cardboard out of it, to say nothing of the creases. "But I was standing right there when Miss Nielsen's call came in and I had a minute . . ." He let the explanation die right there as he smiled at Jolynn, bringing a hint of rose to Jolynn's round cheeks.

Elizabeth raised a brow. "Oh, well, that's fine," she said, not quite sure Yeager was even listening to her. "Jolynn found the mess. You'll probably want to talk to her first."

Jolynn reached into her desk drawer and pulled out a candy bar. "Butterfinger, Agent Yeager?"

Yeager's smile split into a lopsided grin. "A woman after my own heart. Come on, Booze," he called to the Labrador. "We got work to do."

The dog heaved himself to his feet with a groan, and the three of them went off to inspect the back door, which had been left standing open by the perpetrator, leaving Elizabeth to deal with Boyd Ellstrom.

Ellstrom strolled around behind the counter, looking over the damage, nudging the fallen computer monitor with his toe, poking at the deceased fuchsia with a ballpoint pen. Elizabeth stationed herself near the counter, arms folded over the front of her purple silk tank top, eyes slightly wary as she watched him.

"I'm sorry if you had to take heat over the quote," she said, not really caring whether Dane had chewed his butt or not. "I figured you knew your odds."

Ellstrom shot her a look. "I can handle Jantzen."

You and what army? Elizabeth's lips curved into what would have to pass for a smile and shrugged. "Then we're square, I guess."

"I did you a favor," Ellstrom said. He moved toward her, his eyes drawn to the cleavage peeking up above the scoop neck of her blouse. She wore a purple stone on a chain around her neck. The jewel pointed straight to that sweet valley between her breasts. He could almost imagine how soft she would be there, and her nipples were probably as hard as that stone. His cock started twitching just thinking about it. "I did you a favor," he said again. "The way I see it, you owe me."

Elizabeth lifted her chin and narrowed her eyes as he moved in on her, cornering her against the counter. The son of a bitch expected her to give him something, and she didn't have to be Einstein's daughter to figure out what it was. Her skin was already crawling just from the way his gaze lingered on her skin. He stopped his advance a scant six inches from her, the look on his big face at once disdainful and expectant. Elizabeth gave him her stoniest glare.

"If you're looking for free samples, sugar, you better go on down to the Piggly Wiggly, 'cause you ain't gettin' any here."

Heat rose into Ellstrom's face, fueled by humiliation and the sting of rejection. If they had been in a more secluded spot, he might have pushed the issue. The bitch came across for every other man who wagged his dick in front of her. She probably played this hard-to-get game just to salve her conscience. But she sure as hell hadn't saved anything from Jantzen.

"You only give it out to the man with the biggest badge?" he sneered.

Elizabeth had to squeeze her arms against herself to keep from slapping him. Instead, she went for him where it would hurt the most. "Naw, you know what they say, honey—it ain't the size of the badge on the man, it's the size of the man with the badge."

The man with the badge pulled open the door and stepped inside as Ellstrom leaned toward her. The air in the room seemed to drop twenty degrees as Dane stood on the other side of the counter, staring at his deputy.

"Have you finished cataloguing the list of the damages, Deputy?" he asked in a silky voice.

Ellstrom didn't say a word, but turned and went about his business, jerking a notebook and pen from his shirt pocket. Elizabeth blew out a long breath as she turned toward Dane.

"You've got your faults, sugar," she muttered, "but timing isn't one of them. Your deputy isn't terribly fond of me right now."

"Looks like he's part of a club," Dane said dryly as he took in the vandalism.

"Yeah, this is a hell of a town you got here, Sheriff," she drawled sarcastically as she scraped a smashed fuchsia petal off the counter with her fingernail. "Folks here sure know how to make a girl feel welcome."

"Tell me it would be different if I moved down south to some little burg and started stirring things up," Dane challenged her, defending his home as instinctively as he would have defended a family member. "You can't. It would be even worse because I'm a *Yankee* and most of those people never got the message that Lee surrendered to Grant at Appomattox. Hell, they'd probably have me tarred and feathered by now."

"There's an idea." Her laugh was half mocking, half hysterical. "Why don't you go out in the street and holler it up and down? I don't have anything better to do tonight. If this mess is anything to go by, your deputies won't bother to interfere."

Dane clenched his jaw for a second and reined in his temper. She had a right to her anger. What he wasn't quite as sure about was whether or not he had a right to be angry *for* her. She had rejected his offer, but he still caught himself wanting to assume the role of protector, and it didn't have anything to do with her being a taxpayer. It had to do with basic instincts and natural chemistry. "Is there someplace more private where we can talk?"

Elizabeth weighed the evils against one another. It was a no-win deal. They either stood here in full view and earshot of Deputy Dope and had their conversation, or she sequestered herself in a room with a man who was nothing but trouble. She caught Ellstrom glaring at them out of the corner of his beady eye.

"My office," she said. She gathered the beleaguered fuchsia in her arms, heedless of the dirt, and turned to lead the way through the wreckage.

The office was a windowless cubbyhole of a room that smelled like a wet basement regardless of all efforts to freshen it. Elizabeth had taken one look at it and set herself up in the front room with Jolynn. The only thing she used it for was storage. As she swung the door open she discovered that its uselessness hadn't spared it from the vandal's wrath. The floor was a sea of paper that had been spewed forth by the battered file cabinets. It was going to take her a month to clean up. She set her smashed plant on what was left of the desk and fingered the ragged greenery and tattered pink flowers.

"When I was married to Bobby Lee Breland—he's Trace's daddy—I saw one of these once in the window of the little flower shop in Bardette," she said softly. "I asked him if he would get it for me for a present. Next day it was gone out of the window. I went home early, all het up 'cause I figured he bought it for me and that meant he loved me and he'd probably stop runnin' around and . . ." She let her voice trail away. Silly, bringing up old hurts when she had enough new ones to deal with.

"Did he?" Dane asked, knowing the answer. He could see it in the set of her shoulders, in the way she tightened her mouth.

She shook her head.

"Are you all right?" he asked softly.

"Oh, sure," she said. "I like being victimized. I'm funny that way."

He propped his hands at the waist of his jeans and scowled at her. "About last night—"

Elizabeth held up a hand to cut him off. "You don't have to feel responsible for me, Sheriff," she said flatly. "I'm a big girl."

Dane looked down at the mutilated fuchsia and ground his teeth. Dammit, he *did* feel responsible. He felt downright territorial where she was concerned. It was a wonder he hadn't given Ellstrom a bloody nose for coming within a foot of her. The fact that he had been tempted rattled him. Christ, he'd been sleeping with Ann Markham for two years and he'd never given a damn who else went sniffing around her.

"I got an interesting call after you left last night," Elizabeth said, needing to get him off the topic of what had happened between them.

His gaze sharpened and, even though he was standing with one leg bent casually, he seemed to come to attention. "What sort of call?"

"Someone wanting to express their opinion of my character. You know," she said, trying to sound as offhand and unaffected as she could. "Bitch. Whore. That kind of thing."

Blind fury rose up in Dane like a geyser. "Goddammit, why didn't you call me?"

Elizabeth stared up at him, eyes wide with surprise at the strength of his reaction. "They didn't leave a name or number. I don't reckon you could have caught your suspect."

"That's not the point." He wanted to shake her, but worse still, he wanted to hold her. She had to have been frightened, alone in that rattletrap house, knowing a killer was at large. The idea damn near choked him with impotent rage. He tried his best to clear his head and think like a cop. "Was it a man or a woman?"

Elizabeth shuddered inwardly as the voice replayed itself in her mind. "A man . . . I think. I couldn't really tell. It sounded strange. Might have been the same person who trashed this place," she suggested, backing away from him. "Calling to see that I was out of the way. Whoever did this sure as hell felt like they had clear sailing. I find it amazing that a business on Main Street could be tossed like this without anyone seeing anything, without a deputy driving by and looking in."

"Vandals work fast as a rule," Dane said. "That's why it's hard to catch them at it. As bad as this all looks, it probably didn't take more than ten minutes."

"If it was a vandalism."

He arched a brow. "Looking for conspiracies again?"

"Still," she corrected him, crossing her arms against her self. "And don't you dare be amused at me, Dane Jantzen. The article in the special edition speculated as to motive for the killing. Maybe someone thinks we've got evidence here."

Dane rolled his eyes. "And maybe someone doesn't like the fact that you've taken the bridge club minutes out of the paper."

Elizabeth gave him a long, level look. "Either way, you've got some thinking to do, Sheriff. I reckon you didn't expect anyone around here, any of these people you know so well, to vandalize a business or make an obscene phone call. Same way you didn't think any of them might have killed Jarvis.

"It seems to me you see what you want to see," she said. "You see what you grew up seeing, what you expect to see. But I'm walking into this town not knowing anyone from Adam, and I can tell you, there are people here just as greedy, just as corrupt, just as unhinged as there are anyplace else. And one of them is a murderer."

DANE TURNED ELIZABETH'S WORDS OVER IN HIS MIND that afternoon as he stood in a side door looking at the people who had gathered to mourn the untimely demise of Jarrold Jarvis.

He was a good cop. While old popularity and old fame might have helped him get elected, Dane knew he held the job on merit. He had never been inclined to rest on some dusty legend of his youth, like Rich Cannon. He might not have been ambitious, but he was conscientious and dedicated. Despite what Elizabeth seemed to think, he wanted the murder solved regardless of who committed it, and he was working tirelessly to that end. It was true he preferred things simple and neat, but that didn't make him lazy.

His gaze scanned the crowd slowly, taking in the faces

of people he had known his whole life. He had always felt his knowledge of these people made him a better sheriff, not a poorer one. He knew what to watch for, whom to keep an eye on. He knew Till Amstutz got mean when he drank because he always had. He knew that the young Odegard boys drove too fast on the Loring road because the Odegard men had been driving too fast since the days of Henry Ford; fast driving ran in their genes. He knew who was always scraping by to make ends meet and which families had kids who were liable to end up in trouble. He knew Tyler County, knew Still Creek. He didn't want to think that knowledge had become more hindrance than help.

Our Savior's Lutheran Church was full. The sun shone through the huge stained glass window depicting Jesus wringing his hands in the garden of Gethsemane, raining colors down on the heads of those who had come to grieve or gawk. There were both, Dane knew, though he suspected the gawkers outnumbered the grievers by a wide margin.

Helen Jarvis made a production of breaking down beside the closed polished oak casket at the front of the church, half collapsing against it and wailing like a banshee. This outburst was something so out of character for her—or for anybody in the state, for that matter—that no one knew quite how to react. There were a lot of horrified, embarrassed looks. Arnetta McBaine cranked up the volume on the old pipe organ and pounded out the chorus of "How Great Thou Art" so loudly that people actually cringed.

Susie Jarvis Cannon was sitting in the front row in her little black dress and hideous pillbox hat. She had Helen's tiny eyes, Jarrold's hook of a nose and weak chin, the overall effect making her face somewhat parrot-like. Her two bored children sat beside her, swinging their feet and pinching each other. At her mother's outburst Susie turned from her children to her husband with her ears pinned back and all but shoved him out of the pew. Looking sulky rather than solicitous, Rich stood and straightened his dark suit jacket, then took Helen by the arm and tried to lead her to her seat.

Helen had her widow's veil peeled back over a hat with a brim so exaggerated that it looked as though it might have been involved in one of man's early attempts at flight. She presented her stricken visage to the crowd, and this time Dane cringed a little. She looked like Bette Davis in *Whatever Happened to Baby Jane?* Her makeup so overdone she could have been a geisha girl— porcelain-white skin, dots of cherry red on her cheeks and outlining her mouth, long false eyelashes elaborately curled and caked with mascara. Of course, she had cried most of the mascara off into black rivulets that streaked down her face. The dark crescents beneath her eyes gave her the appearance of some odd tribal woman emulating the sacred raccoon.

The overall picture was ghoulish, and no one seemed to know what to make of it. Everyone in town knew Helen and Jarrold had stayed together only out of spite and meanness. Dane doubted either of them had held much capacity to love anyone but themselves. So this was another of Helen's little melodramas, which seemed to be getting stranger and stranger.

"Was it a man or a woman?"

"A man . . . I think. It sounded strange."

Elizabeth's answer whispered through the back of Dane's mind as he watched Helen slump into her seat. He couldn't help but think of the way the woman had looked when she had launched that Jell-O fish at Elizabeth, or the way she had sounded. If Helen was slipping a few gears in the wake of all that had happened, she might have made a call like that. She didn't like anyone stealing her thunder the way Elizabeth had inadvertently done by stumbling across Jarrold's body and triggering an avalanche of gossip. But the vandalism was out of the question. It had taken strength to pry the padlock off the back door of the *Clarion* office, more strength than Helen possessed even in a rage.

Dane pulled his gaze away from the grieving widow,

looking at Rich in his new politician suit, and Susie, who was more concerned with her children making her look bad in public than with the idea of laying her father to rest. In the pews behind them sat a dozen people who owed Jarrold money, and more whom he had cheated in one way or another. Dane looked over this crowd of people he had known since childhood and realized that his perception of them was changing subtly. For the first time he was looking at them as potential suspects, and he didn't like it. He didn't like seeing them that way any more than they liked the idea of crime coming to Still Creek. But times they were achangin', and, like it or not, Dane knew he and the rest of Still Creek would have to change with them.

He slipped into a pew as Reverend Lindgren emerged from the sacristy, and turned his mind to murder as the rest of the crowd turned their hymnals to "Faith of Our Fathers."

ELIZABETH WHEELED HER ELDORADO INTO THE SERvice drive of Shafer Motors and cut the engine. The business was located on the southwest side of town along the highway, to help attract customers, Elizabeth suspected, but there wasn't any sign that the location was doing good today. In fact, most of the town had looked deserted as she drove down Main Street, devoid of locals at any rate. Two tour buses were parked in front of the Coffee Cup, and she had spotted a gaggle of tourists gawking and pointing as an Amish buggy clomped toward Hardware Hank's. But the crowd was down at Our Savior to see Jarrold Jarvis put into the ground, and to feast on ham salad and German chocolate cake in the church basement afterward. All things considered, Elizabeth had decided it prudent to send Jo to observe the ritual.

She climbed out of the Caddy and took a long look at what Garth Shafer had done for himself after the partnership with Jarvis had gone awry. The building that housed the Ford dealership was by no means new or fancy. In fact, the cinder-block building looked badly in need of paint, the sea-green walls having turned a polluted shade over the years. A new gray Thunderbird was parked in the showroom window, but most of the cars on the lot appeared used.

The sign in the door proclaimed the place open, and Elizabeth let herself in quietly, hoping to get a look around before anyone came to sell her a car. The sound of power tools whined and wheezed from what was presumably the service garage. The manager's office stood open and empty. Shafer himself was probably at the funeral with all the other hypocrites, Elizabeth thought, edging toward the office. She was wrong.

He came up behind her, quiet as a cat as she leaned into the office. Suddenly his reflection appeared in the window glass and Elizabeth jumped, clutching her heart, nearly crashing into him. He took a step away and she stumbled around and backed toward the Thunderbird, scrambling to compose herself as her heart rammed into her ribs like a paddle ball.

"Oh, my Lord in heaven, you startled me!" she gasped, trying to laugh it off and seem friendly and innocent all at once.

He didn't apologize, but stood there with a frighteningly large wrench in his hands and a carefully blank look in his dark eyes. He was a tall man, late forties to early fifties, who bore an unfortunate resemblance to Jack Palance. Unbidden, the lines from *City Slickers* came to Elizabeth's mind: "Kill anyone today, Curly?". . . Jack Palance smiles that chilling smile. "Day ain't over yet."

She rubbed her hand over the purse that rested against her hip, trying to take reassurance from the solid weight of the Desert Eagle tucked inside, trying not to imagine a situation where she would actually have to use it.

"Can I help you with something?"

"Well—a—you just might, sugar," she said, pasting on a bright smile. "I might be in the market for a car soon." *Or not.* "Someone told me to come on down and ask for Garth. I don't reckon he's here today, though, what with the funeral and all."

His expression didn't change so much as a blink. "I'm Garth Shafer."

"You are?" She tried to sound more pleasantly surprised than dismayed by the prospect of having this particular conversation with an armed man. "Well, I'm in luck, then, aren't I?"

He didn't seem to have an opinion on that one way or the other. He just stood there in his grimy blue coveralls, twisting that blasted wrench around and around in his greasy hands.

"I'm Elizabeth Stuart."

"That newspaper woman."

"Yes."

He nodded and turned to glance out the door at the Caddy that gleamed as bright and red as a maraschino cherry under the afternoon sun. "Trading in?"

"Could be." She started to circle the Thunderbird slowly, needing to put some distance between herself and that wrench. She shot him a curious look. "Mind if I ask why you aren't at the funeral? I understand you and Jarrold used to be partners."

"I've got a business to run," he said flatly.

He looked like the kind of man who wouldn't take time off to bury his own mother. At any rate, it didn't seem wise to call him on it. She trailed a finger along the side panel of the car and slanted him a sultry smile. "You like selling cars, do you? Better than the road construction business?"

Shafer must have considered the question rhetorical. He didn't say a word.

Elizabeth shrugged and tucked her fingertips into the front pockets of her faded jeans. "Well, you must to have traded one for the other. I mean, selling cars is a feast-or-famine kind of thing, up and down with the economy, which is most always down, if you ask me. Roads, on the other hand, we always need roads. A man can get rich building roads."

"Do you have a point to make here, Mrs. Stuart?" he asked quietly. His face was the same blank mask, but anger now simmered in his eyes. He tapped the wrench against the palm of his left hand methodically.

Elizabeth swallowed. Yes, she had a point to make. That Jarvis knocked up Garth Shafer's wife, screwed Garth in the buyout of the construction business, and left him with a career that would never make him rich while Jarvis had been rolling in dough like pig in pink mud. That was her point, but she couldn't see any tactful way of making it. This investigative stuff always seemed easier in the movies.

She shrugged a little and batted her lashes. "Just making conversation. Is this an automatic?" she asked, sliding a hand along the roof of the Thunderbird.

"Yes. Power steering, power brakes, power windows, air-conditioning, AM/FM stereo." This was delivered in his same flat monotone. A dynamic salesman, Garth. It was a wonder the whole town hadn't converted to horse and buggy.

"Mmm . . . nice." She leaned against the car, looking across at Shafer, her gaze drawn inexorably to the wrench. "That was terrible, Jarrold getting himself killed that way. You must have known him a long time. What do you think about it?"

Shafer didn't move, but the field of tension around him made Elizabeth feel as if he had yanked her closer with it. He seemed suddenly nearer, larger, angrier. His nostrils flared and he drew in a deep breath through his yellowed teeth. The hair on the back of Elizabeth's neck bristled.

"Get out," he snarled, hands twisting harder on the neck of the wrench as he stalked around the hood of the Thunderbird. "I don't have anything to say to you."

Elizabeth backed up slowly, her gaze darting between Shafer's face and the tool in his hands. She thought about the pistol weighing down her purse, but her fingers were clenched on the strap, cold and damp with fear. Swallowing down the lump in her throat, she said, "Mr. Shafer, don't get angry. I was just—"

"Looking for dirt to put in your paper," he said bitterly. "What happened between me and Jarrold was buried twenty years ago. I won't have a tramp like you drag it out again. You're not welcome here—not in my business, not in this town. You've brought nothing but trouble—".

Elizabeth held up a hand to defend herself from his words if not his wrench. "Wait a minute. *I'm* not the one who killed—".

"Get out. Get out," he chanted, backing her toward the door, the volume of his voice rising with each word as his temper finally broke through his stony facade. "Get out!" he yelled, red-faced, the cords in his neck standing out sharply.

He hurled the wrench past her and it hit the block wall, ringing like a horseshoe hitting the stake. Elizabeth ditched her dignity, turned, and ran, jerking the door open and bolting for the Caddy. She jumped into the car and gunned the engine, slamming it into reverse with no regard for the transmission as Shafer came out onto the step to glare at her. She was a half mile down the highway before she stopped feeling those cold, dark eyes on the back of her neck and started thinking about the power of a grudge that had been nursed for twenty years on a diet of bitterness and hate.

TRACE PEDALED TOWARD STILL CREEK, HIS HEAD down, back rounded as he bent over the handlebars of the twelve-speed. The bike had been an expensive toy in Atlanta, a custom-made racer imported from Italy, something for his friends to envy. Here it was his only mode of transportation, which took all the fun out of owning it. For one thing, it wasn't cool for a man to have nothing to get around on but a bike. And the bike was a failure on gravel roads. It seemed to Trace he spent most of his pocket money replacing tire tubes. And, on the narrow two-lane state highway that took him into Still Creek, it seemed he was forever having to dodge farm equipment or Amish buggies or old geezers in boat-size Buicks who drove only as fast as their eyesight allowed.

What he needed was a car. A car would make all the difference in his life. He would be free if he had a car, not at the mercy of Carney or anyone else. Not at the mercy of tire tubes or the weather or eighty-year-old gomers too blind to drive. If he had himself a car, he could whiz by the stupid Amish instead of having their stupid horses breathing down his neck every time he came to a hill. If he had a car, he could be his own man. If he had a car, he might get up the nerve to ask out that girl he'd seen in the courthouse Friday.

Lord, she was pretty. Big blue eyes and long, wild hair and a smile that could have stopped a clock. She'd *smiled* at him. He couldn't quite get over that. She'd looked him right in the eye and smiled at him, as though she didn't think he was some disgusting piece of southern trash. She had smiled and her little nose crinkled up and the freckles on her cheeks seemed to bounce. Trace still got that funny feathery feeling in his belly just thinking about it.

He wanted to see her again, but he didn't know her name so he couldn't call her. Not that he'd ever get up the gumption to do that anyway. It was hard enough to talk to a girl in person, when you could see their faces and kind of half know what they were thinking. As far as he could see, the phone was just an instrument of torture when it came to dealing with women. With his luck, he'd call her up and she would have found out who he was and what he was doing at the courthouse and she'd sit on the other end of the line, not saying anything while she doodled ugly faces and words of rejection on a little pink notepad. No, he'd need to see her in person to talk to her. And it sure would help to have a car to impress her with.

He shifted down for a long hill and stood on the ped-

als, the bike swaying side to side beneath him as he pow-
ered it up. The muscles in his shoulders and thighs
bunched with the effort. Sweat rolled from his forehead
and made his white T-shirt stick to his back.

He would have had a car by now if they had stayed in
Atlanta and his mother had stayed married to Brock.
And it wouldn't have been some crummy old rusted-out
Impala with a coat hanger for a radio antenna like Carney Fox drove either. It would have been something sleek
and sporty, a Miata, maybe, or one of those new Vipers.
Black and shiny as a record album with a Blaupunkt
sound system and a Fuzzbuster. Brock would have had it
ordered for him—not because Brock gave a shit about
what Trace wanted, but because it would have been a
matter of pride to him that "his son" have nice wheels.

But they weren't in Atlanta and his mom wasn't married to Brock anymore. Trace had asked her once about
getting another car, and she'd told him they could barely
afford the one she drove, let alone one for him and the
insurance to go with it. He hadn't asked again. She didn't
think it was any fun being poor either, and it wasn't her
fault old Buttwipe had dumped her. Trace knew the
whole story there—who had done what to whom—and
he sure knew who had gotten the shit end of the stick.

He was just going to have to fend for himself, that was
all. It wasn't as though he was some little kid who
needed his mother to wipe his nose for him. He was a
man. Men fended for themselves, stood up for themselves and their friends, did what had to be done. He
would get himself a job and buy himself a car.

Carney had told him the quickest way to make a buck
was dealing dope. He claimed he had a pipeline from
Austin through some biker down in Loring and he could
get Trace a little if he wanted to sell—just 'cause they
were friends. But Trace told him no. His mother was
already afraid he'd started using again. She'd peel the
hide off him if he got caught dealing, to say nothing of
what the sheriff would do to him. Besides, he didn't see
Carney driving no Viper with a Blaupunkt stereo in it.

Nobody was going to get rich selling dope in a stupid little Amish town like Still Creek. Anyway, he was all through with that stuff. It hadn't been worth the trouble it got him.

He crested the hill and coasted down, sitting back with his arms dangling at his sides, letting the racing bike fly. Still Creek came into view, looking practically like something out of the last century, with its old brick and stone buildings. The grain elevator rose up on the edge of town, all rusted corrugated metal, stark and ugly, with Amish buggies tied up at the hitching rail, as small as toys beside the towering buildings. Trace bypassed Main Street and stuck to the highway as it curved west to skirt the edge of town.

He hadn't had any luck finding a job yet. Jarvis had turned him down at Still Waters, and Arnie at the Red Rooster said he couldn't hire anybody who wasn't old enough to drink. The manager at the Piggly Wiggly claimed they had enough bag boys, though Trace knew for a fact he'd hired on two new guys since then. His options were narrowing down in a hurry. One of the many drawbacks of living in this jerkwater town was that there wasn't a whole lot to pick from jobwise. But he'd heard just last night about a new opening, and he meant to get it.

He turned in at the Texaco station, propped his bike against the side of the building, and ducked into the bathroom to check himself for presentability. He had showered at home and he took a quick sniff of his left armpit to see if any of the Ban roll-on had survived the trek into town. He smelled a little bit, but there wasn't much he could do about it now. Even if he stripped off his shirt and washed up in the tiny sink, he would still have to put the same sweaty shirt back on. Didn't seem worth the effort, but then he reminded himself that a man needed to put his best foot forward in a situation like this.

The faucet wouldn't run hot water. Trace gave up on it after a minute and soaked paper towels in the grungy little sink. Cold would probably help him stop sweating anyway. He took off his glasses and laid them carefully on the little ledge beneath the cheap wall mirror, then proceeded to give himself a sponging off. When he finished, he put his shirt back on and tucked it neatly into the waist of his jeans. He fished his comb out of his hip pocket and gave his hair a going-over. Hair was important to employers. They didn't want to see it long or greasy or like it hadn't been combed in two years. Finally he cleaned his glasses and settled them back in place.

He reckoned he looked as good as he was going to under the circumstances. He probably looked as good as anyone who had done odd jobs at Shafer Motors. He sure looked better than the guy he'd seen last night in the Rooster parking lot, who had quit to go to work at a big hog outfit down on the Iowa border. That guy had definitely looked more suited to hogs than cars. Trace figured he could present himself about a hundred times better, and he *really* wanted this job. To buy himself a car. That would have to count for something with a car dealer.

Working up his confidence, he stepped outside into the warm afternoon sun, climbed back on his bike, and headed down the road toward Shafer's.

AS HE CLEANED AND PACKED HIS TOOLS, AARON LIStened to Elizabeth's tale about the vandalism of the *Clarion* office and her encounter with Garth Shafer. He had fixed the barn door as his last job of the day, and they stood beside the weathered old building, Aaron intent on his task, his face its usual grim mask. Elizabeth leaned back against the building and watched him idly as she spoke. She wouldn't have thought of the Amish as obsessive-compulsive, but that described Aaron to a T. A place for everything and everything in its place. His tools were immaculate and arranged meticulously according to their purpose—screwdrivers, pliers, planes, carving tools. He was as bad as Dane with his pens.

She took a deep drag on her cigarette and exhaled a

stream of exhaust. She didn't want to think about Dane Jantzen just now. Mere mention of him brought all her nerve endings to aching awareness and stirred old fears she would sooner have left dormant. All she wanted now was a little time to wind down. She dropped the cigarette butt in the long grass and crushed it with the toe of her boot.

"I tell you, Aaron, for a state where everyone is supposed to be so calm and stoic, I've sure run into my share of nut cases."

He hummed a note of disapproval as he cleaned his hands on a rag he carried for the purpose. "Better to leave things alone, I say." He gave her a stern look over the rims of his spectacles. "You only are going to get yourself hurt. This will nothing change."

"I want to find the truth. Doesn't it say in the Bible— the truth will set you free?"

"The truth of God and Christ, not the truth of Still Creek. I'm thinking all that will get you is trouble." He picked his carpenter's box off the bed of the old hay wagon he had been using as a workbench. "Now I go. Services are tomorrow. There is much that yet needs doing at home."

A smile pulled at Elizabeth's mouth. She found it kind of sweet the way he translated his thoughts from German to English, not always getting the words in the right order. It made him sound naïve. But he was a man who had lost his family, she reminded herself, thinking of the markers down by the creek. She didn't know if experiences like that could leave a man with much naïveté.

"Monday I put your locks on the house doors," he said, walking toward his buggy.

Elizabeth fell into step beside him, her fingers tucked into the pockets of her jeans. "Thanks, I'll sleep better."

He gave her one of his wry looks as he stowed his gear in the buggy. "Locks don't help nothing if you go out looking for trouble."

"I'll bear that in mind."

He sniffed in disbelief and disgust. She imagined he

didn't know quite what to make of such a willful crea-ture as herself. Amish women were probably much more subtle in how they went about getting their own way.

He muttered something in German, shaking his head, and put his foot on the buggy's step. On impulse, Eliza-beth reached out and stopped him with a hand on his arm. He looked down at her, eyes round with astonish-ment.

"Aaron," she started to say, feeling awkward, not knowing what his customs allowed. "Thanks for caring. It's sweet, really." She raised up on her tiptoes and brushed a quick kiss on his cheek above his beard. "You're a good friend."

She stepped back from him, shrugging a little as she tucked her fingers back into her pockets. He stared at her for a few moments, his face betraying nothing of what he was feeling. Then he turned without a word and hauled himself into his buggy. She watched him drive away, lis-tened to the sounds of his departure—the clomp of hooves, the jangle of harness—and thought they blended in with the natural sounds of the birds and the breeze in the trees. Harmonious, peaceful. Nothing like the roar of Buddy Broan's 4x4 as he came tearing past on his way home from town, kicking up clouds of gravel dust that puffed up high and rolled after him as the wind pushed them east.

It might be kind of nice being Amish, Elizabeth thought. Except for not having indoor plumbing. That was more of a sacrifice than she cared to make for any god. She turned and walked back along the side of the barn, toward the woods, wondering what the odds were of Aaron going English for her. She liked talking to him. Unlike most of the men she'd known, he actually lis-tened—or seemed to. Of course, he probably didn't agree with anything she said. He looked at her sideways most of the time, as if he weren't quite sure she wouldn't bite him if she got the chance.

No, they'd be a disaster together, she thought, bend-ing to pluck a dandelion. That he was any kind of a friend at all was probably a miracle. She wasn't attracted to him anyway, even if he did favor Nick Nolte. She shook her head as she walked along the edge of the woods. Dane was the man she was attracted to—strongly and against her will.

What kind of sense did that make for a liberated woman? None. She had to draw the conclusion that her hormones were hopelessly *un*liberated. Good thing she was too smart to leave them in charge all the time.

She stopped and drew a long breath. The air here, at the edge of the woods, was clean and rich. She could pick out the scent of the damp earth, the trees, the subtle perfume of the wildflowers, and she thought about growing up in West Texas, where the spicy smell of sage and dust had overpowered everything else.

People associated certain smells with home, but Elizabeth didn't feel as if she'd ever had a home, not in the truest sense of the word. She'd grown up in Texas, but "home" had been wherever J.C. hung his hat. There had been no sense of security or comfort. She had tagged after him, wondering half the time if he would miss her if she weren't around. More than once she had thought about running away, but had never carried through on it because of the genuine fear that he wouldn't bother to come after her.

During her marriage to Bobby Lee, she had felt isolated, not by physical bounds but by her youth and motherhood and by the shame of her husband's innumerable infidelities. The house they had shared had never given a sense of home, partly because of its sad state and partly because Bobby Lee had had no compunction about bringing his girlfriends there. It had been more like a nightmare version of a home—close to what she had always longed for, but hopelessly, cruelly twisted. Grim and empty when Bobby was gone to a rodeo, leaving her alone with a baby and no real friends. Full of despair and shattered dreams when he was there, reminding her with every look, every snide remark, that he resented her for tying him down.

For a long time after the marriage had broken up she had abandoned the idea of a real home. She had concentrated all her energy into school and work, promising herself that she would get something better for herself and Trace as a result. San Antonio had offered them that bright, pretty dream again for a time—a promise of peace and home and love—but that had been snatched away from her too, and she and Trace had moved on.

In Atlanta she had never fit in with Brock's snooty crowd, and Brock hadn't allowed her her own set of acquaintances. He had kept her cocooned in his wealth, isolated by prestige and notoriety, never caring that the Atlanta aristocracy wouldn't accept her as one of them. Cinderella in her glass slippers had also felt enclosed by glass walls, invisible barriers. Never quite accepted, but too rich to be spurned—until the divorce.

She had hoped things would be different here, that she and Trace could settle in and make a place for themselves. Disappointment ached through her as she looked across the yard, bright with dandelions, to the sorry old farmhouse. This was supposed to be home, but they weren't welcome in Still Creek and they weren't wanted. Too bad, she thought, because she was too damned stubborn and too damned tired to move on. She would make this her home or die trying.

FOURTEEN

JOLYNN SAT AT HER TINY KITCHEN TABLE IN HER tiny white kitchen, ostensibly going over her notes for the Jarvis case. But her mind was going over the supper she had shared with Bret Yeager. She had run into him in the church basement after the funeral. He was standing in a corner, hunched over a plate of coconut cream pie, the end of his tie lapping up cream filling like a long, synthetic tongue as his eyes scanned the crowd. Not having any desire to mingle with the Jarvis entourage, Jo had struck up a conversation with him about a paper she had read on the requirements for forensic cases. The next thing she'd known, they were sitting across from each other in a booth at the Coffee Cup, sharing French fries and talking shop.

He was a sweet guy. She liked his square, honest face, his rumpled shirts and goofy dog. He seemed amazed that she not only didn't mind talking about things like latent fingerprints and DNA identification, she actually knew something about them. She had impressed him. The idea had pride and pleasure rising like a giddy tide inside her.

The back door swung open and she looked up, half expecting to see him standing there. But the smile died on her face as Rich walked in.

"Not tonight," she groaned, tunneling her fingers

back through her thick hair as the good feelings inside her deflated like a burst balloon. "I have a headache."

He didn't comment on her sarcasm, nor did he pull up a chair. He leaned back against the counter and folded his arms across his chest. Maximizing his height advantage, Jo thought. There were few things Rich liked better than being able to look down on people. He was still dressed in his funeral garb, though he had shed the jacket and loosened his tie. The starch had gone out of his white shirt, taking most of his "young congressman" image with it. It clung limply to his brawny shoulders, making him appear more like overdressed mob muscle. He had rolled the sleeves up to his elbows, revealing forearms that were tan from weekends ramming his power boat up and down the Mississippi and liberally dusted with rusty gold hair.

"I would have thought you'd be consoling your poor grieving wife tonight," Jolynn said dryly.

Rich took a pack of Pall Malls from his shirt pocket and shook one out. "She's busy consoling her poor grieving mother. I've had about all the grieving I can stand for one day myself." He lit up, wreathing his head in smoke, and tossed the match into the sink. "Jesus, I can't believe the show Helen put on at the funeral."

Jolynn shook her head and shoved her empty ice cream dish across the table at him in lieu of an ashtray. "You're the soul of sympathy, Rich. What an advocate for the common folk you'll make."

"It's just so much bullshit," he said derisively. "Nobody feels bad that Jarrold's dead."

"I wouldn't make that comment in front of the wrong people if I were you." She gave the ice cream dish another nudge. "You know, technically, you have to be considered a suspect."

He laughed and choked on a lungful of smoke. "By who?" he asked hoarsely. He picked a fleck of tobacco off his tongue and flicked it away. "*Miz* Stuart, Bitch Queen of the South?"

"Among others." Yeager had asked her a question or

two about good ol' Rich. Whether his interest was genuine or just a cop's way of making conversation, she
wasn't sure. She wanted to suspect the latter, not for
Rich's sake but for her own.

"Like who? You?"

"No. You were too comfortable leeching off him,"
Jolynn said bluntly. "Besides, I don't think you've got the
balls to kill anybody."

Rich's eyes narrowed and hardened. He pointed at her
with the filter end of his cigarette, raining ash down on
the dingy linoleum. "You know, I think you're spending
too much time with that boss of yours. Your mouth is
worse than usual."

"Yeah, well, if you find me so intolerable, you know
where the door is," she snapped. "I didn't exactly invite
you in. And use the goddamn dish, will you? You're getting ashes all over the place. Christ, you're such a pig,"
she complained, stretching out her fingers to catch the
edge of the bowl.

Treating her to a wounded look, Rich grabbed it before she could fling it at him. "Jesus, you're cold tonight.
What are you, on the rag?"

He held the dish away from himself and made a great
show of tapping his cigarette as he leaned over the table
to snoop at her notes.

Jolynn swept the papers into a heap with her arm and
bent across them the way a schoolgirl guards her test
paper from the class cheat. Utter disgust squeezed her
face into a sour knot. "You know, I'm not sure when I
hate you more—when you're being your true obnoxious
self or when you're playing the obsequious, ass-kissing
politician. I am not 'on the rag,' as you so tactlessly put
it. Maybe I'm tired, Rich. Since you've never done a full
or honest day's work in your life, I'm sure the concept is
foreign to you, but I've been putting in some long
hours."

"For what?" he sneered.

"For the truth. For an ideal." She ground her teeth
and clamped her hands on top of her head as if to keep

her brain from exploding. "God, I might as well be speaking French."

He shuffled up to her chair and traced a finger down the side of her throat, his gaze capturing hers. A cocky smile tipped up one corner of his mustache. "You can speak French to me if you want," he said, his voice rumbling low as heat rose in his eyes. "In bed."

His hand trailed down to massage her shoulder, and Jo shrugged him off. Three days ago she had gone to bed with him without a word. Tonight the idea of letting him touch her made her angry. Maybe it had something to do with watching him play the dutiful husband all afternoon. Or maybe Elizabeth had gotten to her with one of her little speeches about independence. Or maybe it was the novel idea that she could have a nice time with a man without having him use her. Whatever the reason, she was in no mood for Rich's antics. She scraped her chair back from the table and went into the living room to put a record on the stereo. With a flick of a switch blues drifted out of the speakers like smoke.

The living room was no better than any other room in the little house. Cramped and cluttered, it was in need of paint and more imagination than Jolynn cared to devote to the task of decorating. A single lamp cast a dim, dusky glow around the room as night tried to creep in through a gap in the drapes. The couch and chairs were the same brown tweed set she had shared with Rich once upon a time, but the upholstery had gone nubby and the cushions were shot. The shelves that held television, stereo, and haphazard piles of books were standard lumber-yard issue she had never gotten around to staining. The one spot of life and color in the room was a silk screen print by a New Mexico artist, a cactus flowering in the desert. It hung above a table that held an array of dead and dying potted plants.

Rich propped himself in the doorway between the two rooms and watched her as she stood with her head down, pretending to read the album notes. She could feel his gaze on her, cool and speculative.

"So why don't you believe Fox killed Jarrold?" he asked casually.

She shot him a glance askance. "I didn't say I didn't believe it."

"Your boss has some cock-and-bull idea about some book of Jarrold's."

Jo shrugged. "If he kept names in it, it stands to reason someone might not have been happy about it. Maybe he was blackmailing someone. He certainly had leverage over a few people who owed him money. What's so fantastic about the idea that one of them wasted him?"

"It's stupid, that's all," he scoffed. "Have you found this famous book?"

She answered him with another shrug.

He rolled his eyes and waved off her theory. "Fox killed him. He's a piece of shit."

"So are you, but that doesn't make you a murderer."

He sauntered across the room with his hands in the pockets of his charcoal trousers. He looked relaxed, but Jo caught the predatory gleam in his eye. She sidled away as he lifted a hand to touch her hair.

"I mean it, Rich. I'm not in the mood."

"Come on, Jolynn," he cajoled, backing her toward the couch. "You're always in the mood."

"Not tonight."

She started to make a break around a coffee table that was heaped with magazines and dust. He cut her off, catching her by one wrist and pulling her up against him. Her shin hit the table, sending a month's worth of *Newsweek* sliding to the floor. Her breath caught in her throat and she looked up at him, not quite certain whether she should let anger or fear take control. Rich stared down at her, heat in his eyes and a hint of cruelty curling the corners of his mouth.

"We both know I can make you want it, Jolynn," he threatened softly.

She started to deny the charge, but the words wouldn't come because they weren't the truth. The truth was, he *could*. He had. Time and again. And she'd let him. She let him use her. She let him degrade her. That was the truth. It churned in her belly, sour and acidic. It was old news, but for some reason it struck her anew as they stood there in her shabby living room with Colin James in the background asking the musical question— "Why'd You Lie?" It struck like a revelation, like a horrible epiphany, knocking down what self-esteem she had. What did she think she was doing, fantasizing about a nice guy like Bret Yeager when she was nothing but Rich Cannon's whore?

All the fight drained out of her, washed away by a tide of despair and inadequacy. She stood there like a zombie, numb, staring at Rich's power tie as he lowered his head and kissed the side of her neck. Jolynn shuddered. The response was shame, not desire, but Rich didn't seem to care.

"You always want it, Jolynn," he murmured, bringing up his free hand to open the top three buttons of her blouse. He pushed aside the cup of her bra and filled his hand with her breast, kneading it, squeezing it, rubbing his thumb across her nipple. "You're always hot for me. You always will be."

Tears rose in her eyes and spilled over to roll down her cheeks. He was right. She had always been hot for him. Always willing. She'd never given him reason to think things would ever change. She had told Elizabeth she enjoyed sex with him. She had told herself it was habit. Maybe it was more a matter of addiction. Or desperation. Either way, it was pathetic. *She* was pathetic.

"Come on, Jolynn," he whispered, his voice as darkly seductive and as smoky as the music that created the undercurrent for it. "You want it."

He didn't seem to notice she wasn't enjoying the proceedings. But then, he had never cared about anything but himself—his pleasure, his satisfaction, his comfort. She was just a convenient means of achieving those ends. His own private toy to use and discard when he was finished.

"Come on," he said. "Let's go to your room. I don't like doing it on your floor, you never vacuum."

"No," she said softly. Whether he didn't hear her or simply chose to ignore her, he took her by the wrist again and started toward the hall. Jo jerked back her hand and dug down inside for a scrap of courage. "I said no."

Rich's eyes narrowed and gleamed with feral light. His upper lip curled into a snarl. "Don't be such a bitch, Jolynn," he growled. "I've got a hardon."

"If you're limber enough, I have a suggestion as to what you can do with it," she said. "Go fuck yourself, Rich. That would have to be the ultimate treat for you."

Color slashed across his cheeks like war paint, and his nostrils flared as he took an aggressive step toward her. His hand snaked out and he caught her wrist in a bone-crunching grip. Jolynn bit her lip to keep from crying out. That she wasn't sure whether he would force her or not frightened her. She'd known him for years and she suddenly wasn't certain what he might be capable of if she made him angry enough.

"You want to have the title 'Rapist' precede your name as you step out onto the campaign trail?" she asked, warding off the pain in her wrist with sarcasm.

The look he gave her was utterly contemptuous. "Who'd believe you?" he sneered, looming over her, slowly twisting her arm.

She bit back a moan, glaring up at him through her tears. "What difference would it make if anyone believed me or not? This is Minnesota. The slightest breath of scandal and you're political road kill."

He swore viciously as he thrust her away from him. She stumbled back against the coffee table, toppling another mountain of magazines. Pulling her injured wrist against her, she rubbed it absently as she watched Rich pace off his frustration.

"You wouldn't do that to me." He stated it as a fact. His eyes were cold and hard as he glared at her.

Jolynn laughed, incredulous. "Why not?"

"There's too much between us."

"Don't make me gag. The only thing that's been between us in the last five years is your penis."

"Jesus, Jolynn." Rich decided to play incredulous too.
The wounded lover. The friend betrayed. "This is my
career we're talking about! This is my *life* we're talking
about!"

She arched a brow in amazement. "And what am I—
an inanimate object? I have a life too, Rich."

He shook his head and laughed to himself. "You're
nobody, Jolynn," he said cruelly, both his gaze and his
words cutting her to the quick. "You and your bitch
queen boss and your stupid little piss-ant newspaper.
You're *nothing*." He tapped a fist to his chest. "I'm going
to be somebody, Jolynn. Don't even think of getting in
my way."

She watched him storm out the back, wincing as the
glass rattled in the door. Tears came for her aching wrist
and for the ache inside her. A jumble of emotions left
over from the confrontation knotted in her chest, and she
cried a little, at a loss as to what to do with them. She felt
alone and unsettled, as if the earth were shifting beneath
her and reality was altering around her.

She wasn't Rich Cannon's wife anymore. She wasn't
Rich Cannon's mistress anymore. She didn't want to
think that she had ever defined herself that way, but she
had. Now she stood in her living room, looking at what
was left of her now that she'd scraped away the layer of
dirt. She looked at her reflection in the glass of the cactus
print and saw herself. Wide-eyed and uncertain. Over-
weight and in need of a new hairdo. She felt raw and
weak . . . and clean. Clean, she marveled. Fresh. Ready
to start over. She smiled a little and shed a tear for herself, for happiness, for a new beginning.

The doorbell jolted her from her trance. She went to
answer it, trying to straighten her clothes and wipe her
tears away with her good hand. She had to look like hell,
but she didn't really give a damn. It wasn't likely to be
anyone but the paper boy coming to collect.

Yeager was standing on the doorstep in rumpled chinos and worn-out purple knit shirt, a strand of sandy hair sticking up in front like an antenna. Yeager and his dog, side by side. The dog cocked his head and gave her a quizzical look that confirmed Jolynn's worst fears about her appearance. Yeager's lazy smile faltered.

"Am I here at a bad time?" he asked softly, concern lighting his dark eyes.

Jolynn shook her head. "No," she said, a secretive smile blossoming on her rosebud mouth and in her heart. "The bad time is over."

"I brought that book over." He lifted a thick, hardbound tome as evidence. *"Arnaut's Science of Blood Spattering."*

Jolynn accepted the offering with a misty smile. She stroked her hand over the cover. "How sweet."

"And I brought cookies," he said, his grin making a comeback as he pulled a giant-size Ziploc bag from behind his back. "Double chocolate chunk with pecans. They're my personal favorite."

"Come on in," she said, stepping back from the door, hugging the book against her. "I think I even have a quart of milk that hasn't gone bad." She turned and headed for the kitchen, waving her good arm at the living room. "Sorry about the mess. I haven't felt like cleaning up for the last two or three years."

"Looks okay to me," he said innocently as he and his four-legged pal followed her into the house, tromping over magazines and past the display of dying plants.

Jolynn cast him a smile over her shoulder. "You're a man after my own heart, Agent Yeager."

Yeager's grin widened. "Yes, ma'am."

FIVE BLOCKS AWAY TROUBLE WAS BREWING IN THE parking lot of the Red Rooster. The building that housed the bar and pool hall, appropriately enough, looked like a chicken coop with a thyroid problem. It had, at one time, been used as a storage shed for the volunteer fire department, then a school bus shed, then a dance hall.

Over the years the building had been modified and up-
dated, never in any way that could have been considered
anything but half-assed. Workmanship and quality mate-
rials had been spared, and tackiness given free rein. The
place looked as though it would have gone over at the
first strong wind, but it had managed to remain standing
for nearly forty years.

The town council had finally shamed Arnie Myers into
painting it—barn red—and Mrs. Myers had contributed
a touch of Still Creek hominess by planting geraniums in
whiskey barrels by the doors. The result was politely
called "quaint" by tourists. Arnie didn't much care. He
had a deficiency of iron and civic pride that melded into a
general kind of apathy. As far as he saw it, it didn't
matter what the tourists thought; he catered to a more
local clientele.

One of the worst of that crowd loitered in the dark
parking lot near the side door. Smoke and noise wafted
out through the screen: the clack of cue balls hitting their
mark, cheers, groans, raucous laughter, glass hitting
glass. The jukebox blasted over it all—Garth Brooks
bragging about having friends in low places. Carney Fox
lit a cigarette and leaned back against his Impala, his
dark eyes gleaming bright as he looked up at Trace Stuart.

"Turned you down, huh?"

Trace laughed, but it was a sound of teenage affront,
not humor. "Shit. Turned me down? He damn near
threw me out with his bare hands."

Thinking of it still made him furious. Old Shafer had
lit into him with his teeth bared, yelling and screaming
that he wouldn't hire Trace for anything, that the Stuarts
weren't anything but trash and troublemakers and no
one wanted them in Still Creek. Well, Trace had news for
him. He didn't want to be in Still Creek either. He would
rather have spent his whole frigging life in Siberia than in
this stinking squarehead Norwegian town. Humiliation
burned inside him as Carney laughed. The rage that he

never seemed to know what to do with reared up and chomped at the bit to be set free.

He hated this place. Hated it, hated it, hated it.

"So, what are you gonna do about it?" Carney asked slyly. He took a drag on his cigarette. The red glow from the tip illuminated his sharp, bony face with eerie light.

Trace scowled at him. "Hell, what can I do? I can't hardly make him give me a job."

And dammit, he'd *wanted* that job. Wanted the money, the independence. Just the *idea* of having that job made him feel more like the man he wanted to be. That and the idea of the car he would have saved for. Now he was stuck with his stupid bike like some stupid little kid.

Carney sucked at the last of his smoke, pinching the filter tip with grubby fingers. He tossed the butt into Carol Myers's geraniums and spread his skinny arms expansively. "No, but you can make him sorry he didn't give it to you." He flashed his crooked teeth in the dim light and trouble hummed in the air around him. "Don't get mad, Trace, my man. Get even."

FIFTEEN

Elizabeth woke with a start, as if her body were aware of something her mind had yet to pick up on. She had fallen asleep on her lumpy beige sofa, curled up in her oldest pair of jeans and a sky-blue Gianni Versace silk shirt —another item she'd stolen from Brock. The lamp on the end table was turned on low, creating a puddle of amber light in the otherwise darkened house. Her three-by-five cards were scattered across the worn brown shag carpet like confetti, notes about the murder—motives, suspects, hunches.

She had sat there all evening, staring at the notes until her eyes refused to focus and her brain had long since given up trying to untangle the threads. She was no detective. Hell, she wasn't even really a reporter. How did she think she was going to solve this mess? How was she supposed to sort fact from fiction, gossip from grounds for murder?

Dismissing the questions, she sat perfectly still, listening until her ears rang from the silence. The Bonnie Raitt tape she had fallen asleep listening to had played itself out, the cassette player had turned itself off. There was nothing in the air, no sound from inside the house, no sound drifting in through the open windows, only a fresh, cool breeze.

She had waited in dread all evening for the phone to ring, but it hung, silent and mocking, on the kitchen wall. According the clock on the VCR it was twelve, twelve, twelve. According to the wind-up alarm clock sitting on the TV it was eleven twenty-five. She thought she might have heard Trace coming in, but there was no sound from the kitchen.

"Paranoid," she mumbled, rubbing her hands over her face.

She pushed herself to her feet and shuffled into the kitchen, trying to rouse her mind from the fog of hard sleep. A bright wedge of moon beamed silvery light down on the countryside and into the kitchen. Pretty night. Quiet night. She poured herself a glass of milk to combat the burn of anxiety and scotch in her stomach, sniffed at it to make sure it hadn't gone bad, and moved to the counter to look out the window.

Everything was still outside. She saw no sign of Trace coming home. There was no light on in the shed. There was no silhouette of him on the road. The idea that he was far away in more ways than just distance made her heart ache. She wanted to be up when he came in, wanted to just sit with him and talk, not fight, which was about all they had been doing recently. Fighting wasn't doing her any good. At this moment he was probably off somewhere with Carney Fox, telling him what a bitch his mother was.

It didn't do her any good to worry about it though. The worry would eat her alive and leave the problem to grow on unhindered. What she wanted to do was get into her car and go after him, track him down and bring him home, but she could well envision the kind of fight that would spark. The need to have him here and safe and free of the influence of people like Carney Fox warred mightily with the logic of letting him go.

He was sixteen. She had been barely a year older when she'd gotten pregnant with him. No one could have told her then that she didn't know everything she needed to know about the world. It might have made a difference if she had had a mother, but it hadn't made a difference to have J.C. The only time he'd taken any interest in her was when she was winning money on the rodeo circuit, barrel racing, or when he was drunk and mistook her for the ghost of the long-dead, long-lamented Victoria. She tried to take some comfort in the knowledge that she was a better parent than J.C. had been, but then, slugs probably made better parents than J. C. Sheldon.

It was hard, she thought, sipping at her milk, so hard for a woman to raise a boy on her own. What Trace needed at this point in his life was a role model, a male to bond with and look up to. She thought of Dane and laughed bitterly at her mind's ability to ferret out ways of justifying a relationship with him.

What she needed was something to occupy her mind until Trace showed up. Something to keep her calm and distracted. Then, when Trace came in, they would have that heart-to-heart and she would try her best to steer him in the right direction without pushing him into an even worse rebellion.

She needed to go over the inventory of damages to the paper office for the insurance company, but she had inadvertently left it in the Caddy out in the shed, and the idea of walking out there in the dead of night didn't appeal. In fact, she shivered at the thought of it.

Coward. The word poked at her, taunted her. Once Aaron got the locks on the doors, she would become a virtual prisoner in her own home, she thought, her mouth curling downward in disgust at her lack of nerve. She would just sit in here every night, petrified, afraid of every sound, afraid to hear the phone ring. What kind of life was that? What self-respecting girl from West Texas lived that way?

Stepping around the sawhorses and over the nomadic pile of shoes that had migrated to a spot near the refrigerator, Elizabeth made her way to the back door. The night was just as quiet from this vantage point. No suspicious sounds, no dark shapes lurking in the shadows of the old buildings. Dane had told her he was sending a car by every hour or so during the night just to keep a lookout. That reminder gave her enough courage to go out onto the back step.

All she had to do was walk across the yard to the lean-to shed at the end of the barn, dig the papers out of the mess she'd left in the car, walk back to the house. Not a tall order. Nothing complicated. Nothing she would hesitate to do in the light of day. Night always seemed more frightening, but the fact of the matter was Jarvis had been killed in broad daylight. He had probably felt perfectly safe—until the blade had sliced across his throat.

Turning that image off before it could rattle her, Elizabeth descended the steps and headed for the shed, picking her way barefoot across the weedy, thistle-strewn yard, glass of milk still clutched in her hand.

The shed was narrow and decrepit, not much wider than the Caddy, with a dirt floor, no windows, and mountains of junk around the sides of it, stuff left by previous Drewes usurpers—old crates of motor oil, rusty tin cans full of rustier nails, amputated car parts, bald tires. The only light was a feeble seventy-five-watt bulb up in the rafters that cast about as much illumination on the mess as a candle, but it was better than nothing. Elizabeth made her way along the wall, feeling for the switch, heart thumping in the base of her throat as something skittered along the floor among the retreads. She flipped the switch and turned toward the Cadillac.

Paper was strewn everywhere. She had dumped much of the mess from the *Clarion* office into the car, planning to sort through it Sunday and get some of the files back in order. Someone had already been sorting—or searching for something. The driver's side door stood ajar, papers spewing out of it in a trail of white onto the hard-packed dirt floor of the shed.

Elizabeth's breath froze in her lungs. The short hairs bristled on the back of her neck. The house suddenly seemed a long, long way away, and tears blurred her vision as she stared through the open door toward it. What good would it do her once she was inside? There were no locks. There were no neighbors near enough to hear screams.

But there was a big pistol in her purse on the kitchen table.

She started to move toward the door, feeling as if she were going in slow motion, when all hell broke loose behind her. Her brain absorbed the action in snatches, as if through the blinding flashes of a strobe light. A figure clad in black. Only the eyes and mouth visible. Eyes wild. Mouth open. It lunged from the dark corner near the hood of the Cadillac, looming up over her shoulder like a specter, one arm raised high.

A scream tore from Elizabeth's throat as the figure lunged at her, arm swinging down. She pitched forward, crying out again as something hard hit her a glancing blow to the shoulder and pain rained all the way down her left arm to her fingertips. The glass of milk dropped from her hand and shattered across the floor of the shed. Stars shooting across her vision, she stumbled, staggered dizzily, and went down to her knees on the hard, lumpy, glass-strewn floor. Glass bit into her right knee, but the pain was there and gone in a white-hot burst as adrenaline swept it away. Her legs felt like rubber and the world seemed to pitch and roll beneath her as unconsciousness beckoned. But from some corner of her mind came a loud, insistent shout—*Move or die! Move! Move! Move!*

She scrambled ahead, frantically, awkwardly, grasping at the side of the car for a handhold that might give her enough leverage to pull herself to her feet. A muffled curse sounded behind her as her assailant struggled with the car door that had become wedged open, caught against the wall of the narrow building. A second blow rang against the Caddy. The door slammed shut as Elizabeth got her feet under her and pushed herself up and forward.

Cold dread washed through her, along with the heat of panic. This was like a nightmare where you ran and ran but never gained any ground, and the harder you tried, the slower you moved. Time became weirdly elastic. Sound came and went through the jet-engine noise of her blood surging through her veins—silence, then deafening sound, snatches of her own mumbled words of panic, the grunt of her assailant as he moved behind her.

She grabbed blindly for a stack of junk to her right and jerked at it as she stumbled past, sending an avalanche of old Coke bottles tumbling into the path of her pursuer. There was a series of crashes and thumps, the rattle and smash of glass bottles, and another loud thump against the Caddy, but she didn't look back to see her attacker fall. Lungs burning, ears roaring, heart choking her as it lodged in her throat, she hurled herself away from the car, away from the building. She burst from the shed into the moonlit yard and ran, not thinking about anything—not pain, not death, not anything—except getting to the house and the gun that waited for her inside.

THE SCREAMS CUT THROUGH THE STILL OF THE WOODS like knives singing through the air. Dane's big gray gelding brought his head up and snorted, gathering his legs beneath him in a nervous dance. Dane rose in the stirrups and set his heels to the horse's flanks. The gray bolted forward, plunging through the woods on the narrow, overgrown trail with Dane leaning over the horse's neck, ducking limbs as the gelding weaved between trees. His mind was already on the other side of the woods, with Elizabeth, and his heart was in his throat.

Dammit, he should have stationed a deputy at her house, even if the only man available for the job tonight had been Ellstrom. She had gotten a call, her office had been ransacked. Christ, she'd damn near witnessed a murder. And he had left her alone. It didn't matter that he had already been on his way to keep his nightly vigil. He had left her alone for a few hours. Minutes was all it took to kill. Seconds.

What if he were seconds late?

Refusing to think about the possibility, Dane nudged

the gray again with his heels and was rewarded with an additional burst of speed that took them over a fallen log and brought them within sight of the Drewes place. They broke the clearing and raced across the yard toward the house. As Dane shifted his weight back and picked up the reins, the quarter horse went into a skidding, sliding stop, tucking his hind legs beneath him and skating across the lawn, front legs paddling.

Dane was out of the saddle and running for the house before the horse came to a full stop. Pain bit into his left knee like vise grips, but it registered only in a far corner of his mind. Reacting on instinct—a man's instinct, not a cop's —he bounded up the back steps, flung open the screen door, and hurled himself into the house without breaking stride.

If she was hurt, if she was dead—

"Elizabeth!" he shouted as he burst into the kitchen.

The room was dark. Shadows and the hulking shapes of appliances, a slice of moonlight, a figure standing near the table. He focused on the figure just as it wheeled and the moonlight flashed on the silver barrel of a gun.

In his playing days for the Raiders, Dane had been famous for diving catches. Laying out his body, stretching for the ball, his concentration on the catch instead of the pain that would follow. The move came as naturally to him now. He launched himself across the room, his concentration on the gun, hands stretching for it, fingers closing on the wrist of the gunman. The momentum of his body carried them both to the floor, and they bounced hard and skidded across the linoleum, cutting the legs out from under a sawhorse and sending a sheet of heavy plywood crashing to the floor. The gun went off with a deafening explosion, firing into the ceiling, and plaster rained down on them like hailstones.

Gritting his teeth against the pain in his ribs, Dane hauled his upper body up off the prone form beneath him. The weapon had fallen to the floor, and he swept it out of reach as he braced himself up on one hand and looked down.

"Elizabeth!"

She lay beneath him, face stark white with terror.

Anger, relief, belated fear, surged through Dane all at once. He was shaking inside as he started to get to his feet. Anger seemed the safest of the three emotions, the least complicated. He seized it with both hands and gave it free rein.

"Jesus Ever-Loving Christ!" he roared, sitting back on his haunches. "What the hell do you think you're doing—"

Elizabeth didn't wait to hear the rest. She struggled up onto her knees and hurled herself against him. She threw her arms around his neck, nearly knocking him on his butt, and buried her face against his chest.

Dane felt his tirade die inside his chest and something else blossom in its place. He wouldn't acknowledge the feeling, but he couldn't seem to keep himself from putting his arms around her. He couldn't seem to stop himself from holding her or stroking her hair or whispering soft words to her as his lips brushed against her temple. She clung to him, shaking so badly he was afraid she was ill.

"What happened?" he asked. He tipped her head back away from his shoulder and brushed wet hair out of her eyes. "What happened, honey?"

Elizabeth didn't seem to notice the endearment. She was still too shaken. She told him the story in fits and starts, as her breath allowed, ending with her frantic search through her purse for the gun.

Scowling, Dane picked up the Desert Eagle from the floor and ordered her to stay put while he searched outside for any sign of the intruder.

Whoever had been there was long gone. The only signs of life in the old outbuildings were vermin. In the shed where the Cadillac was parked, a possum had come out of hiding to inspect the mess around the car. It sat up on its haunches among the scattered files and stared at Dane with bright little eyes, then turned and shambled away into the mountainous stacks of junk at the front of the building.

If the uninvited guest had been Jarvis's killer, he'd just lost a plum chance to nail the bastard, Dane thought as he walked across the yard to catch his horse. Killer or no, the assailant had been looking for something. Jarvis's book? The idea brought an even grimmer look to Dane's face as he tied the gelding to the utility pole and loosened the girth on his saddle.

When he went back into the house, the kitchen light was on and Elizabeth was trying to clean up some of the mess. She looked swallowed up in a man's dress shirt that hung nearly to her knees. She picked up a stray sneaker and shook the crumbled plaster off it, fighting back tears. Dane took the tennis shoe and tossed it onto the pile by the refrigerator. He turned her by the shoulders and herded her to a chair at the table.

"There's nobody out there."

"There was!" Elizabeth cried. She started to bolt out of the chair, but Dane kept her seated with a hand on her shoulder.

"I believe you," he said. "But he's gone now. I'll call it in, but he could be anywhere by now. We'll dust the car for prints—"

"He was wearing gloves," she said flatly, leaning an elbow on the table and cradling her forehead in her hand.

Dane heaved a sigh. If he'd been a few minutes quicker . . . If he'd been a few minutes later . . . Anger in one of its more impotent and frustrating forms burned through him. He reined it back and went to the phone to make his call. When he finished talking to the dispatcher, he turned back toward Elizabeth. She was still sitting at the table, looking pale and frightened under the glare of the fluorescent light.

"Where did you get this gun?" he asked, pulling the Desert Eagle out of the waistband of his jeans and laying it on the table amid the junk she'd spilled from her handbag.

"Brock."

Dane arched a brow. This wasn't the kind of toy gun a millionaire gave to his lady to keep in her purse. This was no two-shot Derringer or .25-caliber pop gun. This was a cannon, a .357 Magnum automatic, ten inches long, and nearly five pounds, loaded. "He gave you this? As a present?"

"Not exactly," Elizabeth hedged, nibbling her lip. She sniffed and combed back a lock of plaster-powdered hair. "It *was* a present. Some Israeli commando leader gave it to Brock for his collection. *I* stole it."

"Stole—?" The word was choked off. Dane took a step back from the table, ran a hand over his hair, and rubbed his neck. That she had stolen this prize from Brock Stuart shouldn't have been amusing, but he liked the idea of the bastard's frustration over losing his toys.

"Then I suppose it's ridiculous to ask if you have a permit to own a handgun in the state of Minnesota," he said calmly.

Elizabeth sniffed again and wiped a hand across her nose. "I suppose."

"And it's too much to hope that you've had some kind of training in the use and handling of this weapon?"

"I know how to shoot a gun," she said petulantly, insulted.

"This isn't just a gun, Elizabeth," he said. "This is a fucking bazooka. You could shoot a hole in the side of an elephant big enough to drive a Mack truck through with this thing. I'm confiscating it."

"You can't!" Elizabeth cried, grabbing for the Desert Eagle as he picked it up and held it out of her reach.

"Watch me," he threatened softly. "I'm sheriff of this county. You're illegally in possession of a firearm. I could toss your pretty ass in jail if I wanted to."

"Oh, isn't that rich?" Elizabeth sassed, falling back in her chair. "Killers running around loose all over the damn place and you're after me for having one little stolen gun."

Dane's temper boiled up. "Jesus, you could have killed me!"

"Or saved my own life," she argued. "What if that hadn't been you coming in the door?"

"Yeah." He nodded. "What if it hadn't been me? What if it had been Trace? Where the hell is he anyway?"

"Out."

"Great."

Gun still dangling from his right hand, he did a slow turn around the kitchen as he blew out a long breath. This whole mess was smelling worse and worse. And right smack in the middle of the pile was Elizabeth. Elizabeth the near-witness, Elizabeth the stranger in town, Elizabeth the would-be investigative reporter. The only solid suspect they had had Elizabeth's son for an alibi.

Elizabeth watched him pace, growing more weary with every step he took. The aftershocks of what had happened were beginning to set in with a vengeance. Her shoulder ached abominably, the throbbing running all the way to her fingertips. She leaned over on the chair, holding her arm against her middle, wishing it would go numb again. For the first time she noticed the bloody tear in the knee of her jeans. She absently picked at the torn fabric. The cut hurt, but she was too tired to tend to it.

"Elizabeth?" Dane hitched his jeans and squatted down in front of her. He'd been talking for five minutes, lecturing her about the damn gun, and she hadn't heard a word.

"Hey." He reached a hand up and touched her cheeks. Her skin was cold, and what color had come back to her during their argument about the Desert Eagle was gone again. "Are you okay?"

"I hurt," she whispered. "I'm bleeding."

She sounded almost amazed, Dane thought. He thought she might be going into some kind of shock, but he hesitated to go to the phone and call for an ambulance. He wanted to take care of her himself. He didn't want anyone else coming near her. The feeling was strong and instinctive and Dane ignored its implications with the ease of a man accustomed to denying his own feelings.

Gently, he peeled the torn, sodden denim back from her knee and examined the wound under the glare of the kitchen light. There was a gash about an inch long just below the kneecap. It wasn't deep enough to need stitches, but it was bloody and dirty with bits of glass clinging in the sticky mess. It needed cleaning. Her hands and face were streaked with dirt and she was favoring her left shoulder more with every passing second, bending over her arm and rocking herself slowly.

"Come on, honey." He stood slowly, drawing her up with him by her good arm. "Let's get you cleaned up."

"I can do it myself," Elizabeth mumbled. It was a lie, but she felt as if she had to try to preserve at least one small kernel of her dignity.

"Yeah, well, you aren't going to."

"I don't need a nursemaid."

"No," Dane said, pressing a hand against the small of her back. "What you need is a keeper. Which way is the bathroom?"

The room was so small they barely fit in it together. Elizabeth suspected someone had taken the term "water closet" too much to heart when plumbing had been added to the house. The toilet had been wedged in between the wall and the shower stall with the sink directly across from it. Pepto-Bismol-pink paint, so bright it seemed to leap off the walls, added to the sense of being closed in.

"Welcome to my luxurious master bath," she said sarcastically as Dane frowned at the tin shower stall with its cheap plastic curtain and angelfish decals stuck on the side. "I'm fixin' to put in a Jacuzzi real soon."

"It's not exactly what you're used to, I guess," he mumbled.

She shrugged with her good shoulder and glanced away. "I've had more that were this bad or worse than I've had better, Cinderella was a princess for only a little while before the shoe came off, you know."

Before the prince yanked it off her, Dane amended. The thought made him angry. Angry that Brock Stuart had been such a bastard, angry that *he* had been a bastard, angry that he cared one way or the other. He would have preferred indifference.

"Let's get these jeans off," he muttered, reaching for the button at the waist.

Their fingers collided, then their gazes, and the room seemed suddenly even smaller than it was. Dane tried to back up a step, but bumped into the sink. Elizabeth tried to move, but hit the toilet. Dane conceded the round, lifting his hands away and letting her do the job.

He gritted his teeth and told himself there was nothing sexual about this as she popped the button and ran the zipper down. He was only taking care of her, showing a little compassion. But as the denim skimmed down her hips, revealing glimpses of a pair of French-cut coffee-brown lace panties, he was hard pressed not to think of how it had felt to be inside her. Then the ugly cut on her knee came into view, the sight of it zapping him with the cattle prod of guilt. She was hurt and he was getting horny. What a prince of a guy he was.

"Sit," he ordered gruffly.

Elizabeth lowered herself to the stool, demurely pulling the tails of her shirt around her to cover her panties. She felt shy with him. Odd, considering. But then, maybe shy wasn't the right word. Vulnerable. That was it. She didn't like it. After Brock she had vowed not to be vulnerable to a man again. Love hurt, especially when the one you loved felt something less. She didn't want to go through that again.

Not that she was falling in love with Dane Jantzen, she rushed to assure herself. It wasn't that at all.

He cleaned the wound carefully, his big hands as gentle as any mother's as he eased away the dirt and blood and bits of glass. The thought made Elizabeth wonder what kind of father he'd been before Mrs. Jantzen had given him the boot. She wondered if he missed that role. Most of the men she had known wouldn't. J.C., Bobby

Lee, Brock—none of them had ever wanted to be a father except in name only. Somehow, she got the feeling Dane would be different. Maybe it was the fact that the only personal item in his office was that picture of his daughter holding up her sign—I LOVE YOU, DADDY.

His daughter, who was probably at home waiting for him.

"What are you doing here?" Until now it hadn't occurred to her to ask. She'd been too grateful to have him here. He looked up at her, a mixture of surprise and concern in his eyes. She rephrased the question. "Why are you here? How did you get here?"

A hint of a blush rose across his cheeks. He cleared his throat and dropped his head, giving undue attention to the Band-Aid he was fumbling with. "I was riding," he mumbled.

"Riding? At this hour?"

Dane ground his teeth a little and pressed the Band-Aid into place, drawing a wince from Elizabeth. He didn't want to admit he had planned to watch over her from the cover of the woods. Didn't want to admit he had already spent two nights doing just that. He didn't want to think about the fact that he'd been late getting there tonight. Almost too late.

"It helps me unwind," he said. That was one version of the truth. He enjoyed being in the saddle. It was a reasonable explanation, and not as revealing as another version of the truth might have been—that he wanted to be near her, that he wanted to protect her, that he still felt like a cad for what had happened the night before.

"Shouldn't you be home with your daughter?"

He frowned at the reminder that Amy suddenly didn't want to spend any time with him. "She's spending the night with one of her cousins." He forced his gaze away from the shapely leg he'd been tending and stood up. "Come on. Let me take a look at that shoulder."

Elizabeth accepted his hand, letting him steady her as she got to her feet. They were too close again. The memory of last night's intimacy hung in the air around them.

Dane was remembering, too, as he undid the top few buttons of the man's shirt she wore. He was remembering that he hadn't taken the time to do this last night. Christ, what a jerk he'd been. He tried to swallow down the guilt and the surge of desire as he slipped the shirt down over her left shoulder. He deserved this torture.

"Does this hurt?" Carefully he ran a hand along the slope of her shoulder and with his other hand gently manipulated her arm. God, her skin was like silk, and the subtle scent of some expensive perfume drifted up from the curve of her neck to tease his nostrils. He wanted to lower his mouth to the spot where shoulder and neck met, and taste her.

Elizabeth winced a little. The shoulder hurt, but the pain was being overridden by other factors. "Yes," she murmured breathlessly.

"I don't think anything is broken," he said tightly. "Bruised. Do you want an X ray?"

"No," she whispered. A tremor went through her, not from pain but from the feel of his hand on her bare skin. "I just want to go to bed."

Dane bit back a groan. He wanted to take her to bed. But that wasn't going to happen.

He helped her up the stairs to the second floor, putting an arm around her and taking some of her weight against him. When they reached the upstairs hall, he stepped behind her and let her lead the way so she couldn't see how turned on he was.

Elizabeth stopped with her hand on the door of her bedroom and shot a look at Dane over her shoulder. "Don't you dare laugh at my bed," she warned, brows pulling low over her eyes.

"Why would I laugh at your bed?"

"Brock did." She pushed the door open and limped into the room, flipping on the lamp on the nightstand instead of the ceiling light. The room didn't look quite so shabby cast in soft shadows.

Dane stepped into the small, pink-walled room, amazed, but not at all tempted to laugh. He wouldn't have laughed on pain of death. The look she was giving him was too proud, too tender.

The bed dominated the room, barely leaving space for a mismatched dresser and nightstand. Elizabeth walked around it, turning back the eyelet comforter and fluffing ruffled pillows, her chin set at a defiant angle, daring him to comment on the ornate brass headboard and footboard.

"Brock called it my whorehouse bed," she said. "He thought it was vulgar, but I like it and I don't care what anyone else thinks, including you."

The very way she said it made it clear to Dane that she *did* care. She didn't want to be laughed at or teased or talked down to—as Brock Stuart had done. The bastard.

"I think it's beautiful," he said softly.

She shouldn't have thought him sweet. He was a hard man. She'd seen that aspect of him too often to believe anything else.

Her breath caught as he came up behind her and slid a hand beneath her hair to caress the back of her neck.

"I think you're beautiful," he said, stepping closer. He dipped his head and brushed his cheek against her hair. "I don't give a damn what Brock Stuart thinks about anything. It's becoming obvious the man is a fool."

She started to turn toward him, and he captured her mouth with his, kissing her softly, tenderly, trembling inside with the force of restrained passion. He wanted to lay her down across that enormous bed and kiss every inch of her, but he pulled himself back from her, hating the scant inch of space he put between them.

"You need to get some rest," he said, struggling to keep his breathing even. "I'll be downstairs if you need me."

She needed him now, Elizabeth thought. But it looked as if Dane had decided to take a stab at nobility. A part of her admired him for it. Another part cursed him for it. She wanted him to stay, but she couldn't ask him. There was Trace to consider; he would be coming home sooner or later. And there was her pride. She wouldn't beg a man to care no matter how badly she wanted it.

She slipped between the sheets, still wearing Brock's favorite Gianni Versace shirt, and pulled the covers over her legs as she propped her back against the mountain of frilly pillows. Dane started to turn toward the door.

"Dane?" The word had escaped her lips before she could bite it back. She scrambled for something more to say as he looked at her expectantly. "Thank you," she murmured. "For being here."

He nodded and started to turn again.

"Dane?" He arched a brow and waited as pride warred with need inside her. Pride won out. "Thanks for not laughing at my bed."

Dane held her gaze for a long while. Something more complicated than gratitude charged the air between them.

"Dane," she whispered. *Pride be damned.* "Stay."

He turned his back on the door and nobility as her need reached out across the room and touched him. She sat on the edge of the bed, her eyes locked on him as her fingers slowly slipped the rest of her buttons from their moorings. She let the shirt fall back off her shoulders.

"Please stay," she asked. "Just for a little while."

Dane reached out and traced her injured shoulder. "I don't want to hurt you."

She just shook her head, shook off his concern. The pain would come eventually. Not the pain he was thinking of, but something deeper. She had opened the door for it. All she could do now was hold it at bay by taking what he could offer her physically. She thought of Jolynn for a second, understanding for the first time what it was that allowed her to let Rich come back time and again.

Then she didn't think at all. She didn't try to analyze or chastise. She took Dane's hand and guided it to her breast.

Dane watched her eyes drift shut and her head fall back as he touched her. A better man might still have walked away, he told himself, but he wasn't better. He was just a man, a man with simple needs touching a woman whose need was consuming her. He didn't have it in him to walk away from that.

He stripped off his clothes, and the bed dipped as he settled his weight on the mattress. "We'll do things right this time," he whispered, leaning over her. He lowered his head and brushed his lips across hers. "I'll kiss you. Touch you." He cupped her breast in his hand and massaged the nipple with his thumb. "Taste you," he said, kissing her throat, his tongue dipping into the delicate hollow at the base to touch the pulse that fluttered there. "Taste you," he whispered again, sliding down in the bed.

He took her over the edge three times then followed her into oblivion. Release, sweet, hot release.

Elizabeth clung to him, stunned by the intensity of the moment, frightened by the glimpse of what was at the heart of this for her. She closed her eyes against it and buried her face in the curve of Dane's shoulder. Please God, she couldn't love him. It wouldn't work. It never did for her.

Now came the pain. She bit her lip and fought it with every scrap of strength she could scrape together.

"Are you all right?" Dane whispered. "Did I hurt you?"

She didn't trust her voice and shook her head instead.

Dane braced himself over her, leaning on one elbow as he brushed her hair back from her face. He thought of the countless times he had done this with Ann Markham, thought of the almost feral look of carnal satisfaction that gleamed in her eye and heightened the color across her cheeks. Elizabeth didn't look that way. She looked fragile and vulnerable, and Dane knew an almost overwhelming need to comfort and protect her. He leaned down and kissed her temple, and her arms tightened around him again, holding him against her and within her.

"It's all right," he whispered. Whether it was or not,

he wasn't sure himself, but he needed to offer her . . .
tenderness . . . something . . . "It's all right."

He gathered her gently in his arms and rolled onto his
side, content to hold her as her breathing slowed and
evened and she fell asleep, exhausted. Content. It was
something he never felt with Ann. This was usually the
time weakness stole over him and that hollow ache
carved out a hole in his chest. Now he looked down at
the woman cuddled against him, felt her soft breath
against his skin, and felt . . . content.

It rattled him. The independent male in him raised its
head and sniffed the air for danger. He didn't want ties.
He didn't want contentment. He wanted simple, honest,
non-obligatory sex with a woman who didn't need him
for anything other than to scratch a carnal itch. What he
had shared with Elizabeth had gone way beyond the need
to slake a purely physical thirst. Dangerous territory lay
on the near horizon, territory he had vowed to steer clear
of.

He eased away from the warm woman beside him and
turned onto his back. Staring up at the cracked ceiling,
he lay there for a long time, wondering what the hell he'd
gotten himself into, wondering why, when that woman
snuggled close to him and murmured in her sleep, he
didn't leave the bed, but slipped his arm around her and
held her, and felt . . . content.

BONNIE RAITT'S SMOKY, SOULFUL VOICE WHISPERED
through the stereo speakers into the dimly lit living
room. A song about tenuous relationships, transient love.
Too blue and too close to the truth for comfort. Dane
tuned it out and concentrated on the note cards that were
scattered on the floor around his stocking feet. He had
given up on the idea of sleep and sat on the couch,
brooding and sipping a glass of Elizabeth's stolen scotch.
Her ideas, hunches, impressions about the Jarvis murder
were spread out on the carpet like pieces of a puzzle she
couldn't make fit together.

He wasn't making it fit either, Dane reminded himself. He had the suspect he wanted, but no evidence to bind him to the crime. Of all the fingerprints in and on the Lincoln, Carney Fox's had not been among them. That didn't mean he didn't do it; it meant Dane didn't have shit to take to a judge for a warrant. And he had to wonder about that. Carney Fox was no rocket scientist. He was sly and slippery, but he wasn't smart enough not to screw up somewhere along the line.

Dane snarled to himself as the sliver of doubt worked its way under his skin. Elizabeth's allegations came back to him, echoing through his mind. He was lazy. He was trying to pin this murder on a stranger because it was easier and because he didn't want to look at the people he'd known all his life and see them as suspects.

His gaze followed her meandering trail of notes. *Helen Jarvis: Unbalanced. J. cheated on her. Inherits big. Garth Shafer: Creepy! Old grudge. Bitter. Violent temper. Rich Cannon: Jerk. Stood to gain, but has alibi—Jolynn. BLACK BOOK: KEY. Where the hell is it? Who's in it?*

His natural impulse was to dismiss each of her suspects with his personal knowledge of them. Helen had gotten too much mileage out of being Jarrold's wife. Garth's grudge was too old and Garth too deeply immersed in self-pity to do anything about it at this late date. Rich was too complacent, too comfortable with his position as Jarrold's pet.

But Elizabeth saw all of these people through very different eyes, the eyes of a stranger. She had no history with these people, no preconceived beliefs about their characters. Her impressions of them had been drawn instantly and under extreme conditions. Did that make her view of them accurate or exaggerated?

Dane rubbed his eyes and sighed. He wished he didn't have to find out. He wished he didn't have Elizabeth's accusations prodding at him. She was right. He didn't want to look beneath the surface of his town or its people. He wanted everything to go on as it always had.

You're lazy, that's what you are.

And she was ambitious. For the truth, for her paper. He looked around the shabby living room with its cracked plaster walls and sagging ceiling and had to think she was ambitious to get out of here. She had gone from squalor to splendor back to squalor. It wasn't hard to figure which she would prefer. She looked too damn good in French lace to settle for less.

The sound of the back door softly slapping shut instantly derailed Dane's train of thought and put him on alert. He flicked off the lamp and moved silently from the living room, through the dining room to the kitchen, walking on the balls of his feet, breath held fast in his lungs. Ever so gently he toed open the kitchen door and took a peek through the crack.

Trace Stuart was leaning into the refrigerator, reaching for the milk carton.

"Getting home a little late, aren't you?"

The milk carton slipped from Trace's hand and hit the linoleum with a splat, spewing milk in all directions. He wheeled and stared at the man in the doorway, his heart racing like an Indy car right at the base of his throat. The sheriff. Oh, shit. Oh, Christ. What was he supposed to do now?

"It's after two," Dane said evenly. "Where have you been, Trace?"

Trace gulped at the jagged rock of fear in his throat. He was a dead man. Jantzen knew something. Why else would he be here? He knew something; it was there in those spooky blue eyes of his. Trace could feel that gaze on him like a pair of lasers, boring right into his brain.

"Hanging out," he mumbled, rolling his shoulders uncomfortably. "Just hanging out, that's all."

"With who?"

"Some guys."

"Carney Fox?"

"Yeah. So? We weren't doing nothing. Just hanging out."

"So you said."

Dane eased away from the door and lazily crossed the room, watching with interest as a fine sheen of sweat beaded across the kid's forehead. The boy looked like a spooked colt, ready to bolt and run if he got the chance. He was hiding something. As Elizabeth had said, Trace was a failure as a liar. But Dane had nothing to question him on.

He plucked a wadded-up dishtowel off the counter and held it out. "You'd better clean up the mess."

"Yessir." Trace snatched the towel away and squatted down to sop up the milk that was puddling around his sneakers. He wanted to become invisible, maybe miniaturize himself and disappear among the cracks in the linoleum. He wanted to be anywhere but here with this man watching him like a hawk, asking him all kinds of questions in that voice that was just like Clint Eastwood in all the Dirty Harry movies.

Damn Carney. It was all his fault.

"Someone attacked your mother tonight, Trace."

Trace jerked his head up so fast his glasses almost fell off. "What? Shit! Is she okay?"

He abandoned the towel and shot up to his full height, ready to go to her. A different kind of adrenaline surged through him, the kind a man felt when his family was threatened. His mom was all the family he had—or all he counted anyway.

"She's a little shaken up," Dane said. "She's sleeping."

"Oh, man." Trace huffed a sigh and ran a hand over his short-cropped hair. He paced through the milk he'd spilled, tracking it all over the floor.

"Somebody was digging through some papers she left in her car. You wouldn't know anything about that, would you?"

"No." He shook his head, then cast a suspicious look sideways at the sheriff. "Why would I?"

Dane shrugged. He wanted to link Fox to this too, and the vandalism to the *Clarion* office, but he didn't have a motive. The vandalism could have been written off at face value, but now . . . Somebody had been looking

for something and, dammit, Elizabeth's black-book theory was the only thing that made sense.

"Are you saying you think *I* hurt my mom?" Trace
asked defensively, poking himself in the chest with a
forefinger. He raised his chin to a stubborn angle remi-
niscent of his mother and glared at Dane. " 'Cause I
wouldn't."

"Wouldn't you?" Dane asked quietly.

He crossed his arms and leaned a hip against the
counter, his gaze steady on Trace the whole time. He was
a good-looking kid, a boy on the brink of manhood, just
starting to fill in his gangly frame. It seemed like a century ago, but Dane remembered what that age was like.
Like walking down the crack of a sidewalk, teetering one
way, then the other, never quite sure which side you were
going to fall on—boyhood or manhood—and deep down
not sure which side you wanted to be on.

Trace had that look in his eye now, as though he
thought he should live up to being a man but a part of
him was afraid of what that would mean.

"You think it didn't hurt her to have you hauled in
and questioned the other day?" he asked.

Trace glanced away, his jaw tightening. He hadn't
asked to be hauled in and grilled. That was Carney's
fault too. Damn Carney. Some friend he was turning out
to be. Misery tightened into a knot at the back of his
throat and he tried to swallow it down so it could churn
in his stomach with its good pals, guilt and fear.

"She worries about you, Trace."

"She doesn't have to. I can take care of myself," he
mumbled, looking down at his shoes. He was standing in
milk. Wasn't that just the story of his life? Always stepping in something. Well, a man had to take care of his
own messes, he thought as he bent down and reached for
the towel. He reckoned he'd have to find some way to
deal with his.

"Stick around with Carney Fox long enough and

you'll be taking care of yourself in jail. Is that what you want?"

"No, sir."

Dane grabbed another towel off the counter and squatted down to help the boy wipe up the last of the milk. "You've got some choices to make here, Trace," he said quietly. "I hope you make the right ones. For your sake and for your mom's."

Trace pushed his glasses up on his nose and blinked at the hot moisture pressing against the backs of his eyes. "Yessir," he mumbled.

They rose together. Dane took the wet towels and tossed them into the sink. Trace stood with his head down, shoulders hunched, looking like a young pup who'd just gotten chewed out for chasing cars. Poor kid, Dane thought. He didn't have a friend in the world . . . or a father . . .

He reached out and clamped a hand on the boy's shoulder. "Why don't you go on up to bed? There's a softball game at Keillor Field tomorrow. I imagine they could use an extra slugger. But a man can't hit worth a damn if he doesn't get a few hours sleep."

Trace just nodded, too miserable to speak. He doubted anyone would want him on their team. He was that white trash southern kid who talked funny and hung out with Carney Fox. He could probably live here till he was a hundred and no one would want him on their crummy softball team.

He stuck his hands in his pockets and started for the door.

"Trace?"

Jantzen stood watching him, eyes as keen as a wolf's. Trace got the feeling not many people fooled him—or were fool enough to try. His heart sank a little farther into his stomach.

"Your mom says you're a good kid. Don't disappoint her. She's had enough to last her awhile."

"Yessir," Trace whispered. He turned away to slink upstairs like the dog he was, dismal and disconsolate. The way he saw it, if he ever grew up to be the kind of real man Dane Jantzen was, it was going to be a pure damn miracle.

SIXTEEN

THE STRAINS OF A CENTURIES-OLD HYMN ROSE into the rafters of the Hauer barn to mingle with the chirping of the sparrows and pigeons that looked down on the proceedings with bright, curious eyes. The song was "Dos Lob Lied," a song of praise, a song from the *Ausbund,* the Amish hymnal, a book of songs that dated back to the times of the Anabaptist martyrs of sixteenth-century Switzerland. The melody was sung in unison, with no accompaniment, and it bore no resemblance to the songs being sung at that same hour in Our Savior's Lutheran Church or any other church in Still Creek. The verses droned on, medieval in tone and tempo, testaments to faith and suffering in the name of Jesus Christ, sung in the old German dialect.

The floor of the hay loft had been swept clean. Rows of plain wooden benches lined the space. On the right sat the women, young and old, many holding babies on their laps, others holding hands with toddlers that were already squirming in their seats in anticipated boredom of the hours-long service that was to come. The women's dresses, dark blue, dark green, black, fell in graceful folds to their ankles. Over the dresses each wore a long, gauzy white apron that covered the chest and was belted at the waist. They wore no makeup, no jewelry, no elaborate hats. Their hairstyles were identical—parted in the middle, smoothed into coiled braids, and tucked beneath fine mesh prayer *kapps* that tied loosely beneath their chins.

The men occupied the benches on the left, with some of the young boys taking seats on the straw that had been swept to the side and back. Some of the teenage boys stood in the back near the walk-out door, handy to slip out to check on the horses that had been unhitched and tied in the stalls below or put in the dry lot beside the building. Broad-brimmed hats lined the floor beneath the benches. Like the women, the men were in nearly identical dress, only hair color and length of beard giving individuality. Some wore traditional black coats. Others had opted for a Sunday vest only, due to the warm June morning.

Aaron stood near the open door, ready in his role as host to assist any latecomers with their horses. It looked to him that most everyone had arrived. Cyrus Yoder was not in evidence, but Aaron did not expect him. The oldest of Milo Yoder's boys, Cyrus had broken the *Ordnung* in as many ways as he could. The elders had been in conference over it this last week, and it was expected that Cyrus would be expelled, the *Meidung* ordered. He would be shunned as all who left the fold were shunned.

Aaron's gaze fell on old Milo, who had tears streaming into his beard as he strained to sing the old hymn of faith. He could find no compassion in him for the old man. Those who were strong in the *Unserem Weg* raised children who were strong in the *Unserem Weg*. To Aaron's way of thinking, Cyrus deserved to be cast out and a close eye kept on Milo and the rest of his offspring for weakness of spirit.

Weakness of spirit.

Lead me not into temptation.

Guilt stabbed him like a knife in the chest as he thought of his own weakness. Elizabeth Stuart. He had thought of her in ways that were not Christian, but carnal. An English woman. She was a danger to him, to his faith. A test. A test from God. God had brought their lives together to try his strength and conviction.

And he was failing.

He would have to try harder, pray harder for guidance. If he was to be a true instrument of the Lord, then he would have to purge from himself this desire for a woman who was so foreign to all he believed in.

He clasped his hands before him and sang a little louder as the congregation segued into another hymn. ". . . and to God's will commend my life, a tool for thy Lord's justice . . ."

The bishop entered the barn then, followed by two preachers and the deacon. They made their way to the front of the congregation, shaking hands with those they passed along the way. Aaron stayed to the side, not feeling worthy of shaking hands with them this day. This would be his day for prayer and meditation. When the meeting was over and all had gone home, he would go down to the creek, down to his Siri, and remain there in meditation until God provided him with an answer to this turmoil of feelings inside him.

Amos Schrock, small and withered, his graying beard hanging from his chin like Spanish moss from a gnarled oak tree, stepped to the front of the gathering of the *Gemei* and began to preach in his warm, soft voice. "All those who thirst for righteousness shall see the Lord Jesus when he comes, not in the flesh but in the spirit."

He stood before no altar, no effigy of Christ. He wore no elaborate vestments and held only a well-used German Bible for a prop. No stained glass windows spilled color across the heads of those who had gathered to hear his words. Sunlight beamed a shaft of gold from the window in the peak of the loft, falling like a dusty spotlight from heaven on Amos and the chaff-flecked barn wall that served as a simple backdrop.

At the end of the first sermon, all but the most feeble knelt on the barn floor to pray. The straw rustled as the younger boys rolled over onto their bellies and bowed their heads. In the beat of silence that followed, a horse nickered and stamped below; above, a pigeon cooed.

Aaron bowed his head and squeezed his eyes shut. *Father in heaven—*

A sound like a hammer on wood cut through his thoughts, an insistent pounding from some distance that throbbed and reverberated inside his head like the pain of a toothache. He tried to begin his prayer anew, but the pounding only grew louder, then another hammer joined in, and another. The high-pitched whine of a power saw pierced the still Sunday morning air.

Aaron lifted his head and glanced out through the open barn door. Across the road, across from his parents' farm, where the faithful of their district had lined their black buggies along the drive and gathered in their makeshift church to observe the Sabbath, an array of automobiles and pickup trucks were parked. Even from this distance Aaron could see the men working on the resort, swarming over the construction site, a crew of a dozen or more.

The bishop began to read from the New Testament, raising his voice in an attempt to drown out the racket of the English world. The congregation got to their feet. Several heads turned in the direction of the door, faces set in grim scowls. Two of the older boys slipped outside past Aaron. He went after them and caught them gawking at the goings-on across the road.

"See to your chores," he snapped, fury simmering inside him.

The boys ducked their heads and scrambled down the hill and around the corner of the barn to check horses that doubtless needed no checking. Aaron scowled darkly as he stood with his hands on his hips and stared across the road.

They had no respect for nothing, these English. Not their fellow man, not God or the Sabbath. One of their own was not yet even cold in the ground and they worked at his business on a Sunday. It was heresy, a blatant sin, a slap in the face of all those who kept the commandments. *Six days thou shalt labor and do all thy work, but the seventh is the Sabbath of the Lord thy God; in it thou shalt not work.*

"Come inside now, Aaron," Samuel Hauer murmured.

Aaron jerked his head around. His father stood beside him, looking weary and old. Aaron towered over him—had since his teens—but his father had always seemed a pillar of strength to him, physically and spiritually. Samuel was seventy, and the fire within the old man had begun to dim, and the boundless energy that had charged his sturdy frame had been spent, left in the fields over years of hard labor. The righteousness that had once flamed in his blue eyes had softened to a kind of weary wisdom. He offered a gentle smile with it now as he rested his hand on Aaron's rigid forearm.

"Come inside and listen," he said.

Aaron turned back toward Still Waters. "Nothing but the pounding of hammers am I hearing. The godless pounding nails on Sunday."

"Judge not, Aaron," Samuel chastened gently. "They are not of our beliefs."

"They believe in nothing but themselves."

"And so they are for God to save and us to pray for."

Aaron couldn't help the bitterness that soured his tone. He didn't bother to try to hold it back. "They take away our own and yet you pray for them? They take my Siri—"

"God took Siri, Aaron," Samuel said, his blue eyes faded and sad. *"Es waar Gotters Wille."*

God's will. The Lord giveth and the Lord taketh away. Aaron let out a carefully measured breath. He knew too much about God's will. More than most here, he thought. It didn't make him any more tolerant.

He gave his father a hard look. "The *Meidung* is issued on Cyrus Yoder for going out among them."

Samuel shook his head. His bushy, steel-wool brows pulled together in consternation. "We cannot shun the English, Aaron. You know that. Only ours who break with the Church. You do now work yourself for the English. Are you a hypocrite?"

Aaron's jaw tightened at the reminder of Elizabeth. He wanted to tell his father that was different, that there was a higher purpose in it, that it was a test from God, but he kept his own council. He wanted to say that Elizabeth was different, that he felt a kinship with her, but in his heart he didn't feel that kinship was right and so he said nothing.

He stared across the field for a long moment, listening to the syncopated beat of the hammers as the bishop's voice rose and fell inside the barn. Out on the road a car slowed and pulled over, and a fat woman in a bright green dress got out and aimed a camera at him. At that moment he felt the world closing in on him, squeezing in on his way of life until he felt like a bug under glass, a specimen to be stared at and marveled over by people who understood nothing of his faith. His jaw tightened and he turned his back on the fat woman and her camera.

"You pray for them then, Pop," he said, walking away. "I cannot. *Ich kann net.*"

ELIZABETH WOKE ALONE. THE SUN WAS STREAMING IN the window. Birds were singing. She sat up in bed, blinking and confused, and wondered if the night had been a dream. Then she tried to stretch and pain bit into her shoulder and the fog cleared. Aside from her shoulder, she ached in places she'd forgotten could hurt. The scent of man and sex lingered among the tangled sheets. The attack in the shed had been real. Dane Jantzen in her bed had been real. What had passed between them had been . . . beyond words. She would have been blissful about that if she hadn't been so damned scared.

He was no man for her to fall in love with. He was ornery and mule-headed and cynical toward the fair sex in general and toward her in particular. That wasn't what she needed. But as she thought of the time they had spent together in this bed, she couldn't think of a single need he hadn't met. He had offered her more than his body. He had offered tenderness, comfort, his strength.

And now he was gone, and she thought of the one thing he hadn't offered—his heart.

"Just as well he's gone, sugar," she mumbled, combing a hand back through her tangled hair. "Before you get used to him."

She pulled on a robe, gathered some clothes together, and dragged herself downstairs to greet the day. Trace was sitting at the kitchen table as she shuffled in to start the coffeepot. Elizabeth jumped back with a yelp and a hand to her heart as her pulse bolted off like a Kentucky Derby hopeful.

"Oh, my Lord!" she gasped, backing into the counter. "Trace! Honey, you'd like to have given me a heart attack!"

Trace shot up from his chair, concern pulling his brows together above the rims of his Buddy Holly glasses. "Are you all right?" he demanded. "Sheriff Jantzen said somebody attacked you last night."

Elizabeth wrapped her aching left arm against her stomach and pressed her right hand to her lips as she nodded and tried to compose herself. She couldn't remember the last time Trace had expressed any interest in her well-being. He was at an age when self-absorption was a chronic state, one that had been magnified and intensified in Trace by other problems—his lack of a father, his lack of friends, the move to what was proving to be a hostile environment. But now, suddenly, he stood before her, looking very much the young man ready to avenge his family.

"I'll be fine," she murmured, dragging a long breath into her lungs. "Somebody was looking for something. I got in the way and got myself trampled is all. Scared me more than anything."

Trace swore softly and looked away, rubbing the fingers of his left hand through his short dark hair in a gesture he had inherited from Elizabeth. His stomach was churning, partly from the Mountain Dew he was drinking for breakfast, mostly from the stress of the past few days. He still hadn't quite gotten over the shock of coming home and finding the sheriff in his living room. He couldn't believe he hadn't dropped dead on the spot.

"We don't belong here," he said miserably.

Elizabeth reached out and took hold of his hand. For once he didn't pull back from her. His hand made hers look tiny by comparison. He really was getting to be a man, but when she looked up into his eyes there were still signs of the boy there—uncertainty, a need for reassurance, a need for comfort. The sad joke was, she was feeling all the same things and she was supposed to be the grown-up.

"People get attacked everywhere, Trace," she said. "Sad to say, but the world is a violent place."

"It's not just that," he insisted. "Nobody wants us here. We don't fit in. You said things would be better after we left Atlanta, but they're not. They're worse."

"Yeah." Elizabeth sighed, wishing she could refute his statement. She couldn't. "We're in some kind of mess right now, aren't we?"

Trace gave a hoarse, humorless laugh, looking up at the bullet hole in the ceiling. God, he wanted to cry. His mother didn't have any idea what kind of mess he was in. He didn't want to be around when she found out. He wanted to be about a million miles away. In the Brazilian rain forest or on the first manned mission to Mars. Anywhere but within shouting distance of Still Creek, Minnesota. As confused as he was about a lot of things, that was one thing he knew for sure—he wanted out of this place.

"You know, honey," his mother said softly, "I think we're finding out we can't just run away from trouble. There isn't any magic place where nobody has a past and everybody just loves everybody else. Not on this earth, there isn't. This is the spot we've ended up in. All we can do is dig in our heels and make a place for ourselves." She looked up at him, her pretty eyes so tired and sad,

Trace just about couldn't stand it. "I've spent my whole life not belonging anywhere, Trace," she said, her voice ragged with a pain that reached out and squeezed Trace's heart. "I'm tired of it. I'm tired of looking for a place that doesn't exist."

Trace had to choke back a lump in his throat that was about the size of a baseball. Shoot, what kind of a man was he? This move hadn't been easy for his mother. He knew what she had gone through in Atlanta with Butthead Brock and his dirty lies, and the trouble Trace had given her himself with the drugs and all. He knew the kind of mean, spiteful things people said about her around Still Creek, and he knew the long hours she was working trying to make something of the *Clarion*. Now someone had wrecked the office and attacked her. God knew she had problems of her own. She sure as hell didn't need him whining like some stupid snot-nosed little kid who couldn't tie his own shoes.

"I'm sorry, Mom," he whispered, blinking furiously at the moisture that was gathering in his eyes. A man didn't cry at a time like this. Especially not in front of his mother.

Elizabeth looked up at him, her heart aching for him. She couldn't think of a time when Trace hadn't tried to act more grown-up and self-reliant than he really was. She could still see him in her mind's eye, looking up at her, those big glasses perched on his little nose, telling her not to worry about him walking to kindergarten by himself. There was so much she wanted to say to him— that she loved him, that she was sorry, too, for the childhood he'd never really had. But the words all stuck in her throat.

They'd never been good at talking to each other. She could shoot her mouth off to everyone else in the world, but when it came to Trace, everything she felt went so much deeper, she just couldn't dig the words out. She slipped her arms around him instead, and gave him a hug, taking advantage as long as he was being tolerant of having her near him for a change.

When she pulled back, she drew in a big breath and tried to muster a motherly smile. "You look tired," she said, rubbing a thumb against the corner of his mouth, trying to erase the line of worry the way she had done when he'd been a toddler. "You were out late, I guess."

"Yeah."

"Doing what?"

He looked away. "Nothing."

That fast the emotional drawbridge went up before Elizabeth could do more than get a hold with her fingers. She heaved a sigh and let it go, telling herself she should be glad for the moment they'd had. It was more than he'd given her in months.

She went into the bathroom and drained the water heater in a futile attempt to steam away some of the aches in her body. When she finally emerged, Trace was gone. Dane sat in his place at the kitchen table, drinking a Coke and looking too damn tempting. He was in jeans and boots again, his long legs stretched out in front of him. The sleeves of his faded denim work shirt had been rolled neatly to the elbow.

"Taking the day off from crime busting?" she asked.

"No. I've got to meet Yeager in an hour."

His gaze caught hers as he rose lazily from the chair. She stood her ground as he stepped too close and slid his hand under her hair to rub his thumb against the nape of her neck, a gesture that seemed strangely, overwhelmingly possessive.

"Are you all right?" he asked quietly.

Stupid question, Elizabeth thought as she managed to nod. There wasn't anything all right about this. She was finding herself drawn to a man she shouldn't want, wanting things she couldn't have, while the whole world went crazy around her. What was right about any of that?

This, she thought as Dane bent his head and kissed her. The kiss wasn't long or deep, but there was a quality of intimacy about it that was almost shocking. She felt breathless and feverish when he stepped back.

Dane turned away and cleared his throat, reaching

with a hand that wasn't quite steady for the gun he'd left on the table.

"I thought you were gonna take that away from me," Elizabeth said at the sight of the Desert Eagle.

"I was," Dane grumbled. He shot her an irritable look. "Then I started thinking you might have stolen a whole arsenal and this one could be the least of the lot. I decided a lesson might be the better way to go."

"I can shoot a gun, sugar," Elizabeth informed him, propping a hand on one hip. "Where I grew up it was considered an essential life skill."

"Yeah, well, you've never shot this gun, have you?"

She cast a glance at the hole in the ceiling. "Not counting last night? No."

"I didn't think so. Come on."

They went out to the farmyard, where Dane had already set up a target. He had stacked some moldy bales of hay against the side of the tumbledown hog house. Tacked to the bales was a life-size black and white paper print of a snarling man pointing a shotgun at them.

"We're facing east for a reason," he said as he loaded the clip. "There isn't anything east of here but cow pasture for a mile. We don't want any stray bullets dropping some poor Amish kid over at the Hauer place."

Elizabeth looked off to the west, across the fields to the Amish farm. The yard was full of people, looking from this distance like a human patchwork quilt rippling across the grass, the distinctive colors of their costumes vibrant under the midday sun.

"What are they doing over there, throwing a party?"

"Sunday services. They feed their souls all morning and their stomachs all afternoon."

"Listening to preachers for that long would be more likely to ruin my appetite," Elizabeth said with a grimace. She could picture Aaron listening, though, maybe even preaching himself, those somber blue eyes looking out across a sea of devout faces as he spoke of faith and duty She turned back to Dane. "Can you tell me something?"

"Yeah, but knowing you, it won't do any good," he said mildly as he slid the clip into the Desert Eagle.

Elizabeth gave him a look. "Very funny. I'm being serious here. What happened to Aaron's family? He told me his wife was dead, but they had children too, didn't they?"

Dane frowned. "Yeah, they did. Two little girls, Ana and Gemma. They were killed in an accident about a year ago. Siri and the girls were driving home from visiting a neighbor woman who'd just had a baby. It was night. Aaron won't put a reflective sign on his buggy—even now—because it's not Plain. The driver didn't see them until it was too late."

He sighed and shook his head, wishing he could shake off the memory of that terrible night as easily. He could still hear the sickening cries of the buggy horse in its death throes and the shot he had fired himself to silence it. He could still see Aaron, inconsolable in his grief, keening from the depths of his soul as he tried to gather the limp, bloody bodies of his children in his arms.

"I'll never forget that night as long as I live," he said. "That was the most terrible thing that ever happened in this county—murder and mayhem included."

Elizabeth said nothing. She stared across the fields again, watching the Amish as they went about their Sunday ritual. It looked like a scene from the last century—the buggies in the drive, horses tied to every fence post; the women in their fine caps, the summer breeze tugging at the hems of their long dresses as they moved around the tables serving the men and children. They wanted to be separate, to be left alone to their ways. In spite of what had happened in his own life, Aaron still drew definite lines between the worlds of English and Amish. But the lines couldn't remain uncrossed. Their worlds collided on a daily basis.

"Are you ready?"

Dane's voice drew her back from her musings. She turned away from thoughts of the pacifist, isolationist Amish as Dane handed her the gun. He clamped a pair of earphones on her head, effectively blocking out all sound. After putting on his own protective headgear, he took a stance behind her and set her up for the shot—nudging her feet apart, squaring her shoulders, arranging her hands on the grip, raising her arms into position. When he was satisfied, he took a half step back.

Elizabeth glanced at him over her shoulder. He nodded. She gave a little shrug and turned toward the target. She didn't see what the big deal was. She'd done this before. If Dane was expecting her to make a fool of herself, like some simpy little Minnesota gal who didn't know what a gun was, he was in for a letdown.

Feeling smug, she squeezed her left eye shut, took aim at her two-dimensional assailant, and fired.

The gun bucked hard in her hands, jerking her arms up. The force of the explosion literally knocked her off her feet, the recoil sending her stumbling backward into Dane. He caught her and wrapped his arms around her, his big hands closing gently over her white knuckles on the handle of the Desert Eagle.

Elizabeth looked up at him, stunned speechless, eyes wide, mouth hanging open. She had wielded shotguns that didn't pack half the punch. The thing had nearly jumped right out of her hands.

"Jesus Christ in a miniskirt," she mumbled as Dane tugged her headphones down to rest like a collar around her neck.

"Now you know why I don't want you pointing that thing around," Dane said. He peeled her fingers away from the grip of the Desert Eagle. Elizabeth leaned into him, her knees still wobbling. "This is too much gun for you, Dirty Harriett," he said dryly. "Look how the cartridge jammed instead of ejecting clean. If you're not strong enough to hold the gun steady as it fires, this happens." Arms wrapped around her, he manually ejected the spent cartridge. "The gun can't chamber another round until the spent cartridge is out. If this had been a real firefight, you'd be a done bunny by now. You should have stolen something more your own size."

"Sugar," Elizabeth drawled, stroking a finger over the barrel of the gun as she sent him a sultry look, "when you're stealing a man's phallic symbols, you've got to go for the biggest ones, else what's the point?"

Dane narrowed his eyes. "Put your ears back on, Ms. Freud."

After she complied, Dane raised the gun, his arms still wrapped around her, and fired a rapid succession of shots. The acrid scent of gunpowder drifted away on a thin cloud of smoke. The paper gunman's chest was gone, ripped away to expose his hay innards.

Elizabeth shivered at the thought of what those bullets would have done to a real man—what they might have done to Dane the night before if he hadn't knocked her over.

As he reached up with one hand and tugged his headphones down, Elizabeth yanked hers off and tossed them in the grass. "I could have killed you!"

He tipped his head to one side and gave her a sardonic smile. "You had your chance and you blew it."

"Oh, shut up!" she snapped. "I don't know why I should even care. You're mean as cat meat and twice as tough."

And I love you.

It made about as much sense as a snowstorm in July, but it was the terrible truth. Her fatal attraction to men who were hopelessly wrong for her had struck again— with a vengeance and in record time.

"I swore off men," she mumbled.

She sounded so disappointed in herself, Dane had to bite back a chuckle. The gun was too handy. If he made her mad enough, she just might rethink doing away with him.

"It's simple, sweetheart," he murmured as desire stirred inside him. "Chemistry . . . magnetism . . . animal attraction . . . sex . . ."

His beeper went off, shrieking like some kind of moralistic sex alarm.

"If I ever get my hands on the man who invented these things . . ." he snarled, pulling away.

"Give him a kick for me too," Elizabeth grumbled as she watched him walk away to the Bronco. She sat on the ground, and amused herself by unloading the clip from the Desert Eagle while Dane called the station on the radio.

"I have to go," he said a moment later as he stood looking down at her with a grim face. "Somebody trashed Shafer Motors last night. Shafer's saying Trace did it."

SEVENTEEN

TRACE SAT AT THE TABLE IN THE INTERROGATION room, wishing he could just roll his eyes back in his head and die. He'd been in trouble before, down in Atlanta. Worse trouble than this when you came right down to it—caught in a stolen car with a gram of coke in his pocket—but he'd never felt this bad. Then he had cared only about pissing off Brock, embarrassing him, costing him money. Getting in trouble had been worth something to him then, when he'd been just a stupid kid. Now he couldn't see the value in it at all.

His mom was in the sheriff's office, waiting for him. Trace had seen her through the window on his way down the hall, and he didn't think she'd ever looked so angry or so upset, not even when she'd come to him to tell him they had to move out of Stuart Tower. And Sheriff Jantzen sat across from him at the table, just staring at him. Staring and staring with those cold eyes of his. He hadn't said a word in five minutes. Trace would never have thought it possible, but that silence was ten times worse than getting hollered at.

He shifted in his chair and looked down at the hands he clutched together on his lap, thinking he'd wrap them around Carney's throat if he got the chance. Damn Carney and his stupid "get even" philosophy. The only person Trace wanted to get even with now was Carney. It was one thing to trash a mailbox, but wrecking cars was too much. Trace hadn't wanted any part of it, but Carney had goaded him into it, calling him a pussy and a coward, and now his ass was fried. Jantzen knew. He didn't have any proof, but he knew, and for some reason that seemed just as bad as being convicted.

"I don't think much of your alibi, Trace," Dane said softly. He couldn't break it either. There had been no witnesses to the vandalism at Shafer Motors. Trace had given Carney Fox as his alibi and Carney had backed him up, smiling that smug, sly smile of his the whole time. But Dane didn't have any doubts about it. Fox was lying. Trace was lying.

He ran a finger along the edge of the report Garth Shafer had made. Two new cars parked behind the service garage had their windows smashed. Those two and five others at the back of the used car lot had been severely scratched with a knife or some other sharp object, ruining the paint. It wasn't the kind of major damage Dane had expected after the call had come in, but it wasn't something to dismiss lightly either. The law was the law. People couldn't go around in his county thumbing their noses at the rules and just blithely walking away.

He took a long, deep breath and sighed slowly, never taking his eyes off Trace Stuart. The kid had been a nervous wreck when he'd come home last night. He hadn't been the picture of cool defiance the day they had questioned him about Fox's alibi for the Jarvis murder either. Right now he looked as though he was going to be sick. He looked as though he was caught in something he didn't know how to get out of. Elizabeth said he was a good kid with problems. Dane found himself wanting to believe that—for Elizabeth's sake as much as for Trace's.

"Mr. Shafer says you were in the shop yesterday afternoon, making trouble."

Trace's head came up sharply, his face the picture of outraged shock. "That's a lie! I went there looking for a job. He's the one that went off, yelling and—"

"Why? What made him yell at you?"

"I don't know! 'Cause he's nuts or something! I just went to ask him about the job cleaning up in the shop and he started yelling at me and calling me names and saying stuff about my mom—" Trace cut himself off and sat back in his chair, crossing his arms over his chest. He wasn't supposed to say anything. Just deny the charges, stick to the alibi, and get the hell out.

"What did he say about your mom?" Dane asked quietly.

"Nothing," Trace mumbled. He didn't want to talk about it. It was hurtful and embarrassing, and the way he felt about it was personal.

"What'd he say, Trace?" Dane prodded gently.

Trace sniffed and looked at the wall, furious and hurt. "He called her a whore."

The words came out in barely a whisper, so tight with anger and pain that the last one cracked and the boy colored with embarrassment. Dane rubbed the back of his neck and sighed. He shouldn't have felt sympathetic. He would have bet the farm on Trace's guilt. But he couldn't sit here and listen to the boy and watch him stew in misery without feeling bad for him. And for Elizabeth. And he couldn't help but think that the real culprit was Carney Fox. Trace seemed angry and confused and unhappy, but he didn't seem destructive. Fox, on the other hand, liked playing the ringleader, stirring up trouble, then slipping out of it. He had all but laughed in Dane's face as he had provided Trace with an alibi. Trace wasn't laughing.

Dane laid his forearms on the table and leaned ahead. "That kind of talk can make a man pretty mad, can't it?"

"Yessir," Trace mumbled, staring at that same blank spot on the wall, so miserable he would have sold his soul to be anywhere else.

"Mad enough that he might want to get back at who said it."

The boy just pressed his lips together and went on looking at the far wall, his thick black lashes beating like hummingbird wings as he tried to blink back tears.

Dane wanted to sink his teeth into Garth Shafer for starting this chain of events. Where did he get off talking that way about Elizabeth in front of her son? What the hell was the matter with him anyway? *Bitter. Violent temper.* The words from Elizabeth's note cards flashed through his head.

"A man has to learn to rise above that kind of thing, Trace," he said softly. "Revenge, retribution—all that'll get you is in deeper shit. Do you understand me?"

"Yessir."

"And hanging around with Carney Fox is going to get your ass thrown in jail sooner or later. What do you think people would have to say about you and your mom then?"

Trace couldn't hardly believe they could come up with anything worse than what they already said, but he got the message. He could rise above their talk or live down to it.

"You still looking for work?"

"No, sir."

Dane arched a brow. "You found something?"

"No, sir. I pretty much ran out of places to ask."

And no one had hired the kid because his mother was a beautiful divorcee from Texas who wore tight jeans and drove a cherry-red drop-top Cadillac. Dane blew out a breath. The Stuarts were giving him a whole new view of small town life. It didn't exactly make him proud.

"Are you afraid of hard physical labor?" he asked.

Trace gave him a suspicious look, wondering if there were chain gangs in Minnesota. "No, sir."

"Good." Dane pushed his chair back and stood up. "Be at my place tomorrow morning around ten. I've got a crew coming to hay. They can use an extra set of muscles."

Trace scrambled out of his chair, hardly believing his ears. He had expected Jantzen to badger a confession out of him and throw him in a cell to rot away the rest of his youth. The man was offering him a job!

"Sir—um—I—a—" he stammered, his brain racing

faster than his mouth could work. "I don't know nothing about farm work," he blurted out, then blushed at the admission. That was no way to impress a prospective employer. *Good job, Trace. Just open your big mouth and stick your stupid foot down your throat.*

Jantzen's mouth quirked up on one side. "This job needs brawn, not brains. Show me you can take orders and work like a man and I might be able to use you all summer."

Trace bobbed his head, sending his glasses slipping down his nose. "Yessir. Thank you, sir." He nearly tripped over himself as he hurried around the end of the table. "I'll work like a dog, sir, honest." He started to offer Dane his hand, then checked himself and wiped the sweat off his palm on the leg of his jeans first.

Dane took the boy's hand and gave it a manly shake. Garth Shafer was going to howl at the injustice of a young hoodlum getting off scot-free. Maybe he was letting his relationship with Elizabeth cloud his judgment, but the way Dane saw it, offering a chance to a kid headed down the wrong path was serving justice just fine.

ELIZABETH PARKED THE CADDY IN THE YARD, WHERE she would be able to see it from the kitchen window. Without a word she pulled her keys from the ignition and dropped them into her purse. She sat there for a while, carefully checking the lacquer on one fingernail, then got out of the car and slammed the door.

Trace winced. He had a feeling getting interrogated by Jantzen was going to seem like a piece of cake compared to what his mother had in store for him. She hadn't said a word to him. Or to Sheriff Jantzen back at the courthouse either. That was an ominous sign. His mother was a talker. When she didn't have anything to say, that usually meant she was saving up to go on a major tear. Silence in his mother was like the calm before a hurri-

cane—a period of eerie quiet before the fury was unleashed.

He dragged himself out of the car but delayed going
into the house, busying himself putting up the Caddy's
rag top—just in case it rained. Then he walked around
the car to check the tires, 'cause his mother was a woman
and women didn't think to do that kind of thing. There
was a dent in the driver's side door and a whole series of
them across that side of the trunk. From the attack, he
supposed, feeling sick at the thought. He licked a fingertip and tried to rub a scratch out of the paint with spit.

"You gonna do that to all Garth Shafer's cars too?"

His mother's words cracked against Trace's eardrums
like the snap of a bullwhip. She was standing on the back
step with a hand on her hip and fire in her eye. Trace
swallowed hard.

"No, ma'am," he mumbled.

He moved toward the house, his feet dragging as if his
shoes were made of cast iron. His mother went into the
house ahead of him, letting the screen door slam shut in
his face. She waited for him in the kitchen. Waited until
he had come in before she hurled her purse across the
room and bounced it off the refrigerator door beside
him, making him jump.

"Dammit, Trace, how could you do this?" Elizabeth
shouted, her temper erupting with all the ferocity of a
volcanic blast. "How could you do this to us? You whine
to me about how bad things are here and then you go out
and do something like this? Jesus H. Christ, how can you
expect people to like you when you take up with the
worst piece of trash in six counties and run around half
the night smashing up cars and doing God knows what
else?"

Trace just hunched his shoulders and hung his head.

"We came here to start over," she said, clamping her
hands on her hips to keep herself from reaching out and
shaking him till his teeth rattled. "I'm working my tail
off, trying to make a home for us here. And what do you

do? You go out and make friends with someone like Carney Fox!

"I got a look at his file while you were having your little chat with the sheriff. How do you think it made me feel to see he'd been arrested for possession with intent to sell?" She bit her lip against a surge of fear and shook her head as she paced beside the table. Her voice thickened with a mother's terror. "Trace, so help me, if you're using again—"

"I'm not using!" Trace shouted. It was bad enough getting chewed out for things he was guilty of. "Jesus, how many times do I have to tell you?"

"Then what are you doing hanging around with him?"

"He's a friend—"

"With friends like him, you don't need enemies. Look what he's got you mixed up in now!"

"Well, maybe it was my idea," Trace challenged his mother belligerently, his chin coming up a notch. "Did you ever think of that? Maybe I didn't like the way old Shithead Shafer called you a whore to my face and so I smashed up a couple of his stupid cars."

Elizabeth squeezed her eyes shut and put her hands over her face. It was all *her* fault. Everything. She had driven Shafer over the edge, and Trace had tried to defend her honor in this horribly misguided way because she was a rotten mother. If she'd raised him right—If she'd given him a father—If she hadn't had such abominable taste in men—

"So I screwed up," Trace said bitterly. "It's what I do best, isn't it?"

"Trace—"

"No, it's true," he insisted. The feelings and words came spitting up through him from a dark, sad corner of his heart, and rolled out of him, surprising Trace as much as they surprised his mother. "I'm the original fuckup." He said it with incredulity, shaking his head at the revelation. "From day one. My dad got you knocked up with me and life's just been one big mess ever since."

"Honey, that's not true," Elizabeth whispered, the words sticking in her throat.

"Sure it is," he said bitterly. "You married Bobby Breland because of me and he kicked you around. Then you divorced him and you were stuck dragging a little kid around with you, and you probably couldn't get a decent guy because no man wants some other man's kid. And Brock probably wouldn't have dumped you if it hadn't been for me. He never wanted me around, and when I started making trouble for him he kicked us out."

"Oh, Trace . . ."

"I never should have been born," he mumbled.

Before his mother could refute his words, he turned and ran out the back door, jumping down off the step and charging for the woods as fast as his legs could take him. He didn't know where he was running to or why he was running at all, except that he had to do something with the anger and frustration and pain that swelled inside him before he just plain exploded with it. He plunged into the woods and ran down an old trail that was overgrown with bushes. He stumbled over roots and batted branches out of his way and ran until his lungs were on fire and his T-shirt was clinging to him like wet paper.

He slowed then, and walked for a while with his hands jammed at the waist of his jeans. The air in the woods was cooler and darker, sweet with the scent of green leaves and humus. As his pulse slowed and the blood stopped roaring in his ears he began to pick up the sounds of his surroundings—the call of *thief!* from a blue jay as it swooped from the branches of a white oak, the busy twitterings of sparrows, the scratch of squirrel claws against tree bark as they chased one another from trunk to trunk.

As he walked deeper into the woods, he found a spot where an old maple tree had died and keeled over, creating a clearing. He hopped up on the natural bench and sat down to think.

Now that he'd run off all the wild emotions inside, he

felt calmer. He sat there and listened to the quiet sounds of the woods, feeling as though he had reached the biggest crossroads of his life with the glaring spotlight of revelation beating down on him. He could go on screwing up as he had his whole life, acting like a stupid kid and disappointing everyone, or he could take charge of his life and start acting like the man he wanted to be. Like Jantzen had said, he had choices to make, and this was the time to make them.

Trace didn't know how long he'd been sitting there when the sound of something coming through the woods broke the trance he'd fallen into. He looked up just as a little blaze-faced black horse came into the clearing, and his heart jumped up and stuck in his throat as he saw who was riding it—the girl from the courthouse. Amy. He'd seen her in the bleachers at the softball game, heard someone call her by name—Amy. He should have figured she'd have a pretty, sunny kind of a name like that. It went with her smile.

He hadn't gotten near her at the ball field. She had been surrounded by friends, the way a girl like her would be, and Trace had been hanging around the sidelines, wishing he knew somebody well enough so he could ask to play in the game. He was a fair hand with a bat and a pretty good shortstop. He figured he might be able to impress her if he could play, but he didn't know anybody and no one asked him. Then the sheriff came.

Christ, she probably thought he was the biggest troublemaker since Cain.

Her horse spooked a little as it spotted him. Amy's eyes went wide with surprise . . . or shock . . . or maybe it was disgust. Trace couldn't tell. He slid to the ground and straightened his shoulders back.

"I'm sorry," he said softly, "I didn't mean to spook your horse."

It took Amy a moment to find her tongue. She couldn't believe it. He was here, in the woods, practically waiting for her. Her heart bumped so hard against her chest, she thought he could see it moving beneath the oversize work shirt she'd snuck out of her dad's closet. She had seen him at the softball game, standing off to the side, watching everything with his serious eyes, his hands stuck in the pockets of his jeans, shoulders straining the seams of his white T-shirt. He was a loner, a rebel. Moody and quiet. Like James Dean. She had a huge crush on James Dean, even though he was dead and probably would have been old enough to be her father.

"That's okay," she said.

Tinker had recovered admirably from her scare and stood with her head turned to the side, nibbling on the leaves of a wild blackberry bush. Amy swung down off the mare and smoothed the tails of the shirt that hung nearly to her knees. She could have died of embarrassment. She wasn't wearing any makeup and she was sure she looked twelve years old with this shirt swallowing her up. This wasn't at all the way she'd wanted to look when she met *him*.

"I'm sorry if I interrupted your thinking."

Trace shrugged it off, his brain stalling as he tried to think of a cool way to behave. *Act like a man, stupid. Now's your chance.* He tossed away the bit of tree bark he'd been fiddling with and dusted the crud off his hand onto the leg of his jeans.

"Trace Stuart," he said.

Amy took his hand, trying to bite back the ridiculous, giddy smile that was tugging at her mouth. None of the boys she knew had manners enough to shake a girl's hand. It seemed old-fashioned and terribly mature. Tingles ran through her as his big warm hand closed on hers and she thought she might melt. "Amy Jantzen."

"Jantzen?" Trace was pretty sure his heart had stopped. He let go of her hand and took a half step back. "Like Sheriff Jantzen?"

"He's my dad." Most of the guys around Still Creek were impressed when she told them who her father was. They looked up to him—more because he'd been a professional football player than because he was sheriff. But Trace Stuart looked as though she'd just told him her

father was Dracula. She chewed her lip and hoped she
hadn't just scared him off for all time. Idiot. She should
have known a rebel like him would be wary of the law,
especially since she'd seen him at the sheriff's office, and
then today her dad had come to the ball field and they'd
walked away together, neither of them looking very
happy.

"Are you in some kind of trouble with him?" she
asked cautiously.

Trace glanced away, rolling his shoulders. "Uh—sort
of. Well—not really. Kind of." He swallowed hard and
called himself a hundred names. "He—a—he asked me
to come work for him."

Amy's eyes went wide as she looked up at him.
"Really?" she breathed. "Like undercover or something?"

"Putting up hay," Trace said, feeling like the dolt of
the century. If he had been any kind of liar, he could
have told her he was a special agent or something. She
giggled and crinkled her nose, and Trace felt the bottom
drop out of his stomach.

"I guess I have an overactive imagination," she admitted, hoping he didn't think she was an airhead. "That's
what Mike says. Mike's my stepfather."

"Your folks are divorced?"

She nodded as she wrapped her horse's reins around a
branch in the berry bush. "I live in L.A. with my mom
and stepfather. I'm here visiting my dad for a few
weeks."

"Oh."

"How about you?" She walked over to the fallen log
and climbed up on it to sit. "You're not from around
here."

Trace stuffed his hands into his pockets and mentally
cursed his drawl. Everyone around here looked at him
sideways when he talked. Amy already had him pegged
as some dumb hick from the South. She probably
thought he sounded as though he ought to be on *Hee*

Haw or something. "We just moved here," he mumbled. "My mom and me—I. From Atlanta."

She beamed a smile at him. "Atlanta? Cool." She made that cute face where she scrunched up her nose, and Trace's stomach did another cartwheel. "I like the way you talk."

His jaw dropped before he had a chance to catch it. "You do?"

She nodded and tugged on the tails of her shirt. She studied him for a moment with her head tipped to one side, her long, wavy hair hanging down like a curtain. "I like your glasses too. That retro look is so great."

Trace grinned, unable to contain himself. He hauled himself up onto the log to sit beside Amy Jantzen, suddenly thinking that maybe life wasn't quite such a bitch after all.

ELIZABETH SAT ON THE BACK STEP, STARING AT THE woods that had swallowed up her son.

"Every time I think I can't feel any worse, I sink a little lower," she whispered, swirling the ice in her Wile E. Coyote glass. She studied the smirking cartoon character that appeared to be standing ankle-deep in scotch and wished she had the same resiliency the coyote showed when all his big schemes backfired and anvils rained down on his head. Unfortunately, life was not a cartoon and everything that fell on her left a bruise.

She had wanted to run after Trace, but, aside from not having a prayer of keeping up with him, she didn't know what she would say to him if she did catch him. She couldn't tell him he had been planned, because he hadn't. She couldn't tell him it hadn't been hard for her after her marriage to Bobby Lee had fallen apart, because it had been. She wanted to tell him none of it was his fault, but he didn't want to hear it.

She looked over to the west, toward the Hauer farm. The Sunday church festivities had broken up. The buggies were gone. The Amish farm looked like the picture of peace and tranquility, and she wished some of that would drift over her way on the breeze. She could live a simpler life, but nothing had ever been simple for her, and there was no reason to think that fact would change any time soon.

As if to prove her point, Dane's Bronco came rumbling down the road, dust rolling behind it. He slowed and turned in at her drive, parking beside the Caddy. Elizabeth stayed where she was, watching him as he crossed the weedy lawn. It wasn't hard to picture him in a football uniform, those long legs striding down the field, elegant, capable hands stretching out to catch a pass, narrow hips evading tackles with moves that would make a lady's breath catch. But then, she knew exactly what kinds of moves those hips could make, didn't she? And they had indeed made her breath catch, time and again last night. The man might have his faults, but none of them could be found in bed.

He stopped at the bottom step, putting him on eye level with her. "You drink too much of that stuff," he said, settling his hands on his hips.

"What's it to you?" Elizabeth said, but with none of the sass she had intended to show and too much of the vulnerability she wanted to hide. The early evening breeze caught her hair, and she snagged it with one hand and held it at the nape of her neck.

Dane took the glass from her and tossed back the last two fingers of scotch himself, welcoming the smooth fire as it slid down his throat to his belly. He was beat. He was sick of looking at reports and sicker of the reason he had to review them over and over. Having to deal with Carney Fox for another unproductive round of sparring had given him a headache, and Garth Shafer had all but reamed him a new asshole, livid that Trace hadn't been arrested and charged. He deserved a drink.

But then, he thought as he took in Elizabeth's bleak expression, she probably deserved one too.

"How'd it go with Trace?"

"Oh, swell," she said with a phony smile. "I yelled at

him, found out he blames himself for everything that's really my fault, then he ran off. I'm fixing to go on the talk show circuit as an expert on child rearing. I can be my own shining example of what not to do."

He knew the feeling, and he couldn't help but reach out to her in commiseration. "Don't be so hard on yourself," he said, climbing the steps to sit beside her. "He's at a tough age."

The phony smile turned sad and reflective as she scanned back over the past sixteen years in her mind. "In some ways Trace has been at a tough age since conception. Always so somber, so unto himself. I don't think we've ever been on the same wavelength."

"It's not easy being a parent." He looked down into the bottom of the coyote glass to see if there might be another drop of scotch. There wasn't.

Elizabeth gave him a sideways look, taking in the lines of strain and fatigue that were etched around his eyes and mouth, making him look tougher, older, more handsome, more dangerous.

"That sounded like the voice of authority," she said.

Dane's mouth twisted. "I'm on Amy's shit list because I told her she wasn't old enough to date."

"How old is she?"

"Fifteen."

"How old do you think she should be?"

"Thirty-five."

A genuine smile claimed Elizabeth's lips for the first time in what seemed like days, and laughter tumbled out. Poor Dane. He sat there looking gruff and disgruntled, big and tough . . . and vulnerable. Elizabeth couldn't stop herself from reaching out to him; she didn't try. She rubbed the palm of her hand over his back in slow, soothing circles and gave him a sympathetic look. "Are you an overprotective daddy?"

"I guess," he admitted grudgingly. "I missed out on so much of Amy's childhood, I don't want to think of her growing up."

"I wasn't much older than her when I had Trace," Elizabeth mused.

Dane winced, paling visibly. "Oh, Jesus, please don't say that."

"Sorry, sugar, but it's true. 'Course, I was pretty much on my own then, anyway . . ."

Her voice trailed away and she pulled her hand back to band her arms around her knees as she looked out toward the woods again. Dane studied her profile carefully, with a sense of wonder. He had told himself he didn't want to know anything about her, but now, as they sat on the cracked old steps, sharing uncertainties, he wanted to know everything.

"What about your parents?"

The shoulder left bare by her blouse rose and fell in a shrug too casual to be believed. "I don't remember my mother. She died when I was a baby. And J.C.—my daddy"—her mouth turned in a sad smile—"he was kind of lost in a world of his own."

As a child she had often wondered how different her life would have been if her mother had lived. She had fantasized about a real home, a permanent one, with flowers planted around it and a yard with a picket fence to keep in the puppy she would have had. She had envisioned her mama just as she looked in that old photograph of J.C.'s—always beautiful, always smiling that sweet, knowing smile the way angels must smile, always in a pretty flowered dress with a little strand of pearls at her throat. They would have been a real family with enough love to go around, instead of just her and J.C. Him with all his love still bound to a woman who was gone forever, with none left over for the child she'd left behind, the child who, ironically, had grown up to look just like her.

Dane listened as she talked a little about her father, a cowboy who had spent as much time in a bottle as he did in the saddle, by the sound of it. He listened as she painted a picture of a childhood that must have been as emotionally desolate as the West Texas landscape that had provided the backdrop, and felt ashamed of himself for judging her so harshly. His own childhood had been of the Norman Rockwell variety—the perfect family with perfect children living in a perfect small town. He had been given love and advantages in healthy doses, had been raised to believe he could do anything, be anything. Elizabeth had been raised to believe she was an inconvenience. She had grown up hungry—for love, for comforts. That explained a lot about the woman she had become.

"Then you met Trace's father," he said.

"Yep," she murmured, still looking inward, looking back, smiling at the thought of the first time she had set eyes on Bobby Lee, with his thousand-watt smile and wicked green eyes. "Bobby Lee Breland, third best calf roper on the circuit, first-class Romeo. That boy could have sold charm by the gallon and still have buckets left over. We had us a time," she said, but her smile faded as the memories turned sour. "Until we got married, that is. I was seventeen and pregnant and Bobby, he didn't care much for being committed to one woman."

Dane developed an instant loathing for Elizabeth's first husband. He couldn't stand a man who shirked his responsibilities. He damn well would have stood by Elizabeth if she had been carrying his baby. The mental image of her heavy with his child brought a strong sense of possessiveness rising inside him. He tamped it down and turned his full attention back to her story. "Were you scared?"

"Spitless." She laughed at that and shook her head. "I let on like I had the world by the tail, but the truth was I didn't know nothing 'bout birthin' no babies. And Bobby Lee was about as much good as tits on a boar hog. His expertise was the part that came before the baby. Everything after that was not his department."

" 'Course, the great thing about nature is that babies will get born whether their mamas know what to do or not." A stillness came over her as her words sunk in. A frown pulled at the corners of her mouth as she stared out toward the woods. "Maybe Mother Nature ought to think about reworking that one. Could save a lot of babies a lot of grief."

"What happened with Bobby Lee?" Dane asked, needing to pull her back from the emotional ledge she was looking down from.

"He had a fatal attraction to rodeo queens. Which was fine when I was one. After I started to look more like the barrel than the girls who raced around them, his pretty head started turning this way and that until you'd'a thought he'd'a got himself a whiplash. I hung on to him for a while, just out of stubbornness, but it wasn't worth it. Finally, he saddled one filly too many and I left him. The rest, as they say, is history."

She gave him another of her sardonic smiles. Another that didn't come anywhere near banishing the shadows of the past from her eyes. Dane had a feeling the history she was leaving untold was long and unhappy. It couldn't have been easy to strike out on her own with a small child. His gaze caught on the little scar that hooked down from the corner of her mouth, and he reached out and traced it with his thumb.

"How'd you get this?" he asked quietly, his gaze holding hers.

Elizabeth didn't want to tell him. She felt as if he were reaching into her soul and taking little bits of her, pieces he wouldn't bother to return when he left her. But she answered him anyway, not able to escape that steady blue gaze or the need inside her to make some kind of emotional contact with him. "I went home from work early one day and caught Bobby Lee riding Miss Panhandle Rodeo Days. I took after him with a pellet gun we used to shoot rats with and peppered his gorgeous little ass. Then his temper kicked in and he got the pistol away from me and smacked me a good one with it."

"Jesus," Dane whispered, anger knotting like a fist in his gut. He could tell by the matter-of-fact way she related the tale that it was but one of many.

"Trace slept through the whole thing," she said with a sad smile. "He was an awful good baby."

God, Dane thought, she'd been little more than a child herself, dealing with a baby and a husband who treated her like dirt. That unwelcome, unwanted tide of protectiveness rose up inside him again. He let it. He cupped her cheek with his hand and leaned down to kiss the scar.

"I'm sorry," he whispered.

Sorry for what? Elizabeth wondered. For her past or for the future he wouldn't give her? She crushed the thought. Falling in love with him was just an unforeseen hitch she would have to get over on her own.

"Your turn," she said, throwing the ball in his court.

He pulled back, poker-faced. "My turn for what?"

"Details," Elizabeth said, cranking a hand around like a director prompting for action. "I'm not gonna be the only one sitting here with my figurative pants down around my ankles. Spill something, Jantzen."

"Like what?" he asked, scowling at her.

"Like what happened with you and Mrs. Jantzen."

Dane turned his head to look toward the pastureland to the east. His pastureland, where a small herd of Hereford cattle grazed contentedly on the sweet clover and grass. He didn't like having the tables turned, didn't like the idea of sharing parts of himself other than those he had designated for this relationship.

"It didn't work out," he said shortly, paring the story down to its bare bones. "When I was forced to stop playing ball, I decided to come back here. She stayed in L.A. and found someone who could keep her in the style to which she had grown accustomed."

He left out the bitter details. The feelings of betrayal and rejection. The awful sensation of falling from the heights of stardom to the depths of despair, to become an object of pity and ridicule and have even his own wife turn on him. Those were feelings he didn't share ever, not with anyone.

He might have been stingy with his words, but Elizabeth caught the echo of bitterness in his voice. She saw the muscles tense in his square jaw, watched the way his shoulders stiffened. He was a proud man, a man who was accustomed to being in control. She could imagine he wouldn't take well to the idea of dissension in his personal life any more than he did in his professional life, and he wouldn't take well to rejection either.

What kind of woman rejected a man when he needed her most, when he was vulnerable, lost? The kind who deserved to have her hair ripped out by the roots, she decided. She wondered if he was still in love with his ex-wife, but she didn't ask. She didn't want to think of him loving anyone except her, and that was just plain foolish to think about at all.

Of course, that didn't stop her from thinking about it. Dane Jantzen didn't love her, didn't want anything from her but sex. She couldn't make him love her, but she could pretend he did. For a little while. Just long enough to feel something other than loneliness.

"Let's go inside," she whispered.

The house was so quiet it seemed to be holding its breath as the sunlight faded and the day's dust settled on the furniture. Elizabeth led the way upstairs.

Dane suspected what she wanted had little to do with sex—at least not the kind of sex he was used to—hard, wild, recreational sex. This had to do with comfort, with losing yourself in another person's arms for a while. He wanted to give her this time. Not just because he was aching with arousal, but because he was aching in a corner of his heart he had deliberately closed off, a corner Elizabeth had somehow managed to touch when no one else had gotten near.

The cynic in him warned against it. He didn't want anything permanent, and he couldn't see it happening with Elizabeth at any rate. She wouldn't want to stick around here, especially after the kind of welcome she'd been given, and he didn't want to be anyplace else. But he couldn't keep from responding to her, couldn't keep from touching her, tasting her. He could have that, he allowed, as long as he maintained his objectivity.

Keep your head in the game and your heart out of it.

He let the message sink in, then he shut off the voice, shut out everything but Elizabeth and the incredible heat that burned through him every time he touched her.

In the aftermath it came to him. That need he had denied over and over with other women. As he lay in that big brass bed with Elizabeth hugging him, the need stole through him like a thief.

He looked down at her and tried to deny it again. She wasn't for him. Not in any permanent way. They were too different. What was drawing them together had more to do with circumstance than anything. They had been thrown together in a situation where emotions ran high and natural chemistry sparked and ignited a flash fire. Once the case was solved, things would cool off, they would drift apart. Elizabeth would go her own way and his life would fall back into its usual routine.

"There'll be a deputy in your yard tonight," he said, easing out from under her, easing out of bed.

Elizabeth sat up, hair in her eyes, sheet clutched above her breasts in one fist. "Fine," she murmured, watching as Dane zipped his jeans. Her time was up. They had had their interlude of friendship, their hour of sex. Now he went back to being a cop. Such an orderly life he led. She both envied and resented him for it. Her life was a tangled mess, like a ball of yarn, like a snare of vines, like her hair, every strand hopelessly intertwined.

He gave her a look that struck her as being more like pity than regret. "I have to go."

Pride bumped her chin up a notch. Her eyes flashed with anger to hide the pain. "I didn't ask you not to."

She slipped out of bed on the other side and went to the window, the sheet draped around her like a Grecian gown. It was getting dark outside. The farm buildings loomed beyond the yard, their sad gray facades taking on a sinister cast as the sun slipped away. She looked down at the black interior of the open shed and felt a little quiver at the base of her neck. The feeling of being watched crept over her like fingers. Residual creeps, she thought, drawing back from the window.

She found a cigarette on the nightstand and dug a lighter out of the drawer. "Thanks for going easy on Trace," she said, blowing a stream of smoke up at the ceiling.

"I didn't have anything to hold him with," he said, tucking his shirt in.

"You didn't have to give him a job either," she pointed out.

"If he's a good kid, then he deserves a chance to prove it."

Elizabeth forced a smile and looked at her feet. A part of her wanted to hold on to the hope that he had been good to Trace because he cared about her. Silly. Selfish.

She needed a pedicure, she noted absently. Too bad she wasn't going to be able to afford one for another twenty years or so. From the corner of her eye she could see Dane's boots as he moved toward the door. He hesitated, turned back, hesitated again. She didn't look up at him. She didn't want to see that look in his eyes. She didn't want him feeling sorry for her, she thought stubbornly. She didn't want anyone feeling sorry for her, including herself. She took another deep drag on her cigarette and walked back toward the window, trailing a plume of smoke like a plane with a blown engine.

Dane watched her for a minute, at a loss for words. Damn. He never had this kind of trouble leaving Ann Markham, but then, he never wanted to spend the night just holding Ann either. He never much cared how she was feeling, never wondered if she was lonely after he was gone. He looked at Elizabeth, with her chin up and her gaze directed out the window, and he felt the pang of her emptiness as acutely as if it were his own.

Dangerous stuff, emotion. He had played that game before and lost. He was better off without it.

Elizabeth stood at the window, listening to his footfalls on the stairs, listening to the distant slap of the screen door. She watched him walk across the yard, get in the Bronco and drive away, taillights glowing through the dust as he headed into a blazing sunset. She stood there for a long while, staring out into the gathering darkness, never aware that someone was staring back.

EIGHTEEN

B Y THE VIEW THROUGH THE BIG PLATE GLASS window facing Main Street, Dane could see the Coffee Cup was doing its usual breakfast business and then some. He wedged the Bronco into a parking spot behind Yeager's pickup. Yeager parked the way he dressed. His old dirt-brown Ford half-ton had one rear wheel on the curb and a front fender nosing up to a fire hydrant. Boozer hung his head out the open passenger window and woofed softly at Dane as he crossed the sidewalk and climbed the steps to the restaurant.

A blast of sound hit him as he opened the door and stepped inside—conversation, flatware hitting china, the groan and scrape of chairs, the hiss of the grill. And with the sounds came the smells—bacon frying, hot coffee, cinnamon rolls. His gaze scanned the mob for Yeager, who waved at him from a back booth.

A reporter from the *Pioneer Press* popped up from his chair at a front table and attempted to fall into step beside Dane as he wound his way through the maze of tables and harried waitresses. "Sheriff, have you got any new leads—"

"No comment."

"What about the attack on the local paper—"

Dane shot the man a look and the reporter heaved a sigh and fell back. As Dane turned to continue on his path, an arm reached out in front of him like a roadblock at a toll booth. He pulled himself up short, scowling down at Charlie Wilder and Bidy Masters, who were sharing a booth and their concerns over stacks of Phyllis's pancakes. Charlie's round face split with one of his nervous smiles.

"Any word, Dane?"

"You'll be the first to know, Charlie."

Bidy's frown carved an extra pair of lines into his long, lean face. "What's this business Garth Shafer is talking about this morning? That Stuart kid wrecked his business and you didn't arrest him?"

Charlie gave a belly-jiggling chuckle, intended to pretty-up the feelings behind his words. "Those Stuarts are sure stirring up trouble. That woman—"

"I need evidence to make charges stick," Dane said shortly, his temper already fraying and it wasn't even eight o'clock yet. He gave the town fathers a look that had them sliding down a little in their seats. "You tell Garth if he comes up with some hard proof, I'll arrest anyone it points to."

Charlie forced another laugh, drumming his sausage fingers on the tabletop beside his plate of half-eaten pancakes. "Well, jeez, Dane, we didn't mean to cause hard feelings—"

Dane didn't stick around for the platitudes. He ducked around Renita Henning, who had both arms lined with heaping breakfast plates, and slid into the booth across the table from Yeager.

"It's a goddamn obstacle course in here."

Yeager grinned at him. "Spoken like a man in dire need of a cup of Joe." He caught the waitress's eye and beamed a smile at her as well. "Renita honey, could you send someone on back here with a sweet smile and a hot pot of coffee?"

Renita returned his grin. "You bet."

"Aren't you the picture of hospitality this morning," Dane growled.

Yeager shrugged expansively. "Hey, I'm in love. The world is a wonderful place."

"With a killer running around loose in it."

"We're gonna handle that, son. We just got to come at it from a different angle, is all." He swallowed a gulp of orange juice, managing to dribble it on the front of his wrinkled plaid sport shirt.

Dane scowled at him. "Jesus, you're a mess. Don't you own an iron?"

Another idiotic grin. "Nope. Life needs a few wrinkles in it to make it interesting." He sat back while Millicent Witt topped off his coffee and poured a cup for Dane. "You got that rabid-wolf look on you, boy. What'd you get up on the wrong side of the bed this morning?" He shot a wink at Millicent. Her cheeks bloomed red and she moved off with her coffeepot, chuckling.

Dane snarled a little under his breath and lifted his cup, breathing in the vapor like smelling salts. He had gotten up from the wrong bed, after a restless night spent thinking about Elizabeth and the awkward way they had parted. He couldn't remember the last time he'd lost sleep over a woman. It was damned irritating, especially now, when he needed his wits about him and no distractions. He didn't have anything to feel guilty about, he reminded himself. Christ, she had invited him into her bed—twice—without exacting any promises from him.

Phyllis stepped up to the table with a slice of lemon meringue pie for Yeager and a plate of bacon and eggs for Dane. He held a hand up. "Nothing for me, Phyllis. Just coffee."

Her wide thin mouth—painted ruby this morning—twisted into a knot of disapproval. "By the look on your face, I can see I should have brought the stewed prunes and oatmeal," she said, sliding the plate in front of him. She scratched the eraser end of her pencil through her Brillo-pad hair and patted Dane's shoulder with the other gnarled hand. "You can't run on coffee and orneriness. Only I can manage that. Eat up."

Yeager chuckled and dove into his pie as Phyllis swished away on her air-pillow shoes. "She's a trip."

Dane pushed his plate aside and regarded the BCA

agent with disgust. "How can you eat that for break-fast?"

Yeager looked up at him in innocence, a fork of brilliant yellow pie in midair, a gob of meringue clinging to his square chin like a goatee. "It's got eggs in it."

"Judas," Dane grumbled. He pulled his wallet out of his hip pocket and tossed some bills on the table. "Chow down, Sherlock. We've got work to do."

THEY TOOK DANE'S BRONCO AND HEADED FOR STILL Waters with Boozer sitting behind the cage, panting rancid dog breath in Dane's ear. Dane drove while Yeager concentrated on rubbing grape jelly off the end of his tan knit tie.

"Did you talk to Jolynn?"

"Yeah," Yeager said, frowning. "She says Cannon came by around eight-thirty the night of the murder."

"And Rich says it was closer to seven."

"Either way, he had time to do the deed. We can't pinpoint time of death because of the warfarin screwing up the blood. Jarvis could have been killed anytime after the crew left the work site." He lifted his head and stared out through the windshield, seeing nothing of the rolling countryside or the Amish farm wagon they passed. His thoughts were on Jolynn and all the shit her ex-husband had put her through. His dark eyes shone with a rare burning anger. Sweet, good-hearted Jolynn deserved a hell of a lot better than the likes of Rich Cannon. "That guy is a bastard deluxe. I hope he did do it just so I can chase him down and kick the ever-loving shit out of him for resisting arrest."

Dane glanced across the seat, arching a brow. So that was how the wind was blowing. Good for Jolynn. If she could stand Yeager's slovenly ways and his smelly dog he was a great guy.

"My money's still on Fox," he said. "Rich doesn't have the guts to kill anybody."

Yeager set his jaw. "He had motive and opportunity and he's lying about something. That's enough for me."

"What we need is a witness who could put somebody at the scene," Dane said. He eased off the accelerator as they neared the Hauer place. Aaron hadn't given him anything to go on, but then, that was Aaron. *Be ye separate from the world and worldly things.* "Did you see a statement in the file from Samuel Hauer?"

Yeager shook his head. "No."

"Shit. I told Ellstrom to interview every person living on this road. The guy's got his head so far up his ass he can't hear anymore."

They found Samuel Hauer in the barn, trimming the hooves of a massive Belgian workhorse. The old man was bent over, shoulder against the side of the big sorrel gelding, knees clamped around the horse's raised leg. He plied the pinchers with the skill of long practice, nipping off a crescent of hoof, then trading the pinchers for a rasp and filing the edge smooth. Yeager's dog snatched up the discarded piece of hoof and flopped down in the straw to chew on it.

"Samuel," Dane said with a nod.

Hauer lowered the horse's leg and slowly straightened his back, a weary smile lighting his weathered face above his beard. "Dane Jantzen."

The two men shook hands and Dane introduced Yeager. Dane asked after the rest of the Hauer clan—all living away from home now, except Aaron, who had moved back after the accident that had taken his family. They chatted about the weather and the quality of the year's first hay crop. Finally Dane felt he could bring up the subject he had come to discuss without putting off the old Amishman.

Samuel Hauer shook his head, his face grave. "Ruth and I was gone to Michah Zook's that night. Sylvia has the cancer of the stomach, you know."

Dane nodded. "I heard. That's a shame."

"They had her to the Mayo Clinic I don't know how long, but she's home now." He shook his head again as he cleaned his rasp with a rag and slid it into his farrier's box. "She's not long for this world, Sylvia. She'll be with God soon." He sighed. *"Gotters Wille."*

"What time did you get home?"

"After dark. After the commotion had started across the road with the police cars and so on." He unsnapped the gelding's halter and gave the big horse a pat on the rump, sending him clomping down the aisle to the door that opened into the dry lot.

"Aaron was here," Dane said. "Did he say anything to you about it? That he saw something, heard something?"

The old man frowned as he took up a barn broom and slowly began to sweep the scraps of hoof cuttings into the gutter. "No."

"Could you talk to him, Samuel? This is very important. If he saw anything—a man, a car—it could help us catch a killer."

A sad smile bent Hauer's mouth. He reached down into the gutter for a crescent of hoof and tossed it to the yellow dog. The Labrador thumped his tail against the straw and rolled onto his back, groaning in ecstasy. "I'll talk to him, Dane Jantzen, but you know how Aaron is. Your justice is not Aaron's justice."

Dane gave the Amishman a long, level look. "It has to be this time, Samuel. You tell him that."

THEY WERE GOING FULL-TILT AT STILL WATERS. THE peace of the country morning was decapitated by the scream of power saws and the thump of pneumatic hammers. Workmen crawled over the skeleton of the main building like sailors in the rigging of a windjammer, shouting orders and gossip over the blare of Dwight Yokum on the portable boom box.

Rich Cannon came out of the office trailer just as Dane and Yeager climbed down out of the Bronco. His step faltered as he saw them, but he managed to put on a plastic smile and alter his course. He was dressed to impress in brown summer wool trousers and a crisp cream-colored shirt. A silk tie with the stripe of an old British public school he probably couldn't have found on a map was knotted beneath his chin.

He reached out with the tube of blueprints in his hand and tapped Dane on the shoulder in a gesture of camaraderie that seemed overt for their relationship. They had never been friends. They had been teammates half a lifetime ago. But then, considering the importance Rich still put on that time of his life, maybe that meant more to him than it did to Dane. Or maybe the bastard's sucking up to me, Dane thought.

"What brings you guys out this way?" Rich asked, smile in place, gaze moving between the two lawmen.

Yeager gave him a hard look. "You."

Dane cleared his throat. "We just had a few extra questions we thought you could help us with, Rich."

"Sure, a—" He glanced at his watch and shrugged, manufacturing a pained expression. "I haven't got a lot of time. I have to get to Rochester to meet with some party people. I'm launching my campaign during Horse and Buggy Days. You know, take advantage of the extra media coverage."

Yeager made a rude noise in his throat. Dane pretended not to notice. "This won't take long." He nodded toward the building as he leaned a hip against the side of the Bronco. "I see you had a crew out here yesterday. Making up for lost time?"

"Yeah, well, you know, deadlines are deadlines. We have to take advantage of this weather."

"Oh, well, you're good at that," Yeager said. "Taking advantage."

Rich's brows snapped together. "What's that supposed to mean?"

Dane gave an innocent shrug. "It means it looks like Jarrold left the reins in the hands of the right man. Did he happen to leave anything else in your hands?"

"Like what?"

"Like the book where he kept track of who owed him money."

Rich rolled his eyes and staggered back a step, as if the utter lunacy of the question had knocked him off balance. "Oh, Jesus, you're not on that too?" he said, incredulous. "I thought it was bad enough when that bitch at the paper office started in on me."

Dane's jaw tightened. Rich didn't notice. He tucked the tube of blueprints under his arm and dug a pack of Pall Malls out of his shirt pocket. He shook one out and dangled it from his lip as he searched for his lighter. "What's all this cloak-and-dagger bullshit about a black book?"

"It might have given someone a motive," Yeager said.

Rich lit up, exhaling a cloud of smoke as he shook his head, his gaze sliding to the building project. "Fox killed Jarrold for his pocket change. End of story. Catch the little shit and fry him."

"There is no capital punishment in the state of Minnesota," Yeager pointed out.

Rich gave him a belligerent look. "Figure of speech."

"We've been double-checking statements," Dane said, drawing his old teammate's attention back to him. "There's a minor discrepancy you might be able to clear up for us."

"Sure."

"You said you went to Jolynn's around seven. She says it was more like eight-thirty."

"Yeah?" He arched a brow, then shrugged off the importance of the statement, looking away again as he tapped the ash off his cigarette. "Well, she's wrong. What can I say?" He flashed them a cocky grin. "I think her mind was on other things, you know? Some women are big on punctuality. Jo's talents lie elsewhere."

Dane stepped away from the Bronco just in time to block Yeager from hurling himself at Rich. The move seemed totally natural and relaxed, belying the tension that was simmering beneath his calm facade. He shot Yeager a warning glare as he sauntered to the hood of Cannon's Thunderbird and sat down.

"Jolynn seems perfectly capable of reading a clock,"

he said quietly, his gaze catching Rich's and holding it. "You have any reason to lie to me, Rich?"

"No!" Cannon swore and tossed his cigarette down to grind it out with the toe of his wingtip. He paced around in a circle, wagging his head in disbelief. "Jeez, Dane, I can't even believe you're asking me this shit! So maybe I'm wrong about the time. Maybe I'm off by a few minutes. Big deal."

Yeager snagged him by the arm and jerked him to a standstill, leaning into his face. "A man is dead, hotshot. That's a pretty big fucking deal where I come from."

Rich yanked his arm free and stepped back, looking petulant. "Yeah, well, I didn't kill him." He turned and looked Dane straight in the eye. "I didn't kill him." His denial hung in the air with the smell of sawdust and cigarette smoke. He glanced at his watch again. "I have to go."

Dane eased himself off the hood of the Thunderbird and stepped away. Boozer gave the car's right rear wheel an extra spray of pee, then wandered over to flop down at his master's feet.

"Everything about that guy smells like a horse's ass," Yeager growled as they watched Rich Cannon drive away.

"He's hiding something," Dane murmured, his gaze fixed on the retreating car, his mind sifting through theories he never would have wanted to associate with his town. "One thing is clear, partner. We've got to find that book."

ELIZABETH HUNG UP THE PHONE, PRESSED HER FIN-gertips to her temples, and squeezed her eyes closed. The relentless pounding going on outside the *Clarion* office echoed inside her head until she wanted to scream. It had been going on for hours—the pounding outside *and* the headache. The judge's booth for the Horse and Buggy Days parade was being constructed right smack in front of the office, giving the judges a good view and ruining foot traffic into Elizabeth's business all in one fell swoop.

She dug into her bottom desk drawer in search of more aspirin, but came up with nothing but an empty Excedrin bottle and half a bag of M&Ms. The screech of a drill penetrated the plywood covering the broken front window and pierced her eardrums, drilling right into the core of her brain. She dropped the M&Ms on the desktop, plugged her ears with her thumbs, and clamped her fingers down on the top of her head to keep it from splitting open.

God was testing her. As He had that poor slob Job. She never had been able to figure out why Job hadn't gone stark raving mad and hacked his whole family to death with an ax. That was what she was fixing to do to the workmen outside—just as soon as the pain subsided enough for her to regain control of her motor skills.

She had gone to bed with the last of that bottle of scotch Dane said she drank too much of, and gotten up with this lovely pounding head. A condition that had not been improved by five calls from businessmen canceling their advertising in the *Clarion*—most notably Garth Shafer, who had expounded on his reasons for ten ear-splitting minutes.

They were up shit creek, to put it mildly. Advertising was where newspapers—even little piss-ant papers like the *Clarion*—made their money. They couldn't afford to lose five advertisers. Especially when half of their customers hadn't paid their bills since man first landed on the moon. Shafer Motors had been their biggest, most reliable account. Now that money was gone and more was sure to follow if Shafer had his way.

"Life's a bitch and then you die," Elizabeth muttered as the drill started again.

"Omigodyouwon'tbelieveit!" Jolynn squealed as she burst in through the back door.

She charged through the room, sneakers pounding on the old wood floor, not even slowing down until she grabbed the end of the counter and wheeled around to lean against it. Her cheeks were flushed, her bosom heaving beneath her Harley's Texaco shirt. Her eyes were bright as marbles, staring out from beneath a tangled shock of bangs.

"You won't believe it!" she repeated emphatically.

Elizabeth peered up at her, eyes barely slitted open behind the lenses of her Ray-Bans. "I'm at a point where I'll believe just about anything," she said softly, careful not to jar her throbbing head with any undue jaw movements. "White mice cause cancer. Elvis is alive and pumping gas in North Dakota. Go ahead. You can't shock me. I'm fixing to go to work for a tabloid when I get run out of this town. Screw the truth."

"Boyd Ellstrom is doing the wild thing with the Widow Jarvis."

For one blessed moment, absolute silence reigned. Elizabeth shoved her sunglasses on top of her head and squinted at Jolynn as she rose slowly from her chair. Excitement stirred inside her, filling her with a giddy kind of euphoria.

"You liar," she said, fighting a grin.

Jolynn shifted anxiously from foot to foot, like a child in urgent need of a potty chair. "It's true. I stopped by to talk to Helen. You know—get her feelings about the aftermath of Jarrold's death, etcetera, etcetera, see if she knows anything about the book." She snatched a breath, pushed her hair out of her eyes, and pressed on. "So she comes to the door in her bathrobe and she's acting all weird and trying to get rid of me. Says she doesn't know anything about any book and tells me Doc Truman has advised bed rest for her nerves. She gives me the bum's rush, shoos me out onto the porch, and shuts the door. Well, I'm thinking this is strange, even for Helen, and I decide to pull a Columbo—you know, 'Excuse me, ma'am, just one more question.' I open the front door and guess who's standing in the hallway in his BVDs?"

"Christ in a miniskirt!" Elizabeth breathed.

"Close, but much uglier."

"Oh, my soul!" Elizabeth pressed a hand across her

mouth, turned around in a circle, then plunked a hip down on her desk as vertigo threatened.

Jolynn scooted around the end of the counter and snatched up the crumpled bag of M&Ms. "I want hazardous-duty pay for this," she said, chuckling as she poured out a handful of candy. "If God had wanted women to see Boyd Ellstrom naked, He would have created him in the image of Mel Gibson."

"I wonder how long that's been going on," Elizabeth mused. She pulled off her sunglasses and nibbled on the end of one temple as the wheels of possibility turned in her head. The unbalanced Helen with the ambitious Deputy Ellstrom. Ellstrom, who hadn't wanted the BCA called in on the murder.

Jo popped three green M&Ms into her mouth and chewed thoughtfully. "I don't know, but it certainly adds an interesting twist to the story, doesn't it? The plot thickens."

"That it does, my friend," Elizabeth murmured, remembering the predatory look in Ellstrom's eye as he had backed her into a corner in this very room. "That it does."

The drill started in again, and she winced as if the thing had struck a nerve.

"I take it the hangover is hanging on," Jo said.

Elizabeth slid her a look. "You have a real grasp for the obvious, sugar."

"Just call me Scoop Nielsen." She tossed the empty candy wrapper in the trash and moved toward the back door. "Come on, boss, I'll buy you a Coke. We'll go someplace where we can talk without the Black and Decker serenade."

They went to the back entrance of the Coffee Cup, where an assortment of lawn chairs sat in haphazard arrangement on an open porch that served as the employees' lounge during good weather and a sheltered spot for the trash Dumpster in the winter. Elizabeth lowered herself into a web chair, slipped off the camel-and-white spectator pumps she'd had made in Milan, and propped her stocking feet on the low porch rail, grateful for the sanctuary. She was in no mood to face another accusing glare from another native. News of the vandalism at Shafer Motors had run like wildfire through town, and, while Dane might not have had enough to charge Trace with, the citizens of Still Creek had tried him and found him guilty—and her along with him.

Jolynn emerged from the door and held it open while Phyllis stepped outside, a tray of tall iced Cokes in her gnarled hands. The three of them settled back and sat in silence for a moment, savoring their drinks and the quiet. The scenery left a little something to be desired—a weedy, graveled alley that faced the back of Buzz Knutson's welding shop and lawn implement dealership. But someone had hung a trailing pink geranium from one of the porch posts, giving the spot some color and a fresh scent, and the day itself was pretty, if not the surroundings. The sky was a soft, cloudless blue, the breeze warm with just a hint of the humidity Elizabeth had been told would come in July.

She closed her eyes and leaned her head back, pretending she was a thousand miles away, on a secluded beach on Paradise Island, with nothing to do but enjoy the feel of a man's strong hands as they rubbed suntan lotion into her back. Dane's hands.

Cursing her wayward hormones, she snapped her eyes open and shot a sideways look at her companions. Jolynn was off in her own dreamworld. Phyllis, though, was watching her like a hawk, watery brown eyes wide, ruby lips pressed into a thin line.

"What?" Elizabeth asked, sitting ahead and smoothing her long Ralph Lauren safari skirt. She lifted her hand to her cheek. "Have I got ink on me?"

"I'm just wondering if you've got the mettle to stick it out here," Phyllis said, then sucked on her straw. "It's not a bad town, you know. You're just here at the wrong time."

Elizabeth arched a brow. "Murder brings out the worst in people?"

"Adversity makes them close ranks. People are afraid. They band together with their own and leave outsiders to fend for themselves. I ought to know, I was an outsider thirty years ago."

Elizabeth sighed. Not only was she not "closing ranks" with the natives of Still Creek, she was holding up a spotlight to the town's flaws and warts and secrets. That was her job. How would they ever accept her if she insisted on doing it well?

"They had to accept you," she said dryly. "You give them food. All I give them is bad news and grist for the gossip mill."

"Things will settle down once Dane and Yeager nail whoever killed Jarvis," Jolynn said. Still overheated from the excitement of catching Helen Jarvis with Boyd Ellstrom, she raised her glass and brushed it across her forehead, wondering what would become of her fledgling romance with Yeager once the case was solved. As regional agent, Rochester was his base of operations. Rochester wasn't so far away—if you had a car that ran on all cylinders. . . .

"That might happen a little faster if we could get our hands on Jarrold's little book," Elizabeth said. "If we could convince Dane the book exists."

"Oh, he's convinced," Jolynn said, leaning around Phyllis to look at her friend. "Bret told me they were going to take another look at the interior of the Lincoln today in case it got wedged down in between the seats or something. I think you getting attacked convinced him."

Phyllis pricked her ears and went on point like a bird dog scenting a quail. "Bret?"

"Agent Yeager," Jolynn said primly, a hint of color staining her cheeks.

"Well, I'm glad to be of service," Elizabeth said irritably, too caught up in her own problems to catch Jo's reaction "He might have told me he decided to believe me," she grumbled. "That man is the most stone-headed, stubborn, rude—"

"Sounds like someone I know," Jo said dryly.

Elizabeth narrowed her eyes. "I am *not* rude."

"Pardon me."

Phyllis watched her carefully, reading all the nuances of her expression as skillfully as any psychiatrist. She hadn't spent thirty years observing folks without learning a thing or three about human behavior.

"Dane's a good sheriff," she said. "And a good man. Tricia turned him sour when she divorced him, but he's still got a good heart waiting for the right woman."

Elizabeth sniffed, dodging the older woman's sharp gaze. "Don't look at me, honey. I've sworn off men. Besides, there's only one thing Dane Jantzen wants from me, and it is not my hand in matrimony." She took a sip of her Coke and changed the subject. "So, what do you know about the Widow Jarvis and Deputy Dope?"

"There hasn't been anything on the grapevine," Phyllis said. She squared her bony shoulders and lifted her tiny chin to an angle of smugness. "But I've suspected something for a while now. There's something odd about that trio—Jarrold, Helen, Boyd."

"Gruesome, you mean," Jo said, shuddering.

Phyllis ignored her, too caught up in her role as consultant to bother with jokes. "I got the feeling Jarrold had some kind of sway over Boyd."

Jolynn made a face. "Jeez, you don't mean you think they were *all* involved, do you? God, Phyllis, that's disgusting."

"It might not have been that. It might have had to do with business, I don't know. But I wouldn't rule it out just because it paints an ugly picture. Small towns have their share of perversion and depravity too. We just don't like to think about it."

Preconceived ideas. Elizabeth set her glass aside, watching the condensation run in rivulets down the side to puddle on the red tin Dr Pepper tray. No one wanted to see the underbelly. Small towns were supposed to be neat and clean and free of sin. Deputies were good guys. Businessmen were upstanding. Divorced women who drove flashy red cars were trouble on the hoof. People saw what they wanted to, clung to their ideals of small town life, fought against anything that disputed their perceptions. She couldn't say that she blamed them. The more she found out about the truth, the less she wanted to deal with it.

NINETEEN

THE TRUTH. CARNEY FOX HAD DANCED AROUND the edges of it most of his life. From the time he was a little kid he had cultivated the fine art of lying. Like telling people his father had been killed in the famous wreck of the *Edmund Fitzgerald* on Lake Superior when the truth was his father was his mother's uncle, a piss-mean son of a bitch who worked on the docks in Duluth and screwed anything that didn't move fast enough to get away from him. Lying had become as natural to Carney as breathing. He had never been able to figure out why everyone didn't do it. A lie could save your ass every time if you were good at telling it.

It struck him as being wildly funny now that it was the truth that was going to have him rolling in dough.

"I know the truth," he said, his voice pitched to the level of conspiracy. He almost couldn't hear himself above the happy-hour noise in the Red Rooster, even though he was tucked back in the dark, narrow hall by the johns. In the pool room behind him, Gene Harris shot the break for a game of nine-ball and a chorus of shouts went up as balls skittered off in all directions. Garth Brooks was blaring again from the jukebox. *Shameless.* Half a dozen women just off work from the furniture factory joined in with voices like chain saws. Carney stuck a finger in his free ear and pressed his mouth against the receiver. "I saw you there. In Jarvis's car."

He had made this call once before. Just to get his new friend thinking about it, sweating out the possibilities, considering what the going rate for silence might be these days. With this call he would arrange the delivery of the first installment of his fortune. Shit, he was going to be a master at blackmail too, he thought, snickering, smiling against the grubby receiver of the pay phone. Someone flushed a toilet on the other side of the wall and he waited for the noise to subside.

"I think five thousand is a nice wad of cash, don't you?"

TRACE WHEELED HIS BIKE INTO THE PARKING LOT OF the Red Rooster and parked it next to the Pepsi machine. He dug a pair of quarters out of the pocket of his jeans and bought himself a Mountain Dew, which he slammed down in half a dozen gulps, Adam's apple bobbing. The soda cleared the dust from his throat and hit his stomach with an explosion of bubbles that came bursting back up in the form of an enormous belch.

No one was around to hear it. Happy Hour was in its final raucous minutes. Everyone was in the bar sopping up the last of the cheap beer. Trace wished he could join them. A man liked to toss back a brewski or two after a long hard day in the fields—or so he was told.

He had lived up to his promise to Sheriff Jantzen and worked like a dog, first laboring under the sun on the back of a hay wagon, stacking bales until the muscles in his arms and shoulders were hard as rock, then standing up in the hay mow, where the air was stifling and dusty, stacking the bales as fast as the elevator ran them up.

He'd never worked so hard in his life. His hands ached from lugging countless sixty-pound bales by the twine that bound them. Truth to tell, his whole body ached as if someone had beat him from head to toe with the narrow edge of a yardstick. By the end of the day his clothes had been drenched in sweat, as wet as if he'd stood out in a downpour. Chaff had covered him, sticking to every inch of exposed skin. The stuff was embedded in his hair and in his ears and fine bits of it were still working out of his eyes.

He had gathered from the grumblings of his co-workers that haying was no one's favorite job. The heat, the dirt, the backbreaking endlessness of it got to every-one except the lucky dog who got to drive the tractor—a job reserved for females or men with seniority. The latter had been the case at the Jantzen place. Pete Carlson had supervised the work. His two sons and Trace had pro-vided the muscle.

Pretty good guys, the Carlson boys. Ryan and Keith. Seventeen and fifteen respectively. They had shown Trace the ropes. They had teased him about being a city kid, but it had been a good-natured kind of teasing. By the end of the day they had all been kidding around like old buddies. Ryan had even invited him to come to the VFW baseball game that night. The team was pretty well set, he'd said, but they could always use some extra guys for practice.

That was where Trace was headed. Never mind that he was so exhausted he could have lay down and slept for a week. He had his mind set on playing baseball—and seeing Amy.

Amy. His stomach did a double clutch at the thought of her. Man, she was pretty. She had brought them all lemonade that afternoon. Ryan and Keith had eyes for her too—what man wouldn't?—but she had let Trace know, just by the sparkle in her eyes and the way she crinkled her nose when she smiled at him, that he was the guy for her. He shook his head at the wonder of it. Quick as he could snap his fingers, his whole life seemed to be turning around.

He crushed the pop can and tossed it into the trash barrel ten feet away, pretending he was Larry Bird sink-ing a game winner at the buzzer. The Rooster's side door swung open and Carney Fox ambled out with a can of Old Mil in one hand and a cigarette in the other.

"Hey, kid, where ya been all day?"

Trace cursed his luck. He hadn't planned on running into Carney, had hoped to avoid him for the rest of his life actually. He leaned back against the Pepsi machine and tucked his fingertips in the pockets of his worn jeans.

"Working," he said.

Carney sucked on his beer and belched derisively. "Working?" he sneered. "Working for who? I didn't think anyone in this shit town would hire you."

"Yeah, no thanks to you," Trace grumbled.

"Hey, you were swinging that pipe same as I was."

"It was your idea."

Carney took a step back, as if Trace's change of heart was a personal affront. He cocked his pointy chin to a truculent angle. "Jesus, what are you now—some pussy won't stand up for himself? I thought you had balls. Maybe I was wrong."

Trace just glared at him.

Carney took a long drag on his cigarette and exhaled twin streams of exhaust through his nostrils. "So, who ya workin' for?"

The answer stuck hard in Trace's throat. He didn't have to be a genius to know Carney wasn't going to think much of him working for the sheriff. Tough shit. A man had the right to work where he wanted, where he could.

"I was putting up hay at Jantzen's."

"Shit!" Carney jumped back, his sneakers scraping on the gravel. He tossed his cigarette aside. "The sheriff? What are you—stupid? The sheriff! Christ!"

He wagged his head in disbelief, then jerked it up and took an aggressive step toward Trace, his dark eyes gleaming with a feral brightness. "You didn't tell him nothing, did you?" he asked quietly, menacingly, leaning up into Trace's face.

Trace grimaced. "Jesus, what'd you eat for supper—shit sandwiches?"

Carney's expression hardened, tightening the skin over his bony face. He poked Trace in the sternum with a grubby forefinger. "Did you tell him something?"

"No."

"Then why'd he hire you? He thinks you're a jerkoff juvenile delinquent."

A part of Trace wanted to refute the statement. Dane Jantzen thought he was decent, had called him a man, had given him a chance. But he held his tongue. You couldn't win an argument with a guy like Carney. Better to just keep your mouth shut.

He sidled away from the pop machine, away from Carney and his rancid breath, and moved toward his bike. "I gotta go."

"Where?" Carney challenged. "Off to suck up to the sheriff some more?" His expression twisted from snottiness to a leer that curled his lip and showed off his crooked teeth. "Or is it his daughter you want to suck?"

Trace stopped in his tracks, protective instincts stirring to life inside him.

Carney cackled a malicious little laugh. "Oh, yeah, you got your pecker primed for her, don't you, Trace? I'll bet she's got some sweet hot pussy. She give you a taste yet?"

"Back off, Carney," Trace said softly, turning slowly around. His hands curled into fists at his sides and his temper rose inside him like steam in a pressure cooker.

Carney laughed again, flashing his crooked teeth. "Come on, Trace, tell me. She let you get in her panties yet?"

"It's none of your business," Trace snarled.

Swaggering a little closer, Carney tipped his head back and snickered again. "Afraid to fuck her, virgin?"

The taunt struck a nerve, jolting Trace like a bolt of lightning. How could he ever have thought this creep was his friend? Why would he ever have wanted to?

"Maybe you need a real man to show you how," Carney sneered. "I wouldn't mind taking a poke at her. She's just my type—"

The rest of his monologue rushed out of him in a grunt as Trace barreled into him, head down, and hit him square in the chest with his shoulder. Carney sailed backward, landing on his ass and skidding back another five feet on the gravel. His beer spewed out of the can he still hung on to, white foam flowing down over his hand like lava from a miniature volcano. He hurled it aside and scrambled to his feet, his eyes narrowing, mouth twisting into a grotesque grimace.

"You little shit!" he hissed, spittle spraying.

He came at Trace with both fists flying, catching him in the belly with one and the nose with the other. Trace's glasses went flying. He doubled over as blood spurted from both nostrils in a hot red stream. Through the haze of pain he saw Carney's knee coming up and he grabbed it and shoved, sending Carney sprawling backward again.

All the pent-up rage came rolling out like floodwaters from a burst dam. Trace didn't try to stem the flow. He'd been holding it back so long, he was sick of it. He let it all pour out, all the anger, all the hurt, all the fury he'd been storing up for years. And he focused it all on Carney, letting Carney take the fall for everyone who had ever hurt him or let him down—his father, Brock, Shafer, everyone.

He fell on Carney, swinging, and landed two hard blows before Carney reversed their positions. They rolled across the parking lot, grunting and swearing, each straining for the upper hand. Trace was bigger and stronger, but Carney had grown up scrapping to survive. The patrons of the Rooster streamed out of the bar to watch and cheer. Trace didn't see them, didn't hear them. All he was aware of was the blood roaring in his ears and the acid burn of anger in his veins. He fought blindly, not really seeing Carney Fox's face even when he rolled on top of him again and started swinging at his head. He didn't see the police car skid to a stop on the lot either, didn't hear the doors slam or Deputy Ellstrom yell at him.

Ellstrom grabbed him by the back of his neck and hauled him to his feet with a series of rough jerks. Carney scuttled out of harm's way and got to his feet, jabbing a bloody finger in Trace's direction.

"You're fucking crazy, man!" His lip was split, his nose was bleeding. Beneath a shock of greasy red hair that had fallen across his forehead his left eye was already beginning to puff up and darken. Half the buttons had been ripped off the front of his thin brown plaid shirt, and the tails hung out, making him look even skinnier and more weasellike than ever.

Trace had fared no better. The front of his white T-shirt was spattered with the blood still flowing from his nose. An inch-long cut angled across his cheekbone. His knuckles were scraped and bleeding. The left knee of his jeans had ripped wide open, the tear framing a kneecap that was bloody and dotted with bits of gravel. He figured he looked as though he'd just gotten the shit kicked out of him. Swell. He couldn't go to the baseball game like this. He couldn't let Amy see him this way. Damn Carney. All that bastard had given him was trouble from the word go. Trace couldn't believe he'd ever been desperate enough to want him as a friend.

Ellstrom gave him a rough shake. "I said, what the hell started this?"

The two combatants exchanged glances. Carney sucked in a mouthful of blood, turned his head, and spat. Trace tried to stem the flow of blood from his nose with his forearm.

"Nothing," he mumbled. He bent to retrieve his glasses—a half-formed blob on the ground by his left foot—and put them on as he stood, cursing mentally at the cracked lens that fractured the view from his right eye. His mother would have a fit when she saw this. Damn Carney.

"You two dickheads want to kick the shit out of each other, take it out of town," Ellstrom growled. He stepped between them like a referee, his right hand resting on the butt of his nightstick. "I've got a goddamn town full of tourists. I don't need trash like the two of you rolling around in the street. I ought to run you both in and let you rot in jail for a week."

"I didn't do nothing!" Carney protested, jabbing his finger at Trace like a bony exclamation mark. "He started it. He fucking tried to kill me!"

Trace didn't say anything. Carney would have given up his own mother to keep his skinny ass out of jail. Jerk.

Ellstrom looked at the Stuart kid, his eyes narrowed. The kid was nothing but trouble—him and his mother too. The bitch. She had wheedled that statement out of him, got his dick in a wringer for him, then walked away as though she didn't owe him a thing. Then her partner had caught him with his pants down—literally. Things were not going his way—Jantzen was on his case, he hadn't found that damned notebook, his bowels were in knots—and, the way he saw it, the trouble all came back around to Elizabeth Stuart. He reached out and gave her kid a rough shove that knocked him off balance.

"Go on, get out of here. If I catch you screwing up again, you're dead meat. That goes for you too," he said, shooting a glare at Carney Fox as he dug a Gas-X tablet out of his pocket and popped it into his mouth.

Carney lifted his bloody nose a notch, instantly smug over the prospect of escaping a night in jail. "Yeah, I'll go," he said, a sly gleam in his eye as he smiled at Ellstrom. "I got more *profitable* things to do tonight."

He chuckled a little as Ellstrom stared at him, then turned and swaggered away. Screw Trace Stuart. He had bigger fish to fry.

THE MOON WAS HIGH OVER THE SKELETON OF STILL Waters. Carney sat on the tongue of the office trailer, picking his nose. He congratulated himself on his choice of meeting spots. The scene of the crime. What better place to remind someone just how much shit was hanging over his head by a thread?

It was a creepy place, though, he thought, eyes darting

around as the wind moaned through the trees that towered around the building site. Just being here made his skin crawl. An image of old Jarvis getting his throat cut flashed in his mind. He hadn't known the guy was dead when he'd first seen them from the cover near the creek. Jarvis had been sitting behind the wheel of that big honking Lincoln, as always. Carney had figured they were having a meeting. Then it had slowly dawned on him that Jarvis wasn't moving while Jarvis's companion was busy rifling through the car.

Carney thanked his lucky stars that day had gone the way it had. He had decided to park his Impala in a field and walk up the creek to Still Waters. That way no one could tie anything to him without catching him red-handed. He had planned to do some damage to pay back Jarvis for not hiring him. But the damage had already been done by the time Carney got there. As much damage as one person could do to another person. He hadn't seen the deed done, but he'd seen the second best thing—who had done it.

With the hush money he planned to collect he would make a big buy from his connection in Austin and triple his investment selling dope in Rochester, where all the kids had money and parents who were doctors at the Mayo Clinic. It was a sweet deal all the way around. Smart as he was, Carney figured he'd be a millionaire before he turned thirty. He'd have money up the butt and a bitchin' babe on each arm.

Something crackled in the woods behind him. Carney sprang to his feet and swung around, pulling his finger out of his nose and reaching for the .38 he had tucked into the waistband of his jeans. A possum lumbered out of the undergrowth, peered at him with eyes as beady as his own, then trundled off.

"Fuck." The tension drained out of him on a sigh. He let his hand fall away from the butt of the pistol and turned around just in time to see the club a split second before it smashed his skull open.

TWENTY

ELIZABETH SAT BACK IN HER SQUEAKY DESK CHAIR and rubbed her hands over her face, obliterating the last remnants of her makeup. She savored the silence in the office. If there was one thing to be said for working late it was this—peace. No abusive phone calls, no people dropping in to cancel their subscriptions and demand their money back, no Horse and Buggy Days workers pounding up a storm outside. Now, in the quiet, she could pretend all was right with the world—as long as she didn't look at the plywood in the front window or the empty spot on the desk where her computer had once been.

She had missed supper and her stomach was complaining about it. She had missed her nightly chat with Aaron. *Really* missed it. It was getting to be a regular habit for her to hash over the events of the day with her Amish friend. Not that he ever had much to contribute, but he was a good listener and he had such a stoicism about him he never failed to calm her down.

Of course, she thought with a frown, he hadn't seemed in the best of moods when he had arrived that morning. She suspected his temper had something to do with the renewed construction at Still Waters, but she hadn't asked him about it. The look he'd given her when she had asked him if she could fix him a cup of coffee had been so hostile she had thought it wise to leave more volatile subjects alone. She supposed Amish people got up on the wrong side of the bed some days too, just like everybody else. Being a religious fanatic didn't necessarily spare a person from having moods.

"Burning the midnight oil?"

Elizabeth bolted in her chair, swiveling around toward the back of the room. Dane stood by the door, near the greasy old Linotype machine, leaning a shoulder against the door frame.

"What's that?" she asked about the plant he held. A pink fuchsia plant, like the one the vandal had killed.

Dane shrugged, moving into the room. Now that he was here with the thing, he felt stupid for bringing it. He had told himself all day he didn't have anything to apologize for. If he hadn't seen the light on in the office, he probably would have just gone home and given the plant to Mrs. Cranston.

"I—a—a peace offering," he mumbled, holding it out to her.

Elizabeth rose and took the plant from him, curling one arm around the pot and lifting the other hand to touch the pretty green leaves. "I gave you a piece, you give me a plant—is that it?" she said, one corner of her mouth curling up in a bitter imitation of a smile.

"I didn't deserve that," Dane said evenly, his gaze holding hers until she blinked and glanced away.

"No, you didn't," she murmured. She turned back toward her desk and set the pot down. "I'm sorry," she said, rubbing two fingers against her right temple. "I'm just feeling . . . beat up . . . used up. It's not your fault."

Dane stepped behind her. "I don't want anything permanent. I decided that a long time ago. It doesn't have anything to do with you."

"That's a comfort." Before he could comment, she turned toward him with a brittle, valiant smile. "You don't need to worry about me, sugar. I just got rid of a husband. I'm sure as hell not angling for another. I swore off men, remember?"

"Yeah," he said. "I remember."

And he remembered very well how she'd stuck to her vow. Just as she remembered.

"She did a real number on you, didn't she?"

"This isn't about Tricia." That was a lie and Dane knew it, but he plowed on past it, the master of denial. "I like my life the way it is."

"Well, you're the lucky one, then, aren't you?" Elizabeth said, looking straight past his macho bullshit. "The rest of us are scared of what we want, reaching for things we can't have. You've got it all together. The man in command. Your ducks are all in a row. Your pigeons are all in their little compartments. I'll bet that's what drives you craziest about this murder—it doesn't fit into your neat little scheme of things."

Direct hit—Stuart. Dane tightened his jaw but said nothing.

Elizabeth turned away and blew out a long breath. Her gaze fell on the plant. She wanted it to mean something that he had brought this plant to her. She wanted to mean something to him. Lord, she was as bad as Jolynn letting Rich use her. The man felt guilty so he brought her a present; it was a story as old as time. Just because it was a fuchsia plant, just because he'd held her while she cried, just because he'd made love to her with a kind of tenderness and passion she'd never known . . . It didn't mean anything.

Just as well too. She didn't need a man in her life. She didn't need complications.

"Don't worry about your precious world order," she said. "I don't want anything from you, Sheriff."

She was lying. She didn't do any better at it than Trace. Dane couldn't believe he'd ever taken her for an actress. Elizabeth might have put on any number of acts, but she was as transparent as glass.

"We can be friends," he offered. "Lovers."

Elizabeth looked up at him and laughed her hoarse, bawdy laugh. "You've never been friends with a woman in your life."

He flashed her a grin. "There's a first time for everything."

"Sure, why not? Want a candy bar, *friend*? Jolynn's got a stash in her desk."

"No, thanks."

Elizabeth gave him a look as she crossed the space between the two desks and helped herself to a Snickers. "Don't you have any vices—besides me, that is?"

"Sure." He leaned a hip against her desk, crossed his arms, and smiled. "I leave the toilet seat up."

"Oh, well, now I know you're not the man for me," she quipped. "That's a habit I just purely hate. I once fell into a toilet because a man had left the seat up."

She peeled the candy wrapper and took a bite, closing her eyes and moaning appreciatively at the taste of chocolate melting on her tongue. She swallowed and shot him a sideways glance, licking a fleck of chocolate from the corner of her mouth. "Find anything in the Lincoln today?"

"Nope."

"Would you tell me if you had?"

"Nope."

Elizabeth sniffed. "Some friend you are. I've got half a mind to keep to myself the fact that your Deputy Dunderhead Ellstrom is doing the old bump and grind with Helen Jarvis."

Dane narrowed his eyes. "Where did you hear that?"

"Oh, I didn't just hear it, sugar. I got me a witness. Unless your deputies are going around conducting police business in their skivvies, it's a plain fact."

"Great." Dane rolled his eyes heavenward. Helen and Boyd. Talk about strange bedfellows . . . or partners in crime? He fought off a yawn and tried to shut off his cop mode for the night. It was past eleven. Nothing was going to get solved at this hour.

"Well," he said, straightening away from the desk, "he can screw her all night for all I care. I'm going home. Come on, Mata Hari, lock up and I'll give you a police escort."

Elizabeth locked the front door, gathered her purse, her keys, the pack of photographs she'd gotten back from the drugstore that afternoon. She picked up her plant and headed for the Caddy parked in the alley. Dane double-checked the new lock on the back door, then followed her home, where Kenny Spencer was dozing in his cruiser in the driveway.

Dane reached into the car through the open window and hit the horn, jolting the deputy awake.

"You're on duty, Deputy."

Kenny straightened his shoulders back and swallowed hard. "Yes, sir."

Elizabeth gave the young deputy a sympathetic smile. "I'll bring you out a cup of coffee, sugar."

Spencer smiled shyly. "Thanks, ma'am. That'd be just the thing."

Dane snorted as they walked toward the house. "Is there a man in my department you haven't charmed?"

"Sure," she said, stopping on the top step and turning to face him. "You."

Not true, Dane thought, but he didn't correct her. It wouldn't have been the smart thing, and he prided himself on being a smart man.

"Thanks for the plant," Elizabeth said, tamping down the hurt flaring inside. When he started to shrug off her gratitude, she raised a hand and pressed her fingers against his lips, lips that had kissed her, loved her, whispered to her in the night. "Don't say it was nothing," she whispered. "Just don't say it."

And she turned and left him standing there before he could leave her.

THE NEXT MORNING ELIZABETH MOVED AROUND THE obstacle course that had become her kitchen, searching for a clean coffee cup. Her head was aching from another night with too little sleep. After taking a tour through her empty house, she had given in to the urge to go looking for Trace, leaving Kenny Spencer in her yard with a thermos of coffee. She hadn't returned until nearly one A.M., tired, upset, and without her son. She sat up, waiting on the sofa, watching a video of an old Tracy-Hepburn movie, determined to have it out with Trace about his nocturnal wanderings the minute he came home.

When she hadn't been thinking about all her problems with her son, she'd been stewing on thoughts of Dane. The movie had rolled on, without generating much interest. The last thing she remembered was Katharine Hepburn sassing off to Spencer and old Spencer kissing her socks off. Then the sun had come streaming in the window and she had awakened to white noise hissing out of the television.

"A masochist—that's what I'm turning into, Aaron," she mumbled, snagging a handful of hair out of her eyes. She had crawled off the sofa, up the stairs, and into a pair of age-faded cutoff jeans and her old UTEP T-shirt. She frowned now as she glanced down and caught sight of a new hole wearing through the cotton in the vicinity of her belly button.

"Do y'all have masochists in your group?" she asked, looking down at the Amishman who knelt on her kitchen floor doing something to the cupboard with a vicious-looking pry bar. "People who punish themselves over and over until you just want to take and slap the snot right out of them?"

Aaron glanced up at her, up what seemed to be an endless length of shapely bare leg, his mouth curving with disapproval even as desire stirred in the pit of his belly. Punishment. That was what he deserved for wanting her. It was what she deserved for tempting him, for going around half naked, her legs bare for all the world to see and covet. But punishment was for God to decide, he reminded himself, jerking his head back down to focus on his work. He picked up the pry bar and started loosening nails.

Elizabeth arched a brow at his nonresponse and continued on her search, picking up a stoneware souvenir mug from the Great Smoky Mountains and peering into its depths. "I reckon people have wanted things they couldn't have since Eve got her heart set on that damned apple, but I'm about sick of it myself."

She hit the jackpot, finding a pair of china cups that had belonged to the Stuarts for a hundred fifty years and gave a little whoop of triumph. She ducked down, coming almost face-to-face with Aaron as he plied the pry bar. "You want a cup of coffee, sugar? Served in a cup Great-grandma Stuart hid from the Yankees during the War?"

Aaron paused in his work, staring at the nail head. She was too close. He could smell her, the fragrance she wore, the soap she used on her hair, and beneath it all—woman. Warm, wicked, English woman. It was just this moment he had spent hours in meditation on since the Sabbath. Hours of wrestling with conscience and heart and bodily desires and spiritual needs. Gritting his teeth, he brought his weight against the pry bar and the nail came free with a horrible screech.

"I don't want nothing from you, English," he said.

His tone was as sharp as the nail he pulled from the cupboard. Elizabeth straightened and stepped back, feeling more hurt than she probably had a right to. After all, he had come to her for work, not friendship. And she was English. English, like the people putting up their garish resort right across the road from his house.

"They're going hot and heavy at Still Waters again," she said, pouring herself a dose of hot black caffeine. "I guess you're not too happy about that."

"They do what they will," he mumbled, flinging the bent nail away.

"Yeah, well . . ." Elizabeth took in the grim set of his mouth and the bleak cast to his eyes and poured him a cup too. She handed it down to him and he accepted it without a word. "That doesn't mean you have to like it."

Her attention drifted away from Aaron as Trace shuffled into the room in his sock feet, hair standing on end at the back of his head. His glasses were broken and his face was an artist's palette of blue and purple with sickly yellow tinges. Elizabeth nearly dropped her cup.

"Trace! Honey, what happened?" she asked, slopping hot coffee over her hand as she scooted around Aaron's toolbox to get to her son. She set the cup on the table and took hold of him by the arms, her expression twisting with a mother's sympathy pains and concern as she took in the damage to her baby.

Trace ducked his head in embarrassment. "I got into a little fight, is all," he mumbled. He wished he could have just stayed in bed until his mother had gone, but he had to get to work, therefore he had to suffer the inevitable fuss.

"A little fight?" Elizabeth reached up to touch the gash on his cheek and he jerked away from her. "You look like you took on a Mack truck!"

"It's nothing," he said, sidling away from her. He eased himself down on a chair, aching more from the work he'd done than from the fight, and reached for his high-top Air Jordans that crowned the pile of shoes on the floor. "Don't make a big deal out of it, Mom."

"Nothing?" Elizabeth parroted, bringing her hands up to rub her temples. Exasperation and concern rose in her like a pair of tidal waves. "How can you say it's nothing?"

" 'Cause—"

A knock sounded at the back door, forestalling Trace's explanation. Elizabeth huffed a sigh and turned as the kitchen door swung open and the frame filled with the bulk of Boyd Ellstrom. An instant burst of instinctive wariness shot through her as she looked at the deputy.

"What are you doing here?" she demanded, abandoning her usual southern charm. She liked this man less and less, and she'd pretty much loathed him to begin with. She couldn't look at him without picturing him and Helen, and if that wasn't enough to turn a stomach, nothing was.

Ellstrom let his gaze roam down over her, and she instantly wished she were wearing something less revealing—like a suit of armor. From the corner of her eye she could see Aaron straighten from his work and regard the deputy with a cold look. Ellstrom dismissed him with a glance.

"I'm here to see your son," he said at last.

Elizabeth turned toward Trace, her heart thudding in her chest.

Trace met the deputy's gaze, a terrible sense of foreboding sliding down through his stomach.

"Trace Stuart," Ellstrom said, shouldering past Elizabeth as he pulled a pair of handcuffs off his belt. "You're under arrest for the murder of Carney Fox."

TWENTY-ONE

I CAN'T BELIEVE YOU DID THIS," DANE SAID IN A dangerous whisper that had the other men in his office exchanging nervous glances. Kaufman cracked his knuckles. Yeager's dog whined a little and scuttled farther under his master's chair.

Ellstrom raised his double chins a notch. "I was out that way when the call came in about Fox. Stuart killed him, sure as I'm standing here. He probably would have finished the job in the parking lot at the Rooster if I hadn't pulled him off. The kid was pounding the shit out of Fox—"

"I can't believe it," Dane growled.

Ellstrom gave a snort of indignant disbelief. "There were fifty witnesses—"

Dane cut him off with a look. He pressed his hands on his immaculate blotter and rose slowly from his chair, never taking his eyes off his deputy. "You just took it upon yourself to barge in there without a warrant, without consulting me—"

"I'm a cop," Ellstrom barked. "I had grounds to believe Stuart committed a felony. I don't need your permission to do my job."

"You do if you want to keep it."

"You don't scare me, Jantzen," Ellstrom sneered.

Faster than he could draw breath, Dane was around the desk and in his face, those arctic-blue eyes boring into his. Boyd had to fight the urgent desire to back away. A healthy dose of fear clawed up his throat, belying his tough talk. Sweat popped out across his brow like dew beading on the skin of a pumpkin. His intestines curled into a writhing knot.

"I've had it with you, Ellstrom," Dane snarled through his teeth. "You mouth off to the press, disobey orders, slack off on the job—"

"*Me,* slack off?" He swallowed down the bile in his throat and went on the offensive. "What about you, *Sheriff*? Everybody knows the Stuart kid busted up Shafer's and you let him off. Now he kills a man and you're chewing *me* out! *I'm* doing my job while you stand back and let that black-haired bitch lead you around by your dick," he said bitterly, envy joining the ranks of the sour emotions churning in his belly. "What's the price to beat a murder rap, a great blowjob? I'll bet she wrote the book on it."

Dane's temper snapped. The cool control he was so famous for cracked like thin ice beneath the weight of Ellstrom's taunt. In a move from his football days he brought his forearm up and caught the deputy beneath the chin. Ellstrom's teeth closed with an audible snap and he slammed against the wall with enough force that the framed commendations jumped on their pegs.

The logical half of Dane's brain told him to back off, that Ellstrom had been within his rights to arrest Trace Stuart, that he should have been able to keep himself in check better than this. But Ellstrom had crossed too many boundaries that had nothing to do with logic and everything to do with the more primitive side. By badmouthing Elizabeth he had trespassed on Dane's territory. Dane recognized that fact even as he denied its implications.

"You're through here, Ellstrom," he whispered, his face inches from the deputy's.

Boyd choked as his windpipe bowed inward. He could barely hear his own voice above the pounding of the blood in his head. "This is assault," he sputtered, saliva running like water in his mouth, wetting his thick lips and gathering in bubbles at the corners of his mouth.

Jantzen smiled at him, a smile that sent ice through his veins and had his nerves clutching at his guts like frantic hands. "Yeah, too bad you don't have any witnesses."

He rolled his bulging eyes in the direction of Yeager and Kaufman. The blinds on the window behind them were closed, shutting out the dozen or so people who were working on the other side. Kaufman looked at his shoes and cracked his knuckles. Yeager pinched the bridge of his nose and batted his lashes. "I've been meaning to get to an optometrist. I just can't see like I used to."

Ellstrom made a strangling sound and Dane stepped back, easing his arm away from the deputy's throat, reining his temper in an inch at a time. He watched Ellstrom clutch at his windpipe and cough, and was disgusted with himself for letting the man get to him. He rubbed the tension in his neck, wondering if he would have come unhinged if Ellstrom's filthy remark had been about Ann Markham.

"Get out," he growled.

Ellstrom glared at him through watering eyes. "You haven't heard the last of me," he said hoarsely, shaking a warning finger as he backed toward the door. He gulped in a mouthful of air that felt as hard and round as a tennis ball in his throat. "You got elected because you're the goddamn golden boy. Big hero football player. You can't ride on that forever, Jantzen. That Stuart kid killed Fox. I say he killed Jarvis too. And I'll prove it. Then we'll see who the big man around town is."

He turned and stalked out of the office, rubbing his windpipe and ignoring the stares of fellow officers and secretaries as he bulled his way toward the door, leaving a toxic trail of gas in his wake. He would come out of this smelling like a rose, he promised himself. All he needed was a little luck and to find that goddamn book and he'd be sitting on top of the whole fucking world, with Dane Jantzen licking his boots and Elizabeth Stuart begging to lick any other part of him. He'd see to it.

Dane shook his head as he watched Ellstrom shove past Lorraine on his way out. Lorraine straightened her glasses and her bouffant and stamped after him into the hall, snapping at him like an outraged schnauzer. He had never been able to figure out why Ellstrom had stayed here after losing the election. Maybe Helen Jarvis had something to do with it. He didn't know and for the moment he didn't care. Already his thoughts were on Elizabeth. He could have safely bet a bundle she wouldn't take this well—Ellstrom interrupting her breakfast and accusing her son of murder. Hell, she'd probably be ready to kill someone herself.

He had his answer the instant he stepped into the interrogation room. Elizabeth stood with her arms crossed tightly beneath her breasts, her stubborn chin raised to the angle of challenge, eyes flashing as she scorched him with a baleful glare. She was ready to kill all right, and the cross hairs were drawn right between his eyes.

He turned his gaze to Trace, who was slouched at the table looking beat up and miserable. "I'm sorry about the way you were brought in, Trace. Ellstrom was grandstanding. I was busy at the scene. I didn't have any idea what he was up to."

"Does that mean we're free to go?" Elizabeth asked, her cool tone frosting over the fear that was churning inside her like a whirlpool.

"No, I'm afraid not." Dane looked to Trace again, trying to read the boy's expression. "I have to ask you some questions, Trace."

"I didn't kill him," Trace mumbled, staring down at his hands. His knuckles were scraped and bruised from colliding with Carney's bony face, the flesh torn and raw, which was just the way he was feeling inside—as though someone had taken a metal claw and raked it through him. Damn Carney, he thought, fear shaking him from the inside out.

"Shouldn't we have a lawyer present, Sheriff?" Elizabeth asked sharply, boring a hole through Dane with her stare, daring him to defy her as she had dared the young deputy who had tried to deny her access to the interrogation room. The poor man had tried to cite rules and regulations to her and had nearly gotten his throat torn apart for his trouble. Nobody, *nobody* was going to keep her from her son at a time like this. The deputy had backed off, obviously preferring to risk his boss's wrath than Elizabeth's. That boss stood before her now, watching her, calmly, quietly, those keen eyes taking in every aspect of her rage and probably looking right through it to the fear beneath.

"Trace hasn't been formally charged," Dane said, thankful Lorraine had gotten hold of him before Ellstrom had seen fit to book the kid. At least Trace—and Elizabeth—had been spared that process. "If you'd be more comfortable with an attorney present, you're welcome to call one."

Elizabeth glared at him for another minute, trying to decide whether or not he was calling her bluff. He met her gaze evenly.

"It's all right," he murmured, his tone a little too intimate, reminding her of how good it had felt to have him hold her. He wasn't holding her now. He was getting ready to question her son on a charge of murder.

"No, it's not all right," she snapped, backing away from him. "Nothing about this is all right."

She felt frightened and betrayed and all she wanted to do was take her son and get the hell out of here, out of this room, out of this town.

Dane motioned for her to sit down at the table and waited until she gave in before pulling out a chair for himself.

"Pete tells me you put in a good day's work yesterday," he said, his eyes scanning the damage to Trace's face. The boy had taken some licks. But by all accounts he had given as good as he got. Carney's face had shown as much damage; his head had shown worse. The side of his skull had been caved in like a deflated basketball.

"Yessir," Trace mumbled.

"I was glad to hear it. I thought that meant you were all through with Carney Fox."

"Yessir." He hung his head a little lower as heat rose into his face and shame and humiliation crawled around inside him like a pair of whipped dogs. He had been ready to turn himself around; now he had to sit across from the man who had given him a chance and be interrogated like a dirtball. And lie. He was going to have to lie. That was the worst of it. There was a lump the size of a baseball jamming his throat. He tried to swallow around it and nearly choked.

"You and Carney got into it last night." Dane picked up a pencil someone had left on the table and absently tapped the eraser against the smooth white tabletop, his gaze never leaving Trace. "What was that about?"

"Noth—" Trace began, but he caught his mother's glare and started again. "He was riding me about working for you."

"That was what you fought about?"

He nodded, dodging those spooky blue eyes that could probably see through lead walls. He couldn't say anything about Amy, about the dirty things Carney had said about her.

"Where did you go after Ellstrom broke up the fight?"

"Home. I rode my bike home and then I went for a walk in the woods."

"After dark?"

"Yessir."

"Why?"

Trace lifted his aching shoulders in a shrug and studied his fingernails. "It's a good place to think."

"You were alone?"

He tried to swallow again and wished he could be anyplace but here—the bitter, killing cold of the Antarctic, the hottest desert in Arabia, the steamiest, most snake-infested swamp—

"Trace?"

"Yessir," he mumbled, sliding down a little farther in his chair.

Dane drew in a slow, deep breath and sat back, letting it out in a carefully measured sigh. The boy was lying. He might as well have had the word stamped across his forehead. Elizabeth knew it too. She looked on the brink of tears as she dug through her Gucci bag for her cigarettes. Her hands were trembling as she flipped open a pack of Virginia Slims and selected one, then shoved it back in and abandoned the idea.

"That's your story," he said, shifting his gaze back to Trace, drumming the pencil slowly, methodically. "You were out in the woods, alone, until what time?"

"I dunno. Late."

"Elizabeth?"

Elizabeth pressed her fingertips against her lips for a minute, trying to stem the tide of panic rolling through her. The pressure of it built inside her until she thought she might explode. "I don't know," she said miserably. "I didn't hear him come in."

"Trace," he said gravely, "you're not a very good liar. You'd be a lot better off telling me the truth."

Trace held his breath for a minute, afraid that lump in his throat was going to crack any second. He stared down at his Air Jordans and wished he were as good at lying as Michael was at slam dunks.

"You don't have anything else to say?"

He winced inwardly at the disappointment in Jantzen's voice. Damn Carney. This was all his fault. "No, sir."

"All right." Dane tossed the pencil aside and rose from his chair, feeling the long, hard days in every joint and muscle he had and a few he had forgotten about. "I don't have a lot of choice here, Trace. I'm going to have to hold you for a while—"

"No!" Elizabeth exploded, standing up so fast her chair tipped over and bounced against the linoleum.

Dane kept his attention riveted on Trace, who had turned chalky-white. "I want you to think long and hard about this, son. You're a prime suspect and you've got no alibi. Telling me the truth can't be as bad as being charged with a murder."

He went to the door to call in a deputy. Kaufman came in looking sad and apologetic and started to reach for Trace. Elizabeth made the deputy back off with a glare and put her arms around her son. She hugged him for all she was worth, wishing she could just gather him up and hold him as she had when he'd been a little boy with a scraped knee.

"I love you, sweetheart," she whispered, stroking his cheek with a trembling hand.

He looked at her through the cracked lenses of his glasses, his gray-green eyes filled with fear and misery and a half-dozen other emotions he didn't give voice to. And in the back of her mind all Elizabeth could see was that little boy with the great big glasses and sober face telling her not to worry about him walking to school because he could cross the street by himself.

"It'll be all right, Mom," he murmured, wishing with all his heart he didn't have to put her through this, wishing he could go back and undo all the stupid things he'd ever done, wishing Carney Fox had never been born.

Kaufman took him by the arm and led him out, down the long white hall toward the jail and the separate holding area for juvenile offenders. Elizabeth stood in the doorway and watched him go, so heartsick she thought she might die of it. When they turned the corner and disappeared from view, she rounded on Dane, needing to vent some of the fear and frustration and fury.

"How could you do that?" she demanded, blinking furiously at the tears that filled her eyes. "He's just a boy!"

Dane reached past her and pulled the door shut, closing off her tirade from the network of curious ears in the offices beyond. "He's a suspect, Elizabeth. I can't let personal feelings interfere with that. I've got a job to do."

"Oh, right," she sneered, swiping a hand under her nose, struggling against the urge to hurl herself at him

and pummel his chest with her fists. "All your loyal constituents are screaming for his head, so you're just going
to hand it to them on a platter. All nice and neat and easy
for you—"

"It's not easy for me."

"He's innocent!" she shouted.

"He's lying!" Dane shouted back, the thunder of his
voice ringing against the cool white walls. "I can't just let
him go. He had a fight with Fox in front of fifty witnesses, then Fox turns up murdered a mile from your
house, and all Trace can say is he was out in the woods.
Do you know where he was last night, Elizabeth? Do you
know what he was doing?"

Elizabeth pressed a hand across her mouth and fought
back tears. She was Trace's mother. She should have
known where he'd been. She should have known what
he'd been doing. She should have known beyond a
shadow of a doubt that he couldn't have killed another
human being. But she didn't. God help her, she didn't
know that he couldn't have done it. He'd been so angry
lately, so unreachable. She had felt him slipping away
from her, and she had wanted so badly to pull him back,
but she hadn't known how.

"Oh, God," she whispered as the fear rose up to
choke her.

Dane watched her fight for control. A part of him told
him that this was a prime opportunity to sever any ties
between them. He had a job to do and nothing could
interfere with that. But still, he couldn't keep himself
from reaching out to her.

"Come here," he murmured, cupping a hand on her
shoulder.

She shrugged him off and stepped back. "No. You
can't have it both ways, *friend*. You can't break your life
up into neat little pieces—friend, lover, cop—and keep
them all from touching each other. Real life isn't that
tidy. You can't reach out to me when your conscience
pokes at you, then set me back on a shelf. I'm not a doll
for you to play with whenever you feel the need. I'm a

person with a heart, and I'm just sick to fucking death of getting it broken, so back off!"

She didn't wait for him to obey her. She pushed past him and bolted out the door. She ran down the hall and through the open office area with its maze of metal desks. Through the blur of tears she could see distorted faces staring at her, mouths moving, but she couldn't make them out, couldn't hear them. Voices and office sounds ran together into discordant noise that assaulted her ears. Standing near the front desk, Yeager's dog barked at her, and the agent reached out a hand toward her, but Elizabeth dodged him, slammed open the door, and ran down the hall that led to the parking lot. Clutching her purse against her, she barreled up the steps, out the door, and smack into Boyd Ellstrom.

He caught her by the arms and held her against him for a second before she could jerk back from the feel of his big soft body touching hers.

"Should have made friends with me when you had the chance," he said darkly.

Elizabeth glared at him, wrenching herself free of his grasp. "Fuck you," she snapped, backing away from him.

"Sorry, babe," he sneered, something cold and mean flashing in his eyes. "You missed your chance. Be sure you spell my name right when you print the story about me arresting your son, the killer."

Elizabeth whirled as a covey of reporters rushed in on her, shouting questions and brandishing tape recorders and cameras. She pushed past them and ran to the Caddy, tossing her purse on the seat and slamming the door without regard for any fingers that might have gotten in the way. The low-slung undercarriage of the car scraped the street with a shower of sparks as she hit the gas and roared out of the parking lot. Horns sounded as a pickup and a car coming from opposite directions screeched to a halt to avoid a collision with her.

She didn't spare a glance for the other drivers. She punched the accelerator and the Eldorado jumped ahead, leaving a smoking line of black rubber behind on the pavement. The Horse and Buggy Days workers paused in their construction of the parade judge's stand to watch her pass, and a bevy of senior citizens paused on their way to morning coffee at the Coffee Cup. An Amish mother grabbed her two small children at the corner of Main and Itasca and pulled them in against her long skirts as the Cadillac sped past.

Elizabeth saw all of them in her peripheral vision, but she dismissed them. She needed to think, not about Still Creek or what it citizens thought of her, but about Trace. She needed to clear the panic from her mind and wrestle the doubts into submission. No one else was going to come to her rescue or Trace's. She needed to think calmly and clearly.

The wind tore through her hair as the convertible shot down the highway like a bright red torpedo. The sun was shining, the sky was an incredible shade of blue. On one side of the road a herd of white-faced cattle grazed as their calves bucked and chased each other. On the other side, a field of corn lifted wide, money-green leaves to the sun. The day was altogether too beautiful for something like this to be happening. The weather should have been dark and stormy with a cold rain and a brutal wind.

Choosing a side road at random, she hit the blinker and swerved off the highway, the back end of the Caddy skidding sideways as the wheels hit the gravel. She straightened the nose of the car, eased off on the gas, and let the big car rumble down the road. When she felt she was far enough away from civilization, she pulled off onto a field drive and cut the engine.

Her first instinct had been to go home, but Aaron was there. Aaron the Righteous, who probably already thought she was the worst mother of the worst kid in the Western Hemisphere. She felt guilty enough without having the face of God staring down at her through Aaron Hauer's stoic countenance.

As her heartbeat slowed and her breathing returned to normal, she took a look at her surroundings. She was in the area known as the Hudson Woods, probably named after another family that had died out with the Drewes. The land was hilly and heavily wooded with a narrow strip of pasture running along the twisting path of Still Creek. From where she sat there wasn't a building of any kind to be seen, no sign of man at all except for the decrepit barbed wire fence that kept the cattle from wandering onto the road. A good place to think.

Like the woods behind her place, where Trace said he had been at the time Carney Fox had met his end.

He was lying. Elizabeth's heart sank at the thought. She brought her hands up and covered her face, pressing her fingers against her eyes until balls of color burst and swam in the darkness. He wouldn't lie unless he had something to hide. What did he have to hide?

Murder.

No. No, she thought, her mother's resolve taking hold of the fear inside her and squeezing it with an iron fist. Trace couldn't have killed anybody. She wouldn't, *couldn't,* believe he had. Yes, he had been sullen since the move—since before the move. Yes, he had seemed angry. Yes, he had been in trouble before, but never like this. The trouble he had gotten into in Atlanta had stemmed from a resentment toward Brock. The trouble he had gotten into at Shafer's had been to somehow avenge her honor. He had unleashed some of his youthful fury on inanimate objects, but Trace had never physically hurt anyone.

Until last night. His face and four dozen witnesses would testify to the fact that he'd had a donnybrook with Carney Fox in the Red Rooster parking lot.

But he wasn't a killer. He couldn't be a killer. Now that she had beaten back the fear, Elizabeth knew it with a certainty that went soul deep. Trace was her baby, her flesh and blood. She might not have known everything that was going on in the turbulent heart of a boy struggling to become a man, but she knew that at the center of the turmoil his heart was good. He couldn't have killed anybody.

Then why was he lying?

She groaned and leaned her forehead on the steering wheel as her thoughts chased each other around. The truth. She needed to find the truth. She was growing to hate that word more with each passing day.

Sniffling, she turned and reached into her purse for a tissue, but came out with the small manila envelope that held Trace's personal effects. Wanting to feel closer to him, she opened the flap and dumped the contents into her lap. Pocket comb, two pieces of Bazooka bubble gum, and his wallet. She stroked a hand over the fine calfskin wallet and smiled a sad smile. She had given it to him for his fourteenth birthday. Not a happy day either. Brock had promised to take him to a Braves game, then reneged when the opportunity had arisen to be seen at a big diplomatic do for the Japanese minister of trade. Business was more important than a boy's birthday, Brock said. Not to the boy.

Absently, she opened the wallet, snooping through it more out of habit than in the hope of finding anything. Seven dollars and a coupon for a jumbo popcorn at the State Theater. His student ID from the snotty prep school Brock had insisted he attend in Atlanta.

Tucked behind the ID was an old, dog-eared snapshot. Elizabeth plucked it out carefully, a wistful smile turning her lips. It was a picture of herself and Trace. They stood in front of a big old bright yellow Victorian house with green shutters and white trim on the wide porch. Elizabeth was wearing navy shorts that revealed a mile of tanned leg, a sky-blue T-shirt from Six Flags amusement park, and the biggest, brightest smile. Lord, had she ever really looked that young, felt that happy? Her hair was its usual wild mess and her sunglasses were crooked, and she stood behind Trace with her arms wrapped around him. He was grinning and gangly, his smile a checkerboard mix of baby teeth, permanent teeth, and no teeth. He wore the same Six Flags T-shirt, and he was clutching an inflatable brontosaurus by its long skinny neck.

Happier times. Elizabeth could easily picture the man

behind the camera. Donner Price. A big gentle bear of a man. A Methodist minister, of all things. They had known him for a summer down in San Antonio. The best summer of her life, not counting the summer she had fallen in love with Bobby Lee. That summer had been filled with hope and possibilities. Then Donner had been killed in a plane crash, flying medical supplies to the poor in Guatemala, and she had taken Trace and her broken heart and moved to Atlanta for a fresh start and a job at Stuart Communications.

She flipped to the next window in the wallet, shuffling past the memories and regrets. Her heart gave a thump and her melancholy vaporized. Another photograph. A school picture of a girl with rumpled chestnut hair and freckles on her pixie nose. She smiled out at the camera, her eyes a warm shade of blue, sweet and tinted with a sparkle of mischief.

Amy Jantzen.

THE REPORTERS FOLLOWED DANE FROM THE COURT-room like a swarm of gnats, hovering and buzzing but never getting close enough to bat away. He had just finished his second press conference in a week. Two too many for a man who had never been able to stand the sight of a press pass. Bunch of goddamn vultures. With no fresh meat on the Jarvis murder, the flock had begun to disperse, but they were back in full force today, with pencils sharpened and hunger in their eyes. Two murders in a week might not have impressed New Yorkers, but it was big news when it happened in the sticks. He could see the headline now: *Reign of Terror in Tourist Town.*

At the stairs to the law enforcement offices a pair of husky deputies stepped in behind him and planted themselves like oak trees, effectively stopping the mob. Dane breathed a short sigh of relief that ended on a groan as Charlie Wilder and Bidy Masters met him in the lower hall. He didn't so much as check his stride, hoping that they would get the hint and let him pass. They fell in beside him, rushing at his heels, trying to make eye contact, their faces creased with lines of worry.

"Dane, can't you do something?" Charlie said, not bothering to butter up his demand with his usual smile and chuckle. He was huffing and puffing at the pace, his round face going red from the effort and the stress. "There are news crews using the Horse and Buggy Days parade stand as a backdrop for stories about a murder spree! Do you have any idea what this is going to do to attendance?"

"Kill it?" Dane asked sardonically.

Bidy turned a shade of ash. "This is no joking matter."

"No," Dane agreed, "murder isn't." He stopped in front of the door to the offices and gave the pair a cool look. "I've got better things to worry about than the decline in revenues at the bingo tent."

Bidy bobbed his head down between his shoulders like a vulture, his dark eyes dead serious. "Like your job."

"You were elected to protect the community," Charlie said. "There hadn't been a murder here in thirty-three years, now we've had two in a week!"

"Well, I didn't kill them, gentlemen," Dane said softly, his gaze never wavering. "And maybe, if you'd quit hounding me about this penny-ante Podunk festival, I could direct my attention to finding out who did."

They stepped back as one, stiffening with affront. Not smart, offending the town fathers, Dane thought as he left them standing in the hall, mouths agape. But he was at a point where he didn't really care. His prime suspect in the Jarvis murder was at this moment stretched out at Davidson's Funeral Home with a skull that resembled a squashed pumpkin. Trace Stuart was cooling his heels in the holding cell, hiding something. And Elizabeth was out there somewhere, cursing the day they'd met.

The office was louder than the press conference had been. Telephones rang incessantly. Officers and office personnel alike were rushing back and forth, in and out. A steady stream of noise ran in an undercurrent beneath staccato bursts of conversation. Lorraine was manning her post with a fierce look. In front of her desk stood a uniformed bus driver and a blonde in short shorts and a tube top. Dane took them in at a glance. The bus driver was forty-five and fat. The blonde looked like a twenty-five-dollar date with too much makeup and half a can of mousse in her hair.

Lorraine rushed out from behind the desk. "Dane, the phone has been ringing off the hook for you."

"I'm incommunicado, Lorraine," he said, heading for his office. "Have you spoken with the coroner?"

She rushed along beside him, the chain on her cat-eye spectacles swinging. "Yes, and Doc Truman too. I left the messages on your desk."

"Good. Thanks."

"There's a bus driver here reporting a missing tourist. What should I do?"

Dane flicked another glance at the pair by the desk. Christ, this was all he needed—tourists getting lost. "Have Kenny handle it."

"All right." She dogged his heels another few strides, then stepped in front of him as they reached his office door. Her lips thinned into nothingness and her brows slashed down over her eyes like twin bolts of lightning. "That Stuart woman is waiting for you. With Amy."

"With . . . ?" Elizabeth and Amy? They had never even met. They were two very separate parts of his life. He shook his head at the thought that they had somehow come together without his knowledge or consent. "All right," he mumbled.

Lorraine sniffed indignantly and marched back to her post.

Dane swung the door open on his sanctuary and stepped inside. Elizabeth sat on the edge of his desk, long legs crossed, smoking a cigarette and wearing her best poker face. Amy sat in the visitor's chair in a bright pink T-shirt and faded denim shorts, her hands folded in her lap, looking like a truant awaiting the arrival of the principal. She turned her face up to him, her eyes wide, freckles standing out against her pale cheeks like nutmeg sprinkled on milk.

"Daddy," she said softly, looking as if she were bracing herself for a terrible blow, "I have something to tell you. . . ."

TWENTY-TWO

I'LL LEAVE YOU ALONE," ELIZABETH SAID, SLIDING from the desk. She stubbed her cigarette out in the Mount Rushmore ashtray and handed it to Dane, her gaze locking on his. "Seems the two of you have a whole lot to talk about."

Dane couldn't read anything in her expression. An ominous sign, he thought, wariness stirring instinctively inside him. He turned toward his daughter. Amy cast a worried look up at Elizabeth, who paused and patted the girl's shoulder.

"It was nice meeting you, honey," she murmured, smiling softly with sympathy and encouragement.

"You too, Mrs. Stuart." Amy bit her lip as nerves did a tap dance in her stomach. "Do you really have to go?"

Elizabeth stroked a hand over the girl's chestnut hair, remembering vividly what it had been like to be fifteen and in love—or at least infatuated. It had been difficult to differentiate between the two, all emotions being magnified enormously by that first mad rush of hormones. "I think it's best. You have to go this round with him, sweetie. It's part of the process."

"What process?" Dane asked as Elizabeth slipped out of the office and closed the door.

"Growing up," Amy mumbled, staring down at the nails her cousin had painted hot pink for her over the weekend. She would have given just about anything to avoid this conversation. She hadn't spoken more than a dozen sentences to her father since their blow-up over the dating issue. She had held her silent vigil, bolstered by the sure knowledge that he had wronged her. But now not only was she going to have to talk to him, she was going to have start out by telling him something he wasn't going to want to hear, something that made her feel more like the guilty one instead of one unjustly oppressed.

Dane took Elizabeth's place on the desk, sitting back against the smooth oak, hands braced on either side of him. "What's this all about?"

"Trace was with me." She blurted out the words, heart thundering, eyes trained on her fingernails, hoping that her father would be calm and rational and understanding.

There was a long beat of silence, during which a dozen different scenarios flashed through her head. Then came his voice—low, tight, deceptively soft, like the first distant rumble of thunder before a storm. "What?"

She lifted her chin and faced him, thinking that now she knew what it must have been like for French underground spies to be interrogated by the SS. He stared at her, his face taut, anger simmering in the depths of his eyes. "Trace couldn't have killed that person because he was with me when it happened."

Dane held himself perfectly, utterly still, tension tightening every muscle, every sinew, skimming across his nerve endings like a razor. "How could he have been with you? You were home in bed." Mrs. Cranston had told him that when he had come in. He had even gone up to check on her, only to find her door locked for the second night in a row.

Amy took a deep breath and told the story from beginning to end. How she and Trace had met. How she had been at the VFW baseball game, waiting for him to come, when news of the fight at the Rooster had hit the stands. How she had found Trace at their spot in the woods and invited him to the house to talk. How she had talked him into climbing the oak tree outside her bed-room window.

"We were only talking," she said, knotting her hands in her lap. "Trace is so sweet and I really care about him. I hated to see him hurting—"

Dane cut her off with a motion of his hand. "After I expressly forbade you to date—"

She bounced ahead on her chair, her face earnest. "It wasn't a date. We were just—"

"Dammit, Amy, don't try to argue technicalities with me!" he thundered, pushing himself off the desk. "You knew what I meant."

"Yes," she shouted back. "You meant you thought I was a child. Well, I'm not, Daddy!" She came up out of her chair, trembling with anger and fear, her long hair swinging around her shoulders like a rumpled veil. "I'm fifteen. I'm a young woman. Mom understands that, Mike understands, why can't you—"

Dane saw red at the mention of the man who had usurped his place in his daughter's life. "I don't give a damn what Mike Manetti understands," he snarled. "*I'm* your father—"

"My *father,* not my keeper," Amy said, refusing to back down now that the fight was on. "You can't force me to stay a child. That's one thing you can't manipulate and control, Daddy. I'm going to grow up whether you like it or not."

"You call asking a boy to sneak into your bedroom growing up?" Dane asked, arching a brow. "I call it childish."

"I call it trying to have a life when my father doesn't want to allow it."

"Oh, and I suppose Saint Mike would allow it?" he sneered, old resentments seeping up through old wounds to burn and sting like acid. "What the hell else does he allow *my* daughter to do? Throw orgies in the pool house?"

Amy rolled her eyes. "God, now who's being child-ish?" she said, shaking her head. She planted her hands on her slim hips, in unconscious imitation of her father's stance, and took a deep breath to try to calm the emotions roiling inside her, to try to ease the lump of tears in her throat. "Mike sees me for who I am and he trusts me," she said. "You don't know who I am. You see only what you want to see. You want me be your little pal, your little 'peanut,' for the rest of my life, because that's the niche I fit into in your life and God forbid you should have to change or compromise or not get your own way."

Dane narrowed his eyes. "What's that supposed to mean?"

"It means you didn't want to live in L.A., so you left. Never mind what Mom wanted or might have compromised on. Never mind that I got left out—"

"Amy, you were a baby!" he exclaimed, wondering how they had veered onto this topic. Wondering how to get off it before all the memories and emotions he had kept penned up inside him all these years found their way out. "You don't know anything about what went on between your mother and me."

She stared up at him through a sheen of tears and hurt. "I know you left."

"Your mother could have come with me. I wanted you with me. Hell, I *fought* to get you!"

"You fought *over* me," Amy declared, feeling that same helplessness, the same worthless frustration and pain she had felt during the divorce. She remembered realizing that Mommy and Daddy had stopped loving each other, and wondering if they would stop loving her too. Tears rolled off her lashes and down her cheeks. She wiped them with the back of her hand. "Like I was a toy or something," she muttered bitterly. "A prize. Well, I'm not a prize, I'm a person, and I'm growing and changing and having relationships with other people, and if you're not willing to accept that, Daddy, maybe I should just go home!"

Choking back a sob, she grabbed her purse from the

back of the chair and stormed out of the office, slamming
the door behind her.

Dane stood there like a statue, feeling old and weak as
the anger ebbed away. He heaved a sigh and slicked his
hands back over his hair. Why did life have to be so
damned complicated, every issue tangling with the next,
clouding the big picture, confusing, confounding? One of
the things he missed most about football was the simplic-
ity of it, the orderliness. The field was clearly defined, the
boundaries absolute, the rules unbending, the enemy instantly recognizable. Goals were set and gone after with
logical precision. Why couldn't life be more like that?

He didn't think it was an unreasonable request. None
of the things he asked for in life seemed out of line—
peace, order, his farm, his job, his daughter.

*God forbid you should have to change or compromise
or not get your own way.*

He lifted the picture frame off his desk and stared at
his little girl, frozen at eleven, happy, smiling, holding up
her hand-lettered sign. I LOVE YOU, DADDY.

His fingers tightened on the frame. That was what he
wanted most—for his daughter to love him. He didn't
like to think he had emotional needs, but he couldn't
deny that one. He had been robbed of Amy's childhood,
her presence had been stolen from his daily life. All he
got to have of her were photographs and snatches of
time. It didn't seem unreasonable to want to prolong that
time in any way he could.

Growing up couldn't happen fast enough as far as
Amy was concerned. She was eager to experience, to
sample life, to become an adult. But for Dane that time
would go by so quickly. A handful of visits. A series of
days. Then she would be gone, with a life of her own, a
family of her own. And he would be left with his little
cache of memories . . . peace, order, his farm, his
job . . .

His job. His mind seized on the words, frantic to escape the emotional mine field. He had a job to do. Drawing in a breath that wasn't quite steady, he blinked to

clear his vision, set the picture frame down, and left the office.

"YOU WERE TOGETHER," DANE SAID TIGHTLY. "TILL when?"

He watched Trace shift uneasily on his chair and swallow hard, his Adam's apple bouncing in his throat. "Till about two-thirty."

Trace watched the muscles work in Sheriff Jantzen's jaw. He was a dead man now. Messing with the sheriff's daughter. Jantzen looked mad enough to pull out a big ol' .44 Magnum, like Dirty Harry, and plug him right between the eyes. He had told Amy they would get in trouble, but she had begged him to stay, just a little while, and he couldn't see how any man could look into those big blue eyes of hers and refuse her anything. He couldn't. He didn't want to. He was up to his ears in love with her. It was wonderful and terrifying, and now he was going to get his butt kicked because of it.

"We didn't do anything, Sheriff," he said, scrambling to allay a father's worst fears. "Honest, we didn't. I mean—well, I *kissed* her—" Jantzen's nostrils flared. Trace gulped down another knot of fear. "But that was all. My hand to God," he swore, raising his right hand like a pledge. "We mostly just talked."

He was telling the truth. That was one thing about Trace, Dane thought as he sat back and rubbed a hand against the band of tension tightening across his forehead. He wouldn't have had any trouble catching the kid in a lie. Trace was positively beaming with honesty, his eyes wide and imploring Dane to believe him. Dane drummed his fingers against the tabletop and glanced at Elizabeth, who stood off to the side with her arms crossed. She hadn't had much of anything to say throughout the interview. Hadn't had a single word for him. She offered nothing now, not anger, not sympathy, nothing.

"Why didn't you tell me this before, Trace?"

Trace rocked ahead on his chair, pushing his broken glasses up on his nose. "I didn't want to get Amy in trouble. She said you were being a real hard-ass—" He bit off the word and cursed himself for being dumber than dirt. His face flushed scarlet and he tried again. "I mean, that you thought she was too young and all."

"Trace, you could have been charged with murder—"

"But I didn't do it!" he said emphatically. "I figured you'd catch who did and then that would be the end of it. I'd go free and Amy wouldn't get in trouble with you. All we did was talk . . . mostly—"

Dane lifted a hand to hold off any more revelations. On the scale of bad days, this had to rank up there with the 1979 game against Seattle that could have won the Raiders a wild card berth in the playoffs. He had dropped a sure thing on the twenty-yard line and blown his knee in the ensuing collision with the Seahawks free safety. They lost the game 29 to 24 and he spent the next six months in rehab.

"Please don't be too mad at Amy, Sheriff," Trace said earnestly, his young heart aching at the idea of his sweet little Amy weathering the kind of storm her father could undoubtedly unleash. "I take full responsibility. I mean, I'm older than her, and I should have known better, but I . . ."

He shrugged and looked down at his fingernails, not quite able to put into words what he felt when he was with Amy. She was so sunny and sweet, and she got him talking about things he didn't ever talk about with anybody. Like how he wanted to go to college to become an aerospace engineer, and how much it had hurt to have Brock Stuart reject him. In the few days he'd known her, Amy had become the best friend he'd ever had—besides his mom, and moms fit into a category of their own, so that didn't count. He wanted to make Jantzen understand, but he had a feeling that wasn't going to happen, him being Amy's dad and all.

"I just wanted to be with her," he mumbled, tamping down all the grand and frightening feelings of first love and compressing them into that one statement. He glanced up at Jantzen through his eyelashes. "I'll understand if you don't want me to work for you anymore."

Dane heaved a sigh. How could he come down hard on a kid who had been willing to go to jail to protect his daughter's honor? It wasn't Trace he was disappointed in, but Amy. And maybe not so much Amy as fate, the fate that had separated him from his daughter, the factors that had driven Tricia to want things he couldn't give her. All of it weighed down on him like a millstone, making him feel too vulnerable, too mortal. None of that was Trace Stuart's fault.

"I don't want you climbing in my upstairs windows," he growled. "But you're not fired. Amy, however, is likely to be grounded for the rest of her natural life."

"But Sheriff—"

Dane cut him off with a look. "Don't push it, Trace."

"Yessir. Thank you, sir."

Dane pushed his chair back and rose, feeling old and tired, responsibility hanging on him like a wet woolen robe. He had two murders to solve and a private life that was tumbling around him like a house of cards in a stiff wind. "You're free to go."

He looked at Elizabeth, who was still watching him with that even, emotionless expression. "I'd like to talk to your mom for a minute in private."

Elizabeth pushed herself away from the wall and stepped ahead, nodding to her son. "Wait for me in the car, Trace."

"Yes, ma'am."

Trace slid out of his chair and followed Deputy Kaufman out of the interrogation room. The door closed and for a moment silence hung like humidity in the air, thick and oppressive. Finally Dane shrugged.

"I'm sorry."

Elizabeth gave him a smile and shook her head. "It's not your fault your daughter is growing up to be sweet and beautiful. In fact, I can't see that you had much of anything to do with that—especially the sweet part."

"That's not what I meant."

"I know what you meant." She slung her purse strap over her shoulder and started for the door, the last scene they had played out in this room too fresh in her mind. She had all but told him she was in love with him. It didn't seem smart to stick around and further endanger her dignity. "I've got to go," she said, looking past him. "I've got a paper to get out."

He should have let her go A smart man would have. "I'm sorry about this mess with Trace. I wouldn't have put you through it if I could have helped it."

"You were just doing your job."

Somehow, when she said it, it didn't sound like a very good excuse, Dane thought. The separate strands of his life had crossed and tangled—job, fatherhood, friendship, sex. This was just the kind of mess he had diligently avoided for most of his adult life, the kind of mess he would avoid again as soon as he got the lines uncrossed and straightened out.

"I'm sorry if you got the wrong idea—about our relationship."

Elizabeth bit down on her pain and managed another brave smile. "We don't have a relationship. We have sex. See there?" she asked, meeting his gaze for one brief, painful second. "Now you've got me doing it. Cutting up my life into neat little chunks. Next thing you know, I won't be able to let any of my foods touch on my plate."

She sauntered to the door, throwing him a sultry look over her shoulder as she went. "See ya 'round, cowboy. Catch yourself a bad guy. Maybe you'll get your name in the paper."

She walked out of the station with her head up and her eyes forward, ignoring the male heads she turned and ignoring the pernicious glare of the ever-diligent Mrs. Worth. She cut through the mob of reporters waiting outside the door, blocking out the noise of the questions they hurled at her, blocking out the feral looks in their eyes with her Ray-Bans.

Trace waited for her in the Eldorado. He had raised

the top on the car, shut the windows, and locked the doors to keep the press at bay. Elizabeth slid in behind the wheel, started the engine and the air-conditioning. Without a word she put the car in gear and piloted it away from the courthouse. Neither of them said anything until they were out of town. Then Elizabeth pulled off on a side road and stopped the car.

Trace looked at her, bracing himself for the worst. "I guess you're pretty pissed at me, huh?"

"I'm not proud that you lied," Elizabeth said, pulling off her sunglasses and setting them on the dash. She turned toward him with love in her eyes. "But I'm kind of proud of the reason you did it. It wasn't smart, but your heart was in the right place."

His brows shot up above the rims of his glasses. "You're not mad?"

"I don't want to be mad right now," she whispered, reaching out to brush his short dark hair. "Right now I just want to be glad to have you sitting here with me instead of in some cell. I want to tell you that in spite of all the mistakes we've both made, I'm glad you're my son."

Tears brimmed in her eyes and in her throat, thickening her voice. She caught his hand with hers and squeezed it hard, as if she might be able to pass her feelings to him through touch. "Don't *ever* think you messed up my life, Trace. Don't *ever* think I didn't want you," she whispered. "God knows I haven't had the greatest life to date, but you are the one bright spot. You're the best thing that ever happened to me, honey. I wouldn't trade you for anyone or anything in the world."

A big ball of tears wadded up at the back of Trace's throat and he knew he had to say something stupid or start crying like a baby. One corner of his mouth hooked upward in a lopsided smile. "Not even for a million dollars and new Ferrari?"

Elizabeth shook her head, laughing and spilling tears to be quickly wiped away with her free hand. "Not even."

She leaned over and rested her head on his shoulder, struck anew by how broad it was getting, how strong. The knowledge that he wouldn't be a boy much longer struck her like a spear. He had already begun the struggle toward manhood, was already feeling his way along to find the right path. At that moment, perhaps more than any other, she wished she had made better choices for him, wished she could have given him a stable home, a father who loved him, a man who could help him take the right steps on that climb. But she hadn't. She would have to live with the choices she had made, and with the knowledge that Trace would be grown-up and gone soon, making his own choices.

"Mom, please don't cry," he said softly.

She heard the embarrassment in his voice, but she heard the love too, and the concern. It had always upset him to see her cry. He had always tried to talk her out of it. The memories of other times, other tears brought a bittersweet smile to her lips. She lifted her head and looked him in the eye through the cracked lenses of his glasses.

"I'll always be your mama, and I'll always have the right to cry over you, even when I'm a hundred and you're old enough to keep your teeth in a glass at night," she told him, blinking to hold her tears at bay. "Don't you forget it, mister."

He grinned a lopsided grin he had inherited from her and glanced away to hide the fact that his eyes were shiny too. "Yes, ma'am."

Elizabeth sniffed and turned her attention back to driving, putting the Caddy in gear and pointing it in the general direction of home. "I'll drop you off," she said as all the feelings settled like dust inside her. "You can do penance by cleaning up your room." She shot him a sideways look. "And don't forget the ashtray under the bed."

Trace ducked his head and smiled to himself. "Yes, ma'am."

TWENTY·THREE

THE WORDS ON THE SCREEN OF THE RENTED COM-
puter blurred together, solidifying into a white blob the
shape of a snowman. Elizabeth sat back and rubbed her
eyes, fighting a yawn. She had dropped Trace off at
home, then come back to town, sticking to the side
streets to avoid any attention from the out-of-town
press—or from the citizens of Still Creek, for that matter.
News of Trace's arrest and release would not be popular
with the locals. They were frightened and angry at the
violence that had so thoroughly disrupted their lives, and
they were looking for someone to blame, someone they
could see and point at and envision in their minds as
being the embodiment of that violence. They saw Trace
as a likely candidate. Someone from outside their world,
outside the realm of their influence and experience,
someone safe to hate.

As much as she wished it weren't her son they had
singled out, Elizabeth understood their reasons. If they
looked to their own, if someone they knew and trusted
had turned on them, then their whole world would tilt
on its axis and they would be left with nothing to cling
to, nothing to believe in, no one to trust. They would
each be left alone in a sense, and she understood the
dread of that better than most.

She hoped for everyone's sake the case would be
solved soon. Once the real killer was caught and the

truth was known, the healing process could begin. The town would never be quite the same again, but the wounds would scar over and life would settle back almost in place. The hoopla surrounding the Stuarts would die down and Elizabeth would be able to print a softer kind of truth in the *Clarion*—the truth as it normally stood around Still Creek. The minutes from the PTA. The news of whose relatives had visited on the weekend. No murders, no conspiracies, no dark secrets.

She glanced at the little wind-up clock she had brought in and wondered what was taking Jolynn so long. She had gone on a food run at eight-thirty. It was now nearly nine. Through what was left of the front window Elizabeth could see the last remnants of daylight fading into night. They had three articles to finish and typeset, and the paste-up to do. If Jo didn't get back soon, they would be working right through the night in order to get done in time to make it to Grafton for the printing of the regular weekly edition.

"What we need is another pair of hands," Elizabeth muttered. Of course, there was no money for additional employees. If the advertisers kept pulling out and the circulation kept dropping, there wouldn't be a paper.

Life's a bitch and then you die . . . alone.

It would have been so nice to have someone to lean on, just a little bit, right now. A pair of strong hands to rub her shoulders after a day like today, or to pat her back in consolation. But that wasn't in the cards for her.

"You swore off men, sugar," she muttered to herself, clicking out another few words at the prompting of the blinking cursor on the screen. "Stick to your word."

Dane Jantzen wasn't going to make a go of things for her here. Only she could do that. And she would give her best shot. She glanced again at the clock. If Jolynn would ever get back . . .

She breathed a sigh of relief at the sound of the back door creaking open and slapping shut.

"Well, it's about time you got—" Her words died in

her throat as she swiveled her chair toward the back of
the room.

Leaning against the greasy old Linotype machine was
Boyd Ellstrom.

JOLYNN SLIPPED INSIDE THE OPEN GATE AT BILL WA-
terman's junkyard, shaking her head at the lack of security. Situated half a mile out of town, on the back road to
the Hudson Woods, the space was rented by the county
and used as an impound lot because the yard was surrounded by a chain-link fence —never mind that Waterman never bothered to lock the gate. Of course, most of
the time there wasn't anything here worth stealing. Tonight there was something that at least one man may
have died for—Jarrold Jarvis's book.

The yard was deserted and spooky-looking, ringed by
trees and lit by a single mercury vapor light on a tall bare
pole. Mountains of metal sat rusting, oxidizing into dust
while Waterman put off hauling it away. In the center of
the scrap heaps stood the corrugated tin shed where dead
cars were dissected for their parts and where Waterman
kept an office of sorts. The Lincoln would be parked
around back.

Jolynn thought she would be eternally grateful to
Phyllis for running out of barbecued potato chips. If not
for that, she would never have stopped in at the Rooster,
would never have struck up a conversation with a disgruntled Harley Cole. Harley, of Harley's Texaco fame,
who had bid for the contract on the county impound
yard and lost because he didn't have an adequate fence.
Harley, who felt entitled to keep Jarrold Jarvis's powder
yellow Lincoln Town Car at his place since he had done
every bit of service work on it—including installation of
an oversize key box on the undercarriage.

If Jolynn's hunch was right, Harley's handiwork
wasn't a key box at all, but a neat little hidey-hole. She
was going to find out. She crossed her fingers and offered
up a little prayer as she wound her way among the stacks

of rusted junk. If she was right, and she found the book, the *Clarion* could scoop the city papers. She would get back to the office and spend the night working on the story. The weekly edition would be run in the morning and on the stands before anyone else would have time to substantiate the rumor that the book even existed.

The phrase *tampering with evidence* drifted through her head, but she dismissed it. She had no intention of taking the book with her. All she wanted was a peek at what was in it. Then she would call Yeager in.

The two of them had stayed up half the night racking their brains over the whereabouts of the book. Bret had bet on a hiding spot at Still Waters, somewhere in or around the office trailer, but the search today had proved futile. Jolynn smiled at the prospect of outsnooping him. He would owe her a hot fudge sundae. And a back rub. Most of all, she smiled at the prospect of being the one to crack the case. Elizabeth would be proud of her, Bret would be proud of her. She would be proud of herself for the first time in a long time.

That thought gave her the courage to shake off the jitters creeping in on her from the shadows of the junk piles. She had wasted too much time mourning the loss of her marital status. Her worth was in herself, not in being Mrs. Rich Cannon. She hadn't lost any of her talent or intelligence when she had lost Rich. All she had lost was dead weight. He had never encouraged her or seen any worth in her abilities. Her sole purpose in his life had been to pay homage to him, to see to his comfort and needs.

Susie Jarvis could have him. The man Jolynn could love would share interests with her, would see her for the bright, capable person she was, would treat her with both passion and compassion, and most of all respect.

She had a sneaking suspicion his name would be Bret Yeager.

The nose of the Lincoln came into sight as she rounded the corner of the building, and Jolynn set her mind to the matter at hand. The box was right where

Harley had told her—within easy reach of the driver's seat, just under the side panel. The ease with which it came loose gave a clue as to how frequently Jarvis had used it. Not remarkable in itself, the black metal box was no more than four inches by five inches and less than an inch thick. The notebook inside —carefully wrapped in plastic—was equally unimpressive. A simple black binder holding pages of blue-ruled paper. The value of the thing lay in the neatly printed notes.

Jolynn sat down on the gravel with her back against the Lincoln and began scanning the pages by the beam of a pocket flashlight she had brought along for the purpose. Most of the names on the pages were familiar. Townsfolk who had gone to Jarvis in time of need. Ivan Stovich, who was on the brink of losing his farm because of his alcoholism. Todd Morrison, who had already failed in three different business ventures. Verne Syverson, who played the commodities market with no skill and less sense. Boyd Ellstrom—

Boyd Ellstrom: $18,700.00—gambling debt.

"Holy shit," Jolynn whispered. Apparently, Deputy Ellstrom wasn't any better at betting than he was at law enforcement.

As she turned to the next page her eyes widened and her stomach dropped. She scanned the narrow beam of her flashlight down the column of dates and figures, then flicked it back up to the name at the top of the page, her heart pounding as adrenaline and dread shot through her.

"Jeez Louise . . ." Her voice trailed off as she flipped to the next page and the next, her gaze racing over the names and dates. She felt as if she had just opened Pandora's box and found snakes writhing inside it, and the excitement that had burst to life within her struggled to bob above the surface of an overwhelming tide. She suddenly felt like a toddler who had fallen into the deep end of the pool.

"Hand it over, Jolynn."

Her heart thudding, she jerked her head up. She

hadn't heard him approach, she'd been so engrossed in her reading, but he was standing not five feet away from her, near enough that she could see his face clearly in the fading light. "Rich."

Slowly, she rose to her feet, her back pressed against the door of the Lincoln, her eyes fast on her ex-husband. Elizabeth had always said he bore some resemblance to Robert Redford as the Sundance Kid, with his square face, rumpled sandy hair, and mustache. But in this setting, with shadows falling across his face and his mouth set in a grim line, his strongest resemblance to that character was the aura of danger that radiated from him.

"I'll take the book, Jolynn," he said quietly.

He reached his left hand toward her expectantly, assuming she would give him what he wanted. As she always had.

"Not this time, Rich," she murmured, shaking her head.

Anger, dark and cold, flashed in his eyes. He took another step toward her, left hand outstretched. In his right he clutched a tire iron.

HE WAS DRUNK. ELIZABETH COULD SMELL THE WHIS-key on him. She got up from her chair slowly, as careful not to make any sudden moves as if she were facing off with a grizzly bear.

"Were you waiting for me?" Ellstrom asked, his mouth twisting into a leer. "Or were you waiting for Great Dane, big man on campus?" He straightened away from the Linotype, swaying a little on his feet, frowning at the smear of grease the machine left on the sleeve of his rumpled uniform shirt.

"Dane," Elizabeth said automatically. "He should be here any minute."

Ellstrom chuckled and wagged a finger at her, shuffling slowly toward her. "You lying bitch. He's not coming here. He's on a call."

He let his gaze slide down over her body, lingering on

every womanly curve, savoring the idea of touching those curves. "Jantzen," he sneered, his mouth curving down as if the name left a bad taste. "Thinks he's so fucking smart. He's nothing but a washed-up jock. He doesn't know shit about Jarvis or anything else."

"And you do?" Elizabeth ventured, reaching behind her to feel across the desk for something to defend herself with. Her fingers brushed her purse and she thought longingly of the Desert Eagle, but she had stuck the gun back in her nightstand after her lesson with Dane, afraid of the power of it and the potential for disaster.

Ellstrom ignored her question, his attention homing in on the way the fabric of her T-shirt snugged across her breasts as she reached back, zeroing in on the way the U of UTEP outlined her right nipple. Lust brought color to his fleshy face. He shuffled another step closer. "Jantzen's not coming, but I'm gonna," he snickered, reaching a hand between his legs and cupping himself suggestively.

Elizabeth backed away from him slowly, never taking her eyes off him. She moved from the desk and the counter, where he had cornered her days before. The wheels in her mind were spinning in high gear. His drunkenness might give her the edge in quickness, but it definitely gave him an edge in the danger category. Whatever inhibitions he might have normally regarding use of force had been washed away by booze. He was a big man—not just heavy, but big-framed. She would have been a fool to think there wasn't physical strength beneath the flab. And he was angry. He had decided she was somehow responsible for all the problems in his life. She and Dane. He wanted restitution. He wanted what most of the men in this town believed she gave away for a smile and a pat on the fanny.

"You owe me," he said, his expression hardening.

"I know," Elizabeth murmured, buying time. She took another step backward, fighting the urge to look over her shoulder to see how close her goal was. "I've been waiting for you."

He blinked in confusion and his step faltered, his motor skills seizing up as his brain tried to direct energy elsewhere. "You told me to fuck off."

She sent him what she hoped was a sultry smile and moved back another step toward the private office she never used. "Oh, come on, sugar. Can't you tell when a lady is playing hard to get?"

She held her breath while he stared at her long and hard, trying to reason through the fog of alcohol whether or not she was playing on the level. She was betting his ego would win out—maybe betting her life. Ellstrom had been involved with Jarvis somehow. With Helen at the very least. And there was something fishy about his arresting Trace for the Fox murder. He had claimed he was just in the area when the call came, and that he had known there was bad blood between Trace and Carney. But he could have killed Carney Fox himself and set Trace up to take the fall. Maybe Fox had seen him kill Jarvis. Maybe Boyd Ellstrom was just plain crazy.

Elizabeth swallowed hard at her fear. She had learned at an early age to think on her feet and save her own ass. In her experience, white knights didn't charge in for a last-second rescue. A woman was on her own in this world, and she either saved her bacon or became a victim.

She tossed her hair over her shoulder and crossed her arms beneath her breasts, plumping them up beneath the thin, soft fabric of her T-shirt.

"I was just teasing you, big guy," she said, batting her lashes. "Don't you like to be teased? It's one of my specialties."

Her back hit the doorjamb and Ellstrom moved in a step closer. Elizabeth fought to grab a breath through the smell of sweat, cheap liquor and bad gas. Her heart jammed at the base of her throat and pounded there like a fist against a door.

"How about a blowjob?" he asked, his gaze glued on her mouth. He could already see those ruby-red lips wrapped around his cock. Just the thought of it had him stretching his shorts. "I'll bet that's one of your specialties too."

She struggled to bend a grimace into a wry smile. "Ever seen *Deep Throat*?"

Her voice was husky and breathless from straining against the need to gag—on her fear, on the smell of him, on what he was suggesting. Ellstrom took it as part of her seduction, and he snickered like an overgrown teenager. He was no more than a foot away from her. His prick was at full attention, straining against the fly of his black trousers. Thinking she would rather wrap her hand around a rattlesnake, Elizabeth forced herself to reach down and touch him. She ran her fingers down the length of him, shuddering inwardly, laughing to cover her disgust.

"Why, Deputy, is this a gun in your pocket or are you just happy to see me?"

Ellstrom groaned and thrust himself against her touch. Jantzen had always been the one to get everything in this town—praise, adoration, the sheriff's job, his pick of the women. That was going to change. Starting now.

He reached for his belt buckle.

Elizabeth grabbed his hand. "Not right here, sugar," she murmured, looking up at him through her lashes. "In the office. You can sit in my chair while I make you happy."

He was sold. She could tell by the glazed look in his eyes. Hormones and whiskey had fogged what little common sense he had. She slid her hands up his chest to his shoulders and backed him into the cramped, cluttered office, wondering if he had been the one who'd tossed the place.

"Take off your blouse," he ordered. "I want to see your tits."

She slanted him a smile. "In a minute, honey. What's your hurry? We've got all the time in the world."

He snickered again, tickled at the prospect of spending the night screwing her. Jantzen would shit a brick when he found out. And he *would* find out. Boyd would make sure of it. Just as he would be sure of finding that damned book of Jarvis's. It was all going to work out for him. He deserved it.

"This is gonna be good," he mumbled, reaching up with the intention of taking hold of one of those big full breasts. She dodged his touch, laughing her sultry, smoky laugh. Teasing him, as she said. His fingertips grazed her nipple and his cock jumped in his pants. He was going to go off like a damned rocket the minute she took him in her mouth.

"Oh, yeah," he groaned. "This is gonna be great. I've been looking forward to this."

"Mmm . . . me too," Elizabeth purred. They didn't mean the same thing, but Deputy Dope didn't know that. She rain her hands over his sloping shoulders and shuffled a little closer to him. "I've been wanting to do this for days."

"Yeah?" His eyes gleamed with the glassy light of intoxication and carnal desire. "Me too. I deserve it."

"You sure do, sugar."

Elizabeth smiled up at him, her prettiest, most man-dazzling smile, then brought her knee up with all the force she could muster, visualizing ramming his balls all the way up to his throat. She connected with a solid blow, and Ellstrom's breath left him in a gust as he doubled over, clutching himself.

"You bitch!" he croaked. "You fucking bitch!" he sputtered, spittle spraying, his voice strangled, his face flushing burgundy. He glared at her through bulging, tear-filled eyes and tried to lunge at her, but he couldn't straighten and wouldn't let go of himself. "I'll kill you! I'll fucking kill you for this!"

Elizabeth bolted out of the office, slamming the door shut on Ellstrom's tirade as she went. She ran for the back door, not wasting time on a look over her shoulder. She could hear him bellowing like a wounded moose. If he caught her before she could get help, she had little doubt but that he would indeed kill her, or make her wish that he had.

But she didn't even make it out of the building in her search for a cop. Just as she reached the door Mark Kaufman pulled it open.

"Ms. Stuart, I need you to come with me," he said softly, his brown eyes shining with concern as he took in her wild expression and the obscenities being shouted from somewhere behind her. "Um—there's been an accident," he stammered, his attention bouncing back and forth like a spectator's at a tennis match.

"An accident?" Elizabeth repeated, her thoughts going instantly to Trace as a rush of fear crested in her chest. "Is it my son? Is it Trace?"

"No," Kaufman said, dragging his gaze back to her. "It's Jolynn."

TWENTY·FOUR

THE STILL CREEK COMMUNITY HOSPITAL WAS A new one-story brick building on the outskirts of town, directly across the street from the Good Shepherd Home for the Elderly. Built partly on the revenues of tourism, the waiting room had been decorated accordingly with an Amish motif. The work of a local artist depicted everyday Amish life in oils and watercolors in frames made of rough-sawn barn siding. The rockers and settees looked as though they might have come from Aaron Haurer's shop. The atmosphere was altogether too homey for a place where people waited with white knuckles and churning stomachs.

Elizabeth paced back and forth on a long braided rug, smoldering cigarette in hand, blatantly ignoring the no-smoking signs. She flicked a glance at the bitchy old cow behind the admissions desk and paused in her pacing to tap her ash into the pot of a thriving ficus. The woman glared at her, her small eyes glittering above fat cheeks, but she said nothing.

Just let her say something, Elizabeth thought, spoiling for a fight—anything to get her mind off her fears for Jolynn. She was in no mood to take shit from anybody. She was at the end of her rope. Her back was against the proverbial wall. She was ready to tear into someone, anyone. But the Minnesotans around her had retreated behind their cool reserve and their good manners, so she was forced to stew.

No wonder people went crazy in this place. Everyone repressing their feelings, holding everything in all the time. Anger and bitterness and God knew what else all boiling inside them, building like steam in a radiator until they just went off. Like Helen Jarvis. Like Garth Shafer. Like whoever had slit Jarrold Jarvis's throat and bashed in Carney Fox's head. Not even Scandinavian stoicism could hold back that kind of rage. It ripped through everything, like shrapnel tearing through steel.

The pendulum clock that hung above a shelf of painted wooden Amish figurines showed 10:30. More than an hour since Kaufman had shown up at the office. Elizabeth had left him to deal with Ellstrom and driven herself to the hospital. She had demanded to be taken to Jolynn, but Nurse Ratchet had confined her to the waiting room. So she paced and prayed and wondered what the hell had happened.

She had nearly made up her mind to go on the offensive again and storm the desk, when Doc Truman came strolling down the hall from the examination area. A small man, he nonetheless exuded an aura of confidence and paternal wisdom. His face was lean and lined with character, and he had a full head of snow-white hair which he wore combed neatly back. A stethoscope hung around his neck. The chest piece was tucked into the breast pocket of the loose white lab jacket he wore over a blue dress shirt and dark trousers. Elizabeth's eyes went immediately to the smears of blood staining the cuff of one sleeve. Her heart picked up a beat and the bottom dropped out of her stomach.

"Oh, my God, Jolynn," she breathed, lifting a hand to her mouth. Her vision blurred with tears.

"You're Elizabeth?" the doctor asked.

She nodded, abandoning her cigarette to the ficus. "How is she? What happened? Can I see her?"

The questions tumbled out in random order, without space between them for an answer. Jolynn was the closest Elizabeth had ever come to having a sister. She was more like family than J.C. had ever been. She was her best and nearly her only friend in Still Creek. God, if she lost Jolynn . . . An almost overwhelming sense of loneliness swamped her.

Doc Truman flipped back the stainless steel cover of a patient chart and jotted something down in ballpoint. "She's got a concussion and some nasty cuts and bruises," he said calmly. He clicked off the pen and slipped it into his shirt pocket, glancing at Elizabeth from beneath bushy white brows. "We're keeping her overnight for observation, but all in all I'd say she's a very lucky lady."

Relief flooded through Elizabeth and swirled around in dizzying whirlpools with fear and anger and everything else she was feeling. "What happened? Can I see her?"

"You can see her briefly. I'll let Sheriff Jantzen fill you in on the rest."

Like an actor taking his cue, Dane appeared in the wide doorway of the hall the doctor had come down. His expression was stern. Elizabeth went to him. They didn't exchange a word of greeting. Dane turned and Elizabeth fell into step beside him. On the way to the room he curtly went over Jolynn's account of the events, from finding Jarvis's book to Rich's arrival to the harrowing scene that had been played out in Waterman's junkyard.

"He planned to kill her with the tire iron, then put her in her car and run the car off the road. Make it look like an accident," he said flatly. "Jolynn made a run for it. She knew she couldn't get to her car, so she went winding through the maze of junk, trying to lose him. Naturally, Cannon came after her. She managed to tip a heap of scrap iron over on him."

Elizabeth shuddered at the thought. She could imagine the raw terror, the horrible certainty of knowing someone you had once loved was going to kill you. Her imagination played out every step of the chase, every sound, every scent, the coppery taste of fear and the salt of tears.

"Is he dead?" she asked.

"I don't know. He was unconscious when they loaded him on the helicopter. I talked to someone in the trauma unit at St. Mary's a little while ago. They said it didn't look good."

That, Elizabeth thought, all depended on your point of view. She wouldn't have felt a moment's sadness over Rich Cannon's death. He had made Jolynn's life a misery and had set out to kill her. Elizabeth's protective instincts for those close to her and her strong sense of justice would have found Rich's demise a fitting one—crushed by a heap of garbage.

Jolynn lay in the hospital bed, her complexion as white as the over-bleached sheets. Already her eyes were ringed with dark circles. A line of delicate stitches bound an angry-looking slash across her right cheek. She wore a wide gauze bandage around her forehead like a head-band and both hands were wrapped like a mummy's. Yeager sat beside her on the far side of the bed, his head bent down next to hers, an expression of tenderness and concern on his face.

"Hey, kid, how you doin'?" she asked, not able to manage more than a whisper around the lump in her throat. She started to reach out to take Jolynn's hand, but remembered the bandages and curled her fingers around the bed's safety railing instead.

Jolynn looked up at her, glassy-eyed and groggy. "Stupid question," she said weakly, trying to manage a smile despite the lidocaine that deadened her cheek. "You ought to be a reporter."

"Naw," Elizabeth drawled, shaking her head. "I think I might try my hand at nuclear physics though. I know just about as much about it."

"I'm sorry about the weekly edition," Jo mumbled. Because of her they wouldn't be able to make deadline. Why'd she have to go and get caught? Couldn't she do anything without screwing up? Rich's fault, her brain reminded her. Rich's fault. Rich had tried to— The signal shorted out and her brow knit at the confusion. Pain pounded through her skull like hammer blows.

"It's okay, sugar," Elizabeth whispered, tightening her hands on the rail. "I reckon Still Creek can stand to miss a week of bad news."

Guilt assailed her like an avenging angel. If it hadn't been for her determination to print the truth, to ferret out that truth on her own, this never would have happened. They should have left everything to Dane and Yeager. Who in Still Creek gave a rip about reading the truth in their stupid weekly paper anyway? All they wanted to see was the 4-H club news and the specials at the Piggly Wiggly.

"It's not your fault," Jolynn said, accurately reading the look on Elizabeth's face. "You're not God, you know. I went out on my own. I made my own decision and I'm glad I did."

She wasn't glad she'd nearly gotten herself killed, but she couldn't say she regretted anything else that had happened. She had taken charge of her life. She had faced down the specter of her past once and for all. She had saved herself physically and psychologically. While she had been running through the towering mountains of junk at Waterman's, not knowing whether she would escape with her life or not, she had been hit by the strangest feeling of being alive, more alive than she had been in years, and everything had fallen neatly into perspective—who she was, who she could be, what she wanted.

Yeager leaned over her, gently brushing her hair back from her face. "You ought to rest, baby," he whispered, his dark eyes warm and bright with worry.

Jolynn smiled at him—with half of her mouth—as her lashes fluttered down and a heavy weariness pulled her toward sleep. "You're so sweet."

He tried to swallow around the knot of emotion in his throat. "I love you," he murmured, brushing at a lock of brown hair that had escaped the bandages to curl against her cheek.

Dane's hand settled on Elizabeth's shoulder. When she

glanced back at him, he nodded toward the door and they walked out together. Their footfalls on the marble floor was the only sound they made as they wandered back down the dark hallway to the front entrance.

Outside, night had settled fully over the town and countryside. The young corn in the field next to the Good Shepherd home rattled in the breeze. Somewhere down the block a dog gave a single bark, then there was nothing—no traffic sounds, no music drifting from open windows. Peace or a facsimile of it hung in the air with the scent of geraniums and honeysuckle and newly mown grass.

Elizabeth leaned against a brick pillar and stared out at the night, wondering if there was such a thing as peace or if it was just an ideal, something longed for but always out of reach. She thought of Jolynn and the contentment on her face as Yeager had whispered that he loved her, and decided that every once in a while someone got their fingers on the brass ring.

Dane watched her, guilt riding in his gut like a stone. "I'm sorry," he said. "You suspected Cannon from the start and I blew it off. Even after we questioned him again yesterday, I couldn't see him as a killer. I guess I'd just known him too long."

She glanced at him sideways, her gaze sharpening as she broke out of her musings. "You think he killed Jarvis?"

"He admitted to Jolynn he killed Fox. Said that Fox had threatened to blackmail him. Since Fox didn't have the book, it stands to reason that the thing he had on Rich was the murder. He must have seen it happen."

"And his motive for killing Jarvis was the book."

"I just glanced at the thing, but the details are pretty damning. Jarvis was bribing key people in the state legislature to help him get road construction contracts. Rich was his bagman. If that had gotten out, Rich's political aspirations would have turned to dust."

"But why would Jarvis leak that information?" Elizabeth asked. "The truth would have ruined him too. Besides, he would have benefitted by Rich getting elected. Think of the hold he would have had."

Dane shrugged. He tucked his hands into the pockets of his jeans and leaned against the other side of the pillar, staring off into the night. "Maybe that was what did it. Maybe Rich didn't like the idea of being Jarrold's puppet. By killing him he got his freedom, his wife's inheritance. . . .We may never know for sure."

Elizabeth shook her head, doubt stirring uneasily inside her. "I don't know . . ."

Dane's incredulous smile flashed bright in the darkness. He stepped around the pillar, eyes narrowed in disbelief. "What? You were the one who pointed a finger at Cannon in the first place. Now you don't think he did it? After he confessed to one murder and damn near committed another?"

"It's too . . ." She trailed off, then chuckled wearily to herself as she reached up and rubbed a hand back through her hair. "Neat. Just the way you like it."

"That doesn't mean it's not true," he said irritably.

"No, it doesn't." She crossed her arms and hugged herself to ward off a chill that came from within. "I just think of the way Jarvis was killed, and it seems so . . . violent."

"So does a tire iron to the skull."

"Yes, but that's different. One good clunk and it's all over. I think of cutting someone's throat—the way it must feel to hold on to another person and drain his life away . . ." Her thoughts turned inward, throwing the image of the murder scene up on the screen of her imagination like a movie with the scene being shot from the murderer's point of view, the murderer standing behind Jarvis, dragging the blade across his throat, tearing flesh, listening to the sounds— A shudder rattled through her and she shook her head to clear the picture. "It must take an overwhelming kind of hate to do something like that."

"Or no feeling at all," Dane countered.

"It seems like a crime of passion—"

"Or cold-blooded evil."

"There were other people in that book," she reminded him. "Other people with motives." Shafer. Ellstrom.

Elizabeth thought she should probably tell him about Ellstrom's little visit to her office, but she didn't have the energy to deal with any of it. Kaufman had hauled the deputy in. Dane would hear all about it from somebody else, somebody who wouldn't want sympathy or sweet words from him. She looked away and sighed. "You're probably right. I'm just being perverse. Anyway, it's the path of least resistance. If Rich dies, there won't even be a trial. Things will be back to normal around here before the Horse and Buggy Days parade."

Dane scowled into the darkness, not liking what she was hinting at. "There's nothing wrong with that if it's the truth."

"The truth," she murmured, the word dragging down on her like an anchor. "I've had about all the truth I can stand for one day." She pushed herself away from the pillar. "I'm going home."

"Elizabeth." She turned and looked at him expectantly, and whatever words he had thought might come to him didn't. Watching Yeager with Jo had stirred something in him. A need to reach out. A loneliness he had ignored for years. A weakness, he thought, crushing it out ruthlessly. "Do you want me to follow you? Make sure you get home all right?"

Elizabeth almost winced at the sting of disappointment. *What did you expect, sugar—a declaration like the one Jolynn got?* "No. Thanks. You caught your killer. What could happen?"

Dane watched her walk away. He didn't want to need a woman, *any* woman, but especially not Elizabeth. He didn't need her poking at him, stirring up doubts about himself or this case or this town—

No. That wasn't true. She was making him take a look at himself. It wasn't her fault if he didn't like what he saw. She had said he was lazy, that he wanted things neat and easy. He had countered by calling her ambitious and labeling her another Tricia. Nothing could have been further from the truth. Tricia would have found a way to keep her hooks in Brock Stuart, regardless of how many women he went through. Tricia would never have struck out on her own with little money and fewer prospects. She would never have come to a little hole-in-the-wall town like Still Creek or lived in a dump like the Drewes place. She would never have given a shit who killed Jarrold Jarvis so long as it didn't directly affect her.

Elizabeth was nothing like his ex-wife. Dane had looked at her and seen what he wanted to see, what was safest, what was easiest . . . That was the truth.

He had his life arranged to his specifications so there were no disruptions, no demands he didn't want to handle. He had his job, his position in the community, his farm, his neat, emotionless relationship with Ann Markham. The path of least resistance. As Elizabeth had said. As Amy had said. Christ, he was no better than Rich Cannon, resting on past laurels, skating along on his reputation, expecting life to accommodate his schedule. Elizabeth was right—he wanted Rich to be guilty, just as he had wanted Carney Fox to be guilty, because it would be less trouble for him.

He descended the steps and walked across the dew-damp grass to where he had left the Bronco, near the emergency entrance. He climbed in, gunned the engine, and drove out onto the street, turning toward the courthouse instead of home. Maybe there were a few more truths he could uncover tonight.

BOYD SAT ON THE BACK STOOP OF HIS HOUSE WITH his head in his hands and half a pint of regurgitated whiskey pooling around his shoes. Kaufman had hauled him out of the paper office, driven him home, and left him with orders to go sleep it off. No charges had been filed against him. Hell, he thought as his stomach clenched and the ache from his balls shot straight up to the core of his brain, if anyone had cause to file charges, it was him.

That black-haired bitch had lured him in, teased him, promised him heaven, and delivered a pile driver right up his crotch. There were laws against that kind of thing. He ought to know. He was going to be sheriff—

Was going to be. Now his future was looking about as good as the puke seeping around his shoes. The Nielsen woman had found the book. Kaufman had blurted out the whole story on the drive across town, blabbing on and on about how Rich Cannon had tried to kill his ex to get his hands on that book. The damn book nobody else would have thought twice about if it hadn't been for that Stuart bitch.

Boyd leaned over a little farther, doubling into a fat, stinking ball of misery. Tears came blubbering out, along with another ounce of sour acid from his stomach. He cried and swore and wretched and swore some more as his guts knotted into fists of pain and his balls ached and his head throbbed. His life was over. He would never be sheriff here or anywhere. Jantzen would fire his ass and he'd never get another job anywhere except maybe as some pathetic security guard at a shopping mall or something. It wasn't fair. He deserved better. He would have had better if it hadn't been for Elizabeth Stuart.

TRACE WAS SITTING AT THE KITCHEN TABLE, WAITING for her, when Elizabeth finally walked in the back door of her house. He shot up out of his chair, his face a mask of worry. "Are you all right?" he asked, taking two steps toward her, kicking stray shoes out of his path. "You're never this late."

Elizabeth slid her arms around him and gave him a long hug, smiling against his shoulder. "Were you worried about me, sweetheart?"

"Yes."

"Good," she said with a weak chuckle. "It's nice to know somebody cares." She gave him another squeeze, then pulled back.

Trace stood with one leg bent and his hands on his

slim hips, brows pulling low above the rims of his battered glasses. "What happened? Something happened, didn't it?"

"Buy your mama a Coke and I'll tell you all about it."

She let the story pour out as they sat on opposite ends of the sofa with Bruce Hornsby's distinctly southern piano-playing setting a poignant mood in the background. She omitted most of the Ellstrom fiasco, knowing it would upset Trace. The last thing they needed was him calling out a deputy in order to defend her honor. The tale of Jolynn's harrowing adventure was enough to keep his eyes wide and his ears tuned in, at any rate.

"Man," he breathed at the end of the story. "So Cannon meant to kill Miz Nielsen to cover it all up?"

Elizabeth nodded and set her glass aside on the cheap fake-cherry end table, where a dozen white rings marked the spots of glasses that had stood there before it. "Thank God Jolynn's got a head on her shoulders, or she'd be a goner."

The thought rattled through her again like an aftershock, and she wrapped her arms around her knees and held tight against the sensation. She could have lost Jolynn, her best friend. They had done their best to cheer each other on through good times and bad over the past dozen years. Losing her would have left a gaping hole in the fabric of Elizabeth's life.

Trace slowly shook his head in wonder and disgust. "How could a man do something like that to a woman he used to love? I couldn't ever think of hurting Amy—"

He broke off and stared down at the big foot he had planted on the sofa cushion, blushing at the realization of what he had just admitted. It didn't seem cool for a man to tell his mother he was in love. And she'd probably think he was goofy or cute or some other equally intolerable thing because he had fallen in love on such short notice. He waited for her to make some embarrassing mother-type remark, but none came and he finally had to look up at her to see what she was thinking.

Her expression was wistful, almost sad, even though

the corners of her mouth were turning up. The lamplight glowed behind her, setting off her hair. She was so pretty. Suddenly he saw her at Amy's age, at his age, too young to be a mother, carrying him around with her everywhere she went. Somehow, he had never thought of her that way—young, scared, in love. Being a mother had given her instant wisdom in his eyes, had instantly elevated her above having fears or uncertainties. Being a mother had made her infallible to him, but in truth she'd been just a teenager.

Realizing that brought on a profound rush of love for her. She'd gone through hell to have him and raise him. She deserved so much better than what she was getting out of life. He vowed right then and there to give her something better. He would be a better person, work harder in school, make something of himself so he could give her nice things and make her proud.

"She's sweet, your Amy," she said, reaching out to curl her fingers over his where they rested on top of his sneaker. "Pretty. Sweet. I like her."

Trace ducked his head, fighting a ridiculous grin. "She's awful special," he said, choking back the flood of adjectives he would have embarrassed himself with. Amy was the sun and the stars and everything kind and good . . . and she was going to be here for only two more weeks. "I don't guess I'll get to see much of her— Sheriff Jantzen being so hard against her dating and all."

"Oh, you give him a few days, honey," Elizabeth said, squeezing his fingers. "He doesn't want to think his baby's growing up. It makes a parent feel awfully . . . mortal to watch a child turn into a grown person. It seems to happen so fast. . . ."

She looked away, drifted off to another place while Bruce Hornsby sang a vivid, strikingly simple line about roads not taken that seemed to capture the essense of life in a handful of words about choices and regrets.

"Well," she said, snapping herself back to the present and forcing a smile. "I don't need to get any older sitting on this lumpy sofa. I'm going up to bed."

She uncurled her legs, stood, and stretched, feeling every day, every minute of her thirty-four years. Trace rose too, seeming to tower over her.

"Good night, Mama," he murmured, slipping his arms around her for a hug. "I love you."

Elizabeth smiled against the instant bloom of tears and hugged him back, remembering the way she had always answered him when he had given her that last good-night hug before curling up with his teddy bear. "Nothing could give me sweeter dreams than that."

IT WAS PAST ONE WHEN SHE CLIMBED THE STAIRS. SHE undressed for bed, too tired to do more than leave her clothes where they fell to the floor. She pulled on an oversize man's T-shirt that fell to the tops of her thighs, in no mood for a silky, sexy nightgown. Exhaustion pulled on her like a G force, weighing down her arms and legs and heart. She wanted nothing more than to lie down and sleep, but her mind wasn't going to let her. It churned and raced with the events of the day, taking her through a replay of all the emotions and stresses she had endured, leaving her feeling raw and exposed.

She went to the open window and sat down on the sill, leaning her back against the jamb. By the yard light she could see the silhouettes of the outbuildings, her car where she had left it in the yard near the house, the county cruiser parked near the shed. Evidently word of Rich Cannon's presumed guilt hadn't spread down through the ranks. No one had bothered to call the guard off her. She hadn't bothered either. Too tired to argue with a deputy, she had come straight into the house. Let him sit there all night. That was what she paid her taxes for. It was probably Kenny Spencer, and he was probably asleep anyway.

She raised her jelly glass to her lips and took a sip of scotch. The liquor slid in a smooth warm trail to her stomach, but it didn't soothe her nerves or take away her heartache. She stared down into the glass and frowned at

the Highland's finest malt. It wasn't an answer or a pan-
acea. It was just a habit. One she needed to break. She
was on her own. She didn't need a crutch that was more
hindrance than help. Maybe she would ship what was
left of it back to Brock with a little note—*Hope you get
cirrhosis.*

She tried to imagine him sitting next to her hospital
bed, torn up with concern for her, whispering heartfelt
words of love. Never—unless there was a camera trained
on him or a reporter within earshot. She could picture
Dane sitting there, but it would never happen.

She tried to turn her mind to the case, but her heart
wasn't in it. Besides, the pieces fit so nicely the way Dane
put them together; he was probably right.

But as she looked out over the countryside, still and
silent in the summer night, she felt that same insidious
evil lurking that she had felt the night of Jarvis's murder.
A sense of malevolence or madness hanging in the air like
smoke. A feeling of eyes focusing on her, drawing that
evil into a powerful beam and projecting it at her like a
laser as she sat in her window in her underpants and
T-shirt. The feeling crept over her flesh like a snake, and
she shied away from the window and into the shadows,
shaken and thankful for the deputy parked in her lawn.

Imagination, probably, she told herself as she set her
glass on the nightstand and climbed into bed. Leftover
jitters from her encounter with Ellstrom. Paranoia in-
duced by exhaustion and nerves and another missed
meal.

She pulled the sheet up over herself and curled up on
her side, trying to ignore the nagging doubt and the scent
of Dane Jantzen that clung to her pillow.

TWENTY-FIVE

Dane rubbed a hand over his face and back through his hair. His eyes felt as though they were dehydrating into something related to prunes. He looked like a bum. He knew because he hadn't been able to avoid seeing his reflection the last time he'd gone into the men's room to relieve himself of another gallon of bad coffee. His shirt was rumpled and sweat-stained and the man inside it looked downright dangerous. He needed a shower, a shave, a beer, a meal, and nineteen hours sleep—not necessarily in that order. The only thing he was going to get was another cup of stale coffee.

The reports from the BCA lab were spread out on the desk in front of him, the initial complaint report number neatly typed at the top, reducing Jarrold Jarvis's death to eight impersonal digits. He had been over every statement, every angle of every theory. He had read over Jarrold's black book, the Who's Who of sleazy deals in state politics. More heads than Jarrold's were going to roll because of that book. Minnesota was a state of squeaky-clean politics. One whiff of this little pile of shit and voters would be on a rampage. But how exactly the book tied in to Jarvis's death, Dane was no longer sure. His head felt ready to bust as he started the wheels turning again, trying to sort it all out and coming up with an answer that couldn't be argued away as being merely the simplest solution.

Beyond his door he could hear the office coming to life for the day. Even though it was only seven-thirty, people were filing in. The scent of Lorraine's coffee brewing in the break room drifted in. Already the phones were ringing off the hook, and Dane could imagine the news hounds gathering in a ragged, hungry pack outside the courthouse, lying in wait for him.

A sharp rap sounded on his door, then it swung open and Lorraine stuck her head in, her eyes widening in motherly alarm behind the lenses of her glasses.

"My stars, you look like death!" she gasped as she let herself in. She slapped a handful of pink message slips to the bosom of her blue shirtwaist while the other hand carried on efficiently, independently, straightening files, snatching up his coffee mug. "How long have you been here?" She curled her nose at the sludge in the bottom of his cup. "What are you drinking?"

"I think it's motor oil." His weary gaze went to the message slips. "What have you got for me?"

"Mostly calls from reporters." She set the cup down on the edge of the desk and sorted through the notes. "A call from the sheriff in Olmsted County. A call from St. Mary's that says there's been no change in Rich Cannon's condition. Three calls from Charlie Wilder about a special session of the town council set for tonight."

"Calling me on the carpet," Dane mumbled, scratching at his morning beard. "Wanting to know if all the lunatics are going to be locked up in time for the parade."

"I also have someone on the line about that missing tourist."

He looked up, brows drawing together in puzzlement while his brain spun in neutral. "The what? Oh, yeah. Shit. Who's handling it?"

"Mark. I think he wants to talk to you—"

"I don't have time right now. Have him deal with it. I'm not taking calls from anybody. And lose the rest of that crap —except the message from Olmsted. Leave that here." Already his gaze was shifting back to the mess on his usually immaculate desk. "And, Lorraine? I'll be your sex slave for life if you bring me a fresh cup of *your* coffee."

She clucked her tongue at his language, but blushed a bit anyway as she went out into the hall, lifting her nose primly as she passed Yeager.

"Don't try to fight it, Lorraine," he drawled, mouth curling in a lazy grin. "We both know you're wild about me."

She pranced away without comment, and Yeager chuckled as he shuffled wearily into the office. Boozer followed him, nose sniffing the air for a stray scent of food. The dog stuck his head in the wastebasket, rooting down through a ream of crumpled paper, and resurfaced with a half-eaten sandwich.

"Roast beef on whole wheat," Yeager commented, slumping down in the visitor's chair. "Lucky dog." The Labrador scarfed down the sandwich in two bites, belched, and flopped over on the floor to rest. Yeager turned his attention to Dane. "Son, you look like hard times on the hoof."

"I look like I'm related to you," Dane said dryly. Yeager was his usual rumpled self, still in the clothes he had worn yesterday. This morning he had an excuse, Dane reminded himself, taking in the agent's bloodshot eyes and the lines of strain on his square, honest face. "How's Jolynn?"

He sighed and rubbed a crick in his neck. "They finally let her go to sleep. I promised I'd bring her a piece of Phyllis's German chocolate cake for when she wakes up. Thought I'd grab a little breakfast while I was at it. I saw your truck in the lot as I was going by. You want to come?"

The idea of one of Phyllis's cholesterol-laden breakfasts had his stomach grumbling, but Dane shook his head. "No, thanks."

"What's all this mess?"

"I'm going over everything again."

The look on Yeager's face clearly said he thought

Dane had gone over the edge. "Why? Our boy is lying in the hospital in Rochester."

"Maybe."

Yeager's face colored from the gray of exhaustion to a healthy, angry red. He sat ahead on his chair, shoulders squared aggressively. "What maybe? Jesus, he tried to kill Jolynn!"

"I know," Dane said calmly. "But that doesn't mean he killed everybody."

"He admitted to killing Fox."

"But not Jarvis."

Shaking his head in disbelief, Yeager fell back, settling in for a siege. "It follows," he said, checking his temper.

"Does it?" Dane lifted the report on trace evidence. "They found blue cotton fibers on the back of Jarvis's shirt. Blue cotton, like from a work shirt. Rich Cannon never did a lick of physical work in his life."

As much as he wanted Cannon to be guilty, Yeager had to admit he'd never seen the man in anything but his spiffy young-senator outfits. Cannon's fashion sense had irked him because he thought maybe Jolynn went for that sort of man and he could hardly claim to be a candidate for *GQ*. "So maybe he put this work shirt on to keep from getting blood on his sixty-dollar tie. Or maybe he hired someone to do the deed. Maybe he paid Fox to kill Jarrold, then whacked him to keep Fox from blackmailing him. I like that idea. It's—"

"Neat," Dane finished, the word tasting as bitter as stale coffee on his tongue.

"The way cases ought to be," Yeager declared. "What got you going on this? Last night you thought Cannon was our man too."

"Something Elizabeth said." A lot of things Elizabeth had said. About him, about letting his preconceptions cloud his judgment, about taking the easy way out. But also an impression she had gotten looking at the murder from a woman's perspective. "About the way Jarvis was killed. About the kind of hate it would take to kill a man that way. She said it struck her as a crime of passion."

"Yeah. Cannon had a passionate need to rid himself of an overbearing, manipulative father-in-law. He gets out from under Jarvis's thumb and his wife inherits a bundle." He reached across the desk and plucked up the black book. "All the evidence we need is right here."

"There are a lot of names in that book," Dane said. "Ellstrom, for one. He owed Jarrold a wad of money and he's been screwing Helen Jarvis in his spare time."

"Man, there's an ugly thought," Yeager said with a shudder. Dane's expression never altered. He took a deep breath and contemplated for a moment. "You don't really see him as a killer, do you? I mean, Jesus, he's a deputy."

"I didn't see Rich as a killer either," Dane said. He sat back and rubbed his hands over his face, scratching his palms over his morning beard. He was exhausted, not just physically, but emotionally, psychologically. Tired of having his world turned upside down and inside out. Now that Elizabeth had gotten the blinders off him, he saw too many possibilities, too many suspects, too many motives, and all of it saddened him beyond words. It was one thing to know the world could be an ugly, brutal place. It was quite something else to look at your home, your haven, your sanctuary, and see the same ugliness, the same brutality.

"I'm not saying Ellstrom did it. I'm just saying there are more possibilities than the easiest one."

Groaning as he moved joints that had spent a long night in a chair reincarnated from the Spanish Inquisition, Yeager forced himself to his feet. "If you want to go on with this, you'll have to come over to the Cup. I can't think on an empty stomach. My body is a finely tuned machine that needs to be refueled at regular intervals."

"Pass," Dane said absently as yet another possibility began nibbling at the edge of his consciousness. His brows pulled together as he stared at the lab report. *Crime of passion* . . . "I need to go check something out."

Yeager shrugged. "Suit yourself. Let me know if it

pans out. I'll be at the hospital with Jolynn." He paused with his hand on the doorknob and a look of wonder came over his face, easing the lines of strain. "She's the one, you know," he said. "I am well and truly in love."

Dane forced a smile. "Congratulations."

Yeager gave him a long, thoughtful look as he rubbed a hand against his grumbling belly. "You ought to give it a try, son. Might improve that churlish disposition."

Dane offered a rude suggestion and turned back to the report.

"I plan to, buddy." Yeager grinned. "Just as soon as Jolynn feels up to it."

ELIZABETH DRAGGED A HAND THROUGH HER HAIR AND yawned hugely as she poured her first cup of coffee of the day. Getting only four hours sleep was a habit she had every intention of breaking just as soon as things around here settled into some semblance of normalcy. If that ever happened.

She had already put a call in to the hospital to check on Jolynn, and one to St. Mary's to see if she could weasel an update on Rich, but the Rochester hospital system—which included the world-famous Mayo Clinic—was no stranger to celebrities, famous and infamous, and they kept a tighter lid on gossip than the White House staff.

"How's Miz Nielsen?" Trace asked, shuffling into the kitchen. He was already dressed for the day in jeans and white T-shirt, the enduring uniform of the teenage boy. His bruises painted a rainbow across his face. His hair stood up in a little rooster tail at the crown.

Elizabeth resisted the urge to lick her fingers and smooth it down as she had when he'd been little. He wasn't little anymore; he was on the brink of manhood. She was still warmed by the thought that he had actually waited up for her the night before.

"She'll be fine in a few days. What are you doing up?"

He stepped around a sawhorse and went to the refrigerator. "I've gotta get to work. Cleaning calf pens at Carlson's today." He pulled out a carton of orange juice and sniffed at the contents.

"Don't you drink out of that carton, Trace Lee," Elizabeth snapped automatically in Mother's Tongue. He rolled his eyes and went in search of a glass. "Do you need a ride?"

"Naw. It's just a couple miles. I'll ride my bike."

Elizabeth started to say it wouldn't be any trouble, but realized Trace was at an age where it wasn't exactly cool to have your mother drive you around. She watched him out of the corner of her eye as he stood at what was left of the counter, drinking juice and eating Nilla Wafers out of the box. Maybe by next spring they would be able to pool their resources and buy him a secondhand jalopy.

"We have to get you some new glasses," she said, drawing her robe closer together at her throat.

Trace gulped the last of his juice, wiped his mouth with the back of his hand, and bolted, brushing a kiss to her cheek as he passed her on his way to the door. "Tomorrow," he called over his shoulder.

He passed Aaron in the doorway as the Amishman entered, toolbox in hand, and was gone with a slap of the screen door.

Elizabeth's mouth curved in a smile. "Sixteen. Everything seems so urgent at that age. What were you like at sixteen, Aaron?"

He flicked a glance at her as he settled his carryall on the plywood table. She looked as though she had just gotten out of bed. Her hair was rumpled, wild and tempting, a cloud of black silk that fell past her shoulders. Delilah must have had such hair to tempt Samson. She was dressed in a sinfully thin wrap of shimmering emerald green. It fell to her ankles, covering her, but was held together only by a belt at the waist. It parted readily, giving tantalizing glimpses of her long bare legs as she moved idly toward him. She seemed to think nothing of it—how seductive she was, how tempting to a man who had been without a wife for so long. Or perhaps she knew full well . . .

"I worked," he said shortly, forcing his gaze back to his tools. An image flashed through his mind of her stopping in front of him and opening the green wrap, baring her breasts to him. His manhood stirred and he squelched the wicked thoughts ruthlessly. She was not for him—only as a test, and he had vowed to pass all tests God sent to him.

Elizabeth slid onto a kitchen chair, tucking her robe around her legs as best she could. She sipped her coffee and watched as Aaron selected an array of tools for the task of dismantling the last of the lower cupboards. He laid them out in neat order, like a surgeon preparing for a heart transplant. He was clearly in another sour mood, his face as grim as an undertaker's. He seemed to be concentrating very hard on not looking at her. Probably because of what she was wearing, she thought. Well, if a man insisted on showing up at a lady's home before eight o'clock in the morning, he would just have to live with her the way he found her. Still, his coldness stung a little. She had started to think of him as a friend, but he suddenly didn't seem to want anything to do with her.

Determined to draw him out, she launched into a detailed account of what had happened to Jolynn. Aaron said nothing until she had finished the story and had waited a good long minute for him to comment.

"Dane Jantzen, then, has his killer," he said softly, turning to the cupboard with a pry bar.

"So he thinks. I'm not so sure myself." She polished off her coffee, contemplated a second cup, and decided against it. She watched Aaron as he crouched down and peered into the cupboard. He seemed completely unmoved by everything she had told him, as if it had taken place on another planet. His indifference irritated her, rubbing against the frayed ends of her temper like a cool breeze across exposed nerve endings.

"You know," she said sharply, snugging the belt of her robe as she rose, "this is your community too. I don't see how you can just sit back and play with your suspenders and pretend none of this is happening right across the goddamn road from your house."

Aaron jerked to his feet, anger surging through him. He curled his fingers around the pry bar until his knuckles turned white even as his face was flushing red. "Take not the name of the Lord God in vain in my presence!" he thundered.

Elizabeth took a step back, his outburst shocking her heartbeat into a quicker rhythm. "I—I'm sorry," she mumbled.

Aaron went on as if he hadn't heard her. "The *Gemei* is my only community. I answer only to God, not to the English!"

His eyes were blazing behind his spectacles, bright with the fire of zealousness. He seemed suddenly bigger and more alive, as if the man inside him had finally burst through the confining shell of his self-discipline. Elizabeth witnessed the metamorphosis with a sense of wonder tinged with fear. The view she had had of the Amish—of Aaron—was of emotional austerity and quiet control. His show of temper threw her off balance.

It seemed to throw Aaron as well. He stepped back, pulled back within himself, dropped his gaze to the floor.

"Forgive me," he mumbled, staring at Elizabeth's painted toenails as a prayer from childhood ran through his head. *Jesu hor dein kleins kind, vergil mir alle meine Sund. Jesus, hear your little child, forgive all my sins.*

"No," Elizabeth said. "I'm the one who should apologize. I'm running on a real lean mix these days. I'm afraid it doesn't take much to get me to shoot off my mouth." She sighed heavily, suddenly desperate for a cigarette. "I'll let you get to work," she mumbled, backing toward the dining room. Aaron turned away from her without a word.

They would never be friends in the true sense, she thought, her heart sinking. They existed on different planes. Their backgrounds, their philosophies, were too diverse. It would have been easier to bridge the gap between two centuries than the gap between their cultures. Elizabeth knew she would never be able to fully understand his ways, and he would probably never view her as anything other than "English." Just as the people of Still Creek would probably never see her as anything other than "that *southern* woman."

Restless and weary, she padded barefoot through the dining room, where the aroma of mouse was finally starting to fade, into the living room, where her notes on the Jarvis murder were stacked on the coffee table along with a mountain of unopened bills and the pack of photographs she had picked up at Snyder's and never gotten around to looking at. After flicking on a Bonnie Raitt tape, she settled into a corner of the sofa, curling her legs beneath her like a cat. She wanted to shower and shave her legs before going to see Jolynn, but it was too early to get into the hospital and she really hadn't worked up the energy yet anyway.

There was a nearly empty pack of Virginia Slims half buried on the table, and she leaned over to unearth it with the tips of her fingers, ending up with half the junk from the table in her lap and one slightly crushed cigarette dangling from her fingertips.

"Beggars can't be choosers, sugar," she whispered, lighting up and drawing the smoke deep into her lungs. Rotten habit, she thought idly as she blew a stream of exhaust toward the ceiling, just like the scotch. It seemed if she hadn't had bad habits, she wouldn't have had any habits at all Smoking, drinking, men . . .

While Bonnie lamented in her smoky voice that it was too soon to tell, Elizabeth began sorting through the papers and notes in her lap, all her hunches and half-formed theories looking thin and silly in the light of day. Maybe she was just being perverse not accepting Rich as the perpetrator of all evil in Still Creek. Maybe she just didn't want to agree with Dane about anything. Maybe keeping herself at odds with him was a mechanism to keep herself from getting too close. If that was the case, she was a day late and a dollar short.

Cannon had killed Carney Fox without compunction. He had tried to kill Jolynn. Why couldn't she picture him picking up a knife and slitting Jarrold Jarvis's throat?

She set her cigarette to smolder in a Baccarat ashtray with the bent corpses of half a dozen others as a dull headache began to squeeze the backs of her eyeballs. Leave the detecting to the detectives. What she really needed was that second cup of coffee she had passed on. She dumped the papers on the middle cushion of the sofa and rose again. Her gaze caught on the packet of photographs, and on impulse she took it with her as she began to wander back through the house.

The photographs from the night of the murder brought back echoes of the fear that had gripped her, and the nightmarish, surrealistic air that had surrounded the scene after the police and press had descended—the blaze of light around the resort, the cruisers with beacons flashing, the deputies standing guard around the perimeter looking both uncertain and unyielding, and at the center of it all the Lincoln and its owner lying dead on the ground. Even in black and white the scene seemed too real, the crime too brutal. Elizabeth frowned as she looked at the fresh young face of Kenny Spencer, saw his shock, felt his uneasiness as his world rocked beneath his feet.

She shuffled the deck of photographs and came to the ones she had taken Saturday morning. The Amishman trudging along behind his work horses as the sun lifted above the eastern horizon. The series of shots of the construction site. The ones she had taken standing on the spot where Jarvis had died—the creek, the willows draping over the banks.

She bumped the kitchen door open with her hip and stepped into the room as she flipped to the photo she had taken accidentally. The one of Aaron standing, head bowed, hat in hand, praying over the graves of his wife and children. His family, who had died at the hands of the English.

An eye for an eye . . . The verse came to her, unbid-

den, and she shook it off mentally. The Amish were paci-
fists. They didn't kill. They didn't answer violence with
violence. They didn't snap under the pressures of the
modern world, because they divorced themselves from
the modern world. They didn't—

Elizabeth stopped and stood perfectly still except for
the throbbing of her heart. She had patted herself on the
back for having such sharp perceptions, uncluttered by
past experience or preconceptions. But she was doing
exactly what she had accused Dane of time and again—
seeing what she wanted to see, what she had been condi-
tioned to see.

Jarvis's murder had seemed to her like a crime of passion, she had said to Dane. A crime of hate, hate that had
erupted suddenly and uncontrollably. Who would be
more capable of hate than a man whose wife and children had been killed?

Her gaze fell on Aaron's carpenter's box and all the
neatly arranged tools of his trade—hammers, screwdrivers, carving tools with thin curved blades, knives and
chisels and gouges.

As she lifted her head, her gaze met Aaron's and an
instinctive shiver went through her, as cold as ice. He
stared at her steadily, calmly, and his face changed subtly, eerily. The skin seemed to tighten against his skull
and a soft hint of color illuminated his high cheekbones.
Behind the plain, practical lenses of his spectacles, his
blue eyes brightened to the hue and brilliance of sap-
phires. Elizabeth's throat tightened.

"Es waar Gotters Wille," he said softly. "It was God's
will."

TWENTY-SIX

Dane turned the Bronco in at the Hauer drive. He wasn't looking forward to the interview he was about to conduct, but then, it seemed this was a day for unpleasant business. It wasn't even eight o'clock yet and already he had gone one round with Ellstrom, whom he had found passed out on the floor of his garage, reeking of whiskey, sickness, and failure. Now he had to play out a hunch every cell of his being would rather have rejected out of hand.

He climbed out of the Bronco and followed the cracked sidewalk to the neat white farmhouse, setting his personal feelings aside. He was a cop, he needed to think like a cop, not like a local hero or a favorite son or a longtime friend.

Ruth Hauer answered the door, a cotton dishtowel in her hands. She was a sturdy woman, built like an icebox with a face lined by years of hard work and childbearing. Wisps of iron-gray hair had escaped the confines of her bun to curl limply around the edge of her white *kapp,* and her cheeks were flushed from the steam of something cooking on the wood stove. She regarded Dane with the kind of wary shock of someone discovering a long-lost ne'er-do-well cousin on their step. His stomach growled at the heady warm scent of fresh bread wafting out of the tidy kitchen.

"Good morning, Ruth. Is Aaron home?"

"In his shop, I tink, Dane Yahntzen," she said, English stumbling clumsily off her tongue. "Something there is the matter?"

Dane hoped not. With all his heart he hoped not. He gave the old woman a smile. "I just need to ask him a few questions."

He left Ruth to her baking and walked across the yard to the building Aaron had set up for his carpentry shop. The shop smelled unmistakably of fresh-cut lumber, lemon oil and stain and beeswax. A workbench stretched the length of one wall. Tools were neatly hung above it or stored in wooden boxes along the ledge. Works in progress were lined along the wall nearest the bench—a round oak dining room table, a tall wardrobe, cupboards. Several completed pieces sat along the far wall, waiting to be picked up by the people who had commissioned them. Everything was in its place except the carpenter. There was no sign of Aaron.

"He has gone already."

Dane looked up from the table he was examining. Samuel Hauer stood in the doorway, dressed as all Amishmen dressed—in black broadfall trousers and a blue shirt. The brim of his straw hat was gone, leaving something that looked like a down-home version of a fez—his milking hat. Dane straightened and moved to the next piece of furniture, the wardrobe that was taller than he was and sturdy as an oak tree. He ran a hand along the smooth wood of the side the same way he might stroke a horse, absently aware of the qualities of beauty and strength. His gaze remained on Samuel as the old man came into the room. Like his wife, like all of his people who had reached an age, his face was lined by the years like the rings in a tree. The Amish had a hard life devoting themselves to God.

"I spoke to him of your questions, Dane Jantzen. He wants nothing to do with your English justice."

"That won't stop me from doing my job, Samuel."

Something like anguish passed through Hauer's eyes. He rubbed a gnarled, weathered hand over his face and muttered something in German. "He has known such torment. Can you not leave him alone?"

"No," Dane said flatly. "As much as Aaron would like to think otherwise, we live in the same world, in the same county. The same justice applies to everyone. Where is he working today?"

"I don't know," the old man said sadly. There were too many things he didn't know about Aaron these days. His son seemed so angry, so tense, as if there were a spring inside him winding tighter and tighter. The grief over his loss was not fading with time, it was souring and hardening, and Samuel sometimes lay awake nights worrying over what that kind of bitterness might do to a man.

"He left without saying," he said. "Zook's, maybe. Or maybe the English woman's." He stepped closer to the wardrobe and reached out a hand to the wood, touching it fondly, as if he might somehow reach his son through the thing he had created.

"He does good work, doesn't he?" he murmured, thumbing the latch. His thick fingers curled around the handle of the door, and when he swung it open, a dead blonde fell at his feet.

ELIZABETH STOOD ROOTED TO THE SPOT, HORRIBLY mesmerized by the look on Aaron's face, like a small, weak animal caught in the gaze of a predator. Realization arced between them. She knew, and he knew she knew. He would kill her now because of that knowledge.

"He bragged to me of how his resort would bring the tourists," he said softly. "Of how he would block the creek and flood the valley so the tourists might go out on boats.

"Ana and Gemma are buried there. And my Siri. My sweet Siri. Killed by the English and he would yet drown them." He shook his head, that steady blue gaze never leaving Elizabeth's. "He was a wicked man. I was doing only God's work."

He hadn't planned to kill Jarvis. He had gone to the creek to spend some quiet time with his loved ones. At Still Waters the workmen had finished for the day. Only Jarvis had remained. Jarvis had stared down at him from the hill, intruding on his privacy, calling out to him.

He hadn't planned to kill the man. Killing went against everything he had been raised to believe. But pain and fury had boiled up within him as they had stood on that hill overlooking the creek. Like acid, it had burned away everything else, all thought, all conscience. His fingers had closed on the handle of the knife in his pocket, the knife he had used to whittle the little birds for Ana and Gemma, the knife he had used to cut the stems of the wildflowers for Siri's grave.

After, he had been overwhelmed by guilt. But as he had knelt there in the dirt beside the corpse, the answer had come to him, as warm and comforting as sunlight. He had a purpose. This was part of God's plan. God had seized him, had guided his hands.

Calmly he had put Jarvis back in his automobile so the stench of his death wouldn't disturb the pure country air, then he went down to the creek and washed his hands, carefully cleaned his knife. A man kept his tools as he kept his life—neat and orderly. For a long while he had just stood and stared at the creek. Such a beautiful spot, so peaceful. Perfectly designed by God. Nothing for man to tamper with. He had walked home the long way, along the edge of Hudson Woods so he could look for ginseng root for his mother.

The wheels of Elizabeth's mind spun frantically. She needed to get out of the house, but Aaron stood between her and the door. She wasn't quick enough to dart around him, or outrun him even if she could get past him. She took a slow step backward, toward the dining room, as he reached for a long shiny steel chisel.

"The *Gemei* are God's people," he said matter-of-factly. "God would have me protect His folk from the wicked who would hurt us or lead us astray."

Like the tourist woman who had come to his shop

yesterday. Wicked creature. *Windfliegel*. Whore. She had tried to tempt him, had offered herself to him. An English harlot wanting to make sport of the simple Amishman. She had touched him through his trousers and his flesh had responded, but he had seen her for what she was—another test. Like Elizabeth was a test.

"I thought we were friends, Aaron," Elizabeth said, trying to buy time, desperately hoping she might be able to reason with him. She kept her eyes on the chisel as he lifted it out of the box, and ruthlessly squelched the urge to bolt. Timing, timing, she chanted inwardly, and eased back another step.

He arched a brow and his mouth kicked up on one corner in that wry smile she had once found so endearing.

"You are an English whore," he said, hating the pain her betrayal caused him. Or was it his own betrayal of his faith? He had wanted her and she was a sinful wanton. As sinful as Eve tempting Adam. "I have seen you through the window. Tempting men. Fornicating."

His admission hit Elizabeth like a blow to the stomach, knocking the wind from her, nauseating her. He had been watching her. Aaron's eyes were the eyes she had felt. The malevolence was his. The madness was his. Tears and bile crowded her throat at the thought. What she had shared with Dane might not have been love on his part, but it meant a great deal to her. More than it should have. The idea of a madman taking it all in, twisting it into something ugly in his mind was revolting. She felt violated and terrified.

She glanced away from him, in search of a weapon or a shield, anything that might help her save herself. Nothing. The counter was gone. There were no knives within reach, not even a bottle of her bootlegged scotch to throw at him. All she could see was the migratory pile of shoes mounded up in the corner. She moved another step and a kitchen chair came into view. Her gaze flicked back to Aaron.

"God wouldn't be having you kill people, Aaron," she said. "What about the ten commandments?"

" 'Honor the Lord thy God,' " Aaron said, coming around the end of the plywood table. "I am an instrument of God."

Elizabeth swallowed hard, taking another step, reaching blindly for the chair. Her fingers, slick with sweat, connected with the vinyl back and curled over the edge.

"Well, I hate to mess up God's plans," she said, panting, as breathless as if she had run a mile, "but I'm not of mind to get myself killed here, Aaron."

He didn't hear her. She could tell her words had not registered at all. He had retreated to some inner place where he doubtless believed he heard the word of God. Somehow, that was more frightening than listening to his lunatic ramblings. He wouldn't listen to her now. He may not even hear her screams as he plunged the chisel into her. The thin thread that had tethered him to sanity had snapped.

He raised the chisel and stepped toward her. Elizabeth grabbed the chair, meaning to fling it at his lower legs, but the back slipped from her fingers like a slab of ice and the chair clattered to the floor, an obstacle instead of a weapon. Better than nothing. She might not get another opportunity. She wheeled and bolted into the dining room, making a beeline for the living room and the front door nobody ever used.

Aaron followed in no particular hurry. Beyond the roar of her pulse in her ears, Elizabeth could hear the scrape of the chair as he moved it aside, his footfalls as he crossed the hardwood floor of the dining room. He seemed to think she had no hope of escape. The possibility that he was right shot through her like shards of glass, ripping at what composure she had left.

She ran into the living room, where Bonnie Raitt was crooning a tune about broken hearts and second chances. The music was slow and bluesy, the kind of thing she liked to listen to on quiet, lazy nights. Now it added to the surrealism of the moment. Slow, sad love songs playing while a killer stalked her. Inside her everything was racing—her heart, her thoughts. Air pumped in and out of her lungs in hot, ragged gusts, while the world around her moved in slow motion.

She hit her sore knee on the corner of a coffee table and wanted to double over in pain, but she kept going, lunging at the door and salvation. Her hands closed on the knob and tried to turn it. It slipped between her fingers like wet soap. Sobbing, choking for breath, she grasped it harder, turned, and yanked. The door didn't budge. She glanced over her shoulder to see Aaron coming into the living room and glanced back around, her heart stopping as her gaze landed on the brand-new brass dead-bolt key lock he had installed for her.

There wasn't time to try to unlock it. She didn't have the key. He was too near. If she didn't run now, he would have her trapped. A thousand different thoughts ran fast-forward through her mind. What if she managed to get out of the house? Were the keys in the Caddy? What if it wouldn't start? Could she get away in Aaron's buggy? Would he run her down and kill her on the road? Leave her body in the ditch to be discovered by a stranger or by her son on his way home from work. Trace. Trace would be left with no one. Would Dane help him? Would Dane grieve for her?

"Whore!" Aaron shouted as adrenaline shot through him in a dizzying rush. He would kill her now as she stood against the door with her green silken robe gaping open, tempting him to disobey God and his people. He raised the chisel and lunged at her.

Elizabeth couldn't draw breath enough to scream. The blade of the chisel sank into the door as she dodged to the side and tripped over a footstool. Arms and legs moving frantically, she scrambled over an easy chair, grabbed a lamp by the neck, and swung it like a baseball bat at Aaron as he tried to cut off her angle. The base of the lamp caught him square in the chest, and he staggered back a step, roaring in outrage.

She didn't look to see if she had hurt him. She ran for

the stairs, praying she would have enough time. Just like in a nightmare, the steps seemed to go straight up at a horrible pitch and the walls of the stairwell closed in around them like a tunnel. Elizabeth hurled herself up them, stumbled, fell, ran on hands and knees and elbows, tangling and tripping on her robe. Off balance, her mind racing faster than her body could keep up, she hit the second-floor landing and flung herself toward her room.

She could hear Aaron's heavy boots on the stairs, could hear him chanting words in German. She fell to her knees in front of the nightstand and yanked the drawer completely out, spilling a cloud of colorful silk scarves, empty cigarette packs, perfume cards from magazines, the Desert Eagle and its clip of ammunition.

"Oh, please, God. Please, God," she whispered, fumbling for the gun. She grabbed the clip and tried to ram it home, but found she had it backward. Her fingers felt as thick and clumsy as sausages as she grappled with the smooth steel shaft, dropping it as Aaron flung the door open.

"I watched you and waited," he said, breathless, eyes bright, heart pounding. "You could have redeemed yourself."

But she hadn't. He had seen her with the sheriff, had watched them kiss and grope each other like wild, hungry animals. Arousal stirred within him at the memory, and rage followed, leaping up inside him like the fire of salvation. His fingers tightened on the chisel and he stepped into the room. It was fitting that she die here, in her harlot's bed.

The magazine slid into place with a hiss and a snap. Elizabeth bit her lip and jerked the slide back on the gun, chambering the first cartridge. Her hands were shaking violently and tears blurred her vision as she hauled the Desert Eagle up in front of her and squeezed the trigger.

DANE HIT THE BRAKES, AND THE BRONCO SKIDDED sideways, spewing gravel up and spooking the buggy horse that stood tethered to the light pole. His mind kept flashing the image of the dead blonde. Flashing it on and off, like frames in a movie, there and gone before he could will it away. Like a pulse beat—*dead, dead, dead.*

He grabbed his .38 off the seat, flung open the door of the truck, and hit the ground running as a shot split the morning air like a crack of thunder.

Every bit of training he'd had vanished from his head and instinct took control. He had called for backup, but nothing was going to make him wait for it.

He bounded up the back steps and into the house. Kicked open the kitchen door and let the .38 precede him into the room. It was empty. For a second he stood, breathing hard, gathering his wits, taking in the scene. The room was its usual shambles. Cereal boxes on the table, shoes on the floor. Aaron's toolbox sat on the sheet of plywood. A kitchen chair had been overturned. Music drifted in from the living room. Bonnie Raitt. Elizabeth's favorite.

Oh, Jesus, please let her be all right.

As he started to move toward the dining room, a second shot exploded above him. Dane bolted into high gear, vaulting over the fallen chair and bashing the door open with his shoulder. He took the stairs two at a time, blocking out the pain that tore into his knee. He hit the second-floor landing and charged for her bedroom, shouting her name like a war cry.

"Elizabeth!"

THE DAMN GUN HAD JAMMED. JUST AS IT HAD THE day Dane had shown her the kind of damage it could do. Her first shot had gone into the wall, spraying plaster everywhere. The recoil had slammed her head into the frame of her bed. And when she opened her eyes, Aaron was still standing there, unshaken, unaffected. He took another step toward her and she shot again, missing again as he dodged to the side. The bullet hit the pot of the fuchsia plant on the dresser and disintegrated it, sending shards of pottery exploding out like shrapnel. She pulled the trigger a third time and nothing happened. A fourth time. Nothing. Her gaze flicked from the man to the gun and she saw the spent shell caught half in and half out of the chamber.

"You can't kill me," Aaron said knowingly. Behind his spectacles his eyes glowed. His mouth curled at the corners in a smile that shot spears of terror through Elizabeth.

"Elizabeth!"

"Dane!" she screamed, scrambling to get her feet under her as Aaron turned toward the door.

The Amishman wheeled and slashed down with the chisel as Dane rushed in. Blinding pain spiked up Dane's arm as the point of the tool sank into his right wrist. *Stupid,* he cursed himself as his fingers went instantly numb and the .38 dropped to the floor. Only green rookies charged in like something from *Miami Vice.* Running on emotion could damn well get them both killed. *Keep your head in the game and your heart out of it, Jantzen.*

Aaron jerked the chisel free, backed up a step, and came at him again, shrieking like a banshee, madness flashing like lightning in his eyes. Dane raised his injured arm to block the assault, and the chisel sliced across his forearm as he balled his left hand into a fist and slammed it into the Amishman's belly. Aaron grunted and doubled over but swung his weapon again, driving the steel blade to its hilt into Dane's left biceps.

Dane staggered back, swearing, grinding his teeth against the pain, blinking furiously as sweat rolled down his forehead and into his eyes. He tried to reach for the chisel to pull it out, but his right hand hung limp and useless, numb to the commands of his brain. Spotting the .38, he dropped to his knees on the hard wood floor and dove for the revolver, stretching out his left arm to reach for it, bellowing as the chisel dug through muscle and scraped bone.

With a howling cry of triumph Aaron flung himself down on top of the sheriff. He felt wild. Euphoric with the zeal of his duty. Bursting with the power of God. He was an avenging angel, a savior, filled with brilliant white light and radiance. He tore his weapon free and lifted it high above his head, ready to plunge it through Satan's heart.

Dane looked up into the face of his own death and gulped what would be his last breath.

An explosion rent the air.

Aaron rose up higher, arms stretching toward heaven, back arching, mouth tearing open wide as the slug penetrated between his shoulder blades and exited through his chest, ripping a hole the size of a man's fist, spewing blood and tissue in a grisly spray. Dane rolled out of the way as the Amishman fell forward, dead, his hands still clenching the handle of the chisel as the blade sunk into the floor.

An unnatural silence rang in Elizabeth's ears as she knelt on the bed, a powerful absence of sound caused by the concussion of the gun blast against her unprotected eardrums. It seemed fitting though, she thought as she stared in horror at the blood that pooled thick and dark red around Aaron Hauer's lifeless body. A moment of silence for the passing of a life. A moment of absolute stillness in which she had to realize what she had done.

She had killed a man, ended his life in the blink of an eye, without a second's hesitation. He was gone from this world just as she would have been had he caught her, just as Dane would have been if she hadn't gotten the gun working. In those few minutes three different lives had hung in the balance. Any one of them might have been snatched away.

Tears and terror rose up in her throat and choked her as the acrid scent of gunpowder burned her nostrils. She coughed and gagged, sinking down on the comforter as the strength rippled out of her legs. She was shaking violently, but she couldn't seem to let go of the gun. Her fingers were curled tight around the pearl handle, knuckles white as bleached bone, nails as red as Aaron Hauer's blood. Her breath hitched in and out of her lungs in fits and starts, and she looked around wildly for Dane.

He struggled to his feet and came toward her, like something from a nightmare. He was limping. Blood beaded on his face in a thick red mist. Aaron's blood. Wincing, he raised his left forearm and tried to wipe it away. His own blood ran in ribbons from his wrist and from the gashes in his arms. The muscles in his square jaw clenching against the pain, he reached out to her with his left hand.

"Give me the gun, honey," he said softly.

Never taking her eyes off Dane, she lifted her trembling hands. The pistol felt as heavy as an anvil, so heavy she could barely find the strength to lift it, much less hold it still. Dane took it from her and set it aside on the cluttered nightstand.

"It's over," he said, turning back toward her.

"I k-killed him," Elizabeth stammered, her gaze straying against her will to the man who lay dead on her bedroom floor. She shuddered as if her life were trying to ooze out of her too. "I—I killed a man."

"I know," Dane murmured, his eyes strictly on Elizabeth. She was as pale as milk. Her eyes were glassy as she stared at the body.

"Elizabeth," he said, his voice quiet but firm with command. "Elizabeth, look at me. Look at me."

She broke the trance with several sharp blinks and looked up at him. "Aaron killed Jarvis. He—he—" *Was insane. Was watching us.* All of it tumbled through her mind and turned her stomach. Fear curled a fist in her chest and shook her like a rag doll.

"Damn you," she muttered, tears streaming down her face as she looked at Dane. "I thought he was gonna kill you!"

Dane slid his arms around her as best he could and pulled her against him, burying his face in her hair. "Sorry he didn't?" he asked.

Elizabeth pressed her face into his shoulder and sobbed, too overwhelmed for banter. She had been terrified when her own life had been threatened, but that feeling hadn't compared to the terrible wrenching in her heart as she had watched Aaron Hauer rise up above Dane with that chisel in his hand. He would have died. For her. Because of her. She would have lost him forever.

But then, he wasn't hers to lose, was he?

She put her arms around him and hugged him for all she was worth, needing to hold him as long as he would let her.

"I love you," she whispered desperately. "I love you."

"Shh . . ."

She took his murmurs of comfort for censure and shook her head. "I know you don't want to hear it. I don't care, you ornery son of a bitch. I love you."

Dane almost managed a laugh, but the pain dug its talons deeper. He felt as if it were tearing out his strength a chunk at a time, and he wasn't sure how much longer he would be able to stay on his feet, but he fought back the wave of weakness and that blissful dark horizon of unconsciousness for the moment. He wanted—*needed*— to hold this woman who claimed she loved him.

I love you too. The words squeezed past the walls of his defenses and whispered through him, stinging and sweet and terrifying. Words he didn't want to hear to go with the feelings he didn't want to feel.

As a siren whined near, he took a step back from her physically and emotionally. "I'm bleeding on your sheets," he said dimly. He tried to take another step, and pain dug into his left knee, as sharp as cat's teeth. His vision blurred a little and her face went in and out of focus as unconsciousness beckoned again.

Elizabeth sniffed and forced a laugh "You silver-tongued devil." He didn't want her love. No big surprise.

Downstairs the screen door slapped shut and Mark Kaufman's voice called out for Dane.

"Up here, Mark!" Dane called back, not taking his eyes off Elizabeth.

"Who says there's never a cop around when you need one?" she said dryly.

She slid off the bed and crossed the room, wrapping her silk robe around her and retying the sash. She kept her head up. She didn't need him, she just wanted him, and God knew she was used to not getting what she wanted.

"Elizabeth." Dane thought he ought to say something, offer some explanation, make some parting apology.

Pausing in the doorway, she looked back at him over her shoulder as Kaufman came thudding up the stairs. "That's all right, sugar," she murmured. "I'll let you take the easy way out. I've sworn off men anyhow."

TWENTY-SEVEN

"THANK YOU AGAIN FOR MEETING ME HERE, GEN-tlemen." State Attorney General Paul Douglas pushed his chair back from the linen-draped table and rose, buttoning the double-breasted jacket of his immaculately tailored gray suit. Fifty-five, tall, and gracefully built, Douglas was in transition from handsome to distinguished. His hair was fading from dark chestnut to the color of steel with silver wings at his temples. Lines of character were etching deeper into his long, tanned face. He was a man with a brilliant future in state and national politics—a future that loomed even larger and brighter thanks to the case that had just been dropped in his lap. Ferreting out rotten apples in the legislature wasn't going to hurt his popularity at all.

Dane eased his chair back from the table and stood slowly, gingerly straightening his left knee, which was encased in the latest fashion for orthopedic braces. Despite the fact that they were in one of the finest restaurants in Rochester, a town that catered to well-heeled visitors including presidents and heads of state from the world over, the excellent steak on the plate before him remained largely untouched. The events of the past few days had soured his appetite.

Crime had no such effect on Yeager, he noticed. The agent had all but sucked the pattern off the china. He stood now too, along with the Tyler County attorney,

Jim Peterson. Peterson was in his best suit, groomed to impress. Yeager looked like an unmade bed in a yellow dress shirt he had to have slept in and a brown tie with a splotch of ketchup ready to drip off the tip.

As the men shook hands, Ann Markham got up from a table across the room and came toward them. As sleek and graceful as a small shark, Dane thought, taking in the trim teal suit and the predatory gleam in her dark eyes. Her gaze flicked from Dane to the attorney general and held on Paul Douglas's face as she turned up the wattage on her smile.

"Ann." Smiling, Douglas tipped his head and reached out to engulf her hand in his. "Fancy meeting you here."

"Well, they let me out of my cage every once in a while," she said, her voice smooth and slightly breathy. Businesslike with an undercurrent of sex. "How've you been, Paul?"

"Fine. I'd ask the same, but I can see for myself you're looking wonderful." Ann all but purred at the compliment. "I'm afraid I have to run," he said apologetically, "but be sure to call me next time you're in the Cities. We'll have drinks."

"Absolutely."

Douglas and Peterson said their good-byes and went out together. Yeager caught Dane's eye and Dane nodded him off as Ann turned toward him. The agent frowned and backed reluctantly away from the table.

"Yes, fancy meeting you here, Ann," Dane said blandly, sliding his hands into the pockets of his pleated tan trousers.

She sent him a sly, triumphant smile. "There's no sense playing the game if one doesn't intend to win, darling. I all but have a homing device attached to our illustrious Mr. Douglas."

"You'll go far."

"I fully intend to. And what about you, Sheriff Jantzen? Where will all this murder and intrigue take you?" she asked, dark eyes sparkling with surpressed humor.

"To an early grave."

A warm, wholly unsympathetic chuckle bubbled in her throat. "Poor baby," she said. "Care to stop by my house on the way for a nice long soak in the Jacuzzl?" She glanced up at him through her lashes, lust lighting a fire in the depths of her dark, exotic eyes.

Dane wished he could have said yes, but there was no answering flame inside him. A sigh slipped from him as he shook his head. "No. Thanks."

She studied him for a minute, looking surprised for just an instant, then skeptical. Finally her lips twisted into a wry smile. "What's her name?" He gave her a carefully blank look for an answer, and she laughed. "Give me a little credit, Sheriff. I make a very good living out of reading people. What's the name of this wonderful creature you've fallen in love with?"

He didn't want to admit to being in love—not to himself or to Ann Markham—but there seemed no point in prolonging the argument either way. "Elizabeth."

Ann nodded. Now that her prospective boss was out of the room, she felt free to open her calfskin clutch and take out a cigarette. "Is she a soft, sweet, docile-little-housewife type?" she asked, lighting up.

Dane couldn't hold back the automatic burst of laughter that erupted from him, turning heads of diners at several nearby tables. "Hardly."

She took a long drag on her cigarette and blew a stream of smoke toward the ceiling. "Good," she said, slanting him a catty look. "I have to go, Sheriff. I'm nearly standing in the no-smoking section. Don't want to be in violation of any laws, now, do we?" She gave him one last, thoughtful look, her mouth tightening at the prospect of losing. No matter that she hadn't wanted him for anything other than sex. "Have a nice life."

"You too," Dane murmured, but she had already turned and was walking out with her head up and her sights set on the state capital.

Yeager had doubled back around the perimeter of the dining room and stepped out the shadows of a potted palm, his brows tucked down in a grim line of annoy-ance. "Come on, Casanova," he growled. "I told Jolynn I'd be home in time for dessert."

THE OLD CLOCK ON THE LIVING-ROOM MANTEL chimed midnight, the soft dulcet tones drifting out through the screen door. Dane stood on the front porch, leaning a shoulder against a smooth white pillar, his gaze trained to the south. He had shucked his shirt and tie, trading the dress clothes for jeans and boots and a work shirt that hung open despite the cool night. He lifted the bottle of Miller that dangled from his fingertips and took a long pull, then set the bottle aside on the rail.

He could have been in bed—his own or Ann's. For the first time in over a week he could have afforded the lux-ury of a decent night's sleep, but sleep wouldn't come. His insomnia had nothing to do with the relentless ache in his knee or the fact that he had handed over a political time bomb to the attorney general in the form of Jarvis's book. It had to do with perceptions—of himself, of his life.

For years he had kept his life neatly in order, each part separate from the next, carefully compartmentalized and kept in cool perspective. Now he felt as if the ground had shifted beneath him and everything had fallen out of place. He didn't like it. Not one damn bit. Even if he could manage to put everything back the way it had been, nothing would be the same. There would be one stray piece that refused to fit—Elizabeth.

He had let her walk away, had told himself it was best for both of them if they let it end. But he couldn't get her out of his mind . . . or his heart. He couldn't stop him-self from wondering if she was all right, if she was sleep-ing tonight, if she was missing him or cursing his name. It didn't make sense that he should love her, that he should have fallen in love with her so quickly or at all. But there wasn't anything logical about this, and stepping back only left him alone with his future stretching out in front of him like a long, dusty road running to nowhere.

Alone. That was the path he had chosen after his divorce. He had labeled it freedom and stuck to it, fooling himself into thinking he was a lucky man, independent, answering to no one. Now alone felt like just what it was—a void, a vacuum, a black hole where his heart beat out its days and nights in a solitary rhythm.

He wasn't lucky, he was scared. He was a coward. That was the truth. The thought of investing his heart in another relationship scared the hell out of him. He had played that game before and lost big, and he couldn't stand the thought of losing, and he couldn't bear the thought of the pain.

"Daddy?"

Dane jerked his head around at the sound of Amy's voice and the soft creak of the screen door. She stood there in her Raiders jersey, blinking sleepily, long hair a rumpled curtain hanging over one shoulder, arms banded around herself to ward off the chill of midnight. He had scarcely seen her since the fight in his office. The case and its aftermath had consumed his life for the past two days. Now he drank in the sight of his daughter and wished things weren't strained between them.

"Hey, peanut," he murmured. "What are you doing up?"

"I couldn't sleep."

She padded barefoot across the porch to tuck herself against his side, her arms sliding around his waist as she nuzzled her face into the curve of his shoulder. The action was so automatic, Dane couldn't help but wonder if she did this with her stepfather, if Mike Manetti offered her fatherly comfort on the nights she couldn't sleep in California. The thought sliced through his heart like a knife. He wrapped his arm around her and pulled her closer, pressing a kiss to the top of her head.

"Is your knee bothering you?" she asked.

"No," he lied. It hurt like hell. He'd been on it too much today. It felt as if little demons were standing on either side of his kneecap, swinging sledgehammers against what little cartilage was left. He knew it would be a miracle if he got through the week without having to have the fluid aspirated, but his knee wasn't what was keeping him up, so he ignored it.

"I love you, Daddy."

Dane blinked, not in surprise at Amy's words, but at the urgency behind them, urgency that shined up at him from his daughter's eyes through a sheen of tears.

"Hey," he said, brushing his knuckles against her satin-soft cheek.

Amy screwed up her courage and shoved out the words she'd been practicing in her head all day. "When I heard about what happened yesterday, all I could think was that I'd been such a brat and that I'd disappointed you, and you could have died and I never would have had the chance to tell you how sorry I was or how much I loved you." Two fat teardrops rolled over her lashes and started twin streams down her face. "It's so stupid. Everybody wastes so much time being mad or scared or proud— It's just stupid," she said vehemently, sniffling. "If you love somebody, you should tell them and not wait until it's too late to do anything about it."

Out of the mouths of babes, Dane thought.

Life was unpredictable, and it went by so fast, too fast. Even here. Even when he thought he had everything so neatly arranged, so carefully aligned. Amy was the perfect example. She would be grown and gone soon, and so much time had slipped away from them, time that would have been better spent storing up memories than regrets.

Gently, he swept away the tears from her cheek with the pad of his thumb. "Where'd you get to be so smart?" he asked, one corner of his mouth tilting upward.

Amy choked on a giggle, her face brightening under the light of the moon, her heart lifting. "My old man."

"Yeah," he said, his voice thickening. "That's what I thought."

He hugged her tight, rubbing his cheek against the top

of her head, breathing deep the scents of apple-scented shampoo and Love's Baby Soft cologne. He squeezed his eyes shut against the wave of emotion that threatened to crest in his eyes. "I love you too, baby. More than anything."

"I know." She hugged him back for a long moment, then looked up at him through a tangle of bangs, trying gamely to resurrect her pixie smile. "Enough to let me go to the fireworks with Trace tomorrow night?"

Dane laughed automatically, but his smile faded as he took in the face that was thinning from cuteness to elegance, the wide eyes filled with hope and hunger for maturity. He felt her slipping inexorably away and knew there was nothing he could do to stop it.

"We'll see."

IT SHOULD HAVE BEEN RAINING. THE OCCASION WAS so solemn, so sad, it should have been against the law for the sun to shine. But it beamed down on the little knot of mourners, butter-yellow and summer-bright, oblivious to their pain.

Elizabeth straightened the lenses of her Ray-Bans and sighed at the scene being played out on the hillside below her. The Amish were burying their dead. There were only a few in attendance. Aaron's family, she supposed, and not many others. Apparently the Amish weren't very tolerant of killers in their midst. Madness and violence had no place in their world. It seemed they preferred not to acknowledge that kind of trouble when it happened. Maybe they thought if they ignored the bad, it wouldn't be real and they wouldn't have to lie awake nights wondering why or when it might happen again. Elizabeth couldn't say that she blamed them.

She wasn't close enough to hear the words being spoken at the graveside. She stood too far up the hill with the wind pulling at her hair and flattening the soft cotton of her white T-shirt against her. Behind her, at Still Waters, where she had left her car, work went on as usual, the sounds of hammers and saws shattering what peace Aaron Hauer might have found in death. Or maybe down there under the shade of the maple tree, beside his beloved Siri, all he would hear would be the stream gurgling and the bees humming as they hovered above the wildflowers.

A white-haired old man with a flowing beard bent slowly over the grave and threw in a handful of dirt. *Ashes to ashes, dust to dust.* That much never changed. Amish and English, zealots and agnostics, all came to the same end.

Up on the road a tour bus rumbled past, carrying people back to town in time to grab a bite of dinner at the Coffee Cup before the Horse and Buggy Days parade. There had been talk of canceling the festival in light of the tragedies that had marred the past ten days, but economics and a need for something good to happen had overruled.

Life in Still Creek would go on because it had to. The worlds of Amish and English would continue to overlap. The horror of what had happened would fade with time. But nothing would ever be quite the same, Elizabeth thought. A certain innocence had been lost. The truth she had been so determined to dig for had not only hurt, it had left scars. She couldn't help but feel saddened by that.

Sad was getting to be a habit. Rotten habit, she thought, like the smoking, like the scotch.

She hadn't heard a word from Dane since the morning of Aaron Hauer's death. The ubiquitous Lorraine had called with curt messages about statements. Mark Kaufman had stopped by the house several times, puppy-eyed and sweet as pie, for her to sign documents and clarify specific points about "the incident," as he so carefully called it. But there had been no sign of Dane, no call. Nothing but a fresh new fuchsia plant delivered by a pimple-faced boy from Rockwell's Flower Shop. A farewell token. He had, it seemed, taken her at her word and opted for the easy way out. Damn the man. Didn't he recognize reverse psychology when he saw it?

Below her, the gathering of Hauer kin was breaking up. They turned away from the grave site and trudged up the hill in their somber clothes and sober faces, the women carefully holding out the skirts of their long dresses as the high grass snatched at them like long, thin fingers. Only one man remained behind to shovel dirt into the hole Aaron's body had been committed to for eternity.

"Maybe he'll find some peace now."

Elizabeth swung around to find Dane standing not ten feet away. The wind teased the ends of his hair, and his expression was inscrutable, his eyes hidden by mirrored sunglasses. He stood with his hands in the pockets of his faded jeans, the sleeves of his khaki uniform shirt rolled neatly to the elbow. Two pristine white bandages on his right arm and the orthopedic brace on his left knee served as the only signs of his own brush with the great beyond.

"I'd like to think so," Elizabeth said, scolding herself for drinking in the sight of him. Didn't she have any pride at all? She tucked her fingers in the pockets of her snug, faded jeans and turned back toward the funeral procession. "He did some terrible things, but he wasn't a terrible man. Just heartsick and lonely."

She hated to think that loneliness could drive a person to the lengths Aaron had gone to, but that was what had been at the root of his illness—loneliness and grief, bitterness and hate that had steeped and fermented into madness.

"Is that what you'll put in the paper? That he was heartsick and lonely?"

"There won't be a paper this week," she said, watching as the one remaining Amishman took up his shovel and began to fill the grave. "By next week this won't be news."

She thought of Aaron's Amish paper, *The Budget,* and wondered if his death would be included among the crop reports and the scandalous news that someone from the Old Order had gone modern and bought himself a tractor.

"Will there be a paper next week?" Dane asked. He wouldn't blame her if she wanted to leave. Nothing that had happened here could have made her want to stay. As much as he loved this place with its quiet, gentle beauty and honest, hardworking people, Elizabeth had been given a very different, very unattractive view.

She looked at him over her shoulder. "I'm not going anywhere. I'm all done moving on, looking for my life around the next corner. This is home, for better or worse. I'm hoping I'll grow on people eventually. Get 'em so they don't want to kill me or throw bricks through my windows, and then work my way up from there."

"Rich is the one who vandalized the *Clarion* office," Dane said. "He was the one in your garage too. I took his statement yesterday at St. Mary's. He was looking for the book and trying to scare you off at the same time."

"I heard he came to. Pity." She smiled at Dane's arched brow. "Women are vengeful creatures as a rule, sugar."

"I'll bear that in mind," he said sardonically. "Will I be taking my life into my hands if I ask you take a walk with me?"

"I'm unarmed at the moment. Should you be walking on that?" she asked, nodding at the brace on his knee.

"Doesn't matter. I've got a date with an arthroscope next week."

"Well, you've got my social calendar beat all to hell."

Dane reserved comment and started down the hill toward the creek. What he wanted to say could do without the accompaniment of pneumatic power tools or the gloom of a cemetery plot.

"What did Fox have on Rich if not the book?" Elizabeth asked, falling into step beside him, feeling a need to put off whatever was to come. The famous final scene, she supposed. Like Bogey and Ingrid Bergman on the tarmac in *Casablanca.* Only she didn't have Paul Henried waiting in the wings for her.

"Rich came across Jarrold when he was already dead. Instead of calling the cops, he started looking for the book, knowing if we found it first he'd be dead politically and up to his ass in indictments."

He stopped at the water's edge and stared across the creek where a mother wood duck was teaching half a dozen of her fuzzy offspring to swim in the muddy shallows along the far bank. "Fox saw him at the scene. I imagine Carney figured Rich had done the deed, but it didn't really matter one way or the other. Just being able to put him at the scene sealed Carney's fate."

He shook his head at the idea of Rich Cannon killing anyone. He'd known Rich forever, and it turned out that he didn't really know him at all. It was an unsettling thought.

"He didn't say anything about calling you," Dane said, turning his attention back to Elizabeth.

"No," she said. "My money's on Helen for that one, but I don't guess we'll ever know for sure." Somehow, now, in the light of day and in view of everything else that had happened, it didn't seem important.

"What happens next?" she asked, needing to think ahead instead of back.

"Now the wheels of justice turn. The state attorney general is digging into the corruption business. There'll be some empty seats in the legislature before too long, you can bank on that. And there'll be a commendation for the *Clarion.*"

Elizabeth smiled at the irony of that. The state attorney general commending a paper the town fathers had wanted shut down. Charlie Wilder was liable to have a stroke. "It's Jolynn they should honor," she said, plucking up a long, tough shoot of grass to occupy her hands. "She's the one found the book. She damn near lost her life for it. I'd say she deserves the credit."

"Yeager says she's doing okay."

"Oh, yeah." She smiled gamely. Jolynn was doing

swell. She was getting her life together for the first time in a long, long time, and Elizabeth was genuinely happy for her. And jealous of her. And sorry for herself. Two more rotten habits to add to her list of thousands. She wondered if, once she got rid of all her rotten habits, there'd be anything left.

Dane studied her as she methodically split the blade of grass she held. She looked a little pale, a little thin. He wanted to take off her sunglasses so he could see those eyes that mirrored everything she was feeling, but he held himself back, the old wariness too ingrained to just let go. "And how are you doing?"

"Me? Hey, I'm a trooper." She cursed the extra hoarseness that roughened her voice. She should have been tougher than that.

"No. No!" she said. Anger boiled up inside her as she wheeled on him, and she let it have free rein because it was a damn sight better than hurting. "I'm not fine. I killed a man two days ago. There isn't enough bleach in the state of Minnesota to get the bloodstains out of the floor. I can't sleep in my bed because I can still see him laying there. And I couldn't sleep there anyway because all I can think about is you!"

Her hands curled into fists and adrenaline pumped through her. "You made me fall in love, you son of a bitch! And if that wasn't the meanest, dirtiest trick. All I wanted was peace and quiet. I wanted to live like a normal person. And along you come—"

Dane grabbed her arms and hauled her up against him. She squirmed and twisted against his hold, swearing a streak that would have turned a sailor's ears blue.

"Quit!" he ordered her, the weight of the command diluted by his laughter.

Elizabeth's temper spiked upward, and she struggled all the harder. "I will not quit! And don't you dare laugh at me! I don't want you. I never wanted you!"

She kicked him hard in the shin. Dane grunted and wrestled her to the ground, pinning her body beneath his, pinning her arms to the ground above her head. They lay belly to belly, chest to chest, his legs sprawled on either side of hers.

He raised himself up enough to look down at her. Her sunglasses had come off in the fray and she glared up at him with eyes that were bloodshot from lack of sleep and red-rimmed from crying. She tried to be so tough and she was so vulnerable. The combination hit his heart with a one-two punch he couldn't begin to block. She stared up at him, mad as wet cat.

"It's like the Rolling Stones say, sweetheart," he said, fighting for breath. "You can't always get what you want."

"I hate the Rolling Stones," she snarled between her teeth. "And I hate you. You're mean as cat meat and—"

"I love you."

"—twice as—" She broke off in confusion. "What?" she mumbled. "You what?"

"I love you."

She stared up at him for a long moment. Then she worked her right hand free of his hold, reached up slowly and pulled off his sunglasses, tossing them aside.

"Say it again," she whispered, needing to hear the words, needing to see them in the blue of his eyes.

"I love you," he murmured. "If it's any consolation, I didn't want to either."

"You sure know how to make a girl feel special," Elizabeth said. "Maybe you should just shut up and kiss me."

"Yes, ma'am."

He lowered himself over her and settled his mouth against hers softly, tenderly, with a poignancy that came from his heart and a heat that seared her clear to her soul. Their lips clung, tasting, savoring, relearning, remembering. Elizabeth let herself luxuriate, steeped herself in the sweetness of the moment. As moments went, this one was perfect. She would remember every single thing about it as long as she lived.

Dane shifted his weight off her as he ended the kiss. He traced his fingertips along the elegant line of her cheek and touched the little scar that hooked down from the corner of her mouth.

I loved Amy's mother, but she wanted . . . things, so many things I couldn't give her, everything money could buy. I can't offer you that, Elizabeth. I'm just a cop, a beat-up old football player turned cop."

Elizabeth could see it all in his face, the pain, the wariness, the need that reached out to her own. "Oh, Dane," she whispered. "I don't want things. I just want you . . . to love me."

"Well," he said, his lips curving in a gentle smile, "maybe we can get what we want after all."

He lowered his head and kissed her again. "I'd ask you to marry me," he said, grinning like a champion, "but I hear you've sworn off men."

Elizabeth smiled up at him. "Now, sugar," she drawled, batting her lashes as she pulled him back down, "where'd you ever get a crazy idea like that?"